AGENTS OF DARKNESS

CAMPBELL ARMSTRONG

AGENTS OF DARKNESS

HarperCollins*Publishers*

FIRST EDITION

Designed by H. Roberts Design

LIBRARY OF CONGRESS CATALOG CARD NUMBER 90-56106
ISBN 0-06-017917-1

91 92 93 94 95 CC/RRD 10 9 8 7 6 5 4 3 2 1

*This book is dedicated to Rebecca;
redefining love daily*

The author gratefully acknowledges the help of many people over a period of time: in England, David Singer, Adrian Bourne, Bob Cripps, Dennis "Frank Pagan" Le Baigue, Anna Bence-Trower, Brian Levy, Charles Nettleton, and Merric Davidson, sportsman and publicist. In the United States, Bonnie Campbell of Sedona Travel, who makes the world manageable; Shelley McGehee of the Arizona State University Music Library; and Katie Smith, a wonder worker at HarperCollins. In Scotland, Robert Burns, Erl and Anne Wilkie, David Taylor, Jack Dennison, David Cuthbertson, and Leonard Mciklc and Ian Ferguson, wherever on the planet they might be. And in the Philippines various people, living in bad circumstances, who would prefer anonymity.

Very special gratitude is due W. E. Wyatt, for lighting bright lamps on wintry Glasgow afternoons.

We stand with you, sir. . . . We love your adherence to democratic principle and to the democratic processes. And we will not leave you in isolation.

> —George Bush, Vice President of the United States, in a public toast to Ferdinand Marcos, Manila, 1981

Guid sakes I'm in a dreidfu state
I'll hae nae inklin sune
Gin I'm the drinker or the drink
The thistle or the mune.

> —Hugh MacDiarmid, *A Drunk Man Looks At A Thistle*

The political and commercial morals of the United States are not merely food for laughter, they are an entire banquet.

> —Mark Twain, *Mark Twain in Eruption*, January 1907

1

Eugene Costain stepped out of the Manila Hotel into a dusk as intimidatingly humid as the day had been. He had walked only a few yards past white-uniformed flunkies and security guards before his cotton shirt and lightweight pants were sticking to his skin. The air, which smelled of gasoline and swamp and sweetly decaying sewage, hung lifeless around him. On Manila Bay, where the dying sun glowed through the dirty muslin of pollution, five or six decrepit freighters were anchored with the stillness of coffin ships.

Costain moved out of the hotel compound, passing parked taxis and newspaper vendors and shadowy men who eyed him in an ambivalent way. Their looks might have been merely sullen or quietly resentful, even threatening. Costain wasn't sure. He knew only that they made him feel so goddamn *Caucasian* and uncomfortable, a stranger in a city that wasn't altogether strange to him. He'd been coming to Manila for more than five years now, drawn back again and again by an obsession that had nothing to do with the requirements of his business, and the uneasiness grew with each visit.

You imagine things, Costain. Increasingly you create your own little nightmares. More and more some small bird of guilt pecks at your skull. Did it come down to that in the end? Have the Philippines unglued you? He was no expert at surveying his inner terrain. He'd spent his life obeying the orders of other people, which was not conducive to mapping his own valleys and shorelines. The very idea of self-analysis caused him to smile as he moved past the green expanse of Rizal Park, where the unruffled shadows of dense trees concealed more figures—loafers, aimless strollers, lovers, watchers in the twilight.

A casual observer would not have noticed the smile because Gene Costain's face barely altered when it expressed anything. The same observer might have seen nothing more than a slightly paunchy middle-aged American with thick gray hair brushed neatly back across his scalp. If he were really interested, the spectator might ascribe an innocuous profession to Costain, an actuary or a corporate accountant, say. Nobody could have guessed Costain's occupation on the basis of his appearance alone, which was as bland as the look you might see on the faces of nice people scouting retirement homes in Palm Springs or Phoenix.

On Roxas Boulevard, where dusk was thickening finally to night, and dull streetlamps failed to illuminate the true dark of Manila, Costain gazed in the direction of the U.S. Embassy. Quiet now, save for the pathetic few who lingered outside its perimeter to be first in line for the next morning's business, it was besieged daily by applicants for visas or Resident Alien cards, men and women who desperately hoped to escape the massive poverty of the Philippines and enter America the Beautiful, where at least there was a better class of barrio than you would find in Baclaran or Pasay or any other area of metro Manila. The embassy depressed Costain; he'd heard once that the waiting list for residency visas in the United States was forty years long. Forty goddam years! Apply at birth, you might stand a chance of leaving Manila in time for middle age in LA. Welcome to America.

Cars, trucks, crowded jeepneys—some tattooed with fire-spewing dragons and monsters, others adorned by Madonnas and religious symbols—screamed past. The air was impossible. No breeze rose from the bay. Costain wiped sweat from his forehead with the palm of his hand just as the first of the night's solicitors approached him, a well-spoken teenage boy with a sister to sell, very young, sir, very clean, a student. Always clean and always a student, Costain thought. What were all these clean students majoring in anyhow?

Costain dismissed the kid, who persisted the way they usually did in the bustling flesh markets of Manila. *Somebody younger, sir? Somebody very young?* Now there was a break in the traffic and Costain, sucking dank traffic fumes, crossed the boulevard, assailed as soon as he reached the other side by beggars, undernourished women with babies in their arms, blind boys, barefoot children, creatures that shuffled or limped toward him as if he were a bug light against which they would witlessly be zapped out of existence. Costain knew that if you stopped to hand two bits to some shoeless kid suddenly the whole gang devoured you. What you did was ignore the assembly and keep moving.

"Hindi, hindi," he said as he brushed past the supplicants. "Hindi, hindi," with increasing emphasis.

He always remembered how Laforge had put it. *The more you give them, the more they despise you. Don't make the mistake of thinking charity buys affection, or kindness loyalty. It's an error we Americans continue to make, usually on a very large scale.* He had a brief image of Laforge, the delicate face that in a certain light appeared skeletal, the flesh too tensely drawn, the tanned hands, those courtly manners that were distant even as they hinted at the privileged possibility of some future friendship. Laforge, with his horses and his Bucks County estate and his lovely wife who smiled as graciously as a duchess on Dilaudid, awed Costain, whose experience of the American aristocracy was almost nonexistent. But what the hell could Laforge know about this kind of personal confrontation with panhandlers? He never came to the Philippines anymore.

Costain freed himself from the beggars and moved along a narrow, grubby street grandly called United Nations Avenue. In the doorways of money-changing shops armed security guards studied the teeming streets and took the pulse of the place—tense men who played portable radios and sometimes shooed beggars away. Scarcely a business in this paranoid city didn't employ at least one uniformed private guard for protection against robbers or members of the *Bagong Hukbo ng Bayan,* the Communist New People's Army, which for years had been successfully infiltrating Manila from the outlying provinces.

Costain made a right turn on Del Pilar Street, the raucous heart of the Ermita district, a crazy thoroughfare where suddenly the darkness was altered, fragmented by neon, splintered by the roar and thunder of rock music blasting out of strip joints and pick-up bars. He was accosted time and again by laughingly persistent girls in luminous miniskirts who tried to drag him inside. Now and then a door would swing open and he'd see girls dancing under ultraviolet lights, and it was as if their white bikinis glowed with radiation. Beautiful brown girls, thumping music, the night was one great magic oyster open to him, but Costain had his own destination in mind.

He passed a bunch of Australian tourists, loud and horny, who had been boozing in one of the Aussie expatriate pubs where photographs of Queen Elizabeth hung prominently on a wall, a disappointed regal observer of how even *American* imperialism had failed.

Del Pilar Street, razored by flashing lights, had occasional dark blocks, and blackened alleys stretched indeterminately away on either side, perhaps to fade out in places where brick and flimsy tin had yielded to tropical decay and rot. The thick air was fishy, sickening. Somewhere a pipe had broken and stinking green water streamed underfoot. Costain, cursing, spotted it too late. His white canvas shoe absorbed the putrid liquid and squelched, goddammit, as he continued uncomfortably to walk.

Outside a shop selling religious icons, a ten- or eleven-year-old girl with the eyes and voice of a sad zombie said, "I go with you. I go with you," and Costain skipped past her, somehow troubled by the encounter, which was not extraordinary by the standards of Ermita.

The night was wrong, he thought. The night did not have the best of vibes. That high of expectation and unbearable lust he always felt when he headed toward Mabini Street was off center, and he wasn't sure why. The beggars had bothered him more than usual, the kid hooker with the sleepwalking manner skewed him, and now his right shoe was sodden with Christ knows what kind of toxic Filipino bacteria. He was getting little signals from somewhere, but he wasn't sure what they meant.

He stopped moving, leaned against a wall, slid the wet shoe off and shook it irritably, thinking how he hated Manila sometimes because it was like some scabrous oriental version of a big Mexican city. Despite the occasional bamboo conceit of a hotel or café, a Spanish flavor dominated the architecture, especially in the formidable Catholic churches built during the four centuries of Spanish occupation. And the names in the phone book, from Acosta to Zapata, strengthened the impression you'd wandered into a community largely Hispanic. But when you looked at the people you knew this was no clapped-out Central American burg because the faces you saw here were a mixture of Spanish and Chinese and Malay. These juxtapositions, genetic and architectural, still had an unsettling effect at times on Gene Costain, as if he were a man seriously jet-lagged by a flight from Mexico City to Manila.

He put his foot back in the uncomfortable shoe. On Mabini Street he turned right. He passed a vendor with a basket of *balut*, half-boiled duck eggs with the fetal birds, small beaks and feathers included, dead in the shell. Costain had tried one once, but he'd been obliged to spit the watery unborn duckling from his mouth. No thank you. His idea of a snack ran more to a Snickers bar.

Close to where Mabini intersected with Soldado Street, Costain stopped outside a three-story building. Narrow and grubby, it had a variety of illuminated signs hanging from it. RICARDO CHIONG, IMMIGRATION LAWYER, US VISAS AND WORK PERMITS SPECIALIST. UNWANTED HAIR REMOVAL BY ROSALITA "BABY" NUNEZ. The one Costain found particularly ironic advertized a 24-hour VD Clinic equipped to diagnose—in capital letters—VAGINITIS, CHLAMYDIA, HERPES, AIDS. If you thought you'd picked up something nasty in the neighborhood, you popped in here to have your fears confirmed or dispelled. A consumer convenience.

Thinking chlamydia a somewhat poetic name for a venereal disease, one more suited to a pale, consumptive Victorian girl, Costain entered a narrow lobby lit by several unshaded light bulbs. Paint peeled from the uneven walls. Plaster had crumbled and bare electrical wires hung from lathework. He glanced at the security guard in the dark blue uniform, who looked at him with a small smile. The guard had seen Costain here before and knew where the American was headed. For his part, Costain didn't reciprocate this familiarity. He just kept moving toward the stairs.

The humidity forced him to pause. He ran his hand over his face and longed for a shaft of icy air conditioning to slice through the clammy building. He climbed to the VD clinic, where a plump woman sat behind a desk and two young men, already gaunt with their disease, were slumped on a plastic sofa. A teenage girl was talking in Tagalog to the receptionist but she stopped when Costain appeared, and only resumed speaking as soon as he'd moved on, as if she had some terrible secret she didn't want him to hear. *Waste of time, sweetheart,* he thought. His Tagalog was limited to a few tourist phrases, and even those he mispronounced.

Drained by the effort of the stairs, he reached the top floor. He fanned the air with an open hand, felt moisture collect at the back of his knees. There was nothing to breathe up here. Inside May's room there would be an electric fan at least, because he'd given her a two-speed oscillating Black & Decker as a gift last time. Delighted, she'd plugged it into a scary-looking outlet and the blades immediately pushed hot air back and forth: It was hardly better than nothing.

Costain stepped across the landing. He didn't knock on the door. He had already telephoned to say he was coming. Any company May might have had would be gone by this time. Costain always assumed his demands had priority over anything else she might be doing. After all, he practically supported her, sending money orders every two or three months, sometimes wiring cash directly into her account at the National Bank.

He pushed open the door, entered the half-dark room, smelled marijuana smoke. A candle burned beside the empty bed, across which a green spread had been neatly drawn. He passed the shelf where May kept her large collection of stuffed toy animals—giraffes, bears, bug-eyed frogs. Pressed upon the walls were cartoon decals Costain had given her, because they delighted her. Out of the flickering candlelight several of the Seven Dwarves peered at him. It was not a room to wake in with a hangover.

This child-woman bit of May's disconcerted him at times,

but it excited him too. The bright enthusiasms, her unashamed lack of sophistication, the delightfully unexpected shyness she sometimes showed—all this thrilled Costain, whose wife was a scrawny woman in Poughkeepsie who bred cocker spaniels and spent much of her time poring over canine accessories catalogs, page after page advertising beef-flavored rubber bones for teething pups, worm medications, and the very latest in doggie chic, plaid overcoats and suede bootees. Whatever sexual urge his wife had once possessed had been sublimated, God help her, in cocker spaniels. But Costain was in Poughkeepsie less and less these days, and who could blame his wife for going, so to speak, to the dogs?

"May?" he said. His waterlogged canvas shoe squeaked on the floorboards. He called the woman's name a second time. The saucer in which the candle stood contained the remains of a joint covered in stalactites of melted wax.

Costain was touched for just a moment by a familiar sense of unease. He recognized it as the unnerving junction where ignorance of what lay in the dark changed and became the certainty of knowing something dangerous was nearby. He stood very still, holding his breath, hearing the roar of his own blood.

"Gene."

A light went on in the tiny kitchen that adjoined the bedroom. Beyond the kitchen was a cubicle with a water closet. Costain blinked, relieved by the sight of May in the kitchen doorway, but distressed by the way he'd felt fear, conjured it up out of nothing save an empty room and some shadows and the sound of his own voice. Getting old, sunshine. Losing your grip. You shouldn't have come here like this, unarmed, unescorted.

But there was a flip side to these admonitions: How the hell could he possibly stay away from this lovely woman who stood watching him from the kitchen doorway? Self-denial wasn't one of his virtues. Besides, she'd enriched his life, and brightened it, so that when he was trapped in Poughkeepsie on a wintry day with the latest litter yapping from the heated kennels in the yard he could bring her face to his mind and taste her flesh in his memory, and he'd be warm in spite of leaden skies and endless snows. Either it was love or some insane, middle-aged obsession. Maybe there wasn't any difference between the two. Costain didn't stop to interrogate himself. He didn't care.

She was wearing a sea-green satin robe that shimmered in the light. A small woman, with glossy hair so black it suggested some impenetrable midnight, she smiled the smile that electrified Gene Costain in his lonesome winters. Her dark eyes were slightly oriental in shape, her teeth improbably white. The color of her skin was something he could never get quite right. Brown was mundane, and tan didn't do it, and coffee was too dark. Even as he sought the correct word, her skin changed by candlelight anyway. All he knew was he'd never seen a more beautiful woman in his life.

"I thought you weren't here," he said.

She came across the floor, slid her arms around his waist, placed her cheek upon his chest. "But I am always here for you," she said.

She had a sweet, high voice. Her English was sometimes very correct, sometimes lazily broken. Her hair was perfumed. Costain closed his eyes, drifting out on the scent. He slipped a hand inside her robe. Her breasts were smooth, lightly oiled by an aromatic lubricant she spread all across her body, a moisturizer with the taste of sandalwood.

"It has been a long time," she said.

"Four months." With his eyes still shut, Costain had the surprising little thought: *I belong here.* Eugene Costain, born 1935 in Watertown, New York, the only son of a stern Methodist minister, is at home in this small, wretched apartment above a VD clinic on Mabini Street, Manila. *The world turns in absurd ways.* Sometimes he wondered what his wife would say if she found out about May. Probably nothing. She might tell one of her confidantes, *Oh, Gene's got himself some young gook girlfriend, isn't that rich? It's like he's a retarded adolescent or something.* Erica wasn't the confrontational kind. If she suffered, she'd do it quietly, thank you very much, and breed more cockers.

"Four months is too long. Why you no come before?"

"Business," he said.

"Funny business, huh?"

Some time ago he'd made up a story about how he sold securities to rich Filipino businessmen and tried to explain this occupation to her, but because she hadn't grasped the notion at once she lost interest, as he'd known she would. Abstractions eluded and bored her. Although she was at least twenty-two—she liked to lie about her age, varying it anywhere from seventeen to twenty-five—she had the attention span of a fifth-grader. Only when it came to real money, *folding* money, or new clothes, a certain shade of lipstick or what music was current, did she focus as well as anyone he knew. And whenever she read gossip magazines in Tagalog she could become as absorbed as Karl Marx in the reading room of the British Museum.

"Jesus, it's hot," he said. "Where's the fan?"

"Fan broken. No good." She shook her head, made a small gesture of resignation with one hand.

"There was a guarantee," Costain said, but he didn't pursue this line. It was just a fact of life here: Nothing electrical seemed to work for very long. Humidity devoured appliances. Sudden blackouts in the wake of typhoons blew circuits. Daily there were brownouts unexplained by the power company. A cassette player he'd given May a year ago had died five months later and now lay unused among the pile of soft toys.

Costain drew her to the bed, where he sat down. May stood before him, watching him untie the knotted cord of her robe. She had a kind of detached curiosity in her expression, as if she'd never seen anyone do this before and wondered where it would lead. He parted the robe, pressed his face against her belly. She touched his cheek with her thin fingers. He loved the feel of her small hands on his skin.

"I undress you now," she said. "I make you relax. I give you *my* guarantee."

Costain, gratefully kicking off his shoes, sat back. May unbuttoned his shirt and pushed it back from his shoulders. His lust astonished him. At an age when many men were spooked by the long somber slope that led to Epitaph Avenue, Eugene Costain had been reborn, not in some Methodist fervor of his late father's making, but in a fever of desire. Here was as close to any form of heaven as he was going to get.

She unzipped his pants, slid them from his legs along with his underwear. She punched him lightly in the stomach and laughed. "You must exercise."

"You're all the exercise I need, baby," he said. He was aflame with malarial intensity.

"Yeah, I exercise you, all right." She stepped away from him. From the pocket of her robe she took out a small plastic packet containing a condom. She insisted on one. She opened it with her teeth, removed the prophylactic, let the wrapper drift to the floor. She knelt beside the bed, caressed him for a while, took him inside her mouth. She had a way of making a funnel of her tongue that detonated little land mines throughout Costain's brain, blitzing him. When she took her face away she shrugged her shoulders so that her robe slipped from her body as she rolled the condom very slowly over his penis. She straddled him. He looked up into her eyes when he entered her.

There. The night was no longer out of balance. Everything was exactly the way it was supposed to be. Closing his eyes, he was lost inside her. It was another world, safer and sweeter than what lay in the streets. He was rocketed up through unexplored strata of himself, higher and higher, shooting through his own private planetarium.

May Quirante, who had the palms of her hands placed upon Costain's chest as she rocked her body upon his, turned her head to the side and nodded. The tall, slender figure in the kitchen doorway, a young man in black jeans and black T-shirt, stepped into the bedroom. He moved as if all his life had been given to the craft of silence. His handsome brown face was lit momentarily by the candle, and his blue eyes flashed before they were obscured again as he approached the bed. Gene Costain, riding his own comet, was unaware of the intruder. He was going up and up, *Yessir, yessir, ooo yes,* moaning while he rose directly into the molten center of the sun.

The young man stood over the blissful Costain. He looked at May, who rode the American harder. Costain, approaching the red-hot core of himself, groaned now. The young man held a butterfly knife. He opened it with quiet expertise. There was a second when the twin blades reflected the guttering flame, the same second in which Eugene Costain crashed through the roof of his personal galaxy and roared with astonishment and love, the same savage second when May Quirante rolled away from Costain, who opened his eyes in time to see the knife glow in its sharp, senseless descent.

Costain was sliced neatly and deeply from gullet to navel. He tried to sit up, at first more puzzled than pained. He saw May at the foot of the bed. With her mouth open she watched him raise his face. Something here was beyond understanding, Costain thought. He blinked, failed to rise, dropped back again. His head tilted from the edge of the bed so what he saw of the room was upside down, Grumpy and Bashful inverted, all the soft toys floating in defiance of gravity. And there was the stranger, the other, who stood above Costain's head like a pallbearer looking down sadly at a corpse displayed in an obscene open casket.

My killer, Costain thought. He gathered all the broken strands of himself together and made a mighty effort to get up, but his heart was punctured, a useless sponge in his chest. He managed to lift a hand in the air and raise his face one last time. The room dimmed, then his head rolled to the side, his cheek pressed into the blood-soaked silk bedspread.

"I liked him," May Quirante said quietly. "He was good to me."

The killer cleaned the blades of his knife in the folds of silk, then snapped the instrument shut and pocketed it. "Take what you find in his wallet," he said. "When that's gone, you'll have to look after yourself. I'm sure you know how."

"Why did I allow this?" she asked. "Why?"

"You allowed nothing. You had no choice. Do you want me to tell you the truth about your American friend? Do you want to hear that story all over again?"

May Quirante looked down at Eugene Costain. The sight of *kamátayan,* death, sickened her. "Once was enough," she replied. Her eyes filled with tears, which she fought back because she was unaccustomed to crying. Besides, she didn't know what she grieved more—the loss of Eugene Costain's life or his financial assistance. Or was there some other emotion she had no experience in defining?

"Someone will come for the body," the young man said.

He rode in an overcrowded jeepney along Roxas Boulevard, past restaurants and coffee shops, nightclubs, large hotels like the

Silahis and the Admiral. Here and there stood black gutted buildings overgrown with foliage where the homeless found shelter under thin sheets of corrugated tin or slats of cardboard. To his right was Imelda Marcos's monumental legacy to the people of Manila, the Cultural Center beside the bay, built with funds provided twenty years ago by the Lyndon Johnson administration. Having raised political expediency to an experimental art form, a dadaism in which all things are permissible and opposites coexist, the Americans had cheerfully contributed to such grandiose notions of the Marcoses as concert halls and theaters, but apparently saw no anomaly in the fact that while Van Cliburn played Beethoven on one side of the street many thousands of Filipinos on the other had nothing to eat and nowhere to live.

The young man, whose name was Armando Teng although he used a variety of pseudonyms, no longer allowed such inequities to anger him. The poverty, for example, had become so commonplace that its existence intruded on his attention like the thin voices of some chorus too far away to hear. This was neither complacency nor acceptance on his part: far from it. But if he was to do what he demanded of himself and finish what had already been started, then he couldn't afford to become trapped in the quicksands of particular feelings.

The cost of his detachment was high. Often, he was compelled to walk away from situations in which his instincts told him he should act, or tune out of his mind tragedies he saw every day on the streets. He forced himself to ignore the searing contrasts created by social injustice: acres of unspeakable hovels in the district of Tondo where more than a million people lived in massed hopelessness while the rich led opulent lives in the fortressed mansions of Forbes Park; the miserable shantytowns that clung to the banks of the Pasig River a few miles from the Manila Polo Club where the young men of moneyed families rode priceless ponies with harsh indifference to the city bleeding around them. All this, which had once angered and depressed Teng, had become no more than a background blur to his main purpose. Consequently, he lived as if his heart was a shuttered house into which only a chosen amount of light was filtered.

Night obscured Manila Bay. Bright Chinese lanterns, indicating some form of festivity for guests, burned in the grounds of the

Philippine Plaza Hotel. The jeepney roared, starting, stopping, swerving in and out of traffic. The driver, a man tattooed with hook-billed birds and snakes, had a cigarette hanging from his mouth. Frequently he'd hawk up phlegm and spit into the traffic with the extravagance expected of a jeepney driver, which was a profession for men who thought themselves hard. When he wasn't spitting, he sang pop songs in a fair voice.

Teng got out of the crowded vehicle on Taft Avenue. Forever circumspect, slipping through the darkest streets, he found a taxi that took him past the Benigno Aquino International Airport to the suburb of Parañaque. People strolled back and forth on the narrow main thoroughfare. Sare-sare shops and cheap restaurants were lit, but they glowed only dimly. There was darkness within darkness here, layered and secretive, as if the real source of the night were inaccessible.

On Diego Cera Avenue Teng paid off the driver, then walked three blocks before he stopped. He pretended to look in the window of a junk shop. A strip of neon illuminated an array of dusty spark plugs, ancient batteries, oily black metal cylinders with no apparent function.

When he was satisfied he hadn't been followed, he walked until he reached the Church of the Bamboo Organ in Las Piñas. He crossed the courtyard, where several cars were parked. None was the one he wanted. Because he didn't like the notion of loitering without purpose, possibly drawing attention to himself, he went inside the church.

He moved toward the back pews, noticing that the holy water fonts were dry and encrusted with salt. Electric fans blew through the musty air. Worshipers, some nursing fretful children, were still lingering hours after the religious service had been performed. Built on a gallery overhead was the nineteenth century organ that had given the church its name. Bamboo pipes, each meticulously cut to a different length, stretched up into the shadows. A slow hymn was being played, a wistful thing Teng couldn't name but which suggested wind whining through caves. A baby cried, men and women gossiped, a mongrel shuffled near Teng's feet.

Teng looked toward the altar and the glassy-eyed icons erected there, a display of holy suffering meant to reassure a needy congregation that the burden of their pain was shared by saints and martyrs. *Suffering,* Teng thought. *The essential condition of a visa into paradise.* He had no time for this notion. Why couldn't there be justice in this lifetime? Why did you have to wait? He had neither the patience for, nor any belief in, the afterlife, like the devotees around him. The old Spanish friars had done their work well in the Philippines, leaving behind an entrenched legacy of Roman Catholic superstition that during certain holy days rose to insanity. Fanatics, in imitation of Christ, had themselves crucified in public display.

He was aware of a man sitting down beside him. Teng, showing no sign of recognition, rose and went out into the courtyard, where he lit the third of the five cigarettes he allowed himself every day. The other man followed almost at once. He was middle-aged and short and had skin like cracked morocco. He wore a short-sleeved barong made out of *piña.* His right eye, from which some parasitic larva had been surgically removed the day before, was bloodshot. As he walked toward a parked Subaru he did so in the deliberate way of a man who finds walking painful. Teng got into the car on the passenger side. Jovitoe "Joe" Baltazar climbed behind the wheel.

"I'm told you left the girl alive, Armando." When he spoke, Baltazar cracked his knuckles in an agitated way and restlessly scanned the parking lot.

Teng smoked his cigarette a moment. "Why not? Why would I want to kill her?"

"She knows your face."

Teng looked through the fronds of a palm tree at a pallid streetlamp. He was not going to let himself be swayed or irritated by Baltazar, who had a cavalier attitude toward spilling blood that Teng did not share. Before you killed, you had to have good cause. You had to have the fire for it.

"Even if she wanted to, she's too afraid to speak," Teng said.

"Can you count on that, Armando?"

Teng flicked his cigarette away. It floated in the direction of the church. "She's not my enemy."

"But she can point a finger at you." Baltazar shook his head in disapproval of what he obviously considered a strange flaw in Teng, this occasional benevolence, this mercy. An eyewitness was just another adversary. So you cleaned up. You closed the eyes, you sealed the mouth. You made sure.

Teng said, "Costain was the only target in the room. The girl doesn't deserve to die."

"She was the American's whore, Armando."

"The country's filled with whores taking American money." Teng remembered how the girl had sat astride the naked man. Watching from the kitchen, he'd been unexpectedly aroused by that roundness of hip and shadow of breast, the way her glossy hair fell forward against her face as she made love to Costain. It had been a long time since Teng had enjoyed any kind of intimacy with a woman. Months? Years? Time had collapsed around him, and he couldn't track its disintegration. He knew clocks, and punctuality, but he had no way of measuring *real* time, the time of the heart. He had loved once. The memory was a cinder, still too hot to touch.

Baltazar rubbed his bloodshot eye tentatively. "I can get somebody else to deal with her."

"No," Teng said. He stared through the windshield at the church. The organ was silent, the night hushed and motionless. "She doesn't know my name. She doesn't know where to find me. After Baguio, I'll be out of the country anyway."

Baltazar sighed. Momentarily he worried about the things that might go wrong in the northern city of Baguio before Teng even left the Philippines, but he said nothing. He never liked arguing with the younger man, whose stubbornness was as rigid as a wall. He unlocked the glove compartment and took out an envelope. He held it firmly a moment, as if he were undecided about giving it to Teng, as if he wanted to raise some last-minute objection. But then he passed it over, with some relic of reluctance still.

"Everything you need is inside. Passport. Money," Baltazar said. "People will meet you in America. Helpful people. But understand this, Armando: They're not professionals. They're ordinary people and this isn't the kind of thing they do every day. What counts is they're on your side."

Not professionals. Teng thought that if he'd developed skills in the craft of killing it was because circumstances had forced him, not because he had some notion of himself as a professional assassin. He hadn't started out with violence and hatred inside; once, the idea of murder would have been anathema to him, mortal sin. He placed the envelope in his lap without opening it. He closed his hands over it. He saw the interior of the church grow darker as candles began to die, and he had the odd sensation that the sputtering flames were inside his head. They didn't exist in the external world. It was a strange moment, as if a sudden fall from the adrenaline high of killing the American had muddled his sense of reality and now he was slowing down, sailing toward the dark tunnel of sleep. He was conscious too of distances, the miles he had still to cover, the three men who were yet to die.

Baltazar said, "If everything goes well in Baguio . . ." Then he paused and looked uncertainly at Teng.

"Baguio's the easy part," Teng said. "What could possibly go wrong?"

Baltazar's little shrug suggested that the potential hazards were too many to name. His world was a place of a million sinewy cracks, each concealing some hidden risk. "Your leniency concerns me," he said.

"Leniency?"

"You didn't kill the girl. What would you call that?"

Teng smiled, a rare, bright expression. "Economy of style."

He got out of the little car, slammed the door shut, and looked at Baltazar through the open window. The smile was already gone and the eyes were lifeless. Baltazar wondered fretfully if he'd ever see the young man again. He was about to wish Teng good luck, but Armando didn't believe in such a thing. You manufactured your own fortune. Bad luck was the excuse of fools.

Baltazar extended his hand and the young man shook it, and they parted without another word.

2

On the hottest recorded June day in the history of Los Angeles County Charlie Galloway, suspended from both duty and reality, sat in a dark air-conditioned bar on Wilshire and watched traffic pass like hallucinations in the glare of the afternoon light. He ran a fingertip around the rim of his shot glass and turned away from the window. If you looked at the street long enough you could imagine all that concentrated heat seeping through the walls, forcing itself inside the ducts of the cooling system and turning this pleasant oasis arid.

On TV somebody with a purple face was blethering about the weather. The continental United States had become one great hot dry mass. Cities had imposed restrictions on the use of electricity, water shortages had become commonplace, elderly people were dropping dead. Temperatures, as the announcer said in the melodramatic parlance of his profession, "soared": *Records are being broken all the way from Brownsville, Texas, to Hibbing, Minnesota.* There was talk of pressure fronts, but Galloway blanked it out. He had a pressure front moving through the center of his own head, and he didn't much like it.

He finished his drink and pushed the glass toward the bartender, who refilled it with Bell's. Charlie would have preferred an unblended scotch, but there was none to be had here. A few feet away a man in enormous Bermuda shorts and a T-shirt that said *THE FUTURE LIES IN PLANKTON* was talking to an emaciated young woman about the "greenhouse effect." The woman agreed the world didn't have much of a future because, hey, the handwriting was on the wall, right? The man plunged a hand into a silvery dish of peanuts and tossed one in the air, catching it in his open mouth. Crunching, he spoke knowledgeably of ozone layers and fossil fuels.

Galloway finished his scotch in a swift motion, a practiced tilt of the hand. All this doomsday talk bored the arse off him. He was an incurable optimist when it came to the survival of the species. It didn't matter to him that the two gloomies at the bar would have accused him of whistling in the dark. He believed in endurance.

Turning the empty glass in his fingers, he contemplated another shot. He'd reached that point where he could go either way. To stop now involved a complicated procedure of getting down from his stool and going out into that hot, skeletal street. It meant returning to life as he knew it, where his wife might or might not have surfaced. On the other hand, if he continued to drink he could feign a lack of interest in the demands of his life until he'd reached the point where he was no longer faking.

Indecision froze him. He thought he could remain forever balanced on this velveteen stool, which was royal blue and very comfortable. But he couldn't just sit with a dry glass, which was akin to trespass. He placed an elbow on the bar, propped his face upon the palm of his hand, caught an unwelcome glimpse of himself in the bar mirror. He had careless brown hair, a tangled ruin. His face, which sagged a little, was pale, and showed absolutely no evidence of California living. He had a vampire's complexion. Crypts might have been his natural habitat. His eyes were a weary gray-green, the color of a sunless sea. The crumpled cotton jacket and crushed linen pants suggested a man whose idea of style was whatever clothing lay closest to hand on waking. He wore scuffed sneakers with broken laces, no socks.

"You ready?"

Galloway looked at the barman, an ox with long Viking hair held back in a ponytail, a nautical sort of bloke, his skin browned by yo-ho-ho days surfing or sailing. He made Galloway, who pushed the shot glass forward to be filled, feel long dead and worm-riddled.

The door opened and a completely unacceptable square of horrifying sunlight brightened the bar. On the periphery of his vision Galloway was aware of a very familiar figure coming toward him. His instinct was to avoid any contact with the newcomer. *Let us step inside the House of Alcoholic Retreat,* Galloway thought. *We will be safe there, beyond rational speech and logic.* But he wasn't drunk enough to pass himself off as totally chaotic. He didn't quite have the key to his own humiliation yet, although it was nearby.

"Charlie, Charlie," the man said as he slid onto the stool next to Galloway, who realized he was expected to make a response, but a synapse popped almost at once and that part of his brain in which were stored simple social reactions underwent a slippage. A broken rudder: His brain was a beached boat.

"This is disappointing," Clarence Wylie said. One of his hands closed very tightly around Charlie's wrist. Galloway thought that if his lungs were in that wrist he'd need a cylinder of oxygen right away. "What is this going to achieve, Charlie?"

Clarence Wylie, who had retired from the Federal Bureau of Investigation last year at the age of fifty-two, still affected the bureau's sartorial fashion: Mormon chic. The shirt was excruciatingly white and the dark necktie neatly knotted, like that of a man on a mission. He had about him the jowly, off-center look of somebody who has balanced a telephone between shoulder and jaw for long periods of his life.

Charlie Galloway had no immediate answer to Wylie's question, about which he preferred not to think in any event. He reached for his drink, remembering that Clarence had worked directly for the monster called Vanderwolf, who'd built a private fiefdom inside the bureau and encouraged his courtiers to jostle one another for his favors, which he dispensed in a miserly way. On the two occasions when Galloway had met Vanderwolf it had been in the great man's office where the tan carpet perfectly matched the drapes and the three telephones aligned on the desk were the same color as rug and curtains. Vanderwolf himself wore a dark brown suit, dark brown shoes. He had a hunter's fondness for camouflage. If you narrowed your eyes, Galloway had thought, you probably wouldn't see him at all except for his forehead, a massive crag across which both enormous silvery eyebrows had bushed together.

The Wolf was a piece of work, Galloway thought. Mean-hearted, vicious, jealous of his terrain—which was the entire Western region of the FBI. That Clarence had survived his time under the man and retired with kindness and humanity intact was a marvel. Most of Vanderwolf's graduates turned out badly, base little men with gnarled, oaken hearts.

"You know goddam well you're not supposed to be here, Charlie."

"Have you been spying on me?"

Clarence Wylie had a sweet, rather sad little smile. "I went to the clinic to see how you were doing. They said you'd upped and left without so much as a farewell. I tracked you here. That's all. I wasn't spying. You know me better."

Galloway finished his drink, set the glass down, patted the back of Clarence's hand. He'd reached a state where he felt a misty gratitude toward Wylie. About a half mile back inside his tear ducts moisture was gathering. In this malted moment of affection, Charlie thought Wylie was the dearest, kindest friend a man could ever have. He was the cream. The best. Primo. They'd known each other for years, Clarence and Charlie, federal agent and Los Angeles cop, first tossed together in one of those usually awkward investigations where the Feds had been obliged to liaise with the LAPD in an affair involving an enormous quantity of narcotics.

"Drink with me, Clarence," and Charlie's accent thickened from the polite, Scottish-flavored speech he commonly used to the expansive vowels and rolling rrrs of his native Glasgow. *Drrrink wi me, Claaarrrnz.* Alcohol did this to him. It catapulted him back to his origins. It was the great slingshot, the time machine to the source. A few more drinks and he'd be damp-eyed and silly, *oot the gemme* as they used to say.

"You know I don't drink before dark, Charlie."

Galloway snorted. His small empty glass looked forlorn to

him. Clarence Wylie stretched out a hand and locked his palm very firmly around Galloway's elbow.

"Come with me," Wylie said. "Call it quits."

"I did five days, Clarence. I did fivefuckendays in that place without windows. Five, and every one a bastart. I graduated, Clarence. I graduated with honors. And here I am." He waved a hand around the bar, as if it were a club you could join only if you'd put in some quality time at clinics and drunk tanks and black rooms where people screamed because they were being beaten by their dead parents, or eaten by oversized rodents, or because they heard their coffin being carried up the stairs by men with hobnailed boots.

"You were meant to stay four weeks, Charlie. That's what the doctor ordered. Four dry weeks. Then weekly follow-ups. You don't exactly graduate from places like that. You don't get a diploma. What they give you is a kind of daily reprieve, my friend."

Charlie Galloway swayed. Because of his recent abstinence the scotch had burned out his connections quicker than he'd anticipated. A mellow stage had been skipped, the plateau of easy serenity missed. Now he was on the glacier and could feel the slavering huskies yanking on the sled that would take him to the edge. He picked up his empty glass. Wylie plucked it from his fingers and set it down.

"You don't need any more, Charlie. Let's get you out of here."

Galloway couldn't find the energy for combat. He allowed himself to be led away from the bar. He wasn't happy. The idea of the blistering white street paralyzed him. He would be cauterized out there, reduced to primal substance. Shitlike glop on the pavement. Charles Douglas Galloway, scooped up and put in a Ziploc bag and sealed, his remains returned to their point of origin on Govan Road, Glasgow, if Govan Road still existed, if Glasgow still existed. And what if they did? Would anyone in the old street remember C. D. Galloway after fifteen years of exile?

"That wanker at the clinic—Boscoe, Roscoe, whoever he was—asked me why I drink," he said, more to stall the exit than to enrich Wylie's store of knowledge. "Puffed-up wee bugger."

"And what did you tell him, Charlie?"

"The truth, old son. Always the truth."

"And what's the truth?" Wylie steered him gently toward the door.

Galloway had one of those moments of strange lucidity, an ellipse in the path of drunkenness, in which he couldn't understand why he wasn't more vigorously protesting his situation. He wanted to stay in the bar. Here he was safe. Out there were people, situations to confront. Here he could postpone remorse until the dark hour when the law required the bar to shut.

Wylie tugged the door open. The light scorched Galloway's eyeballs. He saw nothing. The heat withered him. He hadn't imagined the universe capable of such an unholy temperature. God was dead. Somebody else was stoking the furnace now. What other explanation could there be? He felt like a lit wax candle.

"You were going to tell me the truth about why you drink, Charlie," Wylie reminded him.

"Aye, so I was, so I was. It's deep, Clarence. Are you up for it?"

"I'm listening," Wylie said, in the manner of a man who has been in the same place too many times.

His throat abruptly dry, Charlie Galloway said, "I drink because I like the taste of the bloody stuff."

"And that's it?"

"That's it."

"Well, hell, that's interesting," was all Wylie said. They moved to the curb, where Wylie had parked a big brown Buick. He opened the passenger door for Galloway.

"Of course, Clarence," Galloway said as he ducked inside the vehicle and struck his head against the rearview mirror, causing a brilliant flash of reflected light. "I can quit anytime."

"I bet you can," Wylie remarked, and he thought of the nights he'd hunted Charlie down in some bar to drive him safely home, or the mornings he'd helped him through manic hangovers when Karen had taken one of her hikes away from her boozed-up husband. He thought of hours spent listening to Charlie ramble in the Sanskrit of the drunk about how he was going to change his world and do everything differently. Yeah o yeah. Clarence had heard it all. And at those times when he wondered why he continued to befriend the accursed Scotsman, Charlie would

throw him a curveball, a surprise, an unexpected month of sobriety and charm and the prospect of better times—only to wreck
it in a sudden binge, swept away on a storm of alcohol. God bless
friendship, Clarence thought. The rough and the smooth. With
Charlie Galloway, who at times had that innocent vulnerability
of a small dog in the middle of a busy freeway, it was all too often
the rough.

Galloway had half expected Clarence to whisk him back to the
clinic, which was situated in one of those plush side streets that
adjoin Sunset Boulevard, and dump him on Dr. Boscoe's doorstep. There would be lectures and Librium and shame. Instead,
Wylie went another way, up and up into the hills above the
canyons, where dense foliage tried to lock out the sunlight and
houses, hidden by mossy trees, came briefly into view before
disappearing again. After a while Galloway realized they were
heading toward his own home, a 1930s two-bedroom place rented
from a Syrian woman who ran a doubtful escort agency for elderly
gentlemen.

"You look like you need rest," Wylie said.

Rest? Rest was what you did when you were dead, for
Christ's sake. What Charlie Galloway wanted was for night to
come and the neon signs of bars to sizzle in the hot dark and
himself on a boozy prowl. He looked through the window. Fierce
sunlight exploded among the trees. He squeezed the bridge of his
nose because a headache had begun to form behind his eyes. It
often happened when he was cut off in mid-drink. The only
known cure was a fresh glass. Sobriety seemed as bleak to him as
a teetotaler's wake.

The Buick continued to climb. The narrow streets, some
barely lanes, twisted unexpectedly. Galloway looked down the
way they'd come, into pale green-brown canyons, abysses that in
wetter seasons were blue-black and luscious. Afloat in the trees
were tiled rooftops, chimney pots, satellite dishes reflecting the
burning sky. He shut his eyes. A pocket of nausea formed in his
stomach and he was dizzy, but he knew this uneasy condition so
well he wrestled it into submission with no great effort.

"You feeling okay?" Wylie asked.

"Never better." He lied with aplomb.

Wylie went into another bend, this one practically a right angle, and Galloway, whose ballast was all wrong, tilted to the side. He recognized this street and understood this turn because he'd negotiated it a thousand times in a variety of physical conditions, but still it surprised him.

Wylie turned the Buick into a driveway and parked under an enormous avocado tree. Home. Home and hearth and heart. Charlie Galloway looked at the small white stucco house with the black wooden shutters. The doorway was arched, a Spanish touch, a bit of olé. It reminded him of a cantina he'd once visited in the Baja with Karen, Dos Equis beer and enchiladas and the smell of things endlessly frying in the same lard. How had so much love distilled itself in memories of refried beans and murderously hot peppers?

Wylie came around the front of the car, opened the passenger door. Galloway stepped out without assistance. He wiped his damp palms on his pants and walked toward the house. According to the landlady, this tiny house had been rented for a month in the 1930s by an actress named Brenda Joyce, whose spurious claim to fame lay in the fact she'd appeared in some Tarzan movies of the late forties. The landlady was very proud of this connection with minor celebrity. And why not? This whole city celebrated celebrity. Millions were spent manufacturing that most perishable commodity of the American century, fame.

As he reached in his pants pocket for his keys, Galloway saw the tiny bird at his feet. It lay upside down against the door, stiff legs drawn in, claws bent, small pale eyes open. He stepped back with a shudder. Death on the doorstep.

"Would you say this was an omen, Clarence?"

Wylie bent, examined the bird. "I'd say it was a dead sparrow."

Galloway stared at the fuzzy little corpse, thinking how death made things shrink, stripped them of size and substance. A deid sparra. Already you could see the outline of the bird's frail skeleton through lackluster feathers. He was reminded suddenly of a canary he'd kept as a boy, a cheerful yellow thing that had sung all day long, passionately courting its own reflection in a mirror. It had chosen Christmas morning, 1952, to die of causes unknown. Charlie Galloway, aged seven, had risen early to catch

Santa at his sly work, but instead had found the bird, far beyond song, at the bottom of its cage.

Galloway's father, a wag, a shipyard worker with a prize fighter's nose, had tried to lift the gloom by suggesting they roast the canary for a Christmas snack. Make a nice change, he'd said. Probably very tasty, mmmmm. Wash the wee bugger down with ginger beer, eh?

Galloway hadn't thought about that Christmas in years. Now he couldn't remember if they'd flushed the bird and gone on with the festivities, or if he'd spent the day moping in his room with the long window that overlooked the smirr clouding the River Clyde and the tangle of shipyard cranes that rose over Glasgow. Something in that rainy arrangement of cranes, those steel grids set against the sky, had suggested a mystery to Charlie, a design he could never fathom.

He couldn't even recollect the damn canary's name. Alcohol and memory played in different leagues. When you drank, everything in the past had a gossamer quality. You reached for it and, whoops, it was gone, leaving only a broken web flapping against your face.

"I wonder what killed it," he said, looking at the sparrow.

Clarence Wylie, kind to dead birds and drunks alike, nudged the dried-out creature gently with his foot on to the parched lawn. "Maybe it couldn't find anything to drink," he said.

"It has my heartfelt sympathy."

Galloway turned the key in the lock. He entered the house reluctantly because there was sadness in these rooms. Lost love, he thought. But this was the city of illusions, and love, like fame, was another commodity with a limited shelf life. Galloway didn't want to believe that, not for a minute.

The living room was dark, the air stuffy. The furniture, chosen by Karen, was Southwestern, the colors pale pinks and turquoises and earth tones. Navajo tapestries hung on the walls. Kachina dolls peered like autistic victims from shelves. The tiled floor was strewn with Indian rugs. There were many wicker baskets, some stuffed with magazines, some with cacti. What the room suggested to Galloway was an upscale wigwam. He'd never felt at home with all this stuff but he'd gone along with Karen's decor because he loved her and love was sometimes a matter of blind compromise in the smallest of things. *Should I hang this picture here, Charlie? Or here?* Wherever pleases you, sweetheart.

He experienced a longing for her so strong it burned into him as surely as acid spilled on his skin. He looked across the room to the doorway that led upstairs, hoping she might materialize there, but there were only shadows and emptiness. He crossed the floor, unlocked the shutters, parting them a few inches to allow a narrow slit of very bright light to penetrate the room.

Followed by Wylie, Galloway went inside the kitchen. He opened the refrigerator. A lonely Pabst beer, attached to a plastic six-pack collar, sat in the center shelf. He reached for it and had it open before Wylie could react. He downed half of it in one swallow. Elixir.

"Hey, no more booze, Charlie," Wylie said, confiscating the can and pouring the liquid into the sink. "We'll play it my way. First, take a shower while I make some coffee. Then you go lie down. You look like shit."

"Bloody bully."

Clarence Wylie said, "I'm a heartless bastard."

With a resigned look of obedience, Charlie Galloway climbed slowly upstairs. The upper part of the house contained three small rooms—two bedrooms, one of them for guests and strays, usually Charlie's inebriated acquaintances, and a bathroom. The larger bedroom was the one he'd shared with Karen. The conjugal bed. If he listened carefully he thought he might hear echoes of lovemaking and passion and an intimacy that had been richer than anything he'd ever dreamed accessible in his life. And what the hell had he done with it? He'd blown it away like the filaments of a dandelion. No. Why be so damned pastoral? What he'd really achieved was the insane derailment of his marriage, strewing wrecked carriages all along twisted tracks—smoke and glass and a shattered locomotive that had gone completely out of control.

An unsteadiness seized him in the hallway between bedroom and bath and he lost his balance a moment, lurching against the wall under the place where Karen had hung framed photographs of their life together. Suspended above Galloway in the gloom was pictorial evidence of a wonderful courtship and a wedding, all bright things done in the lacy sunlight of those days of promise.

In a state of sadness, he slid slowly to the floor, his cheek pressed to the white paintwork. A barb dug deeply into his heart: *How had it come to this?* He squeezed his eyes tightly shut because what he wanted more than anything else was to cry, to shake himself free of sorrow. But alcohol was always an unhappy tunesmith; melancholy's piper. *You could sit here and wallow for a long time, Charlie. Pain, after all, is a comfort all its own. You sick bastard, what are you?*

He pulled himself up and made it inside the bathroom, black and white squares on the floor and a huge bathtub on paws, a simple sink, a simple mirror. There was no clutter here, nothing that invited you to linger. He undressed, tossed his sweaty clothes on the floor, climbed into the tub, and drew the shower curtain. The water pierced and stung him, revitalizing him to a point where the edge of drunkenness was lost, even if he knew it was only a temporary bluntness.

He decided to shave. A daft undertaking. He razored himself badly, bled into the sink, stuck toilet paper over the wounds. He doused redness from his eyes with Murine, then brushed his teeth and gargled. What emerged some minutes later, dressed in a clean silk robe, face studded with tiny cuts, looked arguably human.

He went downstairs. In the kitchen Clarence Wylie had found a jar of instant coffee and two mugs, one of which he pushed toward Galloway.

"What happened to your face, Charlie?"

"Failed suicide attempt."

Wylie replied with a mild joke. "Couldn't quite cut it, huh?"

Galloway smiled politely and peeled the pinkish pieces of paper from his jaw. He reached for the coffee. Already the quick fix of energy from the shower was fading and there was slippage inside him. He'd drifted from his moorings. The coffee was tasteless. It needed something to make it sit up and sing. Vodka. A slug of Gordon's. He slumped in a chair.

"Where's Karen living?" Wylie asked.

"Now, that's a good question, Clarence. She tells me she moves between friends. It's her drifting phase." Galloway pushed the coffee mug aside. He resented the yellow daffodils that decorated it. Drifting phase. "I miss her," he added, and his voice had a break in it. He looked up at the ceiling, where the fan was still and a spider hung from a blade. "I miss her and I wish to God I knew how to get her back," and his tone became strident all at once, loud with desperation.

Wylie gazed across the kitchen, saying nothing. His round, worn face had the contemplative expression of a monk who has encountered too many sorrowful pilgrims. He was a good-natured man who'd asked a sympathetic question. But it was the wrong question at the wrong time, and it had provoked a raw reaction. Galloway had the anemic, disbelieving look of an earthquake victim who finds his whole world vanished in deep crevices. He picked up his coffee and held it to his lips. His eyes were closed. Steam rose into his lashes.

"I'm sorry, Clarence. I didn't mean to shout. I just—" and his voice left him a moment. He pressed his fingertips to his eyelids. "It's the bloody emptiness. And the ghosts get on my nerves."

But you know how to get Karen back, Wylie thought, although he wasn't about to say so. The last thing Charlie Galloway needed was advice on how to reinstate his marriage. Boozers regarded unsolicited counsel with the skepticism reserved by physicians for psychic healers. And Wylie, wary of setting off more depth charges, was quiet for a while before he rose from his chair. "I have to go, Charlie."

"I'll walk you out," Charlie said.

"You don't need to."

Charlie made a small dismissive gesture and opened the door. *The least I can do.*

Outside, even the shade beneath the avocado tree had been breached by heat. Every dry leaf appeared to vibrate with its own fiery energy.

"Now go back to bed, Charlie," Clarence said. "And stay there. Sleep it off. No booze." A finger wagged.

"I will, I will."

"I'll call you later. Just to check in."

I bet, Charlie thought. I bet you will.

Unbalanced, leaning against the doorjamb, he watched

Wylie, jailor and wet nurse, stroll to the Buick. Behind the wheel Clarence raised a clenched fist in the air, though whether as warning or encouragement it was hard to tell. Charlie observed the car go out of the driveway. How dehydrated he felt! Did Clarence really expect him just to go and lie down in a darkened room like a man with migraine? Wily Wylie surely knew better. It would not be beyond Clarence to wait in some hidden place, concealed inside his sweltering Buick, eyeballing the road for a sign of Charlie scudding off to the nearest liquor store or cocktail bar.

Galloway was about to close the door when he realized a figure had appeared near the big tree, a woman of about fifty in a white blouse and baggy red shorts. Her head was covered by a large straw hat, her face in shadow. She carried a canvas bag.

"Ella, how are you?" Galloway asked. He'd forgotten it was Tuesday and that she came every week, same day, same time.

The small Filipina woman approached the doorway, wiped a hand across her damp forehead. She set the canvas bag down. It contained her cleaning materials, jars of this, bottles of that, rags that smelled of furniture polish. She didn't drive. Wherever she had to go she walked or rode a bus. Galloway, who was very fond of Ella Nazarena—indeed had come to consider her a family member, a favorite aunt—felt sorry for her in this weather. He had the urge to hug her. Some quality about her always unleashed in him a profound sympathy. She made him wish he was filthy rich and could transform her life with a shower of coins: Here, Ella, sit down, take the weight off your life, relax, no more hard miserable work for you, my dear. He gazed at the religious symbols around her neck, a crucifix, a St. Francis, and some other saint he didn't recognize.

"Mrs. Galloway is back?" she asked. She must have been very pretty once, Galloway thought. Sometimes when she smiled there was a pale flash of an old beauty and the black-brown eyes suggested a tamped-down fire. It was as if a specter of a former self still occupied the body.

Galloway shook his head. He was distracted by wondering if there was anything in the house to drink. Something stashed. Something he'd planked away.

Mrs. Nazarena said, "Too bad. Don't give up hope. One day

soon, huh? She will come home. She loves you. You love her. It works out in God's own time. It always does."

The woman's simple faith often dumbfounded Galloway. She perceived a logic in God, a balance. God kept the ledgers and everything came out right in the end. A joyful accounting. This uncomplicated belief that sustained her wouldn't have belonged in the Scottish kirks of Charlie's childhood, which tended to be cheerless places designed by men who thought the road to heaven was John Knox Avenue, a gloomy thoroughfare little used. The notion of happiness in religion, if you were a Presbyterian, belonged only to pagans and holy rollers. He remembered trembling a great deal as a boy, appalled by the roar of a certain Reverend McNab, a bony white giant in a high pulpit who offered his congregation either a living hell or a dead one. The minister made Charlie feel guilty of something, only he wasn't sure what. As for grace, which McNab referred to always in the sly whisper of a car salesman with a lemon to get off his hands, that concept eluded Charlie entirely except as the name of a girl who sat in front of him at school and had very big purplish ears.

"You still want me to work today?" Ella asked.

"Of course. The house needs you. I need you. Where would I be without you?" He smiled at her. His affection for her had stemmed originally from a sense they shared of exile from their native countries. Sometimes, when she reminisced about the Philippines, when she remembered a landscape of lagoons where the water, she said, was God's own idea of blue, or valleys so green they suggested the very first hour of creation, when she talked of the wondrous rice terraces of northern Luzon, Galloway became her fellow conspirator in nostalgic attachments to faraway lands where they'd each left the most important parts of themselves. He spoke to her of the rocky Western Islands set in savage black tides, the lonesome greenery of the Borders, mystic Glasgow on a long white summery night. They understood each other's longings.

Once, in a mood of drunken benevolence, he'd danced for her his version of the Highland Fling, arms upraised over his head, feet daringly light—a darting, laughing performance during which he'd caught her around the waist and spun her until she was breathless. At the end of the dance he tried to tell her that in the interests of authenticity he should have worn a kilt, a garment he couldn't altogether explain to her. A skirt? Sort of, Ella. But not really. She'd said the word *kilt* to herself several times, a new discovery.

Later, she told him she'd looked up Scotland in a world atlas at the public library, and for some reason this touched him so much that he reciprocated, studying a map of the Philippines and finding Ella Nazarena's province among a multitude of exotic islands littered in the South China Sea like so many cookie crumbs. He'd taught her some good Glasgow words, like *dreich* and *bauchle* and *pokey-hat,* and in return he'd learned *salámat* and *paálam* and *kumustá.* Theirs was a relationship less of employer and minion than of equals, involving tiny moments of yearning and some of raucous laughter.

"You no work today?" she asked.

"Not today."

"Suspended again?"

Galloway nodded quickly, glossing over the humiliating matter of his unemployment, then stepped back into the blessed shade of the house. In the direct glare of the sun he'd begun to feel like flimsy paper placed beneath a magnifying glass to curl blackly and smolder until total cremation.

Mrs. Nazarena, her face creased by years of monotonous domestic chores in the canyons of Los Angeles, picked up her bag and followed Galloway inside. "How long suspended this time?"

"Three months."

"Without pay?"

"Without pay."

"Bad news." She frowned, bit her lip, then turned her head to the side as if she didn't want to look him directly in the eye. She smells it on me, he thought. The sulfuric perfume of drunken loneliness. But then he realized it was more, that the woman had something on her mind she wanted to say, only she wasn't sure how.

Had he forgotten to pay her? Did he owe her? No, it was more than that. If it had been back pay she would have said so without hesitation. There was an element in her manner he'd never seen before. Fear? Maybe that was too strong. He wasn't sure. Sun and booze had melted his antennae. All the messages that came to him were scrambled in transmission.

"Is something wrong?" he asked.

"Yes. I think so." She looked bone-weary, puckered by heat and depression. "Maybe something bad."

"If you've got a problem, Ella, I might be able to help."

Mrs. Nazarena said, "Maybe later. I think it over. Will you call me tonight?"

"Whatever suits you, Ella. Just remember. Anything I can do. Anything . . ."

"*Salámat.*"

He wondered what Ella could possibly have in mind. *Maybe something bad.* Did she know somebody in trouble with the law? Had one of her many relatives done something illegal? But how could he possibly help *anyone* in his present condition? Dear God. His skull ached. He said he was going up to his room, mumbling something about a nap as he headed, in an uncertain manner, toward the staircase, which appeared unusually steep, peculiarly angled, strange.

"I try to be quiet as I can," Ella called after him.

She stacked dishes in the dishwasher. She sprayed the ceramic work surfaces with Glass Plus, which she wiped off, then she tackled the inside of the oven. God only knew what Mr. Galloway had been eating since Karen had gone; the bottom of the oven was covered with blackened blisters, burnt warts of spilled food that had baked on the enamel. She worked on these for a time with Easy-Off, then cleaned the inside of the microwave where streaks of tomato pulp adhered to the glass. It looked like chicken cacciatore had exploded.

The trapped heat of the house tired her quickly. She drank cold water and went inside the living room. She sat down on the edge of the sofa, balanced in the manner of an uneasy guest. She'd worked six years for the Galloways and they always treated her well, more like a friend than housekeeper. Some of her employers scarcely noticed her presence. Some hardly even spoke to her except to issue commands. They were princesses, their houses kingdoms to be ruled. The Galloways were different. They were human. They had no pretensions, no airs and graces.

She knew Charlie was basically a good man who had his problems. One afternoon she'd found him fully clothed and fast asleep inside the bathtub and Mrs. Galloway had said, *Leave him right there, Ella, let the bastard sleep it off.* It was only natural for Karen to express herself with anger at times. Life with Charlie was no day at the beach, after all. But Karen wasn't the kind of woman who could stay enraged for long. Her heart was too big for that. Too big for grudges, for weights.

Mrs. Nazarena had absolutely no doubt the Galloways loved each other. She knew love when she saw it. But sometimes love alone wasn't strong enough to hold things together. You needed to work hard, and be considerate, and if you were Charlie Galloway you needed above all else to get rid of the weakness that was killing you slowly.

And amen, she thought.

She took her rosary from the pocket of her shorts. The feel of the plain wooden beads comforted her. She closed her eyes and wondered if she'd done the right thing by approaching Mr. Galloway. It hadn't come easily. Last night, when she considered it for the hundredth time, she'd been unable to sleep. Besides, the packs of stray dogs that roamed the neighborhood had been especially active and noisy. There were so many vicious strays now that people had taken to shooting them. Around two A.M. she'd risen to take a sleeping pill. While she waited for the narcotic to affect her, she sat for a long time at the kitchen window and watched the broken-down house across the narrow street where the muscular young man called Luke worked all night long on the motorcycles in his garage. The moon, she recalled, had been coppery with freeway fumes, the night hot and loud, police sirens in the next street, an ambulance cutting through the dark, kids partying along the block, and the dogs, always the dogs.

Was it right or wrong to bring the problem to Mr. Galloway? Why should he take on the *ligalit*, the worry of somebody else? He had enough troubles of his own. But something bad was going on, something that would lead to violence. She hated violence. Even if it was around her all the time, she'd never become immune to it. The notion of one human being inflicting injury or death on another was inconceivable to her. Her life was tempered by mercy.

She didn't want to go to some unfamiliar cop. She trusted Charlie Galloway. He wouldn't expose her. If she showed him Cara's letter which contained the bad news, he'd act with discretion. She was sure of that.

Maybe she should have kept her mouth shut and not bothered him. Dear Jesus, she said to herself, help me. Open my eyes and make me see. Show me the right thing. I am your willing subject, guide me.

She got up from the sofa with some effort, moaning softly. Increasingly these days she was inconvenienced by muscular pains in the back of her legs, but the medication she'd been prescribed killed more than the pain—it made her mind freeze and she forgot things, and sometimes she would stop moving because she couldn't remember where she was headed in any case. She often felt as if she were suspended in midair.

She polished the living room table. She sang quietly as she worked, because it made the labor easier. She had a good clear voice, younger than her years. When she came to the part about troubles melting like lemon drops, she stopped.

She saw her face look up from the gleaming surface of the table. Thirty years ago, before she'd emigrated, she'd been the prettiest girl in her *barangay* in Benguet Province. Dozens of men, not only from her own *barangay* but from other districts, had wanted her. She'd chosen Luiz, the one she considered the brightest, the strongest. In 1960 he had brought her to Los Angeles, where he'd worked in the construction industry. One morning scaffolding collapsed and buried him, and it had taken too long to get him out. They rushed him to a hospital.

DOA, they told her. Tough break. Very tough. In full settlement of the construction company's liabilities, she'd accepted a check for thirty-five hundred dollars. She'd signed a paper, and the company's youthful lawyer—a smooth boy blemished only by a pimple on his forehead; she'd never forget that red zit—had smiled with confidence and charm, and that was the end of it. A check came in the mail two days afterward.

Years later she learned she might have sued for many thousands, perhaps a million dollars, but she'd signed that opportunity away because she hadn't understood the system, how America worked, how big corporations knew all the ways to cheat poor people. There was no more money to be had from Luiz's death. She spent almost all the thirty-five hundred on his funeral expenses. What she had left over was enough to buy a twenty-dollar medallion of St. Rose of Lima, patroness of the Philippines, and a black coat and hat for the church service.

Now look at her. The years had rotted her. But she had Jesus, and the Holy Virgin, and she surrounded herself with saints. She was neither bitter nor lonely.

She even had a gentleman caller, a widower named Freddie Joaquin from Tarlac Province. Freddie always wore highly polished black shoes so that when he moved, his feet were like two flashing mirrors reflecting everything. Freddie had recently spoken of marriage, but Ella couldn't commit herself; she was half in love with the dead. Besides, Freddie wasn't as reliable as she would have liked. Sometimes she caught him out in white lies, sometimes his excuses when he was late for a date weren't always acceptable. Slippery. But kind to her. A small gift here, flowers there. She couldn't deny his generosity, but marriage was something else.

The telephone rang. It was Mrs. Galloway. "Is Charlie there, Ella?" she asked.

Ella said he was. But probably asleep.

"Damn. I wanted to pick up some of my stuff."

"Tell me what you need. I'll get it for you."

"Are you sure?"

"No problem."

As she listened to Karen's list of requirements—some clothing items, a few jewels—Mrs. Nazarena drifted into a daydream in which the Galloways reconciled. She'd pray for them later. There was no marriage counselor like God. And she'd remember to pray for herself at the same time.

3

Some nine thousand miles from Los Angeles, and twenty-four hours before Charlie Galloway escaped from the deprivations of the clinic, Captain Ramon Deduro and two of his men traveled through Baguio City in a Land Rover. The captain rode alone in the back. All three men wore the uniform of the Philippines Constabulary and were armed. Bad-tempered because of the ungodly hour—the red dawn sun had only just begun to burn mist from golf courses and ravines—each man was sullenly withdrawn. They gave the impression that they'd shoot without question the first person who irritated them.

Captain Deduro, who had tubercular shadows under his eyes and the chagrined look of a man disappointed by his rank in life, scrutinized the street as the vehicle went down through the center of the city. Baguio was quiet at this hour. The big public market on Magsaysay Avenue hadn't opened and the stores and cafés on Session Road were shut. The air, unfouled as yet by traffic, was scented by tupalau and almaciga, the pines of the region. The sweet perfume reminded Deduro of a pleasant experience, although he wasn't sure what—a woman's aromatic kiss, a talcumed breast in the palm of his stubby little hand. Something romantic: The captain adored women. He closed his eyes, as if to focus on the exact nature of what the pines suggested, but another memory, specific and far less cheering, intruded.

A few hours ago he'd lost forty-two thousand pesos at the roulette table in the Hyatt Terraces Hotel. In pursuit of the strangely elusive number thirty-three, he'd watched hundreds of pesos vanish at each maddening click of the tiny ball. With a gambler's irrational conviction that sooner or later the fates would bestow upon him the malicious smile they reserved for the obsessed, he stalked thirty-three hour after hour. At three-thirty A.M.—this sinister configuration of threes didn't escape him—he dropped his last hundred and rose blearily from the table.

He was already in debt to various friends and moneylenders. His position in the constabulary allowed him a certain license when it came to repayment. After all, who would be idiot enough to pressure a captain? But he didn't like owing money because his political enemies would seize the fact and distort it, claiming that not only had he amassed gambling debts but had also taken bribes and abused his position. In the old days, the Marcos days, he might have ignored his carping critics. But now, under the watchful eye of Auntie Cory Aquino, you had to exercise some discretion, some care. These were not qualities that came to him naturally. He was more inclined to swagger and bravado.

He'd left the casino and gone back to the house where he lived alone, a two-room cinder-block affair that clung to the side of one of the many hills of Baguio. Jerry-built like most of the housing in the city, it appeared to have been rooted to the ground in such a precarious fashion that any passing wind might blow it away. It hadn't happened yet; it was as if the builder had negotiated a deal with gravity.

Below Deduro's house were buildings of even more questionable construction, shacks, hovels with corrugated metal roofs and tarpaper walls. An incalculable number of barefoot children lived in these dwellings and sent up a daily clamor. Sometimes when he looked from his bedroom window the captain felt fortunate that he had the highest house on this particular hill, one that commanded a fine view over a landscape of pine and bougainvillea, vegetable terraces and deep green valleys—which, if you chose to ignore, as Deduro did, the brittle ugliness of the shacks and the inexpensive laundry hung out to dry, was beautiful.

He'd fed his guard dog and reset the burglar alarm, then drawn the straw blinds in his bedroom. With his pistol under his pillow he lay for a restless hour pondering how to pay off his markers at the casino. Then he slept for another hour before the brisk sound of the telephone made him sit up. The caller, very apologetic about the inconvenience, had found a corpse in a field, obviously a police matter because of the bullet wounds in the dead man's head. Sleepily, Deduro had scribbled down directions in a notepad he kept on a bedside table.

The caller said his name was Arturo Paz. Deduro agreed to meet him at the place where the corpse had been found. It was a damnable nuisance at this or any other hour of the day, but what could he do? In normal circumstances the matter would have been dealt with by the night officer, a churl called Sergeant Almenha, but he'd been sick, so he claimed, for the last few days, and calls were forwarded to Deduro's number. If a murder had been committed, then it had to be investigated. And a corpse, if indeed one existed, could not be left to decay in a field. . . .

Deduro had dressed quickly while he considered the call, questioning it the way he did every piece of information that reached him. The times had made him cautious. Members of the constabulary throughout the republic were killed almost daily for their weapons by gun-hungry adherents of the New People's Army, which Deduro considered an undernourished assortment of Marxist fools, thugs, and misguided peasants.

But you couldn't treat them lightly. Last month, in the adjoining province of Ilocos Sur, four constabulary members and their families had been ambushed inside a church during Mass— an unthinkable sacrilege. You walked with great care these days and you developed eyes in the back of your head and you went nowhere, absolutely nowhere, without your weapons.

Now Deduro stared at Magsaysay Avenue, along which the Land Rover traveled north. On either side of the street were fertilizer and seed supply stores, outlets stocked with cinder blocks and bags of cement, small general stores and drab cafeterias, blacksmiths, radiator shops. Mainly these were dim caverns with dirt floors. Ahead rose the enormous pagoda of the Bell

Temple, whose stairways climbed the side of a steep hill where the sun hadn't yet burned through the mist. The high tower of the Chinese temple was almost obscured from view, a ghostly thing.

The driver turned on the radio. Deduro heard a man sing

Take me home, country roads
To the place I belong

The captain hummed along with the tune. He accepted without question an American song coming out of a car radio in the Benguet Province of the Philippines. There was nothing even slightly incongruous in this for him. All his life he'd been conscious of Americans in his country. He'd worked alongside them on two or three occasions and admired the direct way they did things. They believed in their own worth and were consequently possessed by that clear-eyed righteousness of all true missionaries who, when they cannot convert infidels, prefer to eliminate them. He liked their culture, which they had exported with such vigor that forty-five years after Filipino independence English was still the official language of government in the country, and basketball—a far greater export than language, if you wanted Deduro's opinion—was the number one sport.

He also liked the American military bases in Clark and Subic Bay, especially the manner in which certain goods sometimes "strayed" from these bases into his possession—automobile batteries, tires, spare parts, for which he always found willing buyers. Perhaps a solution to his financial problems lay there. Later, he might make a call to one or another of his connections just to see whether something was scheduled, as the Americans put it, "to fall off a truck."

"Make it louder," Deduro said. "I enjoy this song."

The driver, Gallines, a dark-complexioned man with Negritos blood, obeyed.

West Virginia, mountain hollow . . .
Take me home, country roads.

As he listened to this anthem of a country he'd never known firsthand, Deduro fretted over his debts and continued to observe the landscape. The Land Rover passed the boundary between Baguio and the town of La Trinidad, and the pale green buildings of the state university slipped past. Nobody moved on the campus, where the shadows were long and deep.

"Left," Deduro said, consulting the directions he'd been given. "Did either of you ever hear of this Paz? The name familiar to you?"

Gallines shook his head. In the passenger seat Sergeant Ocampo chewed on the confection called *turrones de casoy* and said he'd once known a Robert Paz in Manila, but that was fifteen years ago.

The Land Rover entered a narrow unpaved street of shacks. A panicked pig scuttled in front of the vehicle and three hens half flew on clumsy wings. Somewhere trash was burning with a vile smell, sending a choking pall of smoke through the open vehicle. Deduro coughed and the driver spluttered. Sergeant Ocampo flapped his hands at the dirty cloud.

"Shit," Deduro said. Somebody was always burning something—garbage, wood, old tires. "Get us the hell away from here, Gallines."

The driver pressed his foot harder on the gas pedal. Dust blew up in torrents from under the wheels and for a moment the Land Rover, itself no paragon of pollution control, was eclipsed by smoke and pulverized dirt. Then the vehicle pulled clear and the smoke drifted away behind it and the dust settled with gritty inevitability. Captain Deduro rubbed his eyes. He couldn't shake his fatigue, which felt like an anchor he was obliged to drag around.

The shacks ended and the street narrowed, fading out in a shallow ravine where sturdy weeds grew and an occasional flame tree, a bright survivor, managed to look faintly festive. The track rose gradually for several kilometers. There were no more homes. Here and there piles of cinder block and wood lay strewn around as if efforts to build had been abandoned; or perhaps these were the ruins of houses flattened by typhoons. How could you tell? Captain Deduro didn't like this place. He wasn't fond of empty landscapes, especially those that came at you suddenly. He took his pistol out of its holster and laid it in his lap before he consulted the directions again.

"Look for a fork in this road," he said. "Bear right for about ten kilometers. That's where this Paz will meet us."

The fork was found, the Land Rover turned right, the land-scape became even quieter. Old bamboo tufts, some rotted by age and insect infestation, slanted along the path. They created a screen against the passage of sound. Silence and bamboo. Twenty-five kilometers from the commerce of Magsaysay Avenue and La Trinidad, and it was another world. Captain Deduro undid the safety catch on his gun.

Gallines drove a little farther, then braked as a tall young man emerged from the bamboos, his slender arms raised in the air, palms turned out. He approached the Land Rover slowly.

"Paz?" Deduro asked.

"Yes."

Sergeant Ocampo stepped out of the vehicle and frisked the young man. "Clean," the sergeant said.

Paz smiled, as if he had passed some test that was important only to the examiners. He had an uncommon face. His cheek-bones were high in the oriental way, his skin light brown, but his other features were Caucasian—that straight, firm nose and small nostrils, those rather thin lips that suggested a slight cynicism more than any lack of generosity. The face, handsome enough, might have passed without much comment had it not been for the truly remarkable eyes, which seized Deduro's attention. Round, long-lashed, the electric blue of a sky on a wintry day, they were astonishing, even unsettling, against the pigmentation of the skin. Deduro felt the surprise of a man startled in a drab landscape by an exotic bird. There was quite a blend of blood in this boy, he thought. He would have guessed a mother of mixed Malay-Spanish heritage, and a father either American or German, perhaps Australian, a mongrel.

Deduro got out of the Land Rover, pistol in hand. "Okay. Where's the corpse?"

Paz looked expressionlessly at the gun. "This way," and he pointed beyond the bamboo.

"How did you happen to come across it?" Deduro asked. He had no intention of going anywhere with Paz until he'd asked questions.

"I was walking—"

"Walking where?"

Paz said, "Nowhere special. For relaxation. Don't you ever do that?"

Deduro hadn't risen this early to answer questions. "At this time of morning?"

"I don't sleep sometimes. I get restless. So I walk."

"Do you work?" Deduro asked.

"Yes. I teach."

"And what do you teach?"

"Arithmetic. English. History. Whatever I'm asked to do."

"Where?"

"In the primary school in La Trinidad."

"Did you recognize the corpse?"

"No."

Deduro had a mild sense of uncertainty. The young man's answers were given without hesitation, but the captain wasn't sure he could read those blue eyes, which were untroubled and clear. Either Paz had nothing to conceal or else he was a fine actor.

Deduro, accustomed to seeing in the most ordinary events shadows of unspeakable menace, glanced at Sergeant Ocampo. With his gun in hand, the sergeant was already moving inquisitively toward the bamboo. Gallines had stepped out of the Land Rover, his FNC automatic rifle crossed upon his chest.

The radio was still tuned to FM 94, the station with "the mellow touch" in distant Manila: *I'm sad to say, I'm on my way, / Won't be back for many a day . . .*

Deduro asked for identification. The young man took a wallet from the hip pocket of his blue jeans and handed it agreeably to the captain. It contained a driver's license and a laminated card identifying Paz as an employee of the Benguet Province school district. Deduro studied these, then shut the wallet and gave it back.

Everything appeared to be in order. A schoolteacher takes a walk in a secluded place, comes upon a body, calls the police—why should there be anything more to it than that? In a sharper frame of mind, less burdened with financial concerns, Deduro might have scrutinized with greater care the young man's background, verified the authenticity of his ID cards. But he made a different decision.

"Lead the way," he said. *Máuna ka sa akin.*

Paz went through the bamboo to a field filled with waist-high grass. A clump of thick trees stood about a quarter of a mile away on the western edge of the meadow. Beyond, a small green hill rose. Against its shoulder a solitary wisp of disintegrating mist hung. The sun was pink now behind the haze.

Paz walked through the long stalks. Deduro was a dozen feet behind him. Ocampo and Gallines strolled a few yards on either side of the captain, surveying the field. The tall grass had a furtive quality that made both men watchful.

Paz stopped, looking toward the trees.

"What's the problem?" Deduro asked.

"I'm trying to remember the exact spot," said the young man, and he turned to the captain with an expression that might have been one of frustration. Why were those blue eyes so shuttered?

Then he moved again, pushing stalks aside as he continued. The dry grass whispered against his thighs. "It was very close to the trees," he said.

"Why didn't you mark the place?" Deduro asked.

"I didn't think," Paz replied calmly. "I literally stumbled across the thing. It's not the kind of sight that makes you react with any clarity, Captain. The smell was terrible. I wanted to hurry away."

Deduro, weary, could imagine more pleasant things than having to deal with a decomposing corpse before breakfast. He was a little out of breath. He smoked too much, burned the candle too often at both ends. He thought he could still hear the whir of the roulette wheel echo inside his head and knew that if he shut his eyes he'd see the croupier's emotionless face and the fake smile of the pit boss, a greasy little man whose courtesy toward him was both endless and sycophantic.

Paz was moving more quickly now. Deduro yawned and tried to keep up with him. It was a chore. Ocampo and Gallines, positioned behind him, had drifted about thirty yards from each other. They flattened the grass with every step, but the stalks sprang up again immediately.

"Here," Paz called out. He had stopped near the trees and was looking down at whatever lay concealed by the dense growth.

Panting, Deduro reached the place.

"Look," Paz said, and he parted the stalks with his hands.

The captain couldn't see what Paz was pointing out to him. A lizard scampered over his shoe and a spider, hanging by a strand of an unfinished web, curled into a protective ball. Where was the corpse?

"What am I supposed to be looking at?" Puzzled and uneasy, Deduro turned to the young man. He was about to press his pistol into Paz's face and demand an explanation, but he didn't get the chance.

Gunfire, destroying the calm of the field, came from the trees. For a moment Deduro mistakenly attributed the sound to some natural phenomena, an earthquake, the roar of thunder. But then he saw Sergeant Ocampo fall and vanish in the grass. At the same time Gallines cried aloud from a place beyond Deduro's vision.

The captain, too slow to absorb events, experienced a fatal moment of indecision. The gunfire continued from the trees and Gallines went on screaming while Paz, moving with quick grace, struck Deduro across the larynx, a savage, chopping gesture that caused the captain to choke. Half conscious, senses disengaged, he dropped his pistol and was struck again, this time in the fibrous place where neck meets shoulder. The pain was vile, intolerable. He went down on his knees, intuitively groping for the fallen pistol as he was hit sharply in the back of the neck. Something yielded in his spine.

He felt distanced from himself, narcotized. The pain that throbbed through him had transported him inside a world of silence. The pinkish tint of the day was strange and dreamy, like something seen through glass the color of salmon flesh. He may have passed out. He wasn't sure. He became aware of the young man slapping his face. He tried to cover himself but somehow his hands had been cuffed behind his back and now he understood that Paz was forcing him to kneel—a position of submission Deduro found intolerable. Paz had Deduro's own pistol in his fist.

"You intend to shoot me?" Deduro asked quietly. He had never been a cowardly man. He had his flaws, but a lack of courage wasn't one of them. He'd always imagined facing death unflinchingly when it came. It was the ultimate act of machismo, this contempt for the last darkness. But he hadn't expected to confront his demise on this particular morning, and he cursed his own carelessness for hurrying here half awake and preoccupied.

"I hate being on my goddamn knees," he said. He was impressively calm, even in pain and danger. He realized that three or four armed men stood directly behind him. They wore bandannas, dark shirts, khaki pants. He wondered why he hadn't already been shot like Ocampo and Gallines. For what purpose had he been handcuffed and kept alive?

"I'm the corpse in the field, I assume. Is that the joke?"

Paz said, "Only if you find it funny." He was quiet for a moment. "Don't you recognize this place?"

"Should I?"

"Have a good look. You're not here by accident."

Deduro gazed in the direction of the hill. The cloud of mist had disintegrated. The sun floated higher. Was there something familiar about that hill? Even vaguely? What the hell did it matter anyway?

He said, "One field is the same as another to me." There was a snarl of defiance in his voice; it concealed the pain that squeezed his spine.

"This one's different," Paz said. "Of course, it was dark the last time you were here. Barely any moon."

"I've never been here in my life."

"Think harder. Take your time."

Deduro stared past the young man. He was defenseless, resigned to the idea of death. There was no notion of struggle, no prospect of fight and escape. He would die here in this wretched field, which for some reason he was supposed to remember. Why? What purpose could he possibly have had for visiting this dreary place?

"Has it come back to you yet?" Paz asked.

It dawned then on Deduro. There was no sudden flash of recognition, merely a quiet memory. He recalled a quarter moon sailing behind the hill and the rotted bamboo and how black and silent the landscape became after all the harshness had gone out of it. He remembered a sense of accomplishment.

"Yes," he said. "It comes back."

"I had a feeling it might." Paz looked toward the hill. "I

wanted you to know why you have to die. I wanted you to remember what happened here.''

Deduro was afraid of nothing. He regretted nothing. It was important for Paz, if that was the boy's true name, to understand the quality of the man he was about to kill.

"I remember it fondly," the captain said, and smiled. "I wouldn't change a thing."

The smile enraged the young man. He raised the pistol to Deduro's face and his hand shook with anger. He thought how it took time and pain to keep fading memories alive, how it needed enormous transfusions of hatred to nourish and maintain the urge for what he considered justice. But it could be done, if you had the will for it. He remembered Eugene Costain momentarily. The image of the overweight American dying was fragile glass that shattered when the gun in his hand exploded and Deduro fell forward. Briefly, the field held the echo of the gunshot, then released it as it might a vapor.

After dark Joe Baltazar drove through the side streets of Parañaque, the clutter of crumbling apartment houses and tiny shops, pedestrians who roamed defiantly in front of his car, staring into his headlights as though challenging him. Lovers with arms linked, sauntering boys, groups of elderly men and women—they moved with total disregard for his vehicle. Manileños generally had the impertinent swagger of people who own the streets, and Baltazar, who came from Benguet Province, had always instinctively disliked them. They thought they were better than anyone else, more sophisticated, tougher. He leaned on his horn time and again, usually with no effect.

The streets became narrower. Small apartment houses were concealed by palms and iron fences against which tangled greenery and vines grew uncontrolled. Baltazar finally parked, locked the doors of the Subaru. He passed under a heavy canopy of palms, pushed open an iron gateway which left a deposit of rust flakes on his hand. He slowly climbed a flight of wooden steps to the upper floor of a concrete apartment house only some three years old but already showing signs of tropical fatigue. A weak light from a window overhead illuminated cracks in the steps; a large furry spider scuttled over Baltazar's shoe and he shivered.

On the top step he paused. The pain between his legs was a constant, sometimes dull, occasionally severe. He never took anodynes of any kind. He wanted the distress as it was, clear and hard in his brain, a souvenir of terror. From his right pocket he removed a small plastic cube in which lay a cat's yellow eye, and he rubbed it because lately he'd come to believe in a form of magic, the power of the amulet, the *anting-anting,* to cure ills. The eye, cut from a cat he'd killed himself, caught the light from the window and seemed momentarily to be infused with life.

But the pain persisted. Tonight there was either no magic or else it had all been used up. Baltazar sighed, put the talisman away and looked out across the darkness. A faint breeze blew the acrid smell of the Parañaque River toward him. He had mixed feelings about Teng going to America. A part of him experienced regret that he wasn't doing the work himself, but since he was practically a cripple, since he could barely walk without flame scorching his nerve endings, how efficient could he be? He'd restricted himself to planning, drawing on his knowledge of the United States and his old connections there, old friends who could be trusted. Even if they were inexperienced in this kind of situation, at least they were loyal, and they weren't being asked to do anything that could endanger them. Besides, why would he want to see the United States again? He'd rather breathe the rancid air of Parañaque than go back. He'd rather die.

He knocked on the door at the top of the stairs. A voice told him to step in. He entered a narrow kitchen, poorly lit and smelling of seafood. On a table the discarded shells of shrimps created a transparent little mountain. Lobster claws had been cracked and tossed aside, lying in disarray like the detached armor of unearthly creatures. Fat Gregory Redlinger, digging meat out of a claw, looked up at Baltazar and wiped his hands on his T-shirt, which had the logo of the Northern Arizona University Lumberjacks. Immense, his eyes very tiny, his big cheeks dimpled in a way that suggested a maleficent cherub, Redlinger raised the corner of his T-shirt to his lips and belched with incongruous gentility, one plump hand lifted to purple lips.

Baltazar sat at the table and watched the American push aside his plate. A Harley-Davidson motorcycle was propped against the wall, leaking oil on spread newspapers. Gregory didn't leave the bike outside because it would have been stolen within thirty seconds, so he hauled it up the stairs whenever he'd ridden it. On the wall a calendar bearing the legend SNAP-ON TOOLS hung aslant. A curvaceous girl in a swimsuit looked somewhat disdainfully down into the kitchen, as if she'd assessed both the fat man and the half-crippled Filipino and found them undesirables.

"Is it done?" Gregory asked.

Baltazar said yes, Teng had telephoned from Baguio, it was done.

"Poor old Costain and now Deduro," said Fat Gregory. "It comes to us all, Joe, baby. You can't avoid the fucking reaper. Swoop. One quick flash of the scythe in the dark and you're yesterday's tortilla. Out of goddamn commission permanent-lee."

Baltazar sometimes had problems with the American's slang and speech rhythms. He watched Gregory clasp his fat hands in a praying gesture. "Let us observe a moment of *silencio* for the departed."

A Filipina woman of about twenty-five appeared and leaned against the doorjamb. She angrily crossed her arms. She was called Amora. She lived with the American in a state of constant discord, a condition both parties appeared, perhaps perversely, to enjoy. Baltazar thought she was very pretty when she smiled, which wasn't often.

"Eat. Make pig of yourself. Blow up. One day you just *boom* explode! Then I scrape you from the floors. Eat, eat, eat." Amora threw up her hands, a dramatic rendition of despair. *"Gihigúgma ko ikáw.* Fat bastard."

Baltazar recognized the Cebuano dialect Amora used. Even as she insulted Gregory, she professed her love for him. In the intricacies of the relationship, abuse and proclamations of love ran together like dogs. Baltazar, who'd had no success with any of his three wives, didn't understand this alliance of war and tenderness between the American and his woman.

"She wants me to diet, Joe. Wants me to shed one hundred and fifty pounds. That's like *a whole goddam person!* Come here, O pretty one." Gregory held out his arms and the woman stepped into the embrace. The fat man slid his hand under her skirt from the back and she laughed as she knocked it away. Then she skipped out of the room, singing to herself, all rage spent as abruptly as it had arisen.

"Adorable little cunt, I do swear." Redlinger looked at Baltazar. "Where were we?"

"The departed."

"Ah. Yeah. Deduro, hell, I don't give a shit about. Costain, now, you couldn't ask for a better friend. Sweet guy. But pussy-whipped from way back. What a weakness." Gregory flexed his thick arms, stretching the T-shirt. He belched once again, as daintily as before. "Did he fight?"

"I have no details, Gregory."

"Pity. I wouldn't have objected to some graphic stuff."

Baltazar had one of those moments in which a tide of distrust rose inside him and he was powerless against it. He had the feeling Fat Gregory was playing a game with him, that somewhere along the way the American was going to prove too costly. After all, Costain had been Gregory's friend, but the fat man had pointed the finger at Costain anyway, as if friendship was something you sucked dry then tossed aside, a husk, a rind, useless. *I know who was involved and I know where you can find them.* Fat Gregory had backed this claim with detail he could only have learned from somebody present that very night in the field beyond La Trinidad. *Lay some bread on me and all will be revealed, Jovitoe, baby.* How could someone so mercenary be trusted? Yet without Gregory's information, expensive as it was, nothing could have been achieved, and Baltazar knew that. He could never have learned the names of the Americans from anyone else. Gregory was both curse and blessing.

Baltazar shut his eyes. He had a bad moment. A darkness invaded his head. He knew this fog. He couldn't think straight when it came. He put his hand in his pocket and covered the cat's eye with his clenched fist, longing for magic to cure him of these attacks. Sometimes he imagined whispers, shapes in corners, men following him along the street. Once, he'd heard his name called on Pedro Gil Street, but saw nobody when he looked around. On an especially lonely night, in a room at the Ryokan Pension House, he imagined he heard somebody say his name over the radio, not once, but twice—and he'd panicked, straddling that fearful terrain between reality and what the mind threw out from its deepest places.

Gregory asked, "When will your man leave?"

"Soon." In fact Teng had left the Philippines more than twelve hours ago, but Baltazar wasn't about to impart this information to the fat man.

"Soon, huh? No date?"

"For reasons of security—"

"Security! Okay. Shut me out, Joe. I don't need to know your plans. No skin off my proboscis. You send Teng whenever you like." Gregory feigned, or seemed to, an expression of hurt. "So don't trust me. I told you who the three Americans were, and I told you where they could be found. I went out on a limb for you, friend. So what? You need to settle some scores of your own, far out, fine with me. Just pay me my balance and we're through."

Baltazar took money from his hip pocket. It was folded in rubber bands. He wanted to get out of here, out into the air, away from Fat Gregory's oppressive presence. Gregory counted the bills, which were American. They totaled five thousand dollars in hundreds.

"You think Teng is up to the task, Joe?"

"I know so." When the fog lifted, what took its place was a depression so terrible Baltazar's head seemed to fill with lead.

"I hope he is," Gregory said. "Tell you what I hear. And this I throw in as a freebie. Gratis. For one night only, no charge. Mr. Kindness." Gregory spotted a piece of crabmeat on the table and swooped on it, scooping it up into his mouth. "Uhhh. Fuck me sideways! Crab's made of rubber."

The fat man spat the offending gob of crustacean into the palm of his hand. "Anyway. What I hear about our friend Laforge is he's been earmarked for something big. New job, Joe. Nothing less than head honcho. If this comes about, then he's gonna have a guard or two. No easy target then. Put that in your pipe."

"I will," Baltazar said.

"Let me phrase it another way. You better send Teng soon. Like *real* soon. Like yesterday."

"Thanks for the information." Baltazar opened the door, gazed into the darkness. The bad time had passed. He felt easy again, almost weightless.

Gregory said, "Hey, sweet dreams, my man."

4

The publication party at the J. W. Marriott Hotel in downtown Washington was held in honor of a book called *An American's Heart* by Senator Byron Truskett of Iowa, chairman of the Joint Select Committee on Intelligence. The book was of a kind familiar to observers of the American political scene, a rags to riches fable appealing to those who believed poverty no obstacle to political achievement in the republic, that it was easier for a poor man to become the President of the United States than a rich man to enter the Kingdom of Heaven.

Byron Truskett's book fudged the truth for the sake of this myth. For example, his father was referred to in the first chapter as "a simple undertaker," though in reality Truskett Senior owned a chain of funeral parlors throughout the Midwest and had enlarged his fortune building tract houses for the lower middle classes. *I box 'em in life, and I box 'em in death,* the old man used to say. Byron Truskett also claimed in chapter five to have worked his way through Northwestern University delivering pizzas, but he actually owned the pizza shop, a gift to him from Truskett Senior, who needed some tax write-offs.

The book also failed to mention Truskett Senior's vision for his son, a deliberate lapse necessitated by a need to appear modest and not some clawed griffin of hideous ambition. Truskett Senior had instilled in Byron the notion that he might one day become the President of the United States. There was no relentless drilling involved, no daily indoctrination, no sense of a father ramming his own failed ambitions into his son's brain. Rather, it was done with quiet persistence: *Anybody can do anything he sets his mind to in these United States, boy, so you aim as high as you care to.* It was a joyful awakening to the unlimited possibilities the great store window of the republic had to offer. I can be the President, Byron Truskett told himself. I can be anything I choose. And if the book didn't mention the fact, nevertheless Truskett Senior had given his son something precious, a manifest destiny all his own, an alignment with the possibilities of history. It helped, of course, that young Truskett, having won a junior achiever's award in a prestigious national competition in 1958, had received his citation and a check for $1,000 from Eisenhower himself inside the Oval Office. He had liked the room as a visitor. How much more might he like it as a long-term tenant? If inside Byron's head there had existed a compass, its needle would never have wavered.

Truth, then, was a matter of degree in Truskett's autohagiography, gently shaded here, turned on its side there, yet always close enough to genuine events to make the book defendable, if anyone bothered to assault it. Nobody did. Reviews were deferential, written for the most part by friends of Truskett, and sales were brisk because many Americans, who thought Truskett had a sensitive finger on the sometimes inaccessible pulse of the nation, were interested in what the senator had to say. Whatever the book's merits, the party was a huge success, attended by five hundred people all speaking at once in voices made bright by martinis or champagne.

Truskett, a big man with the shoulders of a weightlifter, had a concentrated way of looking at other people that made them feel important. *He makes you think you're the most interesting thing in his life,* his constituents often said about him. He possessed that gift as precious to a politician as votes: the common touch. When he shook a hand he didn't withdraw at once, as if fearful of infection, the way some pols did. He'd perfected "the wrap," in which he grasped firmly with his right hand while his left covered the handshake. An extra touch of warmth and intimacy; people remembered such things. He pumped flesh with the same cheer that Truskett Senior had crated the stuff and buried it. Flesh, dead or alive, was Truskett business.

He moved among guests, gripped the hands of fellow senators and, where familiarity allowed it, bussed their wives, exchanged barbed little jokes with this or that columnist or lobbyist, picked at a canapé here, a drumstick there, and balanced a champagne cocktail high in his left hand. He was stalked by the PR lady from the publishing company, a sharp little Australian woman called Callie Cousins who had a whole gang of journalists wanting to interview the senator, because he was generally held to be an unusual American phenomenon: an intelligent conservative. He was considered a comer, a strong presidential possibility down the line—if not at the next election then four years later. Truskett had no intention, however, of patiently waiting the years away. He wanted to occupy the White House by his forty-fifth birthday, if only to give the finger, with firm vigor, to those fogies and superannuated ninnies around Washington who said he was too young for the Big Job, too immature, needed more seasoning. Seasoning! The precedent set by Jack Kennedy had been conveniently overlooked by Truskett's enemies, simpering men who envied him his popularity.

Posters of Truskett hung around the room. They depicted a healthy forty-three-year-old man with a friendly mouth and eyes that shone, a trustworthy face, big and open, bran-fed and Iowan, touched by the honest sunshine of the heartland. Here was a man who ate a nutritious breakfast every day of his life and was faithful to his wife and would never dream of maligning the great democracy he worked for so ably.

He glimpsed Miriam across the room. She was in the company of Carolyn Laforge. The two women, heads inclined together, shared a confidence. Truskett wondered what. Miriam, dark-haired, was shorter than Carolyn. They were roughly the same age, late thirties, although neither showed it.

A flashbulb went off. Miriam Truskett looked surprised; Carolyn merely smiled. Later, the photograph would reveal this marked difference between the women. While Carolyn was grace-ful in the presence of the intrusive cameraman, as if she were bestowing the gift of her lovely image on him, Miriam, the child of immigrant Swedish farmers, was ill at ease, caught off balance. She didn't have the other woman's background, old Pennsylvania money and an expensive finishing school. For a second Byron Truskett yielded to a vague sense of irritation, but it passed as quickly as it had come.

He plunged deeper into the crowd, through clusters of con-gressmen, influential editors, two or three presidential aides, the House Majority Speaker, the Vice President and his tight-lipped little wife with her bleached mustache.

"Who's running the country tonight, Byron?" the senior senator from Nebraska asked. "If we're all here, who's minding the damn store?"

Byron Truskett laughed. "Store's shut, George. America's closed for the night."

"I'll bet she is." The Nebraskan pulled Truskett to one side gently. "Speaking of minding the store, Senator, little birds tell me you're going to make a certain recommendation about a re-placement for our dying friend. . . ."

"It's possible, George."

"You'll get some opposition. Not from me, mind you." The Nebraskan, George Hammer, was an ashen-skinned man who smoked too much. He wheezed when he spoke. "I'll back your boy. He's got experience. Besides, if he's good enough for you . . ."

"I appreciate that."

The Nebraskan said, "Keep one eye open for skeletons, Byron. Damn things won't lay still. There's more goddam archae-ologists on the Hill than in all Egypt. Jesus, they love nothing better than a good dig."

"I'll keep that in mind." Skeletons, Truskett thought. There were always skeletons in this town. This was the city of old bones, of legacies that sometimes were too dangerous to be dragged into the light. He thought for a moment of the man who lay dying from cancer in the Naval Hospital in Bethesda, the man who would have to be replaced as the director of the Central Intelligence Agency. What dark things moved through Alexander

Bach's sedated mind as he died? Truskett wondered. What would the director carry with him to his grave? Truskett turned these thoughts aside even though the word *skeletons* echoed uncomfortably inside him.

"I hear the White House would prefer Jerry Slotten for the post," Hammer remarked. "He's done a pretty fair job deputizing for Sandy Bach, no question."

"Jerry's a good man," Truskett said.

"But he's not your man."

"Exactly."

"One other thing," said Hammer, reaching out to detain Truskett, who was getting urgent signals from the Australian publicist. "Some people like nothing better than to see a high flier come down flat on his ass. Human nature's base, Byron. Some folk just can't stand to see a fella like yourself move ahead of the pack. Makes them envious as all hell."

"Good counsel, George." Truskett smiled, patted the Nebraskan's shoulder. "If it was the Ides of March, believe me, I'd beware."

"Aren't there Ides in June?" Hammer had a slanted grin. "What the hell are Ides anyhow?"

Truskett, still smiling, moved away. Large pyramids of *An American's Heart* had been arranged in the corners of the room. Sometimes people thrust copies into the senator's hand for an autograph, which he gave with pleasure. He finally reached the place where his wife stood with Carolyn Laforge.

Miriam clutched her husband's arm possessively. She was very proud of Byron. She gazed at him like a high school pompom girl with an awesome crush on the star quarterback; she had the satisfied light in her eye that suggested a recent consummation under moon-streaked bleachers. Truskett kissed her on the side of her face even as he glanced at Carolyn Laforge and wondered how anybody could look so unbearably elegant simply holding a glass of Évian. Some optical illusion? Some genetic factor? And those cheekbones—how had those marvels come about? You had to believe Carolyn had been built on one of God's better days.

"Congratulations, Byron. It's a wonderful party. Everybody's here," Carolyn Laforge said. She had a melodic voice, just a little deeper than people somehow expected.

"Everybody but your husband," Truskett said. He noticed how the expensive green dress was almost the color of her eyes. Her yellow hair, simply arranged—as if style were merely the absence of fuss—touched her shoulders. There was a fragile quality to her elegance; she might have been made from something finer, more transparent, than china. If he had learned anything in Washington, Truskett thought, it was how appearance and reality so rarely collided. Deception in this town had as many strata as some ancient rock formation.

"You know how William is," Carolyn said. "He's never at ease in crowds."

"A loner," Miriam Truskett said. She admired Carolyn. Often she telephoned her for advice on paintings or antiques. Carolyn had studied interior design in London and knew about art and art history.

"Not exactly a loner," Carolyn said. "He likes parties only when he has control of them. He's what people call a control freak."

Byron Truskett finished his champagne cocktail. Later, when the party was over, he'd have his drink of choice, some good Kentucky bourbon. He said, "I'd like to see him get around more. It might do him some good."

"I'll tell him that, Byron. I can't promise he'll listen."

Truskett moved a little closer to his wife. Miriam, he noticed, didn't have Carolyn's posture. She was slightly round-shouldered. He wanted to make her straighten her back. But how? He couldn't whisper to her directly. She'd be embarrassed. He laid a hand very lightly on the nape of her neck and made small circular motions with his fingertips. Miriam smiled at what she took to be a display of intimacy in public. She was the great man's wife, and he loved her and obviously didn't care who knew it. She was on fire. Truskett was her sun and moon.

"Are you going back to Pennsylvania tonight?" Truskett asked.

Carolyn shook her head. She had fine straight teeth, lustrous lips. "I'll stay in town. I have some shopping to do in the morning."

Miriam Truskett asked, "Then why don't we all dine together later?"

Before Carolyn could answer, Truskett said, "I'm afraid you'll have to count me out, sweetheart. As soon as I'm through here I have to meet with the committee. I don't think I can get away before midnight. Why don't you two girls go ahead on your own?"

"I'm sorry, I'll have to beg off as well," Carolyn said. "Do you mind, Miriam? I'm a little tired."

Miriam Truskett didn't look disappointed. She had the resigned attitude of a woman who could never make plans without having them altered for reasons beyond her control. "Of course I don't mind," she said.

Carolyn put down her empty glass. "Call me soon."

"Are you leaving already?" Miriam asked. "It's early."

"It's been a long day."

There was an exchange of kisses, quick little connections of lips and cheeks, flurries of hugs.

"A lovely party, Byron," Carolyn said.

"You tell William I'll be in touch," Truskett said. He was aware of the Australian publicist sniffing around behind his back, looking for attention. He'd have to appease her somehow.

"I'll tell him." Carolyn Laforge moved sleekly through the crowd and without a backward look reached the door. And then she was gone, a vision of green and gold some found dazzlingly perfect, others arctic.

It was, Truskett thought, a matter of taste.

"Senator," the little Australian woman said. "You gotta talk to the hounds sooner or later. I can't hold the buggers off any longer."

Byron Truskett smiled. "Bring on the circus," he said, and he squeezed his wife's neck, where his hand still lingered.

William Laforge shaded his eyes and watched the sun slipping behind the stand of birch across the meadow. He saw a raven fly between branches, its wings listlessly beating the dry air. Long brown grass and brittle dandelion and wildflower stalks crackled beneath his feet; everything had been bleached by the relentless summer. He turned from the sun and clasped his hands behind his back. In the distance his house was visible, an eighteenth century farmhouse of whitewashed fieldstone and black shutters, which seemed momentarily to shimmer in the way of a mirage. The gardener had been burning off tenacious crabgrass and thin smoke drifted over the stables beyond the house. A horse whinnied, then fell silent.

Beyond the birch a creek ran through the property. Laforge passed between the trees then walked the incline to the water's edge. The creek, which usually clattered riotously, was quieter and slower than Laforge had ever known it in all the twenty years he'd lived here. He kneeled, plucked a pebble from the water, turned it over in the palm of his hand. Downstream, the tendrils of a willow trailed the surface of water. The lower leaves were green and lovely, but the higher the eye traveled the browner the leaves became, as if the tree were dying from the top down.

This dryness was everywhere on Laforge's two hundred and seventy-one acres. At nights, with the windows open and the sky sometimes starry beyond the deathly pall that reached up from Philadelphia, you could smell the dehydrated earth. He stood up, tossing the pebble into the stream. Was it only last year he'd fished from this very place? This summer he'd seen brook trout only once or twice, runt-sized specimens that pitifully hugged the shallow shadows of the bank.

He rubbed the palm of his damp hand on his cotton pants. He was a trim man with very soft white hair parted to the left, the relic of a boyhood style begun while he was in prep school forty-five years ago. When people looked at Laforge, who had the kind of tanned, well-bred face one often saw in the better marinas of the world, they had the impression of a man who had been put together very well. He was fifty-seven years old and his flesh was unblemished; many men of the same age were concerned with the menacing brown freckles of the decaying process. His stomach was flat, his pectoral muscles firm, no flesh sagged beneath the upper arms. His manner was that of a man who keeps very much to himself and who speaks only when he has something to say. He was a person to whom one would entrust a secret and feel secure about it.

Gossip was anathema to him. Parties like Truskett's were torture. He hated not only the babble and the scream of false laughter but also the pressure of bodies, the touch of strangers. Laforge tended to stand apart from things, always analytical when he observed and careful when he finally chose to participate, whether in a marriage, the purchase of a horse, or one or another of the many tasks he'd undertaken on behalf of the U.S. government. He rarely rushed into anything; he was as much a stranger to the hasty judgment as he was to the unguarded moment of passion. On the very few occasions when he'd acted without due consideration he'd always regretted it.

He walked downstream. An old wooden bridge, covered in moss, precariously straddled the water. It shook when Laforge stepped on its weathered boards. He crossed to the other bank. A stone wall some yards above the bank marked the limits of his property. He climbed up through fern and bramble. When he reached the wall he hoisted himself over without effort. On the other side lay a narrow county road along which very little traffic ever passed. Across this desolate strip of pockmarked blacktop were the somewhat dank woodlands that belonged to Laforge's neighbor, a reclusive billionaire he'd never met.

Laforge knew Railsback would come from the right, from the southwest. He looked at his watch. At the same moment he heard the sound of a car. Railsback, like himself, was a punctual man. Laforge leaned against the wall in a nonchalant way, pleased to see the car was a Ford with no character, dark blue and functional and utterly forgettable. He not only approved of low profiles, he insisted on them.

The car stopped at the side of the road and Thomas Railsback stepped out. He was a man in his middle thirties who wore blue-tinted sunglasses and a short-sleeved white shirt. Like the car, there was nothing exceptional in Railsback's appearance unless one counted the sunglasses. When he took these off he looked very ordinary, as if some important element were missing from his features. His dark brown eyes were lifeless.

Both men shook hands briefly. Railsback was tired. He'd flown that day from Dallas to Philadelphia, where he'd hired the Ford.

"Good timing," Laforge said.

Railsback folded his arms and breathed the warm air into his lungs in the uncertain way of a city man wary of pollen and microbes. "You're looking fit," he said to Laforge. "It must be true what they're saying."

"What exactly are they saying?"

"You know. The job. *The* job."

Laforge felt a surge of excitement at the idea of *the* job: He wanted it, deserved it, he alone had the authority and experience for it. But he shrugged with assumed indifference. "I don't listen to Washington scuttlebutt, Tom. You know me better than that."

Railsback smiled. It was a fast little expression because he was unhappy with the shape of his new bridgework. He'd been thinking about suing his dentist. The country was a carnival of litigation. Lawyers, deafened by their cash registers, bloated by greed, gloated from sea to shining sea. "I heard on the car radio old Sandy Bach's in a coma. His chair's going to get very cold unless they find somebody to sit in it pretty soon."

"Why do you think it might be me, Tom?"

"The smart money says so."

"The smart money is sometimes very dumb." Laforge tried to infuse conviction into his voice. It was difficult to conceal a desire for something one had coveted so many years. But an appearance of detachment was important. It would be the height of bad manners to show even a tic of ambition, whether Sandy Bach was alive or dead.

"Other than you, who else is there? Who else has the experience?" And the friends in high places, Railsback thought.

Laforge didn't answer at once. He gazed across the road at the woods. Faded trespass notices hung on several trees. Sunlight died miserably among the thick trunks. The evening had a wrong feel to it in a way that had nothing to do with the heat. *Those woods,* he thought. *Anybody could come out of that density. Anybody at all.* He wondered if suddenly he was afraid. A new sensation: He'd never felt fear in his life.

Was it age? Did it blemish you in ways other than a general slowing down and a cracking in your joints? Perhaps something on the inside gave way, an essence evaporated, only you didn't know it until you needed the very quality that had disappeared.

He looked at Railsback. "Sandy's a fighter," he said.

"Sometimes you don't come back off the ropes," Railsback

remarked. He was fond of sporting analogies. "Sometimes you've got nothing left."

Laforge laid his hand on the rough stone wall. "I didn't ask you here to talk about Sandy, Tom."

"I gathered that."

"And I'm sorry I had to drag you all the way from Dallas. But I don't trust telephones. I had a message from Manila. Gene Costain's body was found in a garbage dump near the bay."

"Ah, Christ," Railsback said quietly.

"He'd been stabbed to death."

Railsback had liked old Gene, even though he considered it Costain's main flaw that he thought more with his tiny head than his big one. His brain was too close to his balls. He had his lovely little whore in Manila, and she'd absconded with his heart. That was his downfall. Railsback had a flash of Gene, that stern face all the more rigid in death, lying in a mountain of trash, the stench of it all, the putrefaction that ascended with obscene rapacity in the Manila climate.

"I assume there's an investigation," he said.

"In the Philippines you never assume anything. The constabulary do what they can in their ham-fisted fashion. They have some help from the embassy. But I think it highly unlikely the killer will ever be found."

"Has anybody spoken to Gene's girl?"

Laforge sighed. He had disapproved of that relationship and had advised Costain on more than one occasion to end it. "They looked for her. But she'd gone. Of course, nobody knows where she can be reached. Nobody's seen her. The whole thing is dead-ended."

"Do we have any idea who might have killed him?"

"Only in the general sense. We both know the Communists are the most plausible candidates. If you're talking about a specific individual, no."

"Poor old Gene," Railsback said.

Both men were quiet for a time, each remembering Costain in his own way. He was loyal, if not the brightest man around. But loyalty was what counted as far as Laforge was concerned. When you gave Costain an order, he'd always obeyed.

Laforge stared into the woods again. How gloomy they were.

How secretive. He turned his face away. Above, where a solitary bat flew without seeming purpose, the sky was hazy with the imprisoned heat of the day.

Railsback said, "You didn't bring me all this way just to tell me about Costain, did you?"

"No."

Railsback lit a cigarette, a Carlton, which to him was like sucking air, but he was trying to cut down. He felt nervous, the result of many factors—the enigmatic call from Laforge, the death of Costain, and now this eerie sense of anticipation he experienced as he waited for the older man to say what was on his mind.

Suddenly there was music from the distance, discordant and angry, the kind of music made by people who sang out against acid rain and oil spills and shaved their heads or wore their hair in lacquered spikes so that in silhouette they often looked like surreal versions of the Statue of Liberty. Eco-rock, it was called, electric and shrill. Laforge made a face.

"My son's music," he said quietly. "I don't pretend to understand his tastes. What we used to simplemindedly call the generation gap has become something of a dark abyss these days."

Railsback, a single parent, looked sympathetic. He had a teenage daughter, a lovely child called Holly. He'd recently found marijuana seeds in her bedroom and a tiny plant in a window box and Rizla rolling papers inside a school textbook.

"Let's walk a little," Laforge suggested.

Tracked by the thudding music, both men moved down the road. A partridge flew up unexpectedly in front of them, a minor shock for Railsback.

"Captain Deduro has been found murdered north of Baguio," Laforge said.

Railsback absorbed the news without great interest. It all seemed so far away both in time and space.

"Now here's what bothers me," Laforge said. "I can't help thinking of a certain connection between the deaths of Deduro and Costain, Tom."

Railsback stopped walking. He ran a fingertip around the base of his clammy neck. "The only possible connection is Benguet Province."

"Exactly," Laforge said.

"But there were no eyewitnesses."

"What if there were?"

Railsback considered this a moment. He had a flurry of memories, none of which seemed to belong to him anymore—flashlights piercing the dark, the quiet sound of chains, somebody crying in fear. No. There had been no spectators. He was sure of it. He *thought* he was sure of it. He said, "Because both men were in Benguet, it doesn't follow they were killed for their part in that particular affair. Look, we know Deduro had been living on borrowed time. He was a target for the Communists long before the business in Benguet. He'd never exactly been Mr. Popularity with the locals. As for Gene—any American connected with the constabulary is at risk over there. A sparrow comes into Manila and kills Costain because he stands for something certain people hate."

Something certain people hate, Laforge thought. Railsback was being needlessly cryptic. The "certain people" he referred to were the New People's Army represented by one of their assassins, a "sparrow." And the "something" they hated was an American presence on Filipino soil, the military bases. The fact that the Americans were supported by the landowning class, who in turn "exploited" the peasants, according to the Marxist jargon Laforge found so boringly doctrinaire, was where the true grievance lay. The rich got richer; the poor, having lived lives of unbearable hopelessness, died sooner. And somewhere in the jungles the Communists, masters of the drab dialectic of hatred, taught boys and girls how to strip down and rebuild rifles blindfolded in preparation for the Day of Reckoning.

Laforge thought how regrettable it was that the desirable ideals of America—democracy, liberty, a free economy—were so difficult to export. It was a deplorable irony, of course, that the transplantation of solid American values, which he esteemed without question, often required the support of indigenous gangsters, such as that thief, the late Marcos. He may have milked the Filipino treasury and declared martial law to protect his presidency, he may have perceived himself as an emperor, and he was *indisputably* an unprincipled felon, but nevertheless his self-interest happened to coincide with the general American goal of limiting communism in the Orient. That was still a vibrantly unpredictable threat to American interests which, according to Laforge's patriotic logic, were also the interests of all the democracies of the world. Unless special care was taken, the Philippines had the ingredients to become another Cuba, one of which, thank you, was enough.

As if to himself, Laforge said, "I've thought about Benguet often, Tom."

Railsback said nothing. He smoked his cigarette with a funereal look.

"Sometimes circumstances force you to do something you wouldn't normally do," Laforge went on. "And sometimes you have to perform a distasteful act for the general good. You're in a distant country, a remote place, the rules are different. . . ."

Railsback, who had no desire to linger in what was past and done and who sometimes smelled the rancid damp of the Philippines in his dreams, said, "Tell me this. Do you have any hard evidence of a connection between the deaths of Deduro and Costain? Do you have anything we can sink our teeth into? Sure, they were involved together in Benguet, but who knows that? And what happened at that godforsaken place was more than three years ago."

"Hard evidence, no." Laforge closed his eyes a second. He looked like a man in uneasy repose. He had feelings, intuitions; the kind of evidence that might convince Railsback was another matter. "People who want revenge often spend years getting it, Tom. Sometimes they love to anticipate the taste. It's almost as important as the act of vengeance itself. Imagine an eyewitness, say. He doesn't even have to be connected with the NPA. He bides his time. He's learned how to wait, because he understands the delicate beauty of patience."

The delicate beauty of patience. Railsback thought it an odd choice of phrase. He crushed his cigarette underfoot. "Okay, let's say for the sake of argument there's an agent of revenge and he knows the people responsible for what happened in Benguet. He's got a list. He snuffs out two of the names on this list. Is that what you're saying? You think I'm on the list and he's going to come all the way to Texas for me."

"I wanted to discuss the possibility with you," Laforge said. "I wanted you to be aware and to be careful. That's all."

You could have told me all this on the goddam phone,
Railsback thought. He said, "I'm always careful. Force of habit."

"Then be even more so, Tom. That's all I ask."

Railsback smiled. "Nobody is going to get me in my own
backyard. And I mean nobody."

Laforge looked up at the sky and wondered if he'd simply
overreacted to the news of Costain's death, if he'd imagined this
theme of vengeance. But he'd always been suspicious of coinci-
dences. Under scrutiny, more often than not they were seen to
be part of a deliberate design. He'd always asked one question
more than the next man because the answers he got never satisfied him. He couldn't let this one go, this unholy trinity of
Costain and Captain Deduro and Benguet Province. He didn't buy
easy concurrences. He had the feeling something dark lay out
there in the landscape. A presence. Suddenly he realized he'd
been expecting it for a long time. But he could explain none of
this to Tom Railsback. It wasn't specific.

Railsback said, "Even if there's a *remote* possibility of a
revenge situation, how can it touch you? You weren't even
there."

Laforge turned toward the house, saying nothing. The music,
which had stopped for a few minutes, cranked up again, incongruous in the rustic twilight. Laforge found it reassuring now. He was
filled with an awareness of failed love for his son; why hadn't he
worked harder to get close to him? Why was he so divided from
Nick? The answer was simple enough. The boy's music, the
clothing, his derisive attitude to some of the things Laforge held
dear—all this separated father from son. And then there were the
strange little magazines Nick subscribed to, inky sheets traffick-
ing in conspiracy nonsense and anti-American platitudes.

*Tell me one day, Dad, just so I can understand, why the hell
you believe the United States of America has to poke its goddam
nose into other people's business. What makes you so sure
we've found the right path and everybody else has to follow it
or else? Do we have some God-given right to invade a country
like Panama, say, because we don't like the guy who runs it?*

He was naive, of course. At seventeen, how could Nick be
otherwise? Laforge was touched by the peculiar sadness of loss, a
poignant feeling that embarrassed him by its intensity.

He shook Railsback's hand when they walked back to the car.

"You think you made a fool's errand," Laforge said.

"No."

"You do understand my concern, Tom?"

"Sure," Railsback said. He climbed in behind the wheel. He wasn't sure if he felt gratitude or pity. He'd never seen Laforge quite so . . . what was the word? Disturbed? Preoccupied? Uncool? He wondered if Laforge had it in him to go off the deep end one day. Maybe he spent too much time in the countryside imagining enemies and was becoming unglued. More likely he was worried about his record and the need to preserve the appearance of a clean sheet. He couldn't afford to be touched by scandal, especially if he was the front-runner for Sandy Bach's position. There would be congressional inquiries, floodlights turned on his life. Probably Benguet haunted him and he'd repressed his feelings about it. This killer, this hypothetical avenger—such a person was always possible, but Railsback thought it far more likely he was a phantom of Laforge's conscience.

He said, "Thanks for the warning."

"I hope it proves unnecessary."

"I think it will." Railsback turned the key in the ignition. "But I appreciate your consideration. I really do."

"One tries to take care of one's own," Laforge said. "If I hear anything else, you'll be the first to know. Obviously, I don't want anything to come up, in view of . . ." He allowed his voice to fade off.

"I understand."

Laforge watched the Ford go down the road. After it vanished, he listened to the vibrating of the fading engine. He thought that Railsback's argument against the notion of any connection between the two murders should have relaxed him. But it hadn't. The uneasiness wasn't going to dissolve so simply.

He didn't want to think that Benguet had been a moral lapse on his part, an error of judgment. Belief in the rightness of the United States justified anything—wasn't that how the reasoning went? But you couldn't always wrap democratic ideals in the flag and give them away as a present, because not everyone wanted the gift. Often there were no takers. They had to be shown how badly they needed American benefaction. There had to be a dog and pony show, strobe lights, some sleight of hand—and when the flash failed, perhaps coercion. Sometimes the flag got a little grubby, a little muddy. And bloody, even that.

He climbed the wall to his own property, beset by the bizarre feeling that he was trespassing on what belonged to him. He stepped on to the bridge, pausing in the middle to gaze down at the creek. Clouded by the motion of the water, his own reflection looked up at him, for all the world like a putrefying corpse below the surface.

Armando Teng had managed to sleep only three shallow hours during the first leg of the flight from the Philippines to Honolulu. There were dreams, terrors, visitations, somewhere the whisper of Marissa's voice. Before Honolulu he was jarred awake by the notion that she was standing over him and he had only to open his eyes to see her, but he found himself looking up, his expression one of disappointment, into a stewardess's face. She smiled and told him he must fasten his seat belt, the plane was about to land in Hawaii.

Between Hawaii and Los Angeles he failed to sleep at all.

He had only hand luggage. He went through Customs and Immigration without incident, bearing a passport made out in the name of Raymond Cruz. He found a cab that took him to a motel whose address Joe Baltazar had given him. Located about three miles from LAX, it was a pale blue cinder-block building dating from an era of streamlined automobiles with sleek fins. He was given a ground floor room, cramped, dark, a little shabby. A swamp cooler blew humid air. In his fatigue, he was aware of his surroundings only in a limited way. He drew the curtains and lay down on the bed. *Somebody will call you,* Baltazar had said. Teng noticed the beige plastic telephone on the bedside table, then closed his eyes. He slipped down into empty, satisfying sleep, pleasantly dreamless this time, as if the distressing currents that had troubled him on the plane were for the moment still.

5

Charlie Galloway lay down for a time and listened to Ella's singing and the sound of the vacuum running, and he thought of Karen, whose image moved in the shadowy way of something trapped under a surface of thin ice. The telephone rang by the bed at five-thirty.

Leonard Paffett was on the line. Galloway always felt like a truant boy facing the badly strained tolerance of his headmaster when he had to speak to his superior, even though Paffett was not an unkindly man. Indeed he perceived himself as a sort of godfather to the men in his command. He went to their weddings, remembered the names of spouses and offspring, birthdays and anniversaries; he spent a lot of time making his subordinates as contented as they might be in a job whose requirements became daily more demanding in an underworld that turned on its axis with increasing viciousness.

"Well, you've done it again, Charlie," said Paffett in that soft voice which made everything seem like an understatement. "To nobody's surprise, I might say. We're not rolling our eyes downtown, Charlie. We're not exactly *aghast*."

Galloway, thinking *aghast* an odd word for a captain in the LAPD to use, said nothing. What response was there to make in any event? You opened your mouth, you compounded your shame. *Hide, Charlie. Scarper. Duck.*

"I hear the precinct's running a book on how long you can stay sober, Charlie. I find that a sad comment on your situation."

"Well," was all Charlie could think to say after some quick rummaging in the cluttered drawers of his head, which squeaked noticeably as he opened and closed them.

"I figured the clinic would help you, Charlie," Paffett said. "I really did. It came highly recommended. Guy there's had some remarkable results with . . . cases like yourself. Too bad. Too goddam bad. When you checked yourself out—an act I can't possibly condone—he called me to say you're in total denial, Charlie. Won't face up to your problem. Won't accept it. When you jump that hurdle, then you've got a chance. Maybe."

Charlie Galloway crossed his legs and his robe parted. Above his right kneecap was a small pale blue pit of flesh less than a quarter inch in diameter, the relic of a childhood disaster in which he'd ridden his tricycle into the pond in Elder Park in Govan, a reckless moment, a profound splash and a scattering of minnows—and now seemingly a harbinger of all such moments that lay ahead of him. Had the seeds of his future lain inside him some forty years ago? Had they begun even then, unseen in a dank cellar of his self, to sprout?

"I'm genuinely saddened," said Paffett. "I don't know what the hell's wrong with you, but you gotta start thinking about turning your life around."

Turning one's life around. How easy Paffett made that sound. Like moving a piece of furniture, opening a book, scratching your head.

"Here's what it comes down to, Charlie. I'm prolonging your suspension. Breaks my heart."

"Prolonging?" Charlie asked. His being seemed to shoot out of him, an arrow soaring across the sky. He panicked. "How long is prolonged?"

"Six months," Paffett said.

"Gimme a break—"

"You've had all the breaks going, Charlie. When the six

months are up I make a reassessment. If I don't get a clean bill of health from a physician that you've been off the sauce, you're out permanently. It's up to you. If you want to be a loser, be my guest. After that last incident . . ."

Charlie flinched because he didn't want to hear yet another description of what had come to be known in his private mythology as The African Disgrace. "Len, what if I went back to the clinic today?" he asked, hurrying to speak, grasping at whispery little straws, seeking some chink of charity in Leonard Paffett's decision.

"No. I've made the situation clear. Six months. After that, we'll see."

"I'm a damn good cop, you know that—"

"Used to be, Charlie. Past tense."

Fuck you! Was this what it came down to? Washed-up, asleep on parade, fly hanging open? The slovenly life. Abandonment. Former homicide detective drools in shabby retirement, spoon-fed by charity workers. Charlie was quiet for a while. Then, infusing his voice with a confidence he pretended to feel, he said, "I can do six months without drinking. I can do that."

"You're gonna have to show me, Charlie. Words don't cut it."

Six months. Galloway remembered the fifth year of his marriage when he'd gone on the wagon for four dry seasons. Twelve abstemious months. Fifty-two weeks of club soda, with a dash of angostura bitters when he felt daring. Eight thousand seven hundred and sixty hours of saintliness. He'd eaten enormous quantities of very rich ice cream and put on twelve pounds during that very long year in the course of which he'd begun to see the world rather sharply. Things formerly blurred had come into focus, and he hadn't always liked the fact. Six months. Why did the word *drudgery* form in his head right then?

"Len, I know I can do it," he said brightly. "Watch me. Just watch me."

Paffett said, "I'm rooting for you. But you gotta get help, Charlie. Go to AA. Or see a therapist. And get your wife back while you're at it. If she'll come." The captain paused briefly. "Remember this, Charlie. Booze kills."

And so perchance does the lack of it, Charlie Galloway

thought as he put down the receiver and stood in the direct spot where the sun skewered the room, lighting him like a nervous actor in a play whose lines he hasn't learned. Six months. Sackcloth and ashes. Empty glasses and tarpaulins drawn across the carnival rides and every day a funeral. *Tae hell with that.*

Because the house had begun to feel like the inside of a baked apple, he dressed, called a cab and went out, mumbling to Ella Nazarena about an unexpected appointment. He understood she saw through this threadbare ruse, of course. If he'd had an appointment of a sober nature, he would have driven his own car. The cab, he knew, was a dead giveaway. He instructed the driver, an Iraqi whose English was impeccable, just to drive around for a while, it didn't matter where.

When he was absolutely sure he wasn't being tracked by Clarence Wylie—as if Clarence, a happily married man with an attractive wife twenty years his junior, didn't have better things to do than hound-dog a drunk—he stepped from the taxi outside a grubby little cocktail bar, the kind with a piano nobody ever played. Secretive windows, a Schlitz neon, a bleached-out poster promoting a pianist who hadn't been inside the bar for years, so that now his photo looked like that of a man wanted by law enforcement agencies long gone out of existence—this tavern had all the elements that magnetized Galloway, who had no taste for yuppie wine joints or anyplace that served drinks with umbrellas or was adorned with ferns and brass or, Christ forbid, had a Theme.

He liked his bars to remind him a little of the funky haunts in the city of his birth, the kind of pubs where no fern would ever have survived, where the only things that ever grew were the magic of your inebriation and the ardency of your patriotism. Ah, Jesus, didn't you love sweet grubby old Glasgow and Scotland on those glorious long-ago rainy nights? Those ancient pubs had a joyful smell, spilled beer and a million smokes and if you were lucky damp newspaper or sawdust or wet umbrellas, a great spellbinding perfume your lungs relished.

He went inside. A familiar wave flowed over him. If he caught and rode it there was no knowing where the night would lead. He adored the unpredictability of the tide, its powerful undertow, the hidden currents. Drunk, he was usually neither clownlike nor morose, nor did he normally become bellicose. His tendency was to be affable and sentimental, and if he ran into a fellow exile there would be lethal overdoses of nostalgia. You just never knew where booze would lead you.

Now and then he had moments when he slipped into a dark reverie where he couldn't locate the center of himself or get a handle on his own scrambled thoughts, when from a point far above—the lofty position of some puzzled angel—he seemed to be seeing himself seated at the bar. And then he'd break into little fragments, as if all his atoms had exploded and he had no way of gathering them up again. These dislocations were weird, and he'd panic because he felt he'd cracked, his identity gone. At such times he'd look at other faces in the bar and wonder if anyone had noticed a sudden change in him, or if he was being stared at. Then the panic would subside and he'd order another glass and remember his comforting credo. *I drink, therefore I am.*

He placed himself up on a stool. The bartender resembled a whippet, lean, bare arms corded with muscles. "Hot enough for you?" he asked Galloway.

Galloway made a sympathetic sound of agreement. *Shheee.* He ordered a scotch and a beer chaser. When they were set down before him he looked around the room, dark and lovely, isolated from the branding iron of the street. The other customers, three in all, were solitary drinkers like Galloway.

He catalogued them quickly. One was a woman of about forty with too much lipstick. Her teeth were red, her eyes puffy. She was drinking straight vodka in which a pallid cherry floated. Given enough alcohol to suspend his critical faculties and impose amnesia on the fact of his marriage—splintered as it was—Galloway would have fallen coyly in love with her for about twenty minutes. His drunken romanticism was less incurable than chronic.

A few feet from the woman, but closing in, was a skinny man with a battered suitcase, which hinted at a lonesome life on the road, a salesman of some kind. The third drinker, a muscular man in a cowboy hat, was a country-western sociopath who looked inside his beer for long periods without actually drinking. He might have been listening to some maudlin tune playing in the jukebox of his head. *I'll never get over her blue eyes, I see them all the time.*

Charlie Galloway picked up his scotch. At the same instant the skinny man made his move toward the woman and plonked his case on an empty stool, whipping the lid open with a flourish. The case contained a variety of novelty items: plastic dog droppings, fake ice cubes with cockroaches trapped in them, long slinky things you wore like spectacles that had bug eyes attached to the ends. The woman accepted a pair of these and put them on and they drooped about two feet from her eyes and swung when she moved her face.

"I bet I look damn stupid," she said, and laughed, a wonderful barroom laugh that rang like bells on Hogmanay.

"You look terrific," the novelty salesman said.

The woman moved her head from side to side rapidly and the slinkies went with her. She couldn't stop laughing.

"What planet do I look like I'm from?" she asked.

"Jupiter," said the salesman.

The cowboy figure looked up and sourly said, "Ask me, you're from the planet moron."

The woman wasn't perturbed. Nor did she remove the bug eyes. She simply said, *"Chacun à son gout,* cowboy. Up yours."

The man fell silent, looking as if he'd heard something very profound. Charlie Galloway tossed his shot back in one. Then he reached for the beer even as he gestured with his free hand to the bartender that the small glass might kindly be replenished.

He had long ago realized there were two worlds, one inhabited by people such as Paffett, a demanding place where clocks kept accurate time and your life was logged, and this other one he occupied now, a land without limits, a place where loneliness was outlawed in the momentary connection of lives, and a woman had weird metal tubes hanging from her eyes—and yet it all seemed so *damned normal* compared to what Paffett expected of him.

Six months without a drink. He'd show Lennie Paffett.

Tomorrow, he thought. He'd begin tomorrow. What difference did the rest of this day make anyway, because it was already shot, already ruined, a day out of joint? Tomorrow, nice and early, he'd get up with the sun and . . .

And what?

And stop drinking.

He'd do things.

Practical, sober things such as other men did.

Like what?

Karen—he'd start there. He'd woo her all over again. Win her back. *See, my darling lassie, the new Charles Galloway, a changed man, a different person. Reborn. Sober. Redeemed.* Those would be his goals. A wife he loved, and his own self-respect. What was wrong with that? All the alternatives were bleak.

He leaned against the bar, closing his eyes as he considered the suddenly luminescent prospect of changing his life. *I'll turn things around,* he thought. *I'll make things new again.*

He heard the door open and shut as the man in the cowboy hat went out into the sun. The skinny salesman and the woman were talking about another bar and making preparations to go there together. And, goddammit, she'd wear the silly glasses all the way down the street and to hell with it, people could stare if they wanted, it was her life.

She and the salesman stepped out, leaving Galloway alone with the barman, who was reading a racing newspaper. It was that moment of unbearable solitude familiar to drinkers, a time of sudden panic when all life receded from you like the ocean rushing backward, and you were left on your own at the bar after people had hurried to other locations and engagements and the small self-contained promising universe that had existed only minutes before was in smithereens. You were the last person alive. The last one left. Even the barman didn't count because he hadn't been included in the original census, and besides he was sober as a hanging judge. But you needed somebody. Anybody. Another face. Another drinker to offset the solitude.

Galloway had two empty glasses before him now. The question was whether he made his exit or kept on drinking until the bar filled up with other sets of people and different worlds.

The barman looked at him. "Need anything?"

Yes, Galloway thought, *but I can't put a name to it.* "Maybe soon," he said.

The barman turned away.

Galloway looked toward the window. The sun was dying little by little, creating shadows that looked deceptively cool between buildings. The street was lifeless, indifferent to him. He wondered about Karen and where she might be right now. He'd find her and hold her and kiss her and ask forgiveness, and then all would be well. He'd be reinstated in her heart, redeemed.

Sure, Charlie. In what easy, imaginary world? Love didn't have the simplicity of a confessional, and he knew it. You couldn't mouth a few platitudes and hope the tarnished brass of the past would shine like bloody gold. You couldn't just *try* to make things new again. You actually had to go out and *do* it.

But what if it was too late? What then? What if the rest of his life was destined to be lived without her? What if, *what if,* she'd found somebody else? This question terrorized him, an armed guerrilla that took his heart hostage. Karen and Another. Karen's body in another man's bed. Her thighs spread for him. His cock between her lovely lips. Some things you didn't think about, couldn't entertain.

He'd get her back. Yes. He'd find her. He'd be lost forever in this world of isolation and empty bars if he didn't.

He went to the pay phone situated outside the toilets. REST-ROOMS, a euphemistic sign said, as if yawning people stretched out on beds beyond closed doors. He pulled a handful of quarters from his pockets. He removed also his small brown leather address book. Where to begin? In this great overheated labyrinth of a city, where did you look for one specific individual?

He flicked through the names of mutual friends—some half forgotten, others eclipsed by alcohol—dialed their numbers, listened to the recorded messages left on answering machines. Wait for the beep. After the beep. Millions of people all over the world listened to the same ludicrous message every day. The whole planet was waiting for the beep. *I'm looking for Karen,* he'd say. *If she turns up, get her to call me.* He had the impression of people listening as he spoke but choosing not to pick up. Once or twice he'd find a real person at the end of the line. He got Herb Mascott on the first ring. Herb was a homosexual who'd once worked for the same company as Karen. He sounded irritable.

"Have you been drinking again, Charlie?"

"I don't want to talk about that. I want to know if you've seen Karen, that's all."

"Lord, you drag all this negative energy around with you when you drink. Anyhow, I don't want to get involved. I love you both as friends. Just don't ask me to take sides, for heaven's sake."

"I'm not asking you to referee, Jesus—"

"Call me when you're sober."

Snip. One vasectomized phone line.

Suddenly he was tired of the panic in himself, drained by the heat and the loss of Karen, by Paffett and his "prolonged" suspension. He wanted to go up to his small house above the canyons and sleep. But he didn't have a car to drive and he wasn't in a condition to do so anyway.

The last time he'd driven drunk it had led to the disaster, The African Disgrace, when he'd totally bollixed a simple chore, something a chauffeur could do in his sleep. Paffett had charged him with the task of picking up a foreign dignitary from Los Angeles International Airport. The visitor was the chief of police in the city of Lagos, Nigeria, a questionable position in view of that city's unbridled lawlessness. Paffett often entertained foreign law enforcement officers, showing them his computer systems, giving guided tours of the expensive arsenal available to the men in his command. A little PR, a little education; Paffett was humbly proud of his force.

The plane from Nigeria had been very late, and Charlie Galloway had idled away the hours in an airport bar. By the time the Nigerian arrived Galloway had already decided, with a drunk's blind indifference to consequence, that he'd show the African something of Los Angeles before depositing him with Leonard Paffett. The man from Lagos would want to see the fabled film capital of the world, not some computer system in a building that smelled like a locker room. And so they went up into the Hollywood Hills, Galloway careless at the wheel, pointing out this sight and that to the enormous black man in an Armani suit who smiled with restrained terror. Why had this lunatic driver been sent to fetch him? Why didn't he pay attention to the twists and turns in the road? And how did he know where all the famous movie actors lived anyway?

Galloway, tour operator, enthusiast, film historian, madman, was beyond interruption. Enthusiasm devoured him. This was the chosen city of his self-imposed exile, was it not? Look! Myrna Loy had lived there! Loretta Young here! And that was Jack Nicholson's house! As darkness fell and the lights of the city tantalized far below, his driving became more erratic and his determination to show the homes of the famous increasingly persistent. Even if he was making most of it up, or confusing this place with that, even if he was hurtling along on the locomotive of his own inventions, what did it matter to the chief of police from Lagos? Hollywood was a fiction anyway: Here you could take any kind of license you liked with reality. Because it lacked any definition, this city could be reinvented a thousand times a day.

Somewhere above Laurel Canyon where, for a reason he couldn't remember, he was absolutely *convinced* Kirk Douglas had his home, he drove the Dodge over the lip of a cliff and it went plummeting down a leafy ravine, bouncing under branches and over tangled roots, crashing through thick foliage and stubborn fern before finally plowing down a cedar fence and thundering into a backyard where Kirk Douglas didn't live, but a legal assistant to the governor of California did. The following day Galloway, uninjured, was suspended, and the African was treated for a fractured rib and a broken thumb at an expensive hospital, courtesy of the taxpayer.

Charlie Galloway shook his head at the memory. *It didn't happen to me*, he thought. It was that other Galloway, the lookalike who did bad things behind the sober Charlie's back. It was the reckless spirit that sometimes invaded him when he was drunk, the poltergeist, more childlike than malicious, who seized his brain and tossed thoughts and impulses around like loose kitchen objects.

He inserted a quarter into the phone and called a taxi.

When he hung up he stood motionless for a long time. He put the palm of his hand to his forehead. Something nagged him, something he'd promised to do. It was on the tip of his tongue, annoyingly elusive. And it wasn't the idea that had just occurred to him about changing his life, it was some other business from before. Gone.

When his cab arrived he walked with stiff-backed dignity out of the bar and into the early evening sun whose brutal light lay over Los Angeles like the incandescent spore of an unnamed plague.

He woke in hot blackness, fighting his way up from some swampy dream of doom whose images vanished at once. He wore only his underwear. In sleep he'd kicked aside the bedsheet. He looked at the lit panel of the clock-radio on the bedside table. Ten-thirty P.M. precisely. He'd slept for a little more than two hours. Dehydrated, sweating, he moved through darkness toward the bathroom where he dipped his face beneath the cold water tap, flooding his eyes and mouth and nostrils. He straightened up and stood dripping on the tiled floor. A moon, low among the hills, was visible through the bathroom window. Rich and white, it had the terrifying immensity of a giant's eye.

He dried his face, walked back to the bedroom, turned on the lamp. When the taxi had brought him home earlier, he'd come upstairs at once and collapsed in sleep. Now he noticed the wardrobe door was open and Karen's dresses he was sure had hung there only that afternoon were gone—which meant she'd come here in his absence, as she'd done before, because she didn't want to see him. But why was she removing her belongings in stages? Why didn't she just come like a dutiful bailiff and seize everything at once?

When she'd first gone three weeks ago she'd taken only toilet items and jeans and a couple of blouses. Three days later she'd come back for shoes, skirts, underwear. Four days after that most of the jewelry had gone. This piecemeal removal suggested to Charlie Galloway, in his more optimistic moments, that Karen didn't want to make a clean break, that she was repossessing things as if she too thought there might still be some chance of reconciliation. Then why didn't she talk to him? Why didn't she want to sit down at a summit conference? Why scurry around behind his back for her stuff?

They'd spoken once briefly on the telephone the day after her departure, the conversation of embarrassed strangers, Karen reluctant to divulge her plans or whereabouts, Charlie unwilling to beg her to return. She'd said, *I just can't take it anymore, Charlie. I need to get away from you.* He'd underestimated, or chosen to ignore, the fault lines in their relationship, flaws his drinking had both caused and exacerbated. Immunized by alcohol, he'd always thought that he and Karen would stay together no matter what turbulence rocked the seven-year-old marriage. Dear Christ, they were in love, after all!

He had imagined she'd come back within a day or two, perhaps three, a week at the outside. Now, twenty-one days later, his optimism was a sad little flag that fluttered occasionally in his head but hung mainly still.

He went downstairs to the kitchen. There might be a note. Something pinned by a magnet to the refrigerator. A sign. *Keep a candle burning in the window for me, Charlie. Tie a yellow ribbon.* In a pig's arse. There was nothing save the scent of pine cleaner and floor wax and gleaming surfaces where Mrs. Nazarena had been hard at work. He opened the refrigerator, then vaguely recollected that Clarence Wylie had poured the last beer down the sink. Shit.

I just can't take it anymore, Charlie.

He walked inside the living room, which had the appearance of a room in which nobody lived. Mrs. Nazarena's work again, of course—and now he remembered what had nagged him earlier in the bar, and that was the promise he'd made to call her tonight. He opened his address book, flicking the pages even as he wondered how he could possibly help Ella Nazarena when his hand trembled the way it did and his brain had the texture of used toilet paper.

He dialed the number. Mrs. Nazarena answered at once, as if she'd been waiting by the phone. "I am happy you called," she said.

He lay back across the sofa with his eyes shut. "Do you want to discuss . . . whatever it is . . .?"

"I don't like phones. I prefer face-to-face."

Galloway, sighing, wondered why. It was unlike Mrs. Nazarena to be this secretive. "Do you want to meet me tomorrow?"

"Tonight would be better. If convenient."

Tonight, he thought. How could he go out into the world and be exposed under that great full moon? He needed rooms, small manageable spaces he could control. The external world was menacing in his fragile condition.

"Can you come here?" he asked, then remembered she had no car. He, on the other hand, had a Toyota in his garage, although the prospect of driving across Los Angeles with this thudding drum of a hangover was dreadful.

"I could catch a bus," she said. "Or a cab."

"No, I'll come to your house. Give me about half an hour." Bighearted Charlie.

"Don't drive if you've been drinking too much," she said. "I don't want you to do anything unwise."

"I'm fine. I'll be okay."

"You have the address?"

Galloway said he'd find the street. "Did you see Karen when you were here today?" he asked, as if the subject of Karen were an afterthought.

"She telephoned me. She wanted some of her clothing. I took it to her."

"Where?"

"We met at a supermarket. She no want to come to the house."

"Did she say anything? Did she say where she's staying?"

"I shouldn't tell. It's a confidence."

"But you know, right?" He tried to keep his questions light and offhanded, but he could hear tension in his voice.

"She said a name."

"What name?"

"I shouldn't answer."

"What name, Ella?"

"Okay. This one time I tell. But not again. She said Justine."

"Justine Harper?"

"Maybe. I don't remember."

Charlie Galloway thanked her, then set the receiver down. *Justine Harper*, he thought. Why would Karen even have *mentioned* where she was living if she didn't want him to find out from Mrs. Nazarena? It was a hopeful sign; she expected him to make contact. At least that was how he read the situation.

Justine Harper, a colleague of Karen's in the copyright department of a music-publishing company called Monument Incorporated, was a divorcee who lived in Santa Monica. Charlie Galloway had always found her friendly in a somewhat guarded manner, as if she expected all human relationships in the state of California to be temporary at best, so why become too close and vulnerable?

He got up from the sofa. His head ached. He dreaded the freeways, those poisoned bloodstreams of Los Angeles that would take him to Ella Nazarena. But he'd made a promise, the keeping of which seemed a good place to begin if he was thinking in terms of redeeming himself—an odd phrase that made him feel like something left in a pawnshop, something dry and cobwebbed and waiting to be wanted.

Ella lived in a neighborhood of third-world tract housing near LAX. One street looked pretty much like the next, one house practically identical to the other. FOR SALE notices, dried-out lawns, vandalized streetlamps, here and there an abandoned house without windows where squatters moved in with their crack pipes and cokehead girlfriends, glazed cookies who'd suck anything for a buzz. Walkways were strewn with dead kitchen appliances, shattered cars, lampshades, plastic sofas, as if everything was one big sidewalk sale. Something more than despair possessed this district, something against which Charlie Galloway wanted to shut the window of his car as if a toxic vapor were rising invisibly through cracks in the pavement. Desperation was the jailer here.

Dogs, maddened by moon and heat, deranged by changes in planetary rhythms beyond the detection of humans, roamed everywhere. They appeared in front of his headlights, snarling into the beams. They skulked along the sidewalks, scavenged through spilled garbage, yelped and howled and struggled with one another. Some of them might once have been domestic pets abandoned by fleeing owners, but others looked as if they'd always been wild. Black shapes slinked around the corners of Galloway's vision and for a time he wondered if these were figments of his own creation, delirium's menagerie. But the barking and howling were real enough, piercing his brain.

He found the street where Ella lived. It adjoined a large area of darkened wasteland, presumably the kingdom of the dog packs. He parked his Toyota outside her small house, then locked it. Several curs sniffed him in a predatory way. When he hissed at them they backed off and barked with their heads uplifted and their jaws slack. *Creatures of the full moon,* he thought. But it would always be full moon time, always Halloween, in this neighborhood. Punk rock music played loudly and a motorcycle was being made to roar every few seconds before fading, and now and again a girl could be heard laughing in a manner Galloway thought was inspired more by some hilarious dope vision than by happiness.

The yellow light on Ella's porch was obscured by foliage and barely illuminated his path. He pushed open the gate in the chain-link fence surrounding the front yard. The dry stands of brittle oleander were rattling, alive with movement, as if at any moment there might be an explosion of vicious dogs who lay concealed among the leaves. It was not a good night to be abroad, he thought, and he rushed up on the porch where both screen and front door lay unexpectedly open and you could see a TV playing in a corner of the living room, a nighttime soap, a hysterical woman screaming at somebody.

There were dogs in the living room too.

Dogs indoors.

Charlie Galloway didn't move for many chilly minutes. The dialogue on the TV might have been spoken in Estonian, so little sense did it make to him. But nothing made sense in this small tidy room with its floral curtains and framed velvet Christs, nothing, not the open doors that ought to have been closed against the night, certainly not the five or six dogs clustered under the window with heads busily bent.

Everything bewildered him. He couldn't breathe. He took a step toward the dogs, who turned to gaze at him. Blood dripped from their teeth.

His head throbbed. He raised his face to the ceiling. Through small vents damp air blew from the evaporative cooler, which vibrated on the roof. *This isn't what I think it is,* he told himself. *This isn't what I think it is.* The small room shrunk around him. His clothes stuck to his skin. He felt fevered.

He stepped closer to the dogs, who snarled and barked. But they parted in his advance anyway. Sated by their recent meal, they were less belligerent than they might have been. He kept moving. The dogs, black and brown, white and gray, continued to back off, some whining, others growling halfheartedly at him. There was a certain controlled madness in their eyes; at any time they might just go berserk and savage him next.

But he didn't move any nearer. He'd gone close enough. Another step would take him where he didn't want to go.

He'd *seen.*

He began to shake. He needed a drink. Inside the narrow kitchen he searched the refrigerator but found nothing except cold boiled rice and egg salad. He opened one cabinet after another until he came upon a bottle of Gallo red. He wouldn't have chosen it for himself, but there was a drinker's saying: *Any port in a storm.*

He made a phone call from the kitchen. He wondered if the operator understood anything he was telling her because he was asked to repeat his information, which he did in a voice that wasn't strictly his own, but thin and stretched, as though his words were latex. When he hung up he leaned into the sink and stuck a finger deep into his throat. His stomach muscles knotted and his chest ached, but he brought nothing up. He doused his face with cold water, then returned to the living room with the bottle. The dogs had gone, leaving behind the musty smell of fur. On TV a diaper commercial was playing. Babies blew soap bubbles, rainbow-colored spheres, a pristine little world. No dogs.

Charlie Galloway, deflated, slumped on the sofa, the wine bottle jammed between his unsteady legs. He didn't open it, but he kept his palms upon the comforting curve of glass.

6

"And they call them man's best friend," said the lieutenant named Kenneth P. Duffy, who arrived with an entourage in response to Charlie Galloway's phone call.

Friedmann, Duffy's forensic expert, said that Mrs. Nazarena had clearly been shot once in the side of the head before the animals, drawn by blood, had come inside the house to dine. Death was a result of the gunshot wound, not the savagery of dogs. A didactic, unfeeling gnome, Friedmann was a cousin to those clay creatures one occasionally saw lingering with quiet malice on suburban lawns. He prefaced almost everything he said with the word *clearly*.

Charlie Galloway hadn't risen from the sofa for the last hour and still clutched the unopened bottle of Gallo, which tempted and terrified him. He was irritated by the circus of Friedmann and Duffy and the studious fingerprint guy in the seersucker jacket who whistled "If I Were a Blackbird" as he dusted and the two uniformed cops who ransacked the little house with all the finesse of dray horses. Despite himself, Galloway found his eyes drawn to the sight of the white sheet thrown over Mrs. Nazarena.

Blood, blackening now, had soaked through the fiber.

Duffy stepped into the kitchen and spent some time talking quietly on the phone. When he came back he sat on the arm of the sofa and smoked a cigarette. He had a very small ginger mustache. His teeth and fingers were stained with the dull bloom of nicotine. "And you say you just dropped in, Galloway?"

"She was a good family friend," Galloway said. "She wanted to see me about something."

"And you don't know what?"

"When I got here she wasn't in any position to tell me."

Duffy smoked feverishly. He was no cocktail party smoker, no well-mannered nicotine amateur. He was the real thing, a fiercely addicted fiend. Smoke shot through his nostrils, billowed out of his mouth, creating a modest vanishing illusion.

"The story downtown is you walked away from the drunk tank," Duffy said.

"It wasn't exactly a drunk tank, Duffy."

"Clinic then. Whatever. What the hell's in a name? Point is, you haven't licked the old boozeroo problem."

"I'm working on it," Galloway replied reluctantly. He had never liked Duffy and was reluctant to talk about his personal failings in front of the man. Duffy was a locker-room gossip, a broadsheet on the bulletin board. Tell Duffy anything and it was bruited about with abandon.

"I can see you're doing real well." Duffy nodded at the wine bottle, which was like an enormous pacifier in Galloway's lap. "I can tell you're coming to grips with it."

Charlie Galloway ignored the broad sarcasm. Why bother? The bait was bad, not worth taking. He was consumed by weariness and sorrow, even as he was bedeviled by clearheadedness; this was the dead center of some limpid nightmare. He smelled the evaporative cooler blowing musty shafts of lukewarm moisture through the room. He wanted to go back up into the canyons, where the air might be fresher. The frail house rumbled a moment. Overhead, an enormous jumbo jet ferrying people to Japan or Thailand rose into the stars. First-class passengers would already be sipping in-flight cocktails, he thought.

The forensic expert said, "I'm through here. I'll have my report on your desk first thing, Duffy. I'm late for supper. My wife had a humongous roast in the oven when I left." Friedmann looked at Galloway now. "A good meat has to be rare. It spoils if you overcook it."

Part of the continuing nightmare, Galloway thought. A cop with a face made out of smoke. A forensic expert, who'd just examined a bloody corpse, yearning for the taste of underdone animal flesh. Galloway felt he'd fallen through a trapdoor into a greasy subterranean cellar inhabited by persons who were just the wrong side of being securely hinged.

Friedmann departed. Outside, dogs barked at him.

Duffy asked, "Was she in any kind of trouble?"

Galloway observed the fingerprint man dust the window ledge, his head bent over his work. "I don't know."

"Did she have enemies?"

"I'd hardly think so. She was a nice woman. Religious. Good-hearted."

"Nice people sometimes have enemies," Duffy said. "Was there a man in her life? Scorned lover puts bullet in mistress's skull, that kind of thing?"

Galloway said he didn't know. He gazed into the wine bottle. The deep red liquid appeared secretive. Sometimes, inebriated on wine—which was not his drink of choice—he'd experienced a kind of mystical high, affinities with the universe, dizzying insights beyond language, cosmic moments. Unfortunately, wine almost always made him throw up.

Duffy wandered over to the window, looked out into the dark street. He put his hands into his pockets and rattled loose change as he swayed a little on the balls of his feet. "It's a hell of a neighborhood," he said. "It's like some other country out there. Fucking Nicaragua or something. Drive a couple of miles from here in one direction, shit, you're in Beverly Hills. Go in another, Santa Monica."

Charlie Galloway agreed these were baffling contrasts.

"I'd raze the whole goddam area, Galloway, if it was up to me."

Galloway let Duffy's notion of urban redevelopment pass without comment.

Duffy went on, "A lot of things don't make much sense. You find that, Galloway? People murdered for a few nickels. People murdered for nothing but kicks. And this woman"—here Duffy glanced down at the sheet—"who'd want to kill her? It doesn't look like robbery, does it? I don't get the impression the joint's been turned over. What's worth stealing here? You want a velvet portrait of Jesus? A plaster Madonna or two? Rosary beads? Trash. Schlock. Even the TV's ancient. The stereo goes back to when hi-fi was state of the art. All this woman had was crap."

This crude inventory of Mrs. Nazarena's world struck Charlie as needless. Given to a sentimentality that was both the burden and blessing of his race, he understood, and was touched by, how much her religious artifacts had meant to Ella Nazarena. A simple woman without malice, she believed unquestioningly in her religion. She lived a peaceful life. So what could possibly have troubled her so much that she'd needed to talk to him? What was it she didn't want to discuss on the telephone? And why was this clown Duffy demeaning her in death?

"Maybe she did a little dealing on the side, peddled dope, nothing big," Duffy said. "You think that's a possibility? Small-time dealer offed by drug-crazed junkie?"

Galloway shook his head and thought, *Drink the Gallo, Charlie. You've earned it.* People like Duffy were walking tabloids. They thought in headlines. That way their world was concise, smaller, easier to handle. Complexities were rare birds they could neither cage nor categorize.

Duffy said, "You ought to wander off home now, Galloway. Seeing as you're suspended and don't have any official business here, I don't see much point in you staying. We'll probably speak again. If I need you I know where to find you. Toodle-oo."

Charlie Galloway stood up. His legs were leaden. He left the wine on the coffee table. Through an open door he could see into a bedroom where the two uniformed men were rummaging around a closet. A large double bed, covered by a patchwork quilt, dominated the room. On the wall was the inevitable crucifix which, having been disturbed by one of the uniformed cops, hung aslant; Jesus at a bad angle. The cops were discussing a recent baseball game.

Galloway limped outside. The darkness had the texture of a hot flannel pressed against his face. Beyond the fence that surrounded Mrs. Galloway's yard, a few neighbors, drawn by cop cars, silently observed the house. He passed among them, reached his car, got inside. As he turned the key in the ignition he noticed his radio had been taken. *Goddam!* From the vacant slot on the dashboard red and black wires dangled like thin petrified eels of exotic origin. Here, in this neighborhood of murder and mad dogs, he'd been burglarized. It was wondrously symmetrical. A dead woman with something left unspoken. A stolen radio. He had the feeling he'd been cut off from all sources of information in a land of thieves and killers.

Disconcerted, hearing the cossack horsemen of depression thunder across the steppes toward him, he drove back to the freeway.

When he entered his house, Galloway turned on the lights in every room. He dispersed all darkness and stalked the place with the nervous energy of a man who has just been assailed by horror, back and forth, up and down, conscious of how silence was not banished by the blaze of lights but instead underlined: Electricity accentuated everything. He switched the TV on, then off again, assaulted only briefly by the chaotic sadism of the Three Stooges. In the kitchen he found a little stack of mail that Mrs. Nazarena, on the last afternoon of her life, must have placed on the table. He'd overlooked it before. Now he sifted it without interest, imagining the dead woman's hand aligning these envelopes just so. Bills, plastic windows through which he had no desire to peer, a dull assortment. Only one item engaged him, a card from his father in Lennoxtown, Scotland.

Daniel Galloway lived in a rest home on the outskirts of Glasgow, a converted Victorian house at the foot of the Campsie Fells. Daniel, seventy-nine, had been sending postcards to his son for the last three years. Usually these contained enigmatic messages, or random family references. This latest, which had a view of Loch Lomond at sunset, read:

> *Your paternal grandfather is burIED in the GlasgOw Necropolis. He spent three YearS in jail for sTealing coPper from the roof of a cHurCh in Cowcaddens. I'm not sure I ever told you thaT. FamiLy history is the only history there is. Your lovINg father, D Galloway.*

These inconsequential bulletins, strewn with mysterious capitals, always upset Galloway because the father he remembered and worshiped was a big man with focus and vitality, a self-educated Marxist, a gentleman, a bright-eyed singer of the old songs, a wit who could hold his drink with a dignity his son had not quite inherited. Humiliated by age, Daniel was forced now to live a glazed, sedentary life, false teeth in a bedside glass, sleeping pills, starched sheets and bossy nurses, and interminable games of draughts with other inmates. Once a week, got up in his navy blue Sunday suit and infused with downers, he was trotted off stiffly to the local Presbyterian church, an establishment he'd never been able to stomach. *Too many constipated bastards,* he always said. *What the Presbyterian church needs is bloody cascara and a damn good shite.* Now he wrote postcards in which he tampered with historic facts. As far as Charlie knew, his paternal grandfather had been lost at sea, and therefore could not have been buried in the Necropolis.

Charlie Galloway remembered when his father had met Karen for the only time, five years ago in Glasgow just before the old man had begun his decline and Charlie's marriage, after two terrific years, was still solvent, a going concern. The Scottish Honeymoon Period, he called it now. Galloway Senior and the young American beauty had taken to each other immediately. Dan had flirted with her, told old jokes and made them seem fresh, called her his "nut-brown maiden," translated the guttural patois of Glasgow for her, dazzled her with charm, took her arm in bars and tea rooms—a spellbinding performance. Once, in the darkened art-deco splendor of the Rogano restaurant in Exchange Place, he kissed the back of her hand and she laughed with the kind of delight she'd shown less and less in the years since.

The whole trip had been a perfect little family episode, a treasure Charlie took out and polished at times. *Alas.* Now the old man was a half note short of an octave, Karen was gone, and the past was a mildewed photo. What he felt roll through this California house was a tidal wave of loss of the kind that drove men to self-destruction.

He got up from the kitchen table. In the living room he dialed Justine Harper's number. Her answering machine clicked on. Her message was businesslike. After the beep Galloway asked

Karen to call him, if she happened to be there. With tactful lack
of detail, he mentioned the murder of Ella Nazarena, then hung
up. His hands shook. Worse, something he couldn't name trembled inside him, a hitherto unsuspected pulse or some new congregation of nerve endings. He felt suddenly cold.

Yielding to impulse, he explored the barren refrigerator,
checked the places where he sometimes stashed booze—behind
books, inside the laundry basket, under the kitchen sink with the
Pledge and Joy and Lime-A-Way. Thirty minutes of hard searching and *nada.* He must have pillaged his own secret caches at
some other time, although he had no memory of having done so.

He stood at the foot of the narrow stairway and looked up
through gloomy shadows. The absences of the place settled all
around him like falling snow. The house was still and in its
stillness perfect, a framed painting Galloway observed like a man
in a gallery who looks and wonders, *Who lives in that house?
Who leads a life there? Where do those stairs go?*

When he'd had enough of this he walked outside and stood
under the avocado. He leaned against the trunk, felt something
filmy flutter against his face, a web, a delicate insect, something.

Family history is the only history there is, his father had
written. That was all very well if you were lying in a rest home
in the somnolent Scottish countryside and your mind was wandering through the thickets of old blood relationships. *But I have
other concerns,* Charlie Galloway thought. He looked across the
dark canyon, hearing the omnipresent hum of Los Angeles as if
it were a string plucked and doomed to vibrate endlessly, and he
pondered murder. Who killed Ella Nazarena? Did a thief enter
her house, had she surprised the robber? Was it that pointless old
story? He had an ache in his heart thinking of the Filipina woman.
You work hard all your damn life, you hurt nobody, and what do
you get in the end? What is your reward? Behind his eyes the dull
pain of the day's alcohol was coming back to bother him.

He wasn't sure how long he stood beneath the avocado or
whether he dozed in an upright position or drifted into some form
of mental absenteeism, his head against the trunk. What startled
him was the appearance of a car in the driveway and headlights
flashing against his face, illuminating him as if he were a prowler

in his own front yard. A door opened, an interior light blinked on and off, and Karen stepped out.

The car was a late-model Mercedes, bright red with a soft white top, a Hollywood vehicle. As Karen came toward him the only thing he could think to ask was where she'd bought it, at which she laughed rather nervously, as if the idea of owning a Mercedes like this one was preposterous.

"I borrowed it," she said. She took his arm and led him toward the house. "It belongs to Justine."

Indoors, the light blinded Galloway. He was anxious and dry. He wondered if the whites of his eyes were pink. Karen wore a magnificent short skirt, a mini, which rose as she sat on the sofa. He'd dreamed of those legs a few nights ago. He'd dreamed he lay with his face propped against her inner thigh, a happy man, satisfied and contented and smugly sated with love.

The skirt was brown suede, the blouse off-white. Some kind of Navajo necklace, silver and turquoise, hung against her breasts. Her hair was different. The last time he'd seen her it had been shoulder-length and full. Now, cut rather severely and shaped to her skull, it imparted a kind of boyishness he found very appealing. He wondered if there was any significance in this fact, something androgynous lurking in the recesses of his nature. With that small surge of pleasure imperfect people feel when they perceive a flaw in the otherwise flawless, he noticed she'd put on about three pounds around her waist, a consequence of the compulsive eating that afflicted her in times of stress. But she carried it well.

"I came as soon as I got your message," Karen said. She had one of those lovely pale faces that, when exposed to sun, becomes pinkly marbled. So she never ventured into direct sunlight, something she had in common with Charlie, who considered the sun overrated, of benefit only to plants and Californian loonies who lay on beaches in the inexplicable quest for discoloration.

"I can't believe Ella's dead, I just can't believe it." She tilted her face against the back of the sofa, looked up at the ceiling. She was trim, small-breasted, splendid. The impression of fragility she usually emitted was blunted just a little by the few extra pounds on her. Galloway had the off-center feeling that after seven years of marriage and three weeks of separation this was their first date, and it wasn't going anywhere.

"Do you have any idea who killed her?" she asked.

"She was shot, that's all I know." He wasn't about to mention the dogs, that whole barbaric scene.

"I saw her only this afternoon." Karen had the awe in her voice of a person who has cancelled her reservation on a doomed flight. The shadow of tragedy, of tragic figures and possibilities, had touched her. She pressed the tips of her fingers against her eyes, which were damp. "It's so hard to believe. She was a lovely woman, Charlie. I never met anybody more gentle."

"She wanted to talk to me about something," Galloway said. "So I drove over there."

"You *went* to her house? *You* discovered the body?"

Galloway sat on the sofa. He wanted to hold his wife's hand. He was reluctant, a man checked by boundaries. What were the behavioral limitations imposed on an estranged husband anyway? Where did the wire fence begin and end? How high were the watchtowers and would the guards shoot you if you made a wrong move?

"I wish I hadn't," he said.

Karen watched him with sympathy. "I can imagine."

No, you can't. You can't even begin. He got up from the sofa. "What the hell do you think she wanted to tell me?"

Karen looked around the room briefly, as if like any absent wife she expected things to have changed since she'd gone, a vase moved, a rug shifted, perhaps even some breakage caused by a drunken Charlie Galloway.

"Maybe she had a legal problem, Charlie."

"Then she'd see a lawyer."

"Or she was in some kind of trouble."

Galloway sat in an armchair. From this new perspective, Karen's legs appeared longer. The lamplight laid a sheen across the material of her pantyhose. *It was a crime,* he thought. *She goes around looking this way. She's out there in the world looking this gorgeous, this edible. For whom?* he wondered. The trouble with phantom lovers was how they always lived in halls of mirrors where they multiplied and pretty soon they were swarming all over your wife—the studs, the cool young dudes, of your imagination.

"She had a beau," Karen said. "Did you know that? She met him about two months ago. He was apparently very sweet to her. Gifts. Chocolates. Even proposed marriage." Karen tried to smile through the remains of her tears. Galloway sensed that she wasn't talking about Ella Nazarena's boyfriend, but referring obliquely to some earlier, more romantic version of Charlie himself, bearer of candies and flowers, the man she'd married, the one who had become somehow lost with the awful passage of time. *Damn, she always looked attractive with moist eyes,* he thought. He wanted to get up and kiss her, but the six feet of ceramic-tiled floor that separated them might have been booby-trapped, land-mined. He was paralyzed by coyness and uncertainty.

"Do you know his name?" he asked.

"Freddie something or other. I don't remember the last name. It'll come back to me. He's a Filipino. He has his own barbershop. She was very impressed with that. . . . Christ, I still can't believe it! It makes me so goddam . . . I don't know, *enraged.* There are times I hate this loathsome city and the fucking mur-derous freaks in it." She ran her hands through her hair. From her purse she took out a Kleenex and buried her face in its folds a moment. "Are you interested in the beau? Is he a suspect?"

"I don't know the man, and I don't suspect him of anything, but I wouldn't mind talking to him," Galloway said. The clock at the top of the stairs chimed twice. Was it two A.M. already? The day lay behind him like a series of episodes without a common link, as if each had been experienced by a man with recurring amnesia. He looked at Karen and what he felt was love, deep and yet troubled, a pool of very clear water distressed by a ruinous wind.

"Except you're not a cop for the next three months," she said.

"Um. Make that six." And he told her about Paffett, the increased suspension, the clinic, his escape from the shackles of Dr. Boscoe or Roscoe.

She listened, gazing into his face in the open, searching way that was characteristic of her. There was no guile to Karen, no side. What you saw in her expression was all there was. She couldn't hide surprise or disappointment. She couldn't mask hurt or anger. It was an admirable quality that had first drawn Charlie Galloway to her. If his own life was a creaking house with many rooms and odd stairways leading up to concealed turrets or down into basements, a house of secret nooks and dark crannies, a boozer's palace, then Karen's was an open-plan ranch with as few walls as possible and a hundred skylights.

"How are you going to live for six months?" she asked.

"On a very sober budget."

"I'll buy the budget part," she said.

"You don't think I can stop drinking?"

"Don't let's drag out that old one, Charlie. Not now."

"I'm on the wagon." How fake it sounded. Even the way it resonated in his skull was an unconvincing echo.

"Sure, sure, sure. The trouble with all the wagons you ever climbed on is they tend to have square wheels and don't go anywhere. God knows, I'd love to have faith, Charlie. Really I would. But I've watched you ride wagons before. You always fall off. You should have stayed in the clinic."

This time is different, he thought. It was one of those thoughts best left unsaid. As soon as it flew from brain to mouth, then darted from mouth to world, it would sound as convincing as a plea for clemency from a serial murderer caught with bloodied ax in hand.

"You can't have been on this new wagon for very long. You smell like a brewery."

"It was a recent decision," he remarked.

"Oh, screw it. I'm not going to nag, and I'm not going to whine. I'm not up for it and I don't want to rehash old disappointments. They're gone."

Karen became silent. She was in territory so familiar to her she could have traversed it blindfolded, through swamps and quicksands and whirlpools. She could have navigated the crevices and scaled the cliffs without benefit of compass or rope. It was the country of Galloway's good intentions, an allegedly fair land whose shoreline she'd seen only from afar, one that always had a way of receding no matter how hard Charlie tried to reach it. How pathetic of him to announce his umpteenth ascent to the wagon, as though it were a coronation; no vehicle could pull

Charlie out of the bog unless he really wanted to be free—and sometimes she doubted that. It was as if, having become imprisoned by alcohol, he liked the stench of his private lockup, the bars on his windows, the anesthetizing of his heart.

It didn't surprise her to learn he was close to losing his job. It was inevitable. There was always a sense of impending catastrophe when you lived with Charlie Galloway; it was like living under the shadow of a guillotine, and she was sick of waiting for the blade to come down. Love, she'd learned, was not adhesive enough to hold together the infrastructure of her marriage to him.

Two or three times, in an attempt to understand Charlie's compulsion and shore herself up with support, she'd attended Al Anon meetings, well-intentioned gatherings invariably dominated either by tightlipped whining women, whose pain lay visibly on their faces and who were in love with the sound of their own moaning, or the other kind, the vulnerable weepers who spoke in broken voices of broken marriages. Horror stories of violent husbands, guns, battered children, destroyed property— somehow these tales, although impossibly heartrending, didn't address the reason for her attendance, which was to gain an insight into Charlie's problem and how to live with it. She heard a catalog of problems, and never what she wanted—namely, solutions.

For a time she'd entertained the notion that she was herself to blame in some way, but she'd rejected that. Why should she feel guilty? She hadn't contributed to Charlie's condition. She loved him. *She* hadn't suffocated him or defused his ambitions or ruined his self-esteem.

There was an escape artist inside him, a man whose only exit from the locked box of himself was alcohol. Karen knew that much. But what was that box and why was it locked? He suffered periods of homesickness and a melancholy that might have been peculiarly Celtic for all she knew, but how could these be reasons enough for his sickness? He sometimes referred to himself as an exile, as if that might explain everything—but *sweet Christ* what was stopping him from going home to the country he professed so dearly to love, if that was all it might take to stop him from destroying himself? Under scrutiny each possible answer turned into a shallow excuse. Subsequently she'd given up trying to understand why Charlie drank; he did so, and that was as much a fact in her world as gravity. He'd drunk himself out of promotions that might have come his way, then later blamed his boozing on his lack of progress. He reversed the polarities of the world, like every drunk. He confused cause and effect.

"Do you know how much is in our savings account?" she asked.

He wasn't sure.

She said, "Eight thousand dollars and some change."

"Half of which is yours."

"I'm employed, remember. I don't need the money. Why don't you do yourself a good turn, Charlie? Why don't you use some of the cash wisely and turn yourself over to another clinic for a few weeks?"

This generosity touched Galloway, although the notion of a clinic had all the appeal of a funeral on Christmas Day. "I'll think about it," he said.

"What is there to *think* about, Charlie? Do you imagine you can lick the problem alone?"

"Problem," he mumbled, as if this word was new to him. Whenever she referred to his "problem" he became defensive, which was the sign for her to make some sharp reference to his denial. She spoke of denial as if it were a real place, an overgrown garden where he lived his life and was happy to hide and play amid dense shrubbery and unshorn trees, a naked, pagan child worshiping his liquid god. He was fucking sick and tired of hearing about Bloody Denial. *I drink,* he thought. *And I drink more than I should, and I admit it. But I can stop if I want to, without help, without clinics and quacks, without divine intervention. I can stop.*

"*Problem,* Charlie," she said. "What other name would you give it?"

She caught herself again and pulled back. For one thing, she couldn't shake herself free from the horror of Ella Nazarena's death, and so she didn't have the energy for any kind of direct confrontation with Charlie on the subject of his drinking; these scenes were always repetitive in any case. For another, she had to remind herself that she no longer lived here, she'd moved out. That was the hard part. She missed him. She missed him on levels of which she'd never before been truly aware, as if she were descending the steps of her self. She wasn't sorry to skip the crap—the broken engagements, the three-day binges when he'd vanish without a word, the slurred midnight phone calls from some downtown bar where there always seemed to be shrill girls laughing in the background, the displays of public humiliation, the jokes he repeated in drunken amnesia.

No. What she regretted was the absence of his tenderness, because at times he could be the most considerate of men, an unselfish lover. She craved the hours of his sobriety when they'd lie in each other's arms and speak so softly of inconsequential matters in the secret language of lovers that they could hear their own heartbeats. The sweet privacy of their life together, the moments of wonder and intimacy, these she adored—and then, for no reason she could fathom, Charlie would introduce the destructive intruder into their home, his treacherously cheerful old friend alcohol, and everything would change, darken, and finally disintegrate.

After a while you can't go on. You can take only so much. Anything else is masochism. You trade the pain of life with Charlie for the ache of loneliness and you hope the exchange is favorable. All at once she wanted to go to him and hold his face between her hands and look into his eyes for some small sign that he might be serious this time about sobriety. She didn't want to take the risk; she'd see the same old eagerness, once upon a time so convincing, and in the end always disappointing. And she didn't want to be persuaded by the rhetoric of old expressions, decayed promises.

She stood up, smoothed her short skirt down. "I'm going now, Charlie. I'm tired."

"Why don't you stay here?" he asked.

"I wish you hadn't asked that."

"There's a comfortable bed upstairs."

"I remember the bed, Charlie. I know it's comfortable. But I'm in no mood to be pressured. Ella Nazarena was murdered today and that makes me sick to my heart. I'm on a very short fuse right now."

"I get lonely," he said.

"You're not the only one."

"We could get lonely together."

"Give it up," she said. She went toward the door and he tracked her.

"I want to save our marriage," he said. "Or is it too late for that?" He experienced a touch of fear, wondering if he really wanted a straight answer to his question.

"You want a hint, Charlie? If you'd like to save this marriage, start by saving yourself." She kissed his cheek, then turned away.

The screen door swung open and shut, clicking back and forth a couple of times in its frame. Karen walked toward the Mercedes. Charlie Galloway, his face pressed upon the fine mesh of the screen where several winged insects had become trapped, watched her get into the car, which she did with the rare grace of a woman who knew how to wear a miniskirt. He heard the engine, saw the headlights burn among the avocado leaves where a surprised, electric-eyed raccoon scampered up the trunk. Beyond, the flying moon speeded through the sky.

Start by saving yourself, he thought. Wasn't he already trying? Hadn't he already pledged himself to that end?

He turned off all the lights and lay on the living room sofa, the fabric of which had trapped something of Karen's scent. He fell asleep shortly after the upstairs clock struck two-thirty. He dreamed of Ella Nazarena and dogs.

Carolyn Laforge bathed in her Washington hotel suite, then wrapped herself in a beige terry robe with the hotel's monogram. She walked into the bedroom, leaving wet footprints behind her in the thick carpet. She undid the robe and let it fall away from her body.

Byron Truskett never failed to be overwhelmed by her beauty. A bewitching process had taken place, a spell cast, his heart sawn in half. But it was a risky business this wizardry, because there was always the chance of discovery. And in the cold light of day, in the frost of law offices and divorce courts, of scandal and remorse, none of the sorcery would mean a goddam thing. For now, though, you laid back and enjoyed the spectacle because it plain perplexed you and took your breath away.

"You make the bedsheet look like a tent," she said. She sat

on the edge of the bed and laid her fingertips on what was figuratively the tent pole.

Truskett reached for her wrist. Desire was not the word. Lust was inadequate. He was rock hard. He knew she'd only have to whisper *Fuck me, Byron* in his ear and he'd come, he'd lose it even before he was inside her. It had happened last time and they'd laughed about it. The premature ejaculation was something unexpected, a sign of her magic that she could transport him all the way back to the embarrassment of youth. He told her once about the power she had over him, ascribing it to witchcraft. The idea she could arouse this man without even trying pleased her immensely.

"I like being a witch," she'd said at the time.

She slid her hand under the sheet and held him. With the tips of her fingers she delineated the blood-swollen veins of his cock. She watched how he tilted his head back and the way his lips parted. He was in a place beyond speech. His eyes were open but they weren't seeing anything. They seemed to be tuned to an inner vista which no one else could look upon. She drew the sheet back. He was enormous.

"Don't move," she said. "Just be very still."

Byron Truskett, stripped of his political power, was obedient.

She worked her hips slowly. She slid him into her. She licked his neck from throat to chin. She stroked the firm flesh of his buttocks, then her hand wandered around the curve, reaching under his scrotum, the pleasure spot, the crux of his sensitivity— and there, with her flautist's fingers, she played her devastating tune on him. He came with such noise she had to clap her palm over his open mouth and he shuddered so violently she thought he'd fall to pieces. She felt his semen flood warmly inside her, a sweet sensation but no more than that, nothing that made her feel as if she'd been touched where she lived. She couldn't love this man the way she loved William; there had never been any question of that.

Truskett was quiet for a very long time. According to the rules by which Washington governed the country, fucking was just another form of negotiation, another political instrument, something that was infinitely more pleasurable than the chore of trying to pass new legislation. And fucking had the advantage of never getting bogged down in committee. Truskett knew all this. He was a realist who understood how the game was played.

But as he placed his arm across her body he thought how easy it would be to toss everything aside in one act of romantic foolishness and fall in love—God, how he could tumble—with Carolyn Laforge. He examined her golden hair upon the pillow, noticing how each filament consisted of a variety of colors which depended on your angle of perception and the reflection of the bedside lamp. He took a strand and laced it between his fingers. He studied the marvel of her jaw, the fine bone that created a frame for the fabulous mouth. He could watch that mouth all the livelong day.

"Are you well fucked, Senator?"

"Well and truly."

"When does your wife expect you?"

Another of her baffling tricks was the way she could make Miriam vanish entirely from the cabinet of his conscience. He looked at his wristwatch. It was almost three-thirty A.M.

"Soon," he said.

"You come and you go."

"I don't want to leave."

"Then stay."

Truskett pressed his lips to her bare shoulder. "I adore you."

"You have a wife, Senator. A dear friend of mine."

"And you a husband."

"True." She turned her face toward Truskett. "And I'm ambitious for him. Unfortunately, he isn't always his own best advocate. Sometimes he needs me to speak on his behalf."

"Speak? Is that what you do?"

"Among other things."

This was no longer a bedroom. This was the bargaining table now, the bottom line. Truskett said, "I can't give guarantees. It's not that kind of situation. You know that."

"I don't remember ever mentioning *guarantees*, Byron. I'm not that naive. We're talking about your support. Your whole-hearted, unequivocal support. I want to know you'll go all the way for him. I want that much. I need to know you'll shed some blood for him if you have to. He deserves this position. He's worked damn hard for this country. Nobody else has anything like his experience. His loyalty is beyond question."

"His loyalty's not at issue," Truskett said. "I'll do anything in my power, but I can only take him so far. I can't walk that last mile with him, Carolyn. He has to come through a Senate scrutiny smelling like a newborn baby. He has to be so pure you'd want him to hear your confession. If there's a trace, a *smidgen*, of lint in his navel, he's lost."

Carolyn sat upright, pushing her hair away from the sides of her face. "William has nothing to hide, Byron. Absolutely nothing."

"I'm glad to hear it," Truskett said.

"His life has been exemplary."

Truskett looked up at the ceiling and thought, *An exemplary life.* Who had ever known that fabled creature, ridden that winged horse? An exemplary life was what saints were supposed to lead, and Laforge could not have traveled this far unscathed. A good man, definitely, and politically sound as far as Truskett was concerned—otherwise he would never have considered Laforge as a viable candidate to place before the President as a future director of the CIA. But Truskett knew that sainthood was given only to a few, and nobody in his experience had ever been canonized for government service. It was lamentable but realistic to say that running the United States did not call for unselfish angels, boy scouts, do-gooders, bleeding hearts. The men who operated the vast conglomerate known as America had more in common with Roto-Rooter technicians than cherubs of virtue. They sucked drains clear of filth and unclogged pipes of coagulated scum so that the murky waters of government could keep flowing. *Washington* and *exemplary life* were opposites and could not coexist.

Truskett knew there had to be some flaws in Billy Laforge's past. What he dearly hoped was that they were small and manageable, unlikely to cause embarrassment. If they were, he was sure he could swing the nomination Billy's way. But Truskett also realized that something more important than Billy Laforge's nomination was involved—namely, his own reputation. He couldn't champion Laforge's candidacy in the White House if there was the slightest chance of Billy's shit flying into the blades of the public fan. The President of the United States, a man who was arrogantly unapproachable at times, treated unpleasant truths as gate crashers at his private party, unticketed louts in need of a flogging.

Carolyn stretched her arms. "Do we go another round, Senator?"

Truskett was filled with well-being.

"Are you hard or do I have to work on you?" she asked.

"I'm getting there," Truskett remarked.

She rolled on her stomach. Fine golden hair, barely noticeable, grew the length of her spine. Truskett kissed her neck, back, buttocks, thinking how sweet she tasted.

"Take me from behind," she said.

There is bliss and there is bliss, the senator thought. *But this, dear crucified Christ, this is* bliss.

7

At ten-thirty A.M. Charlie Galloway, stiff from having slept on the sofa, telephoned Karen at her office.

"Did you remember the name of Ella's boyfriend?" he asked.

"It's Joaquin," she said. She pronounced it Hwa-keen. She'd taken Spanish in her freshman year at UCLA, where she'd continually changed her major, from philosophy to sociology to business administration, in the quest, as fashionable then as now, for self-definition. "I don't know where he has his shop, though."

Galloway fumbled around, found a pencil and a sheet of paper. "Can you spell Hwa-keen for me?"

"As in San Joaquin Valley. I don't see what difference it makes to you anyway. You can't get involved."

Charlie Galloway admitted as much, but only in a half-hearted manner. He thought of the dogs. The small house in the wretched street. The terrible pattern of dried blood on a sheet. He was already involved, with or without official sanction. How could he not be? Ella Nazarena was dead. A *friend* was dead. Was he supposed to stand back and shake his head sadly, resigning himself to this dreadful fact? Was he expected to do *nothing?*

Karen surely knew better, but she changed the subject in a rather heavy-handed way, as if she didn't want to hear a single word about misadventures and potential disasters in Charlie Galloway's future.

She said, "In the off chance you're interested, I found the name of a good treatment center. It's run by somebody called Oakleigh, an ex-priest who used to be a substance abuser. I'll give you the phone number."

Substance abuser. A whole new vocabulary had been invented by those whose lucrative industry it was to cure people of their "dysfunctions." You couldn't be a doper or a drunk anymore. No, that was too simple. You were a substance abuser, you were chemically dependent; and, God help you, if you drank and drugged together you were said to be "cross-addicted."

Dutifully he wrote down the number, wondering how Karen had found it. He imagined her asking around among her colleagues for a place where her estranged husband might get his scattered act together.

"Stay out of trouble, Charlie."

"I plan on it."

"And call Oakleigh. Please. They say he's terrific."

"I'll think it over." He told her he loved her, then hung up.

A former priest, he thought. Excommunicated for cocaine in the sacristy? A shot of Wild Turkey in the old communion wine? Crack concealed in the vestments?

Charlie made instant coffee and drank it standing by the sink. He parted the slatted blind with a finger, then recoiled at once from the fiery sun that already had the city locked in its bright shackle. It was going to be another grinding doomsday, impossible to move and breathe without effort. California was frying again.

He finished his coffee, went upstairs, found clean lightweight pants and a T-shirt on the back of which a large gibbon glowered. Karen had bought the shirt from a vendor outside the San Diego Zoo a year ago and had given it to Charlie without comment. He'd never worn it until now. The message, the monkey on his back, hadn't endeared him to the garment. Today he didn't care. Today, sunny and infernal, was his new beginning, his genesis. Today he'd stay sober.

Somehow.

Downstairs, he checked the yellow pages under Barbers. Freddie Joaquin was listed as the proprietor of a place called Kwik-Kuts, "established 1976," which in Californian terms made it practically an historic enterprise. Kwik-Kuts had a tiny box to itself in the middle of the page. The location was given as Inglewood, a neighborhood east of the San Diego Freeway. Galloway scribbled the address on the same piece of paper as he'd written Joaquin's name.

He studied the information a moment, as if simple perusal might yield a practical insight. His feelings for Ella Nazarena notwithstanding, was he just trying to find busy work for himself, on the principle that if you were occupied the devil couldn't get you? But if that was all, why didn't he do something easy, like prune the avocado tree or water the long-dead flowers behind the house?

Better still, why didn't he turn himself over to this Oakleigh character and ask to be exorcised? A couple of sober weeks with the former priest might amass him sufficient points to engineer Karen's return, and just for a moment he was tempted to dial the man's number. He'd only have to behave himself for a short period of time under Oakleigh's watchful eye and it would be Homecoming Day and brass bands up here in the hills and all would be well, all heavenly, the house would burn with old love rekindled.

But for how long, Charlie? How long before The Demented Other moved in and Karen out again? No, running off to some ex-priest wasn't Galloway's answer any more than clipping leaves from a dry tree. He was going to have to reach more deeply inside himself to find a place of integrity and character, a reservoir that hadn't evaporated altogether, if such a core still existed.

Yesterday, when he'd drunkenly come up with the idea of a salvage operation to raise himself out of the rut of his being, he'd fully expected it to pass into oblivion with sobriety. All his inebriated notions tended to scurry away, frightened mice in the brassy light of day. But this one hadn't faded at all; even stranger, it had no hollow, counterfeit ring to it. Nor was he deriding himself as he usually did when the ruin of some grandiose scheme, concocted in his cups, rumbled through the accusatory

Greek chorus of a hangover. No matter how hard he listened he couldn't hear the familiar chiding of self-mockery. *You, Charlie? Sober? Har, hardy har, pull the other one.* He was possessed by an unexpected sense of self, as if he'd been delineated by a thick dark edge, like a character in a drawing. He sensed possibilities, fresh directions, huge difficulties.

It was as if the murder of Ella Nazarena were a window through which he could see another version of himself. That younger Charlie, unaffected by booze, the fresh-faced Glasgow policeman who'd come to the United States fifteen years ago and risen to the rank of lieutenant in the LAPD, that optimistic lad who'd perceived the world as a black and white place, justice here, injustice over there, two separate bundles, clean-cut and uncluttered because truth was without ambiguities.

He'd made an impression in the LAPD, distinguishing himself in a newsworthy homicide case, one of those gruesome multiple killings seemingly patented by the state of California. A whole family, husband and wife, grannie and three kids, had been tortured and bludgeoned in a fine house on Mulholland Drive, and Charlie, assisted by doggedness and the unshackled optimism of all young men in pursuit of an ideal, had unearthed the clues that led to the killer, who turned out to be—what else?—a Satanist of sorts, an acid-head with a demonic view of the inequities of the world, somebody who had read Aleister Crowley and Karl Marx and had gotten them mixed up in what was left of his brain.

Charlie Galloway, Lone Ranger.

Later, working with the Narcotics Division, Charlie had rendered immeasurable service to the Federal Bureau of Investigation in two complicated cases involving corruption and cocaine, conspiracies of greed and blood that stretched from South America to Hollywood and points east, dragging in their zigzag paths a well-greased Californian judge, a dozen airline employees, several Mr. Bigs of the LA blow scene, dealers, couriers, and assorted flunkies. Tons of toot were confiscated, its street value estimated by the popular press at many tens of millions of dollars. Success! A promotion within the department! Newspaper stories! Handshakes with chill-fisted, chill-eyed Vanderwolf. A cryptic conversation with the mysterious, powerful Hugo Fletcher, the invisible man who was the assistant director of the FBI. Charlie couldn't remember the talk, only Fletcher's awesome quiet emission of authority, which erected a magical aura around the man. You just knew that Hugo Fletcher, who worried even Vanderwolf, understood the inner workings of the republic; he grasped the complexities of the machine, the engine room, which levers to pull. You wouldn't want to make Hugo your enemy.

Charlie had received a personal thank-you note from John J. Coleman, the titular director of the FBI in Washington. There was a whisper, generated by Vanderwolf, that Charlie might make a good Fed himself in the fullness of time, if he should so choose that direction. The bureau always needed good hard-working men. Something to keep in mind. Something to store.

He was going places, this Charles D. Galloway, formerly of Govan, Glasgow. He was in the land of opportunities where doors were being opened for him and he was stepping into other, brighter rooms, a promise enhanced when he met Karen at a colleague's wedding reception and his heart was enriched by the suddenness of captivity. Her Americanness, that marvelous New World self-assurance coupled with a delightful, airy naïveté, a stray gene left over from hippie times, enchanted him. After marriage, which increased his already unlimited sense of his American future, he fully expected the thermometer of his achievement to go on climbing.

But.

But somehow quicksilver became frozen in the cylinder.

He wasn't quite sure why. Perhaps he expected too much. Perhaps he'd risen too quickly and supposed the rest of his career would be a meteor. When it stalled and no further promotion came his way, he felt the gray shadow of disappointment fall across his life for the first time. Had he deceived himself all along, attributing some lucky breaks in a few important cases to a nonexistent talent for the vicissitudes of police work?

For a while he entertained the idea that his career had come to a dead stop because of his failure to play the game of department politics, his inability to understand how the unwritten rules worked, to hear the drums that signaled who was advancing and who falling and where the real power lay. Maybe his face didn't fit. Maybe he had the wrong friends and didn't drink with the truly influential department characters. But he'd never cultivated people for his own ends, nor was he sure how to begin even if he wanted to. Smarmy wasn't his line. If he had charm it came unforced. When he smiled it was because he felt like it. He couldn't turn these things on and off. Whatever failings he might have, he was no fake.

His job demanded that he spend time increasingly behind a desk. Stultified, he rarely hit the streets himself; instead, he sent a flow of eager young cops out in pursuit of criminals. Thousands of sheets of paper passed between his fingers. He became involved in departmental budget matters, fiscal concerns, dollars and cents. Burning the midnight oil, he turned into a kind of accountant, his soul dulled, his ambition blunted. His life became a paper nightmare. Where were the serial killers? The terrorist threats? Where was the bloody excitement? Why did his responsibilities keep him stuck to a desk? He yearned for the streets, the city, the shadows.

He retreated, at first slowly, then with unintended acceleration, into drink, which provided a consolation of sorts. It reduced boredom, wiped out growing disillusionment, stamped your visa for entry to the land of the living. It took the disenchanting edge off the gradual realization that perhaps you were going no farther than the place you'd reached. This was all there was going to be. His star was seemingly a spent force by his fortieth birthday. Somebody knocks the ladder out from under you so you dangle forever in the one spot and when you look around suddenly you realize you've got a reputation as a man who has become too fond of his lunchtime drinkies and is therefore unreliable.

This sorry perception of his stalemate inevitably led, over a few years, to a cynicism he wouldn't have thought possible before. He saw younger cops join the force and he thought, *Let them believe in justice.* He felt stale and jaded, bruised by a discontent which spread beyond the department to the republic itself. Gradually he began to see injustices wherever he looked. There were no blacks and whites in his world, no constants of truth, nothing cut and dried. What he once naively thought the fairest system yet devised turned out to be a monochromatic business administered by lawyers making deals and soliciting political favors, amoral men. In this galaxy, where illegitimacy reigned, politicians didn't have constituents, they had rich ''clients," on whose behalf they finagled deals and chipped away at the public kitty; here judges were bought and sold and attorneys hacked the carcass of justice from breastbone to blindfold, and wealthy criminals bought freedom and walked the streets because the system had been "manipulated" by advocates and magistrates.

America, which he'd once considered so healthy, a land of good cheer and unbridled possibility, came to seem jaundiced. All the smiles were forced. All the laughter was canned. White paint peeled on picket fences, green meadows glowed at night with the fluorescence of radioactive waste, people didn't have enough to eat in the hollers of Kentucky nor in the middle of Manhattan. The cities collapsed in callous ineptitude, farms fell to ruin, streets clogged with the homeless, the deranged, the deprived, the incurably sick. Bounteous America: It was a cracked bell jar in which Charlie Galloway, God help him, had become trapped.

Now he stepped out of the house and the sun burned on his head as if a furnace door had been left open. In the ravines, pollution formed a fine rust-colored mist. It stung his eyes even before he reached his car and got inside. He turned the key in the ignition and switched on the air-conditioning unit before he'd traveled half a mile. He drove along a twisting road where no other traffic impeded his progress, then suddenly he was stuck in a main thoroughfare going down toward Sunset Boulevard. At a traffic signal, which had broken down, he was surrounded by Mercedes, Porsches, and a Bentley, all driven by impatient men on their way to power encounters with other impatient men.

Galloway drummed the steering wheel with his fingertips and wondered why, given his general condition, he stayed in these United States, why he hadn't gone back to his native land. The question was complex. Karen, of course, was a major part of it; this was her country and she didn't want to leave it. And he had no desire to be six thousand miles away from her, no matter the condition of their marriage.

But there was more. Although he criticized Madam America's blowsy makeup and her hypocrisies and how she tolerated injustices with barely a flutter of her fake eyelashes, there was some element of comfort in her soft, cushion-breasted embrace just the same. After all, he was a naturalized citizen, and she'd welcomed him inside her—how could he be so churlish as to feel ingratitude? But she puzzled him. She tantalized him. The more she teased, the harder he tried to understand her. The harder she was to understand, the more difficult it became to love her.

Who was she really? Under her ambivalent trappings was there a heart of gold? Was she bag lady and dowager and whore simultaneously? She was secretive, yet he knew she waited to be discovered. She was always just around the next corner, a baffling shadow seen from the corner of his eye, a trace of laughter he heard echoing. He became convinced that some important element eluded him.

Perhaps it was all so simple he had difficulty seeing it. Perhaps he no more belonged in America than he did in the LAPD. He was no organization man. Too much disorder had penetrated his life. To be an American, to be a member of the LAPD, maybe you needed something he didn't have—a sense, however loosely arranged, of being comfortably absorbed into the body that was the United States and its assorted institutions. You needed an extra gear in your motor, a tear duct attuned to the "Star-Spangled Banner," a history that involved Roller Derbies, surfboards, and *Leave It to Beaver*, all of which were beyond his experience.

Once, during an evening of drinking when he'd mentioned this feeling to Karen, she had stared at him for a long time without speaking.

Finally she'd said, "You're not missing anything, honey."

"That's easy for you to say. You've spent your entire life here. You know what's going on."

"But there's nothing *going on*, Charlie. I think you're imagining things. You come to a new country and for years you feel out of tune. But it doesn't mean there's some great big secret everybody's keeping from you. What you think you're missing just doesn't exist."

"It's like this: They give you a green card but they don't give you a key."

"A key to what, Charlie? To what?"

"I don't know. That's the mystery."

She had held him then, he remembered that. She'd put her arms around him and rocked him slowly against her, loving and comforting him because she'd seen some tiny drunken distress in his eyes. He'd never felt that close to her before. He recalled the tenderness clearly. He remembered how her hair smelled and the way one of her earrings, an onyx half moon, pressed into the flesh of his cheek.

"Do you get this same feeling in your own country?" she'd asked.

"Scotland's easier to read. She's like some crotchety old spinster who remembers her manners every now and again and offers you a cup of tea and a sliver of shortbread. She's not hiding anything. When she speaks, it's always in plain language. And her makeup's simple. A wee touch of rouge, light lipstick, that's it. Sensible clothes too."

"Tweeds."

"Tweeds and wellies."

"So why did you ever abandon this old dear in the first place?"

"It was the land of no opportunity. Too small for me. Too obsessed with its own history. Too many people who were big fish in a very small pond. I wanted something else."

Something else. I never found it. Why not? Because it lacked definition? Because I didn't know where to look?

Traffic was moving again. He took a turn off the main drag and down through rich side streets. Signs reported that security was in place. Electronic eyes, lasers, arc lights, booby traps. Hollywood under siege.

Galloway took the freeway to Inglewood. He missed the radio. The silence inside the Toyota emphasized the sense of isolation, the vague unease, he always felt on the deranged freeway systems of Los Angeles, those mental asylums of motion.

Freddie Joaquin's barbershop was situated in a small plaza of the kind that proliferated throughout the city. A bakery, a pizza place, a beauty shop, a diet control center, a locksmith, and Kwik-Kuts. An old-fashioned red and white pole hung outside Joaquin's establishment.

Galloway went inside. Two barbers in pale blue smocks smoked cigarettes. A radio played soft rock music, a kind of auditory syrup. The floor was littered with amputated locks and curls. There were no customers. One of the barbers, a Filipino with tinted glasses, stared at Galloway.

"Hay-cut, sir?" he asked.

Galloway shook his head. "I'm looking for Freddie Joaquin."

The small man removed his glasses, wiped them on his sleeve, then replaced them very deliberately. The other barber, also Filipino, had a ragged goatee. He blew out cigarette smoke, which was sucked up and destroyed by the large blades of the ceiling fan.

"Freddie's not here," said the man in the glasses.

"Know where I can find him?"

The one with the wispy beard asked, "Who are you? What you want with him?"

From his hip pocket Galloway fished out his ID, which by some administrative oversight hadn't been taken away from him. The Filipino barbers were not impressed. They lit fresh cigarettes and stared at how stirred air pushed strands of hair around the floor in little vortices.

"This got something to do with Freddie's lady friend that was killed last night?" the one in glasses asked. The other barber tugged at his beard.

"That's right," Galloway said.

"He already talked to the cops first thing this morning. Then he says he's taking the rest of the day off."

"Where can I find him?"

"I'll tell you, as long as you don't tell Freddie where you heard this. You understand me?" He walked to the door, pointed a finger, said Galloway should make a right at the stoplight, drive four blocks east, make another right. There, halfway down the block, he'd find a place called Joolies. Joaquin would be inside.

"You see Freddie, just remember his grief, okay? You treat him good."

"With kid gloves," Galloway said.

He walked to his car. The barber watched him from the doorway. It was one of those odd moments in which the intensity of heat seemed to have expanded space. The parking lot appeared larger, the Toyota farther away than he remembered, and there were no shadows, which heightened a general sense of unreality. When he got behind the wheel of his car he glanced back at

Kwik-Kuts, but the doorway was empty now. The facade of windows in the plaza might have had nothing of substance behind them, as if each little shop were no more than a prop broiling in the stark light.

When he found Joolies it turned out to be a bar with black windows and a sign advertising GIRLS GIRLS GIRLS MORNING TO NIGHT. The front door squealed as he pushed it open. He stepped inside the darkness, which was that of a cave. Accustomed to sunlight, he could see nothing. He had an impression of shadowy figures, and heard music from a jukebox, but it was minutes before he felt enough confidence to move without bumping into anything.

He went down a short flight of steps toward the bar. Emerging from the gloom, a young barman asked, "What can I do for you, friend?"

Galloway longed for ice-cold beer. The inside of his mouth was dry. The chorus in his mind chanted its usual rallying cry. *Beer beer beer! Charlie needs his beer! Give the bugger his suds!*

"Club soda," he said.

"Club soda, you got it." A small sparkling bottle was produced, uncapped, and poured into a glass already filled with ice cubes. You never saw a really good barman make his moves. He was like a magician who pulled everything together at once. A half moon of lime, conjured out of nowhere, floated on the bubbles.

Galloway laid a five-dollar bill on the counter. He looked around the large room. In one corner a stage, enclosed by a silver curtain, had been erected. The floor, which stretched away into deep shadows, had about two hundred tables, some of which were occupied. Your basic cozy pub, he thought. A place for intimate encounters. The music from the jukebox was suddenly loud and the shaft of air from the air conditioner like shaved ice.

The curtain parted. An oriental girl stood there in panties and garter belt and lacy bra beneath a pale yellow spotlight. She looked out at the customers with an expression which, with just a touch more conviction, might have passed as lethargy. She moved her hips, cupped her hands under her breasts, discarded her bra, slid her fingers inside her panties. The homogenized strip. Something seriously bland was taking place. The girl turned her back to the room and showed the cleft of her ass. Peekaboo! The curtain fell in place, the music stopped. Around the room there was some desultory clapping, which faded rapidly out.

Galloway turned to the barman. "I'm looking for Freddie Joaquin. I'm told he might be here." A strange place to be, he thought, if you're working on some grief. On the other hand, maybe it was fine if distraction was your goal. But a familiar Presbyterian ghost in him doubted the propriety of it. You didn't bring your fresh grief, if you had any, to a dump like this. You tended to it in a quiet place, in secrecy, behind drawn curtains.

The barman, a friendly Filipino, nodded across the room. "He's over there," he said. "That table by the fire exit."

Galloway pushed the change from his five-dollar bill toward the young man, then made his way across the floor. Freddie Joaquin sat alone.

"You mind if I join you?"

Joaquin looked up. "You a cop? I talked with cops this morning already."

Galloway sat down, sliding his ID toward Freddie Joaquin, who examined it without expression. "Like I said. I already talked with your colleagues."

Joaquin ran a hand across the surface of his slicked-down black hair. *Dapper* was the word that came into Galloway's mind. Freddie, probably in his middle fifties, was about five feet two inches tall and wore an immaculate black and white pinstriped suit, a white silk shirt, a charcoal-colored tie pierced by a pearl-headed pin. His feet were small, his black shoes as glossy as anything dipped in wet black wax. He had a broad nose, flat cheekbones, very white teeth, one of which was filled with a sliver of gold.

Galloway's first impression was that he couldn't quite imagine this man actively courting Ella Nazarena, who'd been a rather unassuming woman with no particular interest in clothes or makeup. There was a discordant note here, an incongruity. Maybe they had in common an interest he could only guess at. Ballroom dancing, listening to music, how could he know?

The curtain parted again. A big blond girl came out onstage. To scale her huge breasts for the sake of love, Galloway thought, would require ropes and grappling irons and a head for heights.

Her excess flesh shuddered in soft rolls when she moved to the music.

Freddie Joaquin said, "Her name's Brenda. Takes a man's mind off things."

"I'm glad your mind's got somewhere to go," said Galloway, unsettled by Joaquin's concentration on the stripper. Didn't he feel anything about the death of Mrs. Nazarena? Or was he shell-shocked? "Let's talk about Ella, Freddie."

"Don't be fooled by my presence in this joint," Joaquin said, as if he intuited Galloway's misgivings. "I feel grief for Ella right in here," and he thumped his breastbone with his fist even as he continued to observe the stage. "Everything I know I told the cops already."

"I'm anxious for a replay. Tell me."

"She was a saint. She never hurt nobody. Who'd kill a woman like that?"

"It appears robbery wasn't the motive," Galloway said. "So we can rule out a thief."

Joaquin made a gesture with his hand that seemed to suggest he and Galloway, being men of the world, could understand each other. "To guys like you and me, she was a poor woman. To a junkie, hey, maybe a different story. He looks at a TV and he sees his next fix. Know what I mean? There's a struggle. He shoots her. He panics, then splits. Who knows?"

Galloway sipped his club soda. His hand gripped the glass a little too tightly.

Joaquin continued. "I told her a hundred times. Move to a better neighborhood. With what? she asks. I'll pay, that's what I tell her. She was *palalo . . .* proud. She wouldn't take my money. I proposed marriage. She says she needs time to think."

He reached for his drink, mango juice and rum. He glanced over the edge of his glass at Galloway. His dark brown eyes were suddenly wet. *Why am I not touched?* Galloway wondered. *Why do I feel I'm being sold some fake grief?* He knew what was disjointed here—this unenticing place and Joaquin's seedy enthusiasm for Brenda, who had already stripped down to her bald pudendum, which suggested a small endangered creature cruelly exposed.

"Where were you last night?" Galloway asked.

"I stayed home. I watched TV. *Wheel of Fortune. Holly-wood Squares.* I told all this to Lieutenant Duffy."

"You were alone all night?"

"Sure, alone."

"You didn't see Ella yesterday?"

"I called her about seven. She said she was too tired to do anything, didn't want to go out. *Ikáw ang bahalà,* I told her. It's up to you. So I didn't see her."

Galloway said, "She was anxious to talk to me, but I got to her house too late. Do you have any idea what she had to tell me?"

Freddie Joaquin shook his sleek head. "No idea."

"Did she ever mention my name to you?"

"I don't believe so."

The music stopped, the curtain fell. Brenda, pink and glistening, vanished. Before she did she blew a pouting kiss toward Joaquin, who pretended it was meant for someone else. He took a white silk handkerchief from his pants pocket and held it against his face. He blew his nose, a tromboning sound.

"Good friend of yours?" Galloway asked.

"We've, hey, you know, met."

"I could see where she'd help ease your grief, Freddie." Galloway remembered the dogs suddenly. The memory was red and harsh. He had a sick sensation in his stomach. He looked at Joaquin and knew for certain that Freddie had been banging the blond stripper on a regular basis, perhaps even as he pursued his role as Ella Nazarena's "beau."

A monogram adorned the corner of Joaquin's handkerchief. *FJ.* The expensive hand-stitched initials, the man's vanity, the relationship with the stripper—what had Ella seen in him? What had *he* seen in *her?* Galloway couldn't get it fixed in his mind.

"Maybe Ella mentioned Karen, my wife?"

Freddie Joaquin shrugged. "Sometimes she talked, but I didn't listen too close. You know how women are. You sit, you nod your head, yeah yeah. Maybe she mentioned your name. Maybe your wife's. Look. I don't remember. I'm sorry."

Galloway felt an odd disembodied dislike toward Freddie Joaquin; it had the texture of a cold shadow falling upon the back of his neck.

On the stage a drunken overweight man in white T-shirt and droopy blue jeans was hamming a striptease, swiveling his hips as if he were burdened by a hula hoop of solid lead. His cronies, gathered around a nearby table, hooted and clapped and whistled. The drunk, whose behavior reminded Charlie Galloway of certain embarrassing exhibitions of his own, took off his shirt and tossed it in the air.

Joaquin looked at his watch. "I have an appointment," he said. "You have to excuse me."

Galloway put his hand on the man's arm. "Did she have any enemies?"

"Enemies? Ella?" Joaquin smiled. "I told you. She was a saint."

"Somebody didn't think so. Somebody fired a gun into her skull."

"Yeah. Well."

Freddie Joaquin stood up, but Galloway still clutched his wrist. "Don't hold anything back from me, Freddie. If there's something you know, tell me now. Don't waste my time."

"If I knew something, you think I'd keep it to myself? I hear anything, cross my heart, you'll be the first to know. Okay? I give my word."

Freddie Joaquin walked away from the table. *I give my word.* Galloway had the feeling that Freddie's word wasn't something you could take to the bank. It had no collateral. Despite the pinstriped suit, the silk handkerchief, the pearl tie pin, Freddie was sleazy. Perhaps Ella Nazarena never saw this side to him. Maybe he was all flowers and charm to her, all smiles and little gold flashes. Mr. Fidelity, the perfect suitor.

Galloway pushed back his chair and stood up. He was beset by a feeling of uselessness. What could Freddie Joaquin tell him? What difference did it make if the man was a scumbag? How much simpler it would be to go to the bar and drink the rest of the day away and forget the death of Ella Nazarena and all your former resolve to change, which was too demanding. If you started drinking now, you wouldn't be aware of the passage of time because the black windows concealed the outside world. You'd be encapsulated in whatever version of reality you chose. Since you didn't like being the flaw known as Charlie Galloway, you could be anybody else you wanted, pretender to the ancient throne of Scotland, a laird slumming, anybody in the whole damn world.

He reached the bar, paused. Onstage the male stripper stepped out of his jeans, showing a pair of fat white thighs and floppy boxer shorts with a penguin design. His feet became entangled in the legs of his jeans and he fell over. Thudddd. Galloway considered this humiliating display a warning. He pushed the front door open.

Outside, he watched Freddie Joaquin's car, a big gun-metal gray Oldsmobile, back out of the parking lot just a little too quickly. The bitter smell of rubber hung in the air as Charlie Galloway moved toward his Toyota.

Where was Freddie going in such a godawful hurry?

The voice on the telephone had directed Armando Teng to an old-fashioned diner on Venice Boulevard. Inside he ordered coffee and sat down at a table, unfolding yesterday's copy of the *Manila Bulletin,* as he'd been instructed to do. Raising his face, feeling still the weight of a fatigue many hours of sleep hadn't altogether lifted, he looked across the chromium-plated room.

The United States of America, he thought. The country of his father's birth. He had dreamed of this country in an embittered way for almost as long as he could remember. All through his childhood in Benguet Province his mother had talked about the American sailor who'd fathered him and then vanished without a trace. Teng's father, of whom no photograph existed, had apparently been tall and blue-eyed. Very handsome, his mother had said more than once. *Magandáng laláki. You look like him sometimes.* When she spoke of him her eyes always filled with tears, a tendency the young Teng had found irritating.

Teng's mother, Teresita, had met the American sailor in Olongapo City, where she worked as a waitress in a restaurant. She wasn't a whore. She was a naive seventeen-year-old from La Trinidad, a pretty girl who'd gone to Olongapo to find work. She fell in love and fantasized marriage, a life in far-off America, magic kingdom, Mickey Mouse. A house with a TV, a refrigerator, even a car in the driveway. All she knew was what she'd seen in magazine photographs or movies. She adored her sailor's fine blond hair, his white skin and blue eyes. When she lay with him she thought she could hear an angel sing.

It never occurred to her to question the sailor's feelings. When they coupled passionately in the hotel room he rented for the purpose, she believed the intimacy was one of pure love, which inevitably led—as she well knew in her romantic young heart—to marriage. When she told her sailor she was pregnant, he didn't seem distressed. He said he'd marry her. He even seemed happy at the prospect. They went to the hotel on Barretto Street and made love and later he kissed her good-bye. She never saw him again, never heard from him. He left her with an emptiness she'd never been able to fill.

When she was five months pregnant she'd written a letter to the base commander at Subic Bay, asking the whereabouts of the father. She received no answer. Subsequent letters were ignored. After Armando was born, Teresita took more direct action. With the child in her arms she went to Subic, where she was passed from one indifferent officer to another, a demeaning process during which her courage, fragile at best in circumstances that overawed her, was lost entirely. She was a tiny thing and the base vast and unfriendly. Weeping, she was led in the end to a man who wore the dog collar of a chaplain.

The chaplain asked for information about the father, even if he knew there was no real point to it. The child's father, protected by the U.S. Navy whose policy was to transfer men who'd impregnated local girls but didn't want to be daddies, would have been posted thousands of miles away. He went through the motions anyhow. Name? Place of birth in the United States? Teresita didn't know the answer to the second question. The first, though, was easy.

Her sailor was called Walter Cronkite. The chaplain looked away.

Armando Teng was nine when he first realized, from reading a U.S. newspaper, that his father had used a ridiculous *nom d'amour.* The knowledge outraged him and brought more unhappiness into a childhood already tainted by his blue-eyed appearance, which set him apart from his companions and made close friendships difficult. He was relentlessly teased and so turned, as many goaded children do, inward, detached from those around

him. A skein of loneliness lay across his whole youth. He remembered lying awake in the dark and quietly castigating his mother
for her indiscretion, her idiot trust in the sailor, her unshakable
belief that he'd one day return. Fool! Didn't Teresita know he
was never coming back? She kept the faith the way one keeps a
candle burning in a window for a dead love.

Sometimes he imagined his father sharing a mean-spirited
joke with his shipmates about the gullible young Filipina who
believed he was *really* called Walter Cronkite. *Simpleminded
gook cunt.* Would he say something like that? Would they all
laugh? Yes.

For years Teng hated his unknown father with a loathing so
deep and frightening it seemed to stand darkly apart from himself. With the same intensity he also despised the country that
had sent the blue-eyed sailor to the Philippines in the first
place. What were Americans doing on Filipino soil? Why did
they behave with such arrogance, as if the country belonged to
them? Why did they impose themselves so? He could even remember in his early childhood listening to records of American
Christmas carols in the shops of Baguio. *Chestnuts roasting on
an open fire, Jack Frost nipping at your nose . . .* what did this
rubbish mean to any Filipino? What was Jack Frost? What were
reindeers in the snow? Teng couldn't recall ever having seen a
chestnut. American popular culture was duplicated in ham-
burger joints, beauty pageants, fashion, music, cinema. American icons—Presley, Rambo, even George Washington—were accepted into the fabric of a Filipino way of life becoming
threadbare.

The United States had controlled the Philippines for most of
the twentieth century, replacing the Spanish with a different
brand of colonialism, insidious, bloated with the rhetoric of progress. Hundreds of teachers arrived in the early years of the century from America, educational missionaries forced into miserably humid outposts where they underwent discomfort and
dysentery and exotic diseases so that they might hastily supplant
the Spanish language with English, and unselfishly "Christianize" their little brown brothers—a guilty reaction, Teng thought,
to the disastrous war of Filipino independence, during which
hundreds of thousands of Filipinos were killed by fine American

boys from Kentucky and Tennessee and Ohio. (By the time the war was over in 1902, only eight hundred and eighty-three Americans had died. Teng always remembered this. *883.* The number came in his mind to represent American supremacy over the Philippines. It assumed a significance almost supernatural.)

Civilize, Christianize, Americanize. The words were interchangeable. The sentiment was always the same: America was the selfless bringer of gifts, the greatest of which was the Democratic Way of Life—a system that culminated in the person of Ferdinand Marcos.

In his teens Teng flirted with various nationalist movements, many of which fell apart during the years of martial law imposed by this same Marcos, lover of democracy, keeper of the keys to freedom, buddy to one U.S. president after another. The nationalist groups splintered in a confusion of aspirations and acronyms; in the end all that linked them was the fact they detested America.

When he was eighteen something happened to make Teng realize he'd squandered too much of his life in the wastelands of hatred. He fell quite unexpectedly in love. Love transformed him. It burned the chill out of his heart. He came to live in a state of awe and bewilderment, concussed by his own feelings. Love seemed to him a glorious, joyful sickness.

He understood for the first time what his mother must have felt for her American sailor, and he absolved her for his paternity; he realized that where love led you had no choice but to follow. Consuming, fiery, sharp-edged, terrible, love involved a series of wondrous paradoxes—the resolution of which made absolutely no damned difference to the sensation. A leaf in a flood, swept carelessly away. You were reduced to that. Teng would not have thought it possible, the trembling pleasure, the obsession, the terror of heartbreak.

The girl was called Marissa Orosa, a history student at the state university in La Trinidad, where Teng had enrolled to study economics. Small, with long dark hair she wore almost to her waist, she mesmerized him. She was beautiful. (How many lonely, frustrating nights did he spend trying to write poems to that beauty, for which he never had quite the words? He suffered the linguistic grief of all who love with passion and are struck dumb. Love, he understood, has no language, neither in Tagalog nor English nor any other tongue.)

Marissa was both beautiful and political, the magnetic center of a group of students working for an independent Philippines—a democracy, yes, but one that did not rely for its existence on the presence of the United States. Communism was no answer for her. She despised the New People's Army; she was too independent, too high-spirited to accept the imposition of drab Maoism, which had been imported intact from China. As for Marcos, she held him in such low esteem she could hardly mention his name, and Imelda—well, Imelda was a joke, a bad joke, somebody Marissa impersonated, with startling precision, at parties. Teng had never before met a woman with her shrewd intelligence, her unexpected sense of fun.

She regarded Teng's adoration at first with curiosity, keeping him at a distance as if she were unwilling to make an emotional commitment. She had a degree to get. She was busy with politics. What time did she have for love? But his persistence charmed her, and the nervous way he behaved around her was touching. He had all the persuasive, sweet-natured clumsiness of a young man in the crucible of first love. How could she keep saying no to him?

Teng sipped his coffee, closed his eyes. Marissa occupied the most raw area of his heart. It was a place he kept returning to, despite the pain. He wanted to remember her. He lovingly accumulated recollections of her, gathered up and stored each detail he could find—an expression, a motion of her head, the proud way she walked, the wind in her long hair the day they'd climbed the two hundred and twenty-five steps going up Mirador Hill to the Lourdes shrine in Baguio, how she'd lit a votive candle with her small hand cupped protectively around the flame—he preserved these memories, as if he truly believed that from a framework of bare bones he could reconstruct the woman.

His thoughts were interrupted by a man who sat down at his table. Teng opened his eyes.

"*Mabúhay,*" the man said.

"*Mabúhay.*" The greeting was the one Teng expected, but he felt tension tighten inside him. Was this man the one? What if something had already gone wrong and this man had been sent to trap him? *Mabúhay* was a common Tagalog greeting; it was the next part that really counted, the connection of flesh.

"Raymond Cruz?" The man smiled, holding out his hand for Teng to shake it.

Teng did so slowly, relieved to find the handshake correct, the position and pressure of thumb exactly right. It was as Baltazar had said. A sign of flesh, almost masonic.

"I'm Freddie Joaquin. Welcome to America."

Teng folded his copy of the *Bulletin.* The headline had to do with corruption in the Filipino government, everyday news.

Joaquin said, "Follow me."

They walked together out of the diner. Hot concrete burned through the thin soles of Teng's shoes.

"Is everything arranged?" he asked.

Joaquin smiled. "Sure. When Freddie Joaquin runs something, he really runs it. Smooth sailing, my friend."

Armando Teng experienced one of those slowed-down, jet-lagged moments when sunlight seemed to dim, creating the impression that Joaquin had dwindled an inch or so. Then it passed and he felt fine again and everything was the way it had been before.

"I booked you into a hotel. I'll take you there now."

"Another hotel?"

"In a hotel you have privacy. You can be anonymous. Where did you think you'd sleep?"

Joe Baltazar hadn't mentioned a second hotel. Teng had an uneasy sense of having no control over events; his destiny lay in the hands of Baltazar. He knew he couldn't do everything himself—but why did he so dislike being forced to depend, at least some of the time, on others?

Marissa. He'd depended on her. No, it was more than that, more than mere reliance. He'd lived for her. That was the best way to phrase it: *He'd lived for her love.* And now Marissa was gone and he felt as hollow as a gutted building. When she'd first died he thought a light had gone out inside him. Now he knew better. Far more than a simple light had been extinguished; all his wiring had short-circuited.

He shook his head, fighting dizziness. Everything was going to be fine. Nothing would go wrong. What he experienced now was simply the stress of an eight-thousand-mile journey through seven or eight time zones. He followed Freddie Joaquin inside a darkened parking garage across the street, where trapped heat and gasoline fumes and the scorched stench of overheated engines suggested one of the levels of hell.

8

Byron Truskett's chief aide, a solitary man named Larry Deets, had joined the senator's staff directly from his graduate studies at Yale Law School eight years ago. On Truskett's behalf he produced policy papers on intelligence so concise they were comprehensible to almost everybody on Capitol Hill. It was rumored that even the President understood them. An angular figure who Brylcreemed his hair, Deets wore dark three-piece suits and ties that were always the color of battleships. At the age of thirty-five he had dedicated his life to work, ignoring the promptings of heart and hormones.

Byron Truskett knew very little about Deets's personal life. He doubted if Larry had one. Last Christmas, puzzled by what seasonal token to give his aide, Truskett had turned the problem over to his executive secretary, Madge McFarlane. For reasons best known to herself she'd presented Larry with a book of coupons good for a dozen lessons at an Arthur Murray School of Dancing. Because he had no desire to look ungrateful, Deets attended for five utterly miserable weeks and then dropped the course. His teacher was a bossy little senorita from Puerto Rico who made him feel too clumsy for the intricacies of rumbas and mambos, but his want of elegance—he had large feet and knuckles like small pink doorknobs—wasn't something over which he grieved. Dancing was frivolous, and Larry Deets much preferred the serious turns of his mind to the frolicsome turns of his feet.

He had an important job to do, which was to help Byron Truskett build the power base that would secure him the White House at his first attempt. During his initial job interview with Truskett years before, Deets had even then smelled the ambition on the senator as surely as the musk of a predator. If Truskett tended to joke about his presidential yearnings, he did so in a transparently halfhearted way. If he made self-deprecatory comments about his presidential qualifications, it was with no conviction. There could be no mistake: Byron lusted after the presidency. He could taste it in his mouth as if it were a hard candy packed with flavor. He dreamed it at night and pursued it by day, patiently, a brick here, another there, building his edifice in a gradual way. Already he had favors owed him by men and women whom he'd managed to place in influential positions at State, Justice, the Federal Bureau of Investigation, and within his own party's national committee.

What Larry Deets wanted, in a life that was otherwise as empty as a derelict house abandoned even by squatters, was to be indispensable to greatness. He wanted to be the grainy figure in the background of historic photographs who hands the fountain pen to the man signing major treaties. His loyal attachment to Byron Truskett was his best shot at a vicarious immortality.

Deets's office adjoined Truskett's. At eleven-ten on the morning following the senator's tryst with Carolyn Laforge, Deets knocked quietly on the door, then stepped inside Truskett's office when he heard the familiar booming "Come."

Truskett's big room was dark because venetian blinds with unopened slats covered the windows, keeping the sun-blasted view of Washington from sight. A large fan churned hot air around. Overloaded, the air-conditioning system for the entire building had broken down. The backup generator, neglected for years, had also failed, sending a skunklike stench through the ductwork.

The senator's face, sweaty and a little drawn on this particular morning, was lit by a Tiffany desk lamp which Miriam had given him because she thought it added class to his office.

Deets laid a blue cardboard folder on Truskett's desk. "You asked to see this again."

Sighing, Truskett looked at the folder, which contained a record of William Laforge's career. He was already so familiar with it he might have been able to recite it verbatim if pressed, but he kept coming back to these typewritten sheets as if haunted by the sensation that he'd overlooked something important. A man's life, double spaced, rendered on pale bond paper, lost all nuance. There was nothing in these pages to suggest the inner world of Laforge.

Truskett gazed at the top sheet, which assumed a greenish-red tint from the Tiffany lamp. "Is he really our man, Larry? Why do I keep having this damned nagging doubt?"

Deets sat down. He considered Laforge something of a dry old fart, but he'd never utter this opinion to the senator. Old farts were often essential to the correct operation of the nation's institutions anyway. Besides, since the senator was humping Laforge's wife—Deets was rarely in the dark about Truskett's activities—then it was two hundred percent certain that promises had been made to William.

"He has the experience. He knows the agency inside out and upside down and sideways. No doubt of that. He shares many of your political views." Larry Deets put no great enthusiasm in his voice. The trouble with old farts was that they often left a malodorous stink in their passing, which was what worried him. Certain areas in Laforge's history made Deets tense; they resembled snapshots that had come out blurred and discolored. Deets dreaded the notion of *anything* spoiling Truskett's shot at the nomination during the next party convention, which would happen if the senator championed Laforge and Billy turned out to be, well, a rancid choice. Deets could hear the accusations already. *Poor Byron, terrible judge of character. Isn't presidential material. Too bad. We had high hopes for him. Go ride Oblivion Expressway, chump.* Given the number of elder senators who resented Truskett's youth, charisma, and ambition—which contrasted markedly with their own desiccation, dreariness, and utter breakdown of vision—Truskett would be crucified if his support of Laforge didn't go across. *Told you so,* they'd say. *Can't expect a boy to do a man's job.*

Because he feared that the good ship Byron might founder on uncharted rocks, Larry Deets, on his own initiative, had begun to tap into that thriving underground network of information shared by senior House and Senate aides, a question here, an aside there, a whisper over Absolut two-olive cocktails in mahogany-paneled bars, a phone number or a name doodled on a damp napkin. In this fashion Deets had gathered knowledge of his own, which he was prepared to share at the appropriate moment. For the present, though, he'd do what Truskett asked. He'd go through Laforge's record with the appropriate impartiality.

"You don't overflow with passion, Larry," the senator said.

"I've always considered passion dispassionately," Deets remarked. "And I find it a tad overrated. For one thing, it's usually brief. I prefer longevity. For another, it tends to get messy. I think clutter's a sign of a mind in disarray."

Truskett looked at his chief aide and thought that although Deets was bright and insightful he was just a little too tight-assed, in need of loosening up. He needed to get his ashes hauled, to be laid all the way to Delaware Bay and back. But it was hard to imagine Larry in any sexual position, fellatory, cunnilinctual, even missionary. Maybe he was gay. Maybe he made do with masturbation. Was there beneath his pillow a linen handkerchief, stiff and discolored from the affection he poured into it?

Truskett opened Laforge's folder. Jesus, what brought him back time and again to this stuff? *Read between the lines. Look deeply into the spaces. Find the man. Pin the tail on the inscrutable donkey.*

"Let's go over it one last time, Larry. I know we're sick of it, I know it's a chore, but I need to be sure. Let's look at it as objectively as we can." He picked up the top sheet. "Okay. We'll start with dear old Iran. Laforge was assigned to 'assist' there from 1963 until 1965. *Assist.* Not exactly specific, Larry. What if somebody wants more detail?"

"As we concluded before, detail's hard to come by. Laforge advised the Shah's people on gathering intelligence. That's about it. It's not as if he worked directly with the nasties from SAVAK—and even if he happened to come in contact with them, where's the evidence? Records were lost in Khomeini's revolution. And the Ayatollah had a bad habit of fabricating documents that implicated American citizens in the atrocities of the Shah's secret police. Who knows what to believe about Iran? It's like Lewis Carroll loose among the mullahs. I think Laforge can also count on something else—what do I want to call it? The pragmatic amnesia of some of your colleagues in the Senate."

Pragmatic amnesia. Truskett looked unhappy a moment. Iran was a stinking pool he didn't want to stir. The undead, waiting to be dredged up as witnesses, lay motionless under a scummy surface. It was unfortunate Laforge had been in that wretched country because there were those in the House who might focus on his role during the Shah's regime. But Deets, Truskett hoped, was right: Time and bureaucratic chaos had blunted both memories and evidence of the Shah's days. And there were still some in power who had good reason to be stricken by a loss of recall and a measure of guilt when Iran was mentioned. The Shah, an overnight leper, had been drawn and quartered by certain self-righteous U.S. officials when his reign was over, mainly because he'd committed the most heinous crime of which an American ally is capable: He'd outlived his usefulness.

Truskett turned the top sheet over. "At least the Tokyo stuff is uncontroversial."

"Unblemished," said Deets.

"Assistant station chief in Tokyo until 1971. An unremarkable time. He developed a good working knowledge of Japanese, for which the Japs loved him. He transmitted a copious amount of accurate material on anti-American nationalist movements in Japan."

Truskett came to the third page. "Bangkok—1972 through 1976. Station chief. Nobody can fault his performance there. He had an excellent network reaching inside North Vietnam. Some of the information he sent back was priceless. He worked his ass off digging out MIAs. Heroic stuff."

The senator stood up, strolled to the fan, placed his face close to the blades. "This heat's a sonofabitch. Doesn't it bother you, Larry? Don't you ever sweat?"

"I sweat."

"You don't show it. What's your secret, Larry?"

"I want to say it's mind over matter," Deets replied. "But the truth is my sweat glands are underactive. Even as a kid, heat didn't affect me like it does other people."

I knew it, Truskett thought. *He's from another planet.* He walked back to his desk and looked at the folder again just as the Tiffany lamp, interrupted by some dip in the current, blinked. "Okay. Billy goes back to Tokyo as station chief in 1978, after spending a year at Langley running what was then called the Office of Strategic Research. In 1984 he's brought home by Sandy Bach, stays in Virginia for six months, where he works reorganizing the East Asia Division. Then suddenly he's shipped off to Manila in '85. But not as station chief, which is what you'd expect, given his experience. Nor is he connected with the Joint U.S. Military Advisory Group, which would have been another possibility. Instead, he's made special advisor to the chief of the Philippine Constabulary. What's that supposed to mean? Pretend I'm on the Senate committee and convince me it isn't downright sinister."

With the air of a man reciting something learned by rote, Deets said, "Marcos was unhappy with his constabulary. He thought it needed reorganization, especially in its intelligence activities. Remember, he was more than mildly paranoid because in his view the hills and hollows of the Philippines were filled with Commie insurgents. Since that was the dubious basis for his declaration of martial law, he had a duty to see reds everywhere. Hence the need for more and better intelligence because he had to keep finding baddies where they didn't even exist. So Billy did an in-depth study and reshuffled some officers and retired others to beef up 'efficiency,' and I am hanging quotation marks around that word. I really think it was window-dressing to keep Marcos cheerful. Billy was a gift to Ferdinand from Ronnie Reagan. Marcos asked for a good man, and Ronnie, ever anxious to oblige his good pal in Manila, sent Laforge and a small team of assistants steaming off to the Pearl of the Orient."

"*Special advisor* makes me nervous," Truskett said. "The phrase stinks. And the association with Marcos isn't going to win us any cigars."

Deets made some minuscule adjustment to the cuffs of his lead-gray jacket. "In Billy's favor, there's not a shred of evidence he was a buddy of Marcos. They might have shaken hands once, but it's not as if they played rounds of golf at Wack-Wack Country Club or shared a dish of rice and listened to Imelda sing 'The Impossible Dream' at the Malacañang Palace. All Billy did was to obey Sandy Bach and Ronnie Reagan. He was told to do a certain job, and he did it. He's loyal to his bosses, always has been."

"And loyalty scores," Truskett said as he sat down, placing his shoeless feet up on his desk. His socks were dark blue with a thin red stripe. He was very quiet for a long time. The fan suddenly quit, and the lamp went off for about thirty seconds, and the room turned into a suffocating black box, like a capsule hurtled abruptly into deep blind space, before electricity was restored. Truskett shook his head. "We're trying to run a goddam country and we can't run this one building with any fucking semblance of efficiency. Sweet Jesus."

He leaned over the folder once more. "So. After Corazon Aquino's ascendancy in 1986, Billy stayed on in Manila for another nine months at the request of Cory herself, which was a bit of a turnaround that definitely won him bonus points."

Deets said, "Maximum. You don't often get requests from an angel, do you? But Billy surely did. He helped analyze the strengths and weaknesses of Cory's intelligence service, and then he came home, where Sandy Bach appointed him deputy director for Operations. And lo, that's where we find him to this very day." He turned his face toward the fan, enjoying the stream of air. He added, "Laforge is weak in European experience. That could be a minus."

"Sure, but he speaks fluent German and French, and he's an Anglophile into the bargain. I think what's more important than any *sprechen sie Deutsch* or knowing how to spread clotted cream on a scone is that fact he knows his way goddam *blindfolded* around the agency." Truskett removed a sock, wiggled his long white toes as if he were somehow surprised by his feet. "Besides, there's one constant in Laforge's life which I think can swing it for him, and that's his blue-blooded Americanism. When he goes before the Senate, Larry, he's apple pie in a pinstriped suit. He's as red-blooded as the March of Dimes, for Christ's sake. He can't be faulted in the patriotism department. He knows the enemy. He's seen the whites of their eyes."

Deets said nothing.

Truskett asked, "Well, Larry. What is he—a strong candidate or a weak one?"

"Something of both, I think."

"What kind of answer is that?" Truskett wanted to know.

Deets, by virtue of his position, sometimes gave equivocal responses to questions. In Washington, language had been butchered, skinned, gutted, the bones removed from the flesh, the marrow sucked loudly from the bones; sentences and phrases, no matter how artfully arranged, often lacked any nutritional value. Deets stood up. He took a glossy leather wallet from the inside pocket of his jacket and opened it. An array of credit cards was neatly displayed in plastic covers. He removed a piece of paper from a zippered compartment and handed it to the senator.

"Read this," Deets said. "Maybe then you'll have an answer to your question, Senator."

"I hope to God this isn't some last-minute surprise, Larry. You know how I hate that kind of shit."

Deets, maestro of the enigmatic smile, said, "It may clarify things. It may not."

Before Truskett could look at the paper, Madge McFarlane entered the room without knocking. She'd been employed by the Truskett family for thirty years, ever since the beginnings of the dynasty in Cedar Rapids, and she believed her longevity afforded her direct access to the senator. She was family, or liked to think so.

"I thought you'd want to know, Byron. Alexander Bach is dead." She had the face of a woman who loves to deliver death notices and other uplifting items of news such as typhoons, earthquakes, political assassinations. She thrived on bleakness.

Truskett considered this information a moment. He remembered Alexander Bach as a quietly humorous figure of an iconoclastic bent. "When?"

"Fifteen minutes ago. I just got word. He died in his sleep," said Mrs. McFarlane. "Flowers to the family, of course?"

"Of course," Truskett said.

"Lilies, I think."

"Whatever, Madge."

"I have never known lilies to be unappreciated." Mrs. McFarlane went out to arrange the floral tribute and the message of sorrow, which she would compose herself in language that would embarrass a Hallmark copywriter.

Truskett looked at Deets and said, "Let's move quickly. Call Laforge. Tell him I'm on my way to see him at his place. I don't want him to come to Washington, where he might look like some overanxious vulture. Then get me into the Oval Office tomorrow. A.M. if possible."

Deets never made notes. He had a memory like a snare. "Don't forget the paper, Senator. I urge you to read it."

"I will, Larry. On the way up to Bucks County."

What Charlie Galloway longed for as he sat inside his Toyota in the frazzled parking lot of the Palms Hotel near Hollywood Boulevard was the kind of drab cloudy Glasgow day known as *dreich,* when the river emitted an ectoplasmic mist and gulls screeched unseen like phantom birds and dampness soaked through everything. He imagined walking up Buchanan Street from Argyle Street, feeling a chill northern drizzle blow against his face; perhaps he'd turn along West Nile or Bath Street or Sauchiehall, that most famous of Glasgow streets, and head west and walk wherever the urge took him—Kelvingrove Park, the university, Byers Road with the splendid assortment of hostelries he knew so well in those days and nights when alcohol had been a pleasant corollary to life, not the necessity it appeared to have become in these United States.

Remembered scents made him ache. Rain on sandstone tenements. Mildewed churches. A rain-soaked *Glasgow Evening Times* uplifted by a sudden squall and made to stick against a wet iron railing. The rotted timber steps of the old Govan Ferry. He stared across the parking lot, possessed by the strange sensation he existed in two places simultaneously. How was it possible he could smell wet parkland even as he observed the shimmering entrance to a Californian hotel across a stretch of concrete where stationary vehicles reflected light with such hot intensity his eyeballs burned? *Madness, Charlie. Downright bloody insanity. You're not yourself. Take a hundred Librium, lie down, call me in the morning.*

Dr. Boscoe or Roscoe, jaw and chin concealed by a great silver cache of a beard, had told him alcoholism was a disease like any other, save for this distinction: It was progressive. *No known cure, Charlie. You can never drink like other men. You can never be a social drinker. You'll never get better.* The physician had tipped his bald head back to study the ceiling, as if, having just condemned Charlie Galloway to death, he couldn't look at him. *Think of it as one door closing, another opening. Think of it as a chance to learn how to live a better life.*

I'm trying, I'm trying. Galloway wiped sweat from his face. No known cure. This troubled him. This really scrambled his *huevos.* Was he quite incapable of strolling inside some cool tavern and imbibing a solitary cold one and, thus refreshed, stepping out again? Was he a mutant weakling who couldn't stop at a single drink, doomed forever to become a slavering wreck baying like a bloody werewolf at moons of his own making?

Millions of alcoholics lead fully productive lives, Charlie. When you hear a strident voice in your head telling you that YOU can't possibly be an alcoholic, don't pay any attention. Above all, don't pick up that first drink.

Alcoholic, my arse!

Okay. All right. Aye. He admitted it. There was a Problem. Drink wrestled him to the canvas from time to time and throttled him until he was senseless. But the *A* word? That was a toe tag on a body in the morgue, a convenient ID. Dear Jesus, how quacks loved their little labels! The insides of their heads were like very old apothecary cabinets, tiny worm-eaten drawers, each duly designated in copperplate.

He opened the door of the Toyota and gasped as he leaned out. The atmosphere in the parking lot had the heft of a velvet curtain. For a while he'd kept the engine idling to enjoy the benefit of air-conditioning, but the temperature gauge had risen quickly to the red danger zone, so he'd shut the system down. After he'd followed Freddie Joaquin to a diner on Venice Boulevard, where Ella's erstwhile suitor had fallen into the company of a tall man, he'd trailed the Oldsmobile back here, compelled by his own rampant curiosity about Joaquin's conspicuous lack of grief.

Or was it more? Did he suspect Freddie of some kind of complicity in Ella's death? *On what grounds, Charlie Galloway?*

Because Freddie, behind Ella's back, was slipping his willie to a beefy stripper named Brenda at Joolies? Because the wee fellow didn't know how to cry convincingly?

Oh, good solid stuff, Galloway. Just the kind of damning evidence needed to fry Freddie. Quick! Get a judge! Reserve the Chair!

The bottom line was that he had nothing on Freddie Joaquin except for callousness and indifference, and while these might be undesirable qualities they were not capital offenses. He didn't like Freddie, nor could he in a hundred years imagine why the little barber had courted Ella Nazarena—which could well be a short in the fuse box of his own imagination. But something told him otherwise, a voice he hadn't listened to in so long a time that it whispered now in a tongue he could barely understand, a shambles of a language without syntax and a vocabulary suggestive rather than explicit. He knew this voice, he'd heard it a thousand times before, it was a familiar mumble issuing from some ghostly larynx, and it was telling him something about Freddie. *Something.* That word was a bell in a faraway steeple, the clap of iron on iron creating resonant echoes that the more they repeated the less they signified anything. *A drink would clear my mind,* Charlie Galloway thought. *A drink would put an end to all this shite about steeples and bells and a voice in your skull.*

How long had he been here anyway? His watch had stopped. Was it twenty minutes ago or a hundred when Freddie had gone inside the Palms with his companion? And who was the tall blue-eyed man accompanying Joaquin anyhow? Galloway tugged his T-shirt from his pants and raised the hem of the garment to his face, pressing it upon his damp skin. If anything brought him pleasure in this situation it was the fact he hadn't lost the knack of tracking somebody without being seen, despite the deskbound condition imposed upon him in the last few years. Admittedly, he'd lost Freddie twice in traffic, but he'd found him again, a sure indication that some of the old instinct was still intact.

But what now? How could he sit here motionless and wait for the return of Freddie without turning to a human loaf? Minibuses came and went in the parking lot, depositing scores of Japanese tourists, who scampered inside the hotel as fast as they could, some of them making small squealing sounds as the heat pounded them.

From one of the buses a geisha suddenly appeared for no reason Galloway could fathom, gorgeous and porcelain, a white vision in tiny shoes and immaculate black hair of an intricacy beyond Charlie's understanding. She walked like a silken goddess of sunlight to the hotel entrance and vanished beyond the glass doors and, Galloway thought, into another dimension where perfection such as hers was standard.

Did I really see that? Or am I stroked by heat to the point of illusion? Was she some kind of tourist come-on? A walking travel poster? What the hell? She made as much sense as the odd black man Galloway had seen earlier on Hollywood Boulevard, a character with a blue plastic visor and a flowing red lamé cape, purple tights and hair dyed flamingo—a visitor, he was telling pedestrians, from the planet Garga, the undiscovered tenth planet in the solar system. Garga, it seemed, lurked behind Pluto, a temperate planet of palm trees, natural mineral spas, and a social system in which racism was a crime. It had sounded altogether too attractive to Galloway, who'd had the urge to buy a one-way ticket to the place. On nights when the moon was full, the man was saying, cruise vessels left from unspecified locations "very close" to the Hollywood Bowl.

Did the sun bring them out? Did the heat force them from their dark hiding places in the wainscoting of America? Visitors from other planets, crystal gazers, spooks who spoke through long-dead Aztecs or Zunis, pentagram worshipers, pendulum swingers, odd men building rocket ships from galvanized steel in their backyards, time-travel buffs, people who had close personal friendships with winged angels, crazies who perceived cosmic designs in landscapes or anagrams, some of which involved convenient poetic license *(America* rearranged was almost *A Crime. What did that tell you, Charlie?),* loonies who'd had their heads wired to so-called energy-harnessing boxes and heard all the celestial harmonies of the stars—on and on and on, as if what lay at the heart of the continent was a great madhouse whose doors from time to time were left deliberately ajar to alleviate massive overcrowding.

Sweating, he got out of his Toyota, stretched his cramped

legs. He had to seek refuge inside the hotel or die. Lured by the beauty of air-conditioning, he attached himself to a clutch of Japanese tourists and was quickly propelled into the lobby, ice-cool and magnificent, stacked with trunks and suitcases and people who spoke no English. He pushed his way inside the bar, ordered a Coke, gulped it in an unseemly manner, ordered a second. It was then he saw Freddie Joaquin cross the lobby, followed by his tall companion. Galloway waited twenty or thirty seconds, laid some money on the counter, then went back outside in time to see the two men climb inside Freddie's Olds.

Concealed by minibuses, Galloway hurried toward his Toyota. He followed the Olds out into the street, where it made a right-hand turn down the hill in the direction of Sunset Boulevard. There it entered heavy traffic moving sluggishly into Beverly Hills, a suburb Charlie Galloway preferred to negotiate at least half drunk because its rabid opulence offended some part of him, perhaps that left-wing residue inherited from his father, who'd spent years muttering vaguely about some impossible revolution among Scottish shipyard workers.

Greek statues, topiaries, Afghan hounds lolling under shade trees, white houses purified even further by the alchemy of sunlight, gold-roofed cupolas and turrets and Tudor conceits. Galloway wondered if it was the architectural horror that bothered him even more than the wealth, but the former was merely the physical realization of the latter. Bad taste abounded. It attacked you, deadened your spirit.

American excess! Was it this that half the countries of the planet envied? Did the blanketed Indian squatting beside his color TV with the rabbit ears on the edge of a Peruvian jungle lust for premoistened two-ply toilet paper available in earth tones? Did the one-legged kid living in a hole in the ground in bombed-out Beirut dream of stone-washed designer blue jeans?

Beverly Hills made sobriety intolerable, like a penance.

Up ahead, two or three cars away, Freddie Joaquin's enormous Oldsmobile chugged along. Joaquin somehow managed to change lanes and make a left turn, which caused Charlie Galloway a moment of panic. Signaling with one hand thrust defiantly through the open window, he switched recklessly into the left-turn lane, ignoring the horns. He made his turn despite a sudden ruthless charge of oncoming traffic.

Now he was on a narrow street of smaller houses, where a quieter opulence was evident. Despite the water shortage, garden sprinklers busily sprayed the air. Here and there imported Mexican or Salvadoran laborers mowed a lawn or pruned a bush or dug a hole.

Joaquin's car turned right. Slowing, Galloway followed. He had to keep a distance. It was the rule of this game. He went right some thirty seconds after Joaquin.

Ah, shite! Freddie had parked his car and was standing on the grassy verge at the side of the street, his face turned in Galloway's direction. He had one arm raised in greeting and he was smiling. Galloway, cursing the recent delusion of efficiency that had afflicted him, drew his Toyota in directly behind the Oldsmobile and wondered exactly when Freddie had spotted him. He stepped out and stood in the short, brittle grass.

"I thought I saw you in the parking lot of the hotel, Mr. Galloway," Joaquin said. "This is coincidence, right? You don't have any reason for following me, do you?"

"Probably we've got friends in the same neighborhood, Freddie," Galloway said, and looked toward the Olds. Joaquin's passenger stared straight ahead, as if this encounter were too tiresome to consider. All Charlie Galloway could see was the man's profile, which was handsome and a little gaunt. The blueness of the eye was unexpected, like a shiver on a hot day. His black hair was short and combed straight back.

Joaquin smiled. The gold in his teeth caught fire. When he spoke there was a touch of defiance in his voice. He was, after all, an American citizen. The Bill of Rights was probably as familiar to him as the national anthem of the Philippines. More so. "My lawyer taught me a word, Mr. Galloway. *Harass-ment.*"

"Is that a fact? I'm very impressed, Freddie. And you've got your own lawyer too. Well, well."

"Are you harassing me?"

Galloway laid the palm of one hand on Joaquin's shoulder and squeezed it in a friendly way. "Don't be silly, Freddie. This is pure coincidence, my wee friend. You were in the Palms Hotel

and so was I. You were coming along this street and, bob's your
uncle, so was I. Lovely thing, coincidence."

Joaquin had an unsettled look. He wanted to believe in this
marvelous world of coincidence, you could see; but on that other
level of awareness where he lived his life, that half-lit realm
whose monarch was suspicion, he knew coincidence was bullshit.
No cop ever followed you by chance. They always had a reason.
Besides, Galloway's front, a kind sarcastic friendliness, clearly
made him nervous.

Galloway, thinking on his feet, said, "As a matter of fact,
Freddie, I've got a couple of questions I forgot to ask you before."

"Anything you like. I got nothing to hide."

"When did you last see Ella Nazarena alive?"

"Two nights ago. We had dinner at a restaurant on Pico
Boulevard, a Polynesian place. Not very good. You can check."

Galloway looked inside the Olds again. The windows were
tightly closed, the air-conditioning running. The passenger continued to ignore him. The one blue eye visible to Galloway was
unblinking. "Question two. Have you got a police record?"

Freddie Joaquin hesitantly ran the palm of a hand across his
hair.

Galloway said, "You might as well tell me now, because I can
find out, Freddie. I push a button. A computer buzzes. Dead
easy."

"I served some time," Joaquin said quietly. "There was, you
know, what's the word, a misunderstanding?"

"Is that a fact, Freddie? A misunderstanding, eh?"

Joaquin lowered his voice, as if to be sure that his passenger
heard none of this. "It was years ago. It involved stolen goods.
Furs, a little jewelry. I bought them in all innocence, you understand. I'm no criminal. Ha. I'm a barber."

Galloway patted the little man's shoulder, a gesture of consolation. "Oh, it breaks my heart when a man does time and he's
not guilty."

"It's the system," said Freddie.

"Tell me. It sucks."

"Sucks is right. I did two years. Nobody can give me back my
time."

Galloway shook his head as if despair had settled on him like an albatross. "One last question, Freddie. You own a gun?"

"No. Never. Never. No."

"You sure?"

"One hundred percent sure." Freddie Joaquin crossed his heart, a gesture so incongruously childish, so calculated to gratify, that Galloway felt a little twinge of guilt. Was he giving Freddie a needlessly hard time? Was he allowing his instinctive dislike of the man to ascribe possibilities to Freddie that were quite without justification? Was this all the result of the shock of Ella's murder? There was a tangible film of scum on Freddie, and you wouldn't want to touch his skin without a precautionary tetracycline shot, but that didn't make him a criminal, nor did it justify Galloway following him through the streets of Los Angeles.

It keeps you busy, Charlie, he thought. *It keeps you out of bars.* Was that what this was really all about? These are pathetic times. These are the days of barbed-wire fences strung around your urges.

Depressed, Galloway stared up and down the quiet street, listening to piped water falling on the leaves of plants, seeing now and then a transient rainbow on somebody's front lawn. Then, shaking free his melancholy, he slapped his hand on the roof of the Olds and asked, "Who's your pal, Freddie?"

Joaquin said, "A very dear old friend. A fine man. He's visiting from my country."

"Does he have a name?"

And here Charlie Galloway lowered his face to peer directly inside the car at Freddie's passenger, who turned slightly, but with no display of interest, to scan Galloway. The eyes were not entirely cold and humorless, yet Galloway had the thought, *This one kills*—then the notion left him, and he wasn't sure where it had come from in the first place.

He rapped on the closed window and the blue-eyed man rolled it down very slowly, almost as if it were beneath his dignity.

"Charles Galloway," Charlie said.

"Raymond Cruz."

Galloway put his hand through the open window. The handshake with Cruz was tight but not unfriendly, certainly no contest of physical strength. Galloway withdrew his arm and said something politely meaningless about how he hoped Cruz would enjoy his visit, to which the Filipino added something just as trite. Save for the brief flash that had invaded Galloway's mind, that arc of freak lightning, the encounter was not something you'd immediately rush home to record in your diary. He stepped away from the car.

"No more questions?" Joaquin asked.

"No more."

"Good, good."

Galloway nodded. "Cheerio, Freddie."

On the grassy verge, listening to the sound of Angelenos further deplete the city's already diminished supply of water, Charlie Galloway for shade stepped under the nearest tree, whose cracked bark was crammed with thousands of red ants—all eerily motionless and still, as if the genetic impulses that stoked their usual frantic industry had been forced by the heat into a baffling siesta.

For several miles after the encounter with Galloway, Teng remained menacingly silent. And then the questions came, posed in a voice so strictly controlled, so icy, it spooked Freddie. Why was this man Galloway following them? Who was he? Did he know anything?

Freddie pretended to be totally absorbed by the traffic on Santa Monica Boulevard, watching the street, peering into the rearview mirror, busying himself.

"Something unexpected came up," he said eventually.

Teng waited for Joaquin to expand on this vague statement. He put one hand around Joaquin's wrist, a gesture applied without pressure and yet all the more menacing for its gentleness. Freddie Joaquin wondered if his pulse was audible. *I am sending a young man,* Joe Baltazar had written, *in whose veins I don't think you will find any blood.*

Freddie had "face" to consider, honor, his machismo. He spoke in a firm voice. "I had to make a decision. I did what was necessary. Understand?"

Teng calmly told him to park the car at a convenience store. Freddie obeyed. For a long time Teng didn't speak. He looked through the window at the storefront, which advertised a jumbo cup of coffee and donut for ninety-nine cents, the Early Bird Special. A thin young girl stepped from the shop, carrying a six-pack of beer. She wore cutoff shorts and a cotton top through which her small damp nipples were visible. Teng watched her climb inside a dented pickup; she glanced at him as she pulled the door closed. Did she smile? Or was that his imagination?

She was pretty in a slender way. He pressed the palm of his hand upon his forehead a moment. He thought of Marissa. Why did they keep coming back, these memories, surging up even when he didn't want them, like things rejected by a churning sea? He stared at the girl, but she'd turned her face to the side and was backing her truck out of the parking space. He sometimes thought death would be easier than the salvage of remembrance. To close his eyes. To drift. But hatred was a raft. The urge to right terrible wrongs kept him afloat. This was the only clarity. Anything else was muddy and impenetrable.

He looked at Joaquin. "Who employs Galloway?"

Joaquin told him.

Teng said to himself, *Calm, calm.* "And why was he asking you questions?"

Freddie Joaquin busied himself again, adjusting his rearview mirror, running his handkerchief over the steering wheel as if it were dusty. "A woman was murdered," he said quietly.

"Who?"

"It's not important."

"Answer my question."

Joaquin crumpled his handkerchief in the palm of his hand. "She was a cleaner. She'd been working in my shop, couple times a week. She could have harmed you. Okay?"

"How?"

"She knew you were coming."

"How did she know that?"

Joaquin said, "News from Benguet, her province. You know the way the grapevine works. She had a letter from a cousin in La Trinidad."

"What was this cousin's name?"

"Cara Panganiban. Sister of Leo."

Leo Panganiban had been one of the gunmen in the field the

morning of Deduro's assassination. A courageous man, Leo had one unforgivable fault; he liked to tell bloated tales of his own exploits when he'd a few drinks. In an idle, beery moment, he might have hinted to Cara that something was happening in which he'd played a vital part, that he was privy to important information. Cara, in turn, could have written a letter to her cousin Ella Nazarena, relaying this news.

It was all too likely. Teng well understood the elaborate system of family networks that formed the basis of Filipino society, the clans, the ancestral bonds, the responsibilities of blood. Cousins and second cousins, aunts and great-aunts, the close relative and the distant one—there was a consistency, an adhesion between all the members of a family, a tribal quality that persisted no matter how far the members might be scattered. Phone calls, letters, postcards, gossip transmitted from a man in Ormoc City to his sister in Tacloban or his uncle in Catbalogan; news was precious, an antidote to the boredom of poverty, a form of song that filled the silences of despair, and it expanded the more it traveled. It became epic. People hungered for nuggets of information, tales, yarns, bulletins of deaths and marriages, divorces and blighted loves. Given this massive ebb and flow of gossip, secrecy could be maintained only with great difficulty, a fact about which Teng had always been concerned.

"What did the letter say?"

"Somebody was coming to the United States to avenge the *gabi ng kamàtayan.*"

The night of death. That was how it had come to be known.

There had been other such nights elsewhere in the Philippines, other horrors, but when Joaquin mentioned the *gabi ng kamàtayan* he referred only to one night, one specific darkness, one place.

"Was I mentioned by name?" Teng asked.

"Yes."

"What name?"

Joaquin said, "As Armando Teng."

This information troubled Teng, who silently regarded the window of the convenience store, which advertised a Cherry Slurpee. The notion that his real name had come up was a source of concern to him. Again he returned to the realization that secrets, in a society clamoring for family information, were hard to keep. And if Freddie Joaquin knew Raymond Cruz was a pseudonym, a nom de guerre, how many others were also aware?

"The woman was going to show the letter to Galloway," Joaquin said.

"And you believe he could have found me? You believe he could have discovered why I am here?"

"Yes."

"The passport I carry identifies me as Raymond Cruz. I've used dozens of different names over the last few years. How could Galloway have connected me with somebody called Teng?"

The young man's calm smile upset Joaquin, the graph of whose life had brought him from a dirt-floor grain store in Tarlac to a barbershop in Inglewood. Freddie imbued the Los Angeles Police Department with omniscience. It was no backwater constabulary with one telephone, no handful of uniformed drunks with outdated rifles playing cards all day long in a corrugated tin shack somewhere in Ilocos Norte. No. The LAPD had computers and listening devices and infrared cameras and all kinds of high technology at its disposal. It was obvious Teng had absolutely no understanding of the vast resources Galloway could use. How difficult would it be for Galloway to make a connection between Teng and Cruz, and perhaps discover Teng's reason for being in the United States? Cara Panganiban's letter to Ella would have been enough to start a whole process rolling. Freddie wished with all his heart he'd never agreed in the first place to do a "small" favor for Joe Baltazar, his brother-in-law, a man too easy to enrage, more than a little crazy. Back in the early days of Joe's marriage to Freddie's young sister, Joe had been fine, even-tempered, easy to get along with. But all that had changed.

"The LAPD can make inquiries with the Philippines Constabulary. They'd dig and keep digging."

Teng remembered Freddie Joaquin's phrase, *smooth sailing.* How inappropriate it seemed now. "And so the woman had to die, Freddie."

A bleak little expression crossed Freddie Joaquin's face. "I couldn't take the chance. I didn't want her dead. But I didn't want her to show that letter to Galloway. She kept changing her mind. One day she said she'd show it to him. The next day she wouldn't. One day this, next day that. I told her it was nothing, gossip, ignore the goddam letter. I took her to dinner, I bought her flowers, I said I loved her. I even proposed marriage to her! If she was my wife, I thought, it would be easier for me to get the letter. But no, she decided she'd talk to Galloway anyway."

Teng said, "Perhaps she considered it her duty as a citizen of this great country." He made a sweeping gesture with his hand, as if America were no more than a half acre bounded by a tawdry convenience store, a few gas pumps gleaming in the sun, a parking lot, a country where breakfast could be had for ninety-nine cents.

"Maybe," Joaquin said.

"Why didn't you steal the letter?" Teng asked.

"Steal it? She put it in a bank deposit box. How was I meant to steal it? Dynamite?"

"It's still in the bank?"

"Yeah, yeah."

"Then it's secure. Unless some bank clerk reads about the murder and makes the connection."

Joaquin said, "It's in one of those big banks with thousands of deposit boxes, so maybe nothing will happen until it's time for the rental to be paid. When she doesn't pay, then the safe will be opened. That could be months from now. There's also the chance the cops might find out about the box, but I don't think it's likely unless they dig deep. I doubt they give a shit about the murder of a Filipina cleaning woman."

"Where did she keep the key?"

"Who knows? She was always stashing things. She had hundreds of little boxes filled with cheap jewelry and souvenirs and holy things. I couldn't find the key in any of them. She sure as hell didn't wear it around her neck."

Armando Teng considered the letter a moment, then dismissed it as an abstraction, something sealed and locked inside a metal box. He did not think it a danger to him because he expected to complete his business and be gone again in a matter of days. It contributed an element he didn't need, a certain extra source of anxiety, but he'd lived with worse. He told Freddie to drive.

Joaquin continued along Santa Monica Boulevard. When

they were a couple of blocks from the ocean, Teng asked, ''Did you kill the woman yourself?''

Freddie Joaquin made no reply for several minutes. The ocean, placid and blue, suggested a great sheet of neon under the brilliant sun. The boardwalk could be seen reaching out into the water like a primitive prosthetic arm. In the undulating heat the palm trees were reflections in funhouse mirrors.

Joaquin parked the car and walked to a bench on the bluff overlooking the beach. Teng sat down beside him, stretching his long legs. Barely any breeze reached the palisades from the sands. The ocean might have been a thousand miles away and tideless, unaffected by gravity.

''What choice was there?'' Freddie Joaquin said. He'd never killed before. Once, he'd wounded a man in a drunken dispute outside a café in Tarlac. This was different. In recollection, it seemed to him he looked at the murder of Ella from a point so high both victim and assassin were miniatures, meaningless little figures of clay surrounded by the tiny velvet Christs and microscopic plaster Madonnas in Ella's living room. He suffered none of the remorse he'd anticipated. No darkness crowded his head. If there was anxiety it arose only from the possibility of discovery, not from the machinery of conscience. And if it happened that Galloway accused him for some reason, he knew he could deny to eternity the act of murder. It was a matter of convincing yourself you didn't do it, you were elsewhere at the time. Besides, who saw you? You were innocent. A gospel truth.

''Does Galloway suspect you?'' Teng asked.

''I don't see how he could.'' And yet Galloway had asked about a gun. Why?

''Then you have nothing to worry about, do you?''

Down on the sands beefy lifeguards played a game of volleyball. Teng observed them for a time, marveling at their energy in the heat.

''I couldn't think of another way.'' Joaquin stood up, raising one foot on the metal rail at the edge of the bluff. Nearby, a small boy in an LA Rams T-shirt peered through a pay telescope at the Pacific. Joaquin watched the kid a moment, then turned back to Teng, whose face was expressionless.

"You did what you had to," Teng said. "Unfortunate, of course. But now it's finished."

Freddie Joaquin shrugged. A passing gull briefly threw a shadow across his face. "This is where I leave you."

"Leave me?"

"Those are my instructions. Somebody else will meet you."

The idea of Joaquin's departure made Teng feel unexpectedly isolated. For a moment he wondered what would happen if nobody showed up, if Joe Baltazar's chain of "helpful people" was broken and he was doomed to sit here alone. Helpful people. *Ordinary* people. While he'd been assembling his organization, Joe couldn't have foreseen that one of his "ordinary" friends would commit murder.

"Good luck," Joaquin said.

"*Paálam.*" Teng didn't turn to watch Joaquin walk across the grass to his parked car. The little man had come into his life, then out again, a chapter closed, although with more incident than Teng liked.

Alone, he watched the sands, the ocean, the white sails of small boats. A luxury yacht cruised about a mile from shore. Teng closed his eyes. The sun burned on his eyelids.

For a second, he was possessed by the notion that his phantom father was nearby, a few streets away, perhaps even on the sands down there, perhaps a stroller walking the pathway along the bluff. It was such a strong sensation that Teng opened his eyes, half expecting to see the man coming toward him. Ridiculous! How could he have recognized his father? The man might pass him on the street, or brush against him inside a store, and he'd never know. Dead or alive: Even that basic distinction eluded him.

A female jogger in tight silken blue shorts and red T-shirt pounded the pathway toward him. She had long black hair tied back in a rubber band. As she approached the bench she slowed. Bending, placing her hands on her knees for support even as she struggled to catch her breath, she looked at Teng curiously.

"Raymond Cruz?" she asked, sweeping a stray strand of hair from her forehead. He raised his face.

"*Mabùhay,*" she said, and reached out to shake his hand.

9

William Laforge turned the loaded revolver over and over in his hand before placing it carefully in the drawer of his bureau. It was a well-kept gun, frequently oiled. Although he was no aficionado of pistols, he knew how to use one. He liked the feel of the weapon, the sense of security it afforded him. He closed the drawer on it and thought, *Nobody can touch me. Even if somebody means me harm, he will find me prepared.*

He walked to the window of his bedroom, which overlooked a sloping stretch of well-watered green lawn where a yellow and white parasol created shade above a picnic table and chairs. The lawn ended in a stand of brittle old beech trees. Laforge watched a squirrel pick at a crumb under the table and then, startled, scurry toward the trees. Perhaps the music Nick had been playing downstairs for the last hour had finally driven the creature off.

Ever since the news of Alexander Bach's death had been mentioned on one of those dramatic TV flashes the networks so love, the boy had been pointedly playing one Johann Sebastian Bach record after another. Now he was halfway through the Casals version of the Suites for Solo Cello. Laforge understood that the Bach marathon was the boy's way of making some kind of comment, sarcastic, caustic, about the vacancy left by Sandy Bach's demise, and Laforge's own ambition to fill it. It was as if the kid were shouting over and over *Bach's dead, Bach's dead, Bach's dead.*

Carolyn, who had her own bedroom along the hallway, came in, dressed in a simple burgundy cotton dress. "Do we know exactly when he's coming?" she asked. She was referring to Byron Truskett, whose aide Deets had telephoned a couple of hours ago.

Laforge looked at his watch. "He should be here in about thirty minutes."

"Is there anything special we should do? Food? Drinks?"

Laforge took his wife's hand and pressed it between his own. Her skin was cool as usual. Her green eyes were frank and deep. Years ago he had thought of them as emerald: a young man's fancy. Now they suggested an undiscovered gemstone, an older man's whimsical description, ill defined but somehow all the more precise for that. Young men nailed definitions to things. Older men, closer to mortality, resisted such limitations.

"I can't imagine," he said. "He likes bourbon, doesn't he?"

"Yes." Carolyn sat in the window seat. "I wish Nick would change that music. I enjoy Bach as much as anyone, but there are limits."

"It's his weird idea of fun."

"It's not mine, William." She shook her head, as if she were sad.

Laforge saw how his wife's cotton dress had risen above her knees and stayed there through a process of static electricity bonding skin to garment. The air-conditioning unlocked a sudden blast of cold air that made the fine hairs rise on the back of her arms.

"Are there any surprises I should know about?" he asked.

"None. Apparently if you come through the hearings unscathed, you're a shoo-in. Isn't that the expression? Nor must you have any lint in your navel. I quote." She covered her smile with a hand, as if she were amused.

"Last time I looked I saw none," he said. "Did he stay with you long?"

"Four hours, more or less," she replied without turning. She was thinking that the picnic furniture needed a fresh coat of white paint. It was all this endless sunlight that had peeled the old paint. Everything was burning. The countryside. The cities. Everything.

Laforge walked to the window. "You've never really talked much about him," he said.

"You've never really asked, William. What do you want to know?"

"Whatever comes to your mind."

Downstairs, the sound of the cello seemed to fill all available physical space, as if the house itself had become one enormous speaker.

"Byron has . . . stamina," Carolyn said in a matter-of-fact way.

"That hardly surprises me."

"He likes me to take him into my mouth, but not for long, because he comes too quickly."

Laforge, as though he were a chemist listening to the recitation of a formula, a sociologist hearing statistics reflecting a reality of which he has utterly no experience, waited for more. The sexual descriptions of Truskett and his wife didn't thrill him; he wasn't moved, as some men were, by accounts of a wife's infidelity. He got no kick out of it. That would have been sick, kinky. Nor was he eaten by jealousy. It was merely interesting, and it gave him some knowledge about Truskett, but he was detached from the actuality, as though Carolyn were reading to him from a work of fiction whose characters lived lives far removed from his own.

"He likes it from behind," she said. "I don't mean anal intercourse, which isn't my style. Once or twice he's been rather surprisingly premature. He says I bewitch him. He says I have magic powers."

"Probably you do."

"He thinks so."

"How does he feel about making love to another man's wife?"

"I'd say he has absolutely no compunction about it. He neither thinks of you nor Miriam when he's fucking me. You and she don't exist. I think he has all the qualities—ambition, callous indifference and passion in equal measure—that will make him a fine President of the United States."

"I don't doubt it."

"I think he'd like to believe he's in love with me."

Laforge was quiet for a moment. "Do you have feelings for him?"

"You know me better than that, my dear."

In a tentative way, Laforge cupped one hand around his wife's elbow. With this simple touch, he possessed her more completely than Truskett ever could. He possessed her frankness and her honesty, which was more than she ever gave anyone else. She was loyal to him in a way that transcended the banality of sexual infidelity. Truskett might penetrate her deeply but he could never find the source of her because she wasn't there to be discovered by him. That part of her which belonged to Laforge, and to her marriage, that part beyond cunt, beyond the easy intimacies of flesh, was inviolate, a room she kept locked, her cell of privacy.

The relationship between Laforge and his wife, which might have struck many as bizarre, was—at least to the Laforges—an uncomplicated arrangement, and had nothing to do with such outmoded notions as open marriages in which spouses were free to find other sexual partners; nor did it imply that Laforge sought vicarious thrills through Carolyn's exploits, a situation he knew happened sometimes in jaded marriages. Their marriage was not remotely weary. If anything, the bond between them was stronger than it had been eighteen years ago at their wedding, because time had stripped the relationship of all pretense, all the subterfuge and pain that came from structuring a life on the flimsy scaffold of lies that characterized so many marriages.

It was really very simple. William Laforge was one of those people, perhaps less rare than one might suppose from the clamorous attention given sex by the popular culture, who was asexual. He didn't like the sensation of putting his penis inside a woman or a man or even, as he'd once or twice done, his own fist. In his teens, when his lack of sexual curiosity troubled him, he'd gone one night to a homosexual bar in Washington where an elderly man, a congressman named Liddell from Delaware, took him to his apartment and there to bed, where the flabby politician had lain flat on his face and young Laforge mounted and entered him, prick slipping between flaccid buttocks and up and up inside an anus that was wet and slack and horrifying. The sensation Laforge experienced then was that he was being sucked up inside another human body as though the congressman were a vacuum cleaner of a kind, that first the penis would vanish, to be followed by hips and thighs and then everything else. Sexual contact was completely menacing to him.

Years passed, and he drifted from one useless therapist to another, before he allowed himself to try again, this time with Carolyn, a fashion model whom he met at one of those Washington parties to which he was invited when an amiable single man was needed. But he waited, both out of fear and decency, until after they were married. He found the woman charming, delicious to look at, and besides a lovely wife could be an enormous advantage to a career in Laforge's covert world, where bachelors were often suspect and considered vulnerable to the sexual skullduggery of the enemy—in those faraway days the Russians.

In bed, Carolyn was kind and patient and in no apparent hurry to consummate the marriage. She wasn't a virgin and she understood William's nervousness, which at first she attributed to the twenty-year age difference between them and a certain self-consciousness on his part. He had to prove himself capable of satisying a vigorous young wife, and she believed that that was *certainly* stressful enough to make him limp.

The eventual coupling, fortified by huge amounts of brandy, was messy and brief. In a contrary way, Laforge's terror, his lack of élan, endeared him all the more to Carolyn, who now began to perceive the true nature of his problem. He just didn't like sex. Very well, she could be businesslike. She could cope. They would build a life around the obstacle. She understood that William would not deny her the occasional fling if it became essential. Annulment never entered her mind. He was dear to her, and sweet beyond her experience of men, who had usually treated her with a kind of deferential brutality, as if her extraordinary beauty were something to savor before ravaging. Besides, William had a career with dizzying possibilities, and she would help him shape that, and push him harder than he might have pushed himself.

She would be his accessory, his companion, his confidante. She would guide him.

Their marriage, if not founded on a mutual passion, became a kind of conjugal corporation in which William was president and she treasurer and secretary; and in the imaginary articles of incorporation was stated the intended business of Laforge & Laforge, Inc.—the furtherance of William's career. *No matter what.* Carolyn would have been mortified if anyone had accused her of sleeping with Truskett to advance William's career. She did not think of herself as some ambitious whore. Rather she considered it her executive duty to promote William's talents and to see that her husband's hard work and loyalty were duly rewarded. Whether she spread her thighs in the process was not a matter of morality, more one of policy. Her body was a corporate asset.

One drunken night a year or so after his first effort, when Laforge decided to try the possibilities of the flesh another time, Nicholas Bainbridge Laforge was conceived. This accidental offspring was shunted off to boarding school as soon as it was decent to do so. The boy felt like an invader from the start. Resentful of everything and nothing in particular, he bounced from one school to another, expelled with shameful frequency. Between institutions now, he was home, where his presence in the old white farmhouse was a source of irritation to his parents, who kept colliding with him in the kitchen or bumping into him on the stairs or being obliged to listen to the monorhythmic pounding of his stereo.

Carolyn went to the bedroom door, opened it, stepped on to the landing and called downstairs for the boy to reduce the volume. He obliged, but without enthusiasm. Closing the door, she clasped her husband's hands. He looked unrelaxed, concerned by the prospect of Truskett's arrival.

"There's nothing to worry about, William," she said. "The job is practically yours. In return, Truskett expects nothing except your loyalty when it comes to his own presidential bid, which is not a very high price to pay. The longer I hang around politicians, the more I understand pragmatism is the name of the game. When the wind blows one way, a politician suddenly changes his mind. When it blows another, he remembers to change it back again."

She released his hands and went to the window again, where she studied the beeches. She loved this place. Sometimes on sleepless nights she would imagine herself a winged creature, a delicately feathered night owl flying all across the property, from the county road to the fields beyond the beeches, from the creek then across the meadows to the paddock. On these flights she'd pass over the white house in which a window or two would be softly lit and she'd wonder who was lucky enough to live in such a beautiful place. She belonged here. She could conceive of no other life. This was her fortress; she lived her real life here.

"It's not as if there's any great difference between yourself and Byron Truskett anyhow," she added. "You both belong to the same political party. And even if you didn't, you both believe in . . . I think the expression is democratic principles. It shouldn't be difficult to agree with Byron on almost anything. I'll say this much in his favor: I think he's managed to convince himself that he can make a difference to this country. He has certain notions that the party is bound to consider radical. Even heretical. He has social programs he wants to implement. He wants to make a truly enormous dent in Pentagon spending. Speak of the devil."

Truskett's car, a black Chrysler he drove himself—he was a man of the people, didn't believe in chauffeurs and lackeys—turned into the driveway.

"Go down, make him a drink, get your business out of the way," Carolyn said. "Tell him I'm taking a shower and I'll join you both in a bit. Oh, and make Nick turn that stereo off."

Laforge hesitated in the bedroom doorway.

"Go on," Carolyn said. "Byron's on your side."

Laforge watched her step inside the bathroom. The door closed behind her. He felt strangely alone for a moment, as if Carolyn had vanished without trace, one of those inexplicable evaporations that happened from time to time, an ordinary man vanishing on his way to work, a child disappearing between school and home, an average housewife walking into a void on her way to a grocery store. It was a curious apprehension he felt, alleviated finally by the sound of water running in the shower stall. He left the room and went downstairs to greet Byron Truskett.

On the way he crossed the living room, where Nick sat. The

boy, who wore his hair very thick on top of his skull but short along the sides in a fashion one might describe as neo-Mohawk, had a beer can in one hand.

"Don't say it," Nick remarked. "You want me to boogie for a while."

"Boogie?"

"Book, pops. You'd probably say scram. Skedaddle. Make myself scarce. Light out. Leave. Split."

Laforge had problems with the new slang. How had the word *book* evolved into a verb that meant "to depart"? He was missing something. As the century entered its final decade, it caused Laforge to wonder where in time he truly belonged. The fifties? The early part of the sixties? He had liked Eisenhower but not Nixon. He had admired Jack Kennedy to some degree, but not Lyndon Johnson. He'd liked Jimmy Carter for about three months and considered Ford a friendly hack. Reagan was fuzzy, indefinable, an impressionistic sketch. Laforge felt adrift in time, a stranger at this point of history.

"Who's the visitor?" Nick asked.

"Senator Truskett."

"Oooo," the boy said, and winked. "Wonder what brings the mighty up to our little homestead, huh?"

Laforge watched the boy walk toward the stairs. Nick paused and pulled an extraordinary face, thusting his tongue behind his lower front gum to look simian. He swung his arms, apelike. "I'll be up in my cage if you want my advice on anything. Just remember today's the day I get my straw changed," and, dangling his arms, he loped up the steps as if he were a gorilla.

Laforge wished these encounters with his son didn't depress him so. He continued to hope he would grow closer to the boy as time passed, a possibility he sadly doubted. A shadow fell upon his mind. That sense of loss he'd felt yesterday in Railsback's company returned to him. It came down to this simple thing: He wanted to love his son but wasn't sure how. What was a father supposed to do? Share secrets with his kid? Mutual confidants? Buddies? The idea darkened as quickly as it had flared. He didn't know what was expected of him. His life, spent in covert activities, hadn't prepared him for overt demonstrations of affection. *Father and son. Such a mystery.* He'd never been on terrific terms with his own father, a textbook publisher who, as early as the late 1950s, had smelled the wind shifting from the humanities to the sciences. He had been the first publisher to specialize in a line of textbooks on computer technology, which had made him extraordinarily rich.

Laforge went outside as Byron Truskett, smiling his large political smile, breezed toward him, hand extended and eyes bright. Clearly he considered full frontal charm the correct way to greet a man you have cuckolded. Laforge had to admire the senator's brazenness even as it amused him. *You fuck my wife, and you think I don't know.* He had a mischievous urge to say this aloud.

They shook hands firmly. Truskett, brimming with health in his white open-necked shirt and tan pants, reminded Laforge of a golfer in his prime, one of those blonds whose names he could never get right. The senator carried a black leather briefcase embossed with his initials and some kind of family crest, an affectation initiated by Truskett Senior, who'd spent his declining years in a desperate search for an aristocratic connection in his genealogy, as if he needed the imprimatur of good breeding at the end of his life.

"We'll all miss Sandy Bach," Truskett said with a certain convincing solemnity. His smile went out like a dead light bulb.

"Yes," Laforge remarked, thinking how easy it was to become a partner in hypocrisy. He'd worked for Sandy Bach for a long time and had never liked the man. Bach was cynical and irreverent, fond of mocking institutions such as the one he directed himself. A smirker. That was how he'd remember Sandy Bach.

"Let's go indoors. I'll fix a drink," Laforge suggested.

Truskett, shading his eyes, looked up at the hot sun. "If you don't mind, I think I'd like to stretch my legs. Stroll for a while."

"Of course, if you can stand this heat."

Truskett moved across the lawn toward the trees. "It's better here than DC, at least," he said. "Here you don't have the goddam pollution. How's your wife?"

You'd know better than me, Laforge thought. "She's fine. She'll join us later for a drink, if you have the time."

Truskett walked as far as the picnic table, where he laid his briefcase down. Then he sat, gazing into the trees for such a long time that Laforge wondered what had so engrossed him, and followed the line of the senator's vision. He saw only the still beeches. Truskett shook his head, as if to free himself from a reverie, a moment of slippage when his concentration had weakened.

"I was just thinking what a pleasant spread this is," he said.

"We enjoy it," Laforge remarked.

Truskett laid a hand on his briefcase, fingering the embossed crest. It consisted, Laforge noticed, of an eagle's head imposed on two crossed swords.

"You know why I'm here, of course," Truskett said. "I assume you haven't had a change of heart since the last time we talked about the job."

Laforge, with a slight quickening of his pulse, replied, "I feel the same, Senator."

"Good, Billy. I'm glad to hear that." Truskett was all smiles again. Whatever somber thought had touched him seemed to have vanished. He even patted the back of Laforge's arm, one old friend to another, By to Billy, a reassurance built out of a thousand shared experiences. It didn't matter that they knew each other only superficially, because Truskett constructed friendships out of nothing all the time. It came with his territory. Laforge loathed the abbreviation of his name to Billy, even though he knew people used it behind his back all the time. It made him sound like a small child or a parakeet. Truskett, though, was the only person who called him Billy to his face, an impertinence he allowed to pass unchecked.

"Tomorrow, I intend to see the President," Truskett said. "He listens to what I have to say on intelligence matters. I hope that doesn't sound immodest."

"It doesn't," Laforge said. Like all politicians, Truskett understood the need for an appearance of humility. Braggardism didn't win votes.

Truskett took a toothpick from his pocket and snapped it in two, as if he were nervous, causing Laforge to wonder if the senator felt uneasy on account of his relationship with Carolyn or whether he had some other concern he was about to raise, something he was circling.

Truskett looked at the broken toothpick in his palm. "You and I share a belief in this country, Billy. We've talked about this before. We have a way of life other nations—less fortunate than us—would enjoy and profit from. Without fear of contradiction, I'd say we have the best system in the world." Truskett laughed to himself, as if he'd remembered some old, private joke. "When I say patriotic things in public, I admit I sometimes get carried away. And some members of our press think I'm a guts and glory right-wing relic. Typically, they're not telling the whole truth, Billy. If I were to hang a label on myself it wouldn't be Republican or Democrat. That's too simpleminded. I'd call myself a Constitutionalist who believes in freedom of speech and the rights of citizens to live their lives without undue hindrance from the state. I think we spend too much on our military. I don't believe in gun control. I don't believe in cutting Social Security. I think abortion is a woman's private business. I think homelessness is the government's problem. What does that make me, Billy? The way I see it, the answer's simple. It makes me an American."

Laforge wondered where the senator was leading. Was Byron simply yielding to some confessional impulse, knowing he was secure and could sound off as he liked, freed from the confines of the usual party cant?

"Unhappily, our great nation has a few enemies," Truskett said. "And the role of intelligence, as we both see it—correct me if I'm wrong—is to identify those enemies before they can harm our way of life. Am I correct?"

"Yes," said Laforge.

"And sometimes we have to use covert means to undermine such people before they can injure us."

"Sometimes."

"And sometimes these means are violent."

Laforge said nothing. The word *violent*, as though trapped by heat, seemed to hang in the air obtrusively.

Truskett said, "Violence in the national interest should be done, but never seen."

"No covert operation should ever be seen," Laforge said quietly. This was leading somewhere, and although he wasn't sure of the destination, he didn't like the journey. Tense now, he observed Truskett's face.

In a deliberative manner the senator tapped the surface of the table with his fingertips, then opened his briefcase. He removed from it a sheet of paper, which he spread on the table very carefully. It was typewritten and had been folded a couple of times. Gazing at this creased sheet, Laforge felt the rhythm of his heart alter. Somehow this piece of paper alarmed him even before he knew what it was.

Truskett said, "If I place your candidacy before the President, Billy, and he supports you, your name is then presented to the Senate for nomination hearings. Now, in the course of these hearings, I wouldn't want anything to reflect badly on your leadership capabilities, because that in turn puts me in a shitty light, which would make me a very unhappy sonofabitch."

Reflect badly? Apprehension filled Laforge. He'd felt the same way during Railsback's visit, when the gloomy woods had suggested to him a concealed figure, the avenger's shadow, somebody who moved so lightly that no twig, no blade of grass, cracked or snapped underfoot. He gazed at the beeches. Their very familiarity calmed him. They had the solid look of reliable old friends who loaned you money when you needed it and never pressed you for its return.

"Are you talking about something specific, Senator?"

Truskett smiled. "I don't want to hear anybody saying that you failed to control men under your command, Billy. That's exactly the kind of thing that isn't going to do you or me any damn good at all. You understand me."

Laforge asked, "Can you be more direct?"

Truskett did not skip a beat. "Eugene Costain."

Costain. Of course. What else? Laforge felt the movement of a ghost, a presence as clammy as the aftermath of tropical rain. Was it never going to go away? He looked up at the house, *his* house, as if it were under siege by forces he couldn't see. "I remember Gene very well," he said. "I was sorry to hear of his death."

Truskett picked up the paper and looked at it. "Costain was part of a team under your direction that was sent to the Philippines during the last few months of the Marcos regime, with the brief of improving the Marcos intelligence network. Am I right?"

"That was the brief, yes."

"Specifically, Marcos wanted all the information he could get on Communist organizations. Their strengths. Weaknesses. Locations. Correct?"

"You're correct, Senator."

"I've received information from a source I can't name that Eugene Costain, in association with the Philippines Constabulary, participated in an assault against Filipinos suspected of Communist affiliations. Worse, that this attack was unjustified and carried out against unarmed civilians with no Communist connections. Is that correct?"

Laforge shook his head fiercely. "Certainly not! Costain's work was to instruct certain members of the intelligence wing of the constabulary and the armed forces in information-gathering techniques. Infiltration. Night photography. Telephone taps. Methods of interrogation. He took his orders from me and I would *never* have approved his participation in *anything* of that sort. Quite the opposite. Believe me."

"You're saying my information is false?"

"It's a slander."

"You're assuring me of this?"

"Yes, of course." The blue sky shimmered in Laforge's vision. A small cloud, turned by the sun to the color of a penny, floated high over the trees. *Where had Truskett gotten his story?*

"Why would anyone supply this inaccurate material?" Truskett asked. "Why make this up?"

"If its original source is the Philippines, which I guess, it was done to discredit the U.S. Why else?"

Truskett was quiet for a very long time. He stroked the sides of his face in a pensive way. Laforge pictured him caressing Carolyn's flesh in just that manner.

"All I want is your assurance that it's completely untrue, Billy. If this Costain business comes up in the course of your nomination hearings, you have to be so convincing that you'll have senators on their knees begging your forgiveness. On the other hand, if this affair has any truth to it you can kiss off your chances of becoming the head honcho at Langley and spend the rest of your life breeding quarterhorses and playing gentleman farmer."

"The story's false. You have my word, Senator." How easy

it was to say such a thing, to re-create yourself and eliminate history. But it wasn't easy to get beyond the words to a reality that substantiated them, because your life was a series of mildewed rooms through which the restless dead moved, damning you. He looked across the meadow toward the birch, beyond which the depleted creek ran, as if his beloved landscape might yield a means of exorcism, a clue to salvation. But it remained dry as kindling and silent as an empty well.

Carolyn appeared in the doorway of the house, a slim gold vision. She wore a full-length dress of some flimsy material through which could be seen the outline of her body. She walked in the direction of the picnic table as though sunlight had bestowed upon her a certain earthy divinity. The senator, troubled by the information Deets had given him about Costain—where in God's name had Deets dug up this sleaze anyhow?—had been pondering all the way from Washington the wisdom of placing Laforge's name in front of the President. Mud, no matter how thin, had a way of sticking. But the appearance of Carolyn Laforge erased his uncertainty and uplifted his spirits: There was magic in Bucks County, a sorcery whose spell once again bewitched all sense out of him. He imagined her in his bed, the searing of flesh, the flash of that electric connection.

Besides, when you got right down to it, he had an instinct about William Laforge, whom he considered too much of a gentleman to fob anyone off with some barefaced lie. He believed the man. He believed Billy would stand up to the probe of any senatorial proctologist. He was not someone who'd yield to pressure, that was apparent. He had dignity, reserves of strength, and the kind of obvious breeding that Truskett both admired and envied.

Looking at Laforge with the intensity of a man introducing a new bill, he said, "I accept your word, Billy. Tomorrow, I'll put your name and my recommendation before the President."

Laforge felt enormous relief, as if some earthquake had passed by in the next county, creating all manner of havoc but skipping his property altogether. Both men shook hands as Carolyn reached the table.

"Have I missed anything?" she asked.

She sat down and sun shone through the thin chiffon dress and Truskett realized, as she lowered herself and parted her legs, that she wore skimpy panties under the garment. The shadowy outline of her pubic hair was unmistakable. She sat very close to him. The urge to slide his palm under the dress was so intense he became erect. He turned to Billy and wondered if he'd noticed this lustful interest, but Laforge was looking idly elsewhere. Why couldn't Billy take a walk or something? Why couldn't he just fucking *vanish?*

Carolyn glanced deftly at Truskett's groin, then smiled and said, "I have the strongest feeling that I am missing something of huge importance."

By early evening Los Angeles was smogbound. You had to learn how to breathe the metallic stuff, Charlie Galloway thought, because it was the air of the future. Only those without vision covered their faces with scarves or handkerchiefs. Men such as himself, like astronauts brazenly tossing aside their masks on the moon, sucked the scum in anyway, and be damned. He wondered if all this powdered lead had hallucinogenic properties of a cumulative nature. Even now, say, was it lodged secretly in corners of human lungs, rooted like some silent tenant quietly growing, soon to flow from lung to heart and then along the brain freeway to cause madness and wreckage? It explained some things, he thought. Such as the general lunacy of the Californian condition. The freeway snipers, the irascible armed drivers who shot fellow travelers for trivial reasons, the serial killers who loved to leave clues for the cops, as if reality were a television show about to be canceled and needing a boost in the ratings. It was that kind of world here. Things simply did not connect, unless you believed in some underlying disorder, a common malaise as yet undetected. And the leaden air, which gripped the vast city like a mailed fist, was as good an explanation as any for Charlie Galloway.

Even his own musings, Charlie thought, might themselves be the product of the poisons already coursing through his brain. How could you tell? How could you check your idea of reality against reality itself? He parked his car and thought *Ah, fuck it*, as he stepped out in the street where Ella Nazarena had lived. The thoughts weren't worth pursuing. When you had no car radio to listen to, you tended to scan your own internal channels, and some of them were call-in shows where all the callers were mad and the man behind the microphone deranged.

He stepped from the car, locked it. This neighborhood by daylight looked worse than at night, if such a thing were possible. Details concealed by dark were evident. Cracked cinder block and broken roofs. Windows, smashed so often that apathy had replaced any need for glass, were hung with brown paper grocery bags. Fenced yards where old men, mainly of foreign origin—Central America, Eastern Europe, Asia—sat on plastic lawn chairs and pretended with an air of defeat that they were somewhere else. Here and there a drug deal was transacted on a porch or the sidewalk in full view. Not that anyone cared. In this place you either dreamed as the old men did or flew away on the wings of your drug of choice: Crack, Ice, Ecstasy.

The dogs were absent. They would come out, Charlie supposed, only after dark. As he stepped toward Ella's house he was assailed by music from all directions—polkas, Mexican folk songs, salsa, punk rock. He stopped at Ella's fence. The police had hung a length of wide orange tape, most of which had already been scribbled on with the cryptic names of gangs and symbols Galloway couldn't begin to understand. He felt a strangeness here, alienation, a suspicion that cults proliferated, forms of voodoo and ancient amalgams of Catholicism and African gods, *santeria,* all of it commingled with the drug underground, that dark subculture of needles and pipes, passwords and violence. It was as if a very old God and a younger, much more hip Devil had come to an understanding in this neighborhood, a kind of delicate, cracked-glass truce.

Charlie stepped over the tape, walked up on the porch, entered the house. Lieutenant Duffy was in the living room, skimming the pages of Ella's Bible as if he expected to find a stash of dollar bills. The bottle of Gallo wine, still unopened, lay on the floor.

"Charlie Galloway," said Duffy, lighting a cigarette from the butt of a former one. "Better late than never."

"I got your message," Galloway said. *See me at the Nazarena house asap,* was what Duffy had said into the answering machine, his tone that of some minor emperor. Resentful, Charlie hadn't hurried. He'd eaten a late lunch in Barney's Beanery, browsed through Tower Records with the notion of buying Karen a gift of her favorite piece of music, a recording of Prokofiev's Seventh Piano Sonata. It was a cacophony to his ears, but its dark thunder made Karen swoon.

"Turned anything up yet, Duffy?"

Duffy said, "I had four homicides last night. This one doesn't take priority. You know the score. I don't have the manpower. Yadda yadda yadda. It's an old song."

"So," Galloway said. "If nothing new's happening, why did you ask me down here? I've got better things to do with my time, Duffy. I've got trees to trim. Dry earth to water. Sick wee flowers are dying even as we stand here and gab."

"Always the joker," Duffy said. "Always the office wag, huh, Galloway?"

"I like a smile now and then," Galloway said, oppressed by the way this house echoed with violence. He wanted out. The plainness of Ella's life, reflected in the religious icons and artifacts and Goodwill furniture, created a tight sensation at the back of his throat. "It brightens the day."

"Allow me to darken yours a little," said Duffy, looking grim. "Two hours ago I had occasion to interview one Freddie Joaquin, the dead broad's fiancé. Routine stuff. My men had already talked to him, and I was checking up on a couple of facts. Now, Freddie happens to tell me you've been on his case, Galloway, which comes as a bit of a surprise to me, to say the least. You're suspended! You don't even have *a fucking job*! Paffett's pissed off and I'm pissed off. You don't have any rights! You don't have any powers! Your juice is cut off, hotshot."

Powers, thought Charlie. Powers were what comic-book characters had. Plastic Man wrapped himself like a giant condom around buildings and Superman could fly, for Christ's sake. Duffy made it sound as if Charlie had run into a stray piece of kryptonite, or whatever it was that made the Man of Steel a wimp. A current of anger went through him and he clenched his fists in the pockets of his pants; he knew Duffy was correct and he felt diminished by his uselessness. *Worthless dreamer, Charlie. What did you think you could achieve?* With this bleak sensation came a familiar urge, a trumpet blast he'd heard many times before. He wondered where the nearest bar was situated. *Go there forthwith. Travel the galaxies. Check out the stars.* A great wheel of flint seemed to turn inside his head, grinding against the roof of the skull, throwing off sparks and small chips of bone. He felt faint. The word *seizure* lit up in his mind like three-hundred-watt bulbs. Were these withdrawal symptoms? Could he expect hallucinations, cold sweats, dread, the big brass band playing the music of doom inside the echo chambers of his eardrums? Swooning, dimming out, heart failure, a one-way raft trip across the Styx. *Measure me, Mr. Undertaker, see that my wood suit fits.* Give me an ungodly drunken sendoff, the mourners reeking of Tennant's and some fine old malt, a twenty-five-year-old Macallan or a sacred Dallas Dhu, the bottle covered in stour and webs. Give me a paid piper playing that most lachrymose of all Scottish tunes:

Bonnie Charlie's noo awa,
Safely ower the friendly main,
Many a heart will break in twa,
Should he no' come back again.

He gazed at the place where Ella Nazarena had lain. The cheap carpet was bloodstained. Christ, the violence of her death kept him earthbound, anchored him to this whole reality business that he'd taken such pains to avoid in the past. He knew his eyes were about to become embarrassingly moist and he turned his face away because the last thing he wanted was to hear Duffy scoff or come out with a snide remark, because Charlie was sure he'd deck the prat if he said something mindless, which was likely, given the cop's stupidity and insensitivity.

Galloway walked to the door. As if some emotion were locked in his chest without possibility of release, he felt padlocked, tethered to a life he wanted to change. And yet he was being denied the chance by people like Duffy and Leonard Paffett. Frustrated, he stepped onto the porch and slammed the screen door behind him.

Duffy, lighting a fresh cigarette, followed him out. "It also seems there's been some bureaucratic oversight, Galloway. You returned your gun, for which we're all enormously fucking grateful and relieved, but somebody forgot to ask you for your badge back. I'm authorized to do so now."

"I left it at home."

"Mind if I don't believe you?"

"Are you saying you want to frisk me, Duffy?"

"In a word."

Galloway clenched his hands, crossing his arms against his chest. He felt the raw need to do violence to Duffy. He was a mere pulse beat away from it. It would only require Duffy to touch him. Just once. The lieutenant, who clearly didn't like the wild look in Galloway's eye, had had some unhappy experiences dealing with enraged persons. He spread his hands and shrugged, backing off and looking very uneasy.

"Drop the goddam thing off downtown toot sweet. Paffett's orders. And stay the hell away from this. Also Paffett's orders. Am I getting through to you?"

"I hear you." He liked the way Duffy had retreated. It raised his spirits to know you could still menace somebody with a good hard-man Glasgow look—even if it was only a coward and bully like Duffy.

"You get up my nose, Galloway," Duffy said, by way of cutting the losses in his self-respect. "You're a royal fuck-up."

Duffy's words stung. They should have floated overhead, leaving Charlie untouched, but they didn't. He wasn't immune to cruelty. He wanted to come back with a stinger of his own, but he drew a blank. He looked up at the sun, which, obscured by smog, was a fierce disc, and strangely milky, as if it were about to metamorphose into the moon.

As Galloway stepped down from the porch and walked toward his car, he realized he had been sober for almost a day. Was that all? Maybe it was worth celebrating. Did you toast twenty-four hours of sobriety with a brimming glass? *Think it over.* There had to be a system of rewards because stone-cold, graveyard sobriety hadn't been particularly attractive in itself, nor did it fill that indefinable part of him which was astonishingly empty. Where was the triumph in not drinking?

He thought of Karen and wondered what the consequences of calling her might be. Would she consent to see him, hold his hand, smooth away the wrinkles of their combined solitudes? Or would she be distant, her tone like that of an icicle with a voice box?

He wasn't going to chance it. He was in no mood for rejection. *Drinkies, Charlie. The cocktail hour doth descend. Booze would jumpstart your stalled soul.*

He took his keys from his pocket and was reaching for the door lock when somebody poked him in the spine with a hard object. Turning quickly, expecting to see a mugger with a gun, he found himself instead staring at the tip of a walking stick wielded by a person in a World War II gas mask, an odd affair with a long proboscis and bug eyes. For a moment he had no idea whether his assailant was male or female; it wore lime-green polyester pants and a floppy sky-blue shirt and, outside the gas mask, an eyeshade such as card dealers sport. Even when a hoarse, aged voice emerged from behind all this cover, it was hard to reach a conclusion as to the person's gender.

"Wotcher." The accent was English, probably London's East End. "This here's a souvenir. Keeps the bloody smog out yer chest." A spindly hand rose from polyester folds and tapped the gas mask. "From the Blitz, sonny. Before yer time."

Galloway, no longer amazed by the human shells the tides of America had tossed ashore, wondered what diverse pathways had brought this eccentric all the way from Shoreditch or Stepney to the cancerous armpit of Los Angeles. The circuitry of other lives seemed at times as random as rogue cells or signals received from immeasurable stretches of space.

"You Ella's chum?" the person asked. "The Scotchman?"

"That's right," said Galloway. "I'm the Scotsman." He stared at the mask, possessed by the feeling he was having a chat with some creature as yet unclassified by zoologists. The walking stick was raised and pressed very gently into his stomach.

"Then you're Galloway."

"That's me."

"The one what drinks."

"The one what drinks, right."

"Listen, sonny. Me and Ella were close. What we didn't know about each other wasn't worth knowing. We was like sisters. She mentioned she had a china from the old country." The masked person stepped closer and the proboscis swayed like the trunk of a small elephant. "Name's Thompson. Evelyn Thompson. Been here for sixty years. Used to be in the motion pictures. Before the talkies ruined the whole bloody thing for me. Couldn't get rid of me accent, know what I mean? Had la-di-bloody-da elocution lessons, speech therapy, dialogue coaches, the lot. You name it, didn't make a blind bit of difference. Can't make a silk purse, dearie. Wasn't no whatchermacaller. Liza Doolittle."

Galloway was still wondering about the location of the nearest tavern. Beer frothed in his head, a cold one, frosted glass. The old woman, determined to detain him, offered him a hand, a brittle white shell he took politely.

"Ella was ever such a dear," the woman said.

"I know."

"They're lovely people, them Filipinos. They got their faults, course. Well, who hasn't, right?" Evelyn Thompson sniffed. "Watcher got to do, Galloway, is catch the effin killer. Catch the sod and give him the bleedin' chair."

"It's a job for the local police," he said, a little shamed by the feebleness of his response.

"What the hell are you then? The bleedin' fire brigade?"

"I told you—"

"My arse," Evelyn Thompson said. "Get up off yer duff and pull that bloody killer in for some hard questions, dearie."

"I will, I promise," said Galloway, and he felt infinitely weary, as if he'd been born with a secondhand soul that had already done too much mileage under its first owner. "As soon as I know who's responsible."

"Oh, I can tell you that, love," Evelyn Thompson said in her muffled voice. "I can name Ella's killer before you can sing 'Lloyd George Knew My Father.' "

10

The girl's name was Lizzie Honculada. Barefoot, she drove Teng in a yellow VW convertible to a house in a quiet back street no more than a mile from the palisades. She said nothing on the way, as if she were involved in Teng's business reluctantly; the less she spoke the more distance she'd maintain. He glanced once or twice at her, thinking how her dark forceful eyes made her attractive. Released from the rubber band, her straight black hair flowed over her shoulders. Her brown calves were slender and firm. He assumed she was a second generation immigrant, perhaps even third. She drove with a confidence that came from belonging completely in one's environment. *An American.*

He envied her this facility. Increasingly he was losing touch with himself, confused by unfamiliar streets and signs and architecture, even by the scents in the air. He had no perception of how one street related to the next, one boulevard to another. He'd lost north and south; the planet might have tilted on its axis. This very strangeness made him ill at ease. He was also unhappy having to depend on people he didn't know, like Joaquin and this Lizzie Honculada. He needed sleep now, he realized that. But when was he going to get the chance? Was he to be passed continually from one person to the next, trapped in the blueprint of Baltazar's connections? He should have made his own arrangements, but how could he? Joe Baltazar, who had spent five years of his life in the United States as an illegal alien, was the one with all the associations in this country.

He shut his eyes, drifted, dreaming for a moment he was in Manila and riding in dense, oily traffic along the smoky Epifanio de los Santos, EDSA, the street of the so-called People's Revolution, Cory Aquino leading the masses in her yellow dress—yellow and bright, the color of eventual disappointment—but then he was jolted back into awareness when the girl stopped the car outside a large white house surrounded by palm trees. It reminded him of the great houses in Forbes Park, except there were no uniformed gunmen standing guard to protect the wealthy, nothing save a small sign advertising an electronic security system.

"Our stop," she said.

He followed her through an arched metal gate and across a courtyard which, though leafy and shaded, was insufferably hot. She opened a mahogany door, each panel of which depicted the martyred face of a saint cut by Filipino woodcarvers. Inside a vaulted white room where light was filtered by stained-glass windows, the girl led Teng down into a sunken sitting room. The paintings on the walls were the works of Filipino artists, primitive seascapes, fishing villages; on shelves stood religious relics, antiques carved from wood that had darkened centuries ago.

"Sit down if you like," said the girl.

Teng did so. What happened next? What role did the girl play in this business? She walked to the fireplace and sat crosslegged on a rug created in the brightly striped Bontoc fashion of Northern Luzon. She was gazing at him with what he considered impolite curiosity. There was an independent quality to her. She didn't give a damn what other people thought of her, Teng included.

"Welcome to my home," said a voice from behind Teng, who turned round in his chair to see a middle-aged man in white linen slacks and an expensive *polo barong* made from very fine *piña*, exquisitely stitched. The man introduced himself as James Honculada and held out his hand for Teng to shake.

"Can I have Lizzie make you a drink?" He gestured toward the girl, who didn't look happy at the idea of playing maid.

Teng, wondering if they were father and daughter or husband and wife, declined.

Honculada sat on the arm of a sofa. "At least tell me you're hungry."

Teng said he wasn't. Unable to hide his disappointment, Honculada remarked that he'd prepared a number of native dishes: *tinola, utak-utak, taberac* as a dessert. Since it was bad etiquette to refuse hospitality, Teng fought a wave of fatigue that rolled across him and amiably agreed to eat. The girl, with some slight reluctance, went out of the room to fetch the food.

"How was Joe Baltazar when you last saw him?" Honculada asked. His English had hardly any trace of an accent.

"He was fine. He'd had some minor eye surgery, but apart from that . . ." Teng set aside his impatience for the sake of this small talk, but his mind was elsewhere. What was planned for him? When was he supposed to fulfill his task? After Joaquin, was Honculada the one who'd point the way? Or was he merely another brick in Baltazar's architecture?

Honculada whispered, "My daughter doesn't know why you've come here. So far as she's concerned, you're somebody on vacation, a friend of a friend. You're passing through and we're being helpful because you're from my old *barangay*. The less she knows, the better for her."

Teng, wondering if Honculada, like Freddie Joaquin, knew Cruz was an assumed name, signaled his understanding just as the girl returned with a tray, which she set on a smoked-glass coffee table. Teng spooned a small portion of the fish soup, *tinola*, and picked at the peppery *utak-utak*. He hardly touched dessert. His hosts joined him, but only the man appeared to have an appetite. The girl pushed the food around, as if it disgusted her. After eating, Honculada lit a cigarette.

"Food from the old country is always a pleasure," he said. "Here it's hamburgers. Barbecued steaks. Fried chicken. Everything's American, including my daughter, who was born in Los Angeles and is very proud of the fact. She went to Manila about five years ago when she was fifteen. Two hours later she wanted to come home. Hated it."

"It's the pits," the girl remarked. She made an ugly face, shuddering as she did so, as if she were remembering a horror movie that had scared her as a child.

Teng despised the girl's gesture, which implied a lack of sensitivity, a failure to understand the plight of the Philippines. But she was American, and as far as Teng was concerned all the Americans he'd met were self-absorbed. They had no curiosity about what lay beyond their own boundaries except as tourists, isolated from reality in buses and taxicabs and expensive hotels. They strutted the globe, driven by a lust to accumulate the indigenous artifacts of the third-world poor that became conversation pieces, dinner party fodder. *Sweetie, the filthy little shop where we bought that adorable statue, you wouldn't believe! There was meat covered with flies in a window and cow dung everywhere. The way some people live.*

In Manila and Baguio Teng had seen Americans glide past like absentee landlords running a disapproving eye over how their property had been mismanaged. Or you saw old GIs in Bataan and Corregidor, half drunk and embarrassingly sentimental, filled with self-delusion about their brave stand against the Japanese in the name of liberty—liberty for themselves, as it turned out, not for their Filipino allies who had made incalculable sacrifices in that same war. How many Americans realized that Manila, next to Warsaw, was the city most destroyed in the Second World War? For that matter, how many knew where the Philippines were located? It was said of President McKinley, after the Americans "liberated" the country from the Spanish in 1898, that he had no idea where the islands were situated. Nothing, it seemed to Teng, had changed in that attitude since.

He smiled politely at Lizzie and said, "Manila's a poor city in a poor country. What can you expect?"

"For starters, electricity that doesn't keep going out. Clean rivers. Streetlights. Pollution control. No beggars. No child whores."

"And better shopping malls?" Teng asked. "Bigger discos?"

"I hate being patronized."

"I'm only trying to point out that your expectations are

colored by your own experiences," Teng said quietly. "You can't go to the Philippines and expect to find America. Excuse me for saying so, but it's naive and unrealistic."

"They try hard enough to be Americans over there," Lizzie said defensively. She was clearly unaccustomed to men arguing with her. "They copy our music, our dances, our clothes, our whole style."

"Which you export with the same impressive vigor that accompanies all your enterprises," Teng replied, a small barbed note in his voice. The girl's superficiality irritated but did not surprise him. His impression was that Lizzie Honculada's entire society was constructed on the basis of image, a country whose political leaders took as their only guide to international policy neither truth nor reason but narcissism.

James Honculada said, "America has been kind to us. Look at this house. I worked hard in real estate, sure, but the opportunity was here to take. Under Marcos I had nothing, including hope. When I saw the direction his regime was taking I had no choice except to flee. So who can blame Lizzie for thinking the U.S. is the only place on God's planet? She wouldn't dream of living anywhere else. She's a true blue patriot."

"Does Mr. Cruz see anything wrong with that?" Lizzie asked.

Teng said, "Absolutely nothing. All good Americans believe in justice and liberty, don't they? The eternal virtues."

Lizzie smiled at him with dazzling insincerity. "You can't say anything without mocking, can you?"

"Was I doing that?" Teng looked at one of the stained-glass panels. Sunlight, rearranged in red and yellow abstracts, slid softly into the room.

"That's how it sounded to me," the girl said.

"Then I apologize."

Lizzie Honculada looked unconvinced. "I don't know if I accept your apology, Mr. Cruz. It doesn't have the right ring to it. In this country we expect an apology to have a certain *tone.*"

"Then allow me to be sorry in my own language," he answered. *"Dinarandam ko.* There. Is that the tone of remorse you desire?"

"You're a hell of an actor, I must say."

Teng inclined his head, an acknowledgment of her sarcasm. He fell silent. He didn't have the energy to goad or be goaded.

He observed the girl for a time, thinking how many times he'd seen faces similar to hers on the streets of Manila or Quezon City or Cebu, the same color of skin, eyes of precisely that shape, hair just as black. The similarities were all superficial. Lizzie Honculada was the product of the USA, a country that reduced a person to bland unquestioning chauvinism. He'd seen it in Olongapo and Angeles City on the arrogant faces of the droves of short-haired young men, marines, tattooed sailors, fliers, who drank themselves into a mass stupor and tunelessly roared "Born in the USA" in bars and clubs where they treated every Filipina like a whore and every Filipino like a menial, a steward. It was an attitude obviously drummed into their young skulls at schools. Home of the brave and free, land of the superior. Americans acted like people who had God's telephone number.

Teng looked at James Honculada. Was he any better than his daughter? Even if he did cling to some of the old things, such as the food and the shirt he wore, were they anything more than quaint to him, dead souvenirs of a world he'd left long ago? Teng experienced an inexplicable sadness he attributed to fatigue. He had to get out of this place and return to his hotel and lie down in darkness with his eyes shut.

He looked at Lizzie Honculada and he was struck by the unthinkable: *She resembles Marissa.* He realized with a shock that this was where his sorrow lay, in this tiny resemblance, this almost imperceptible likeness. More than her speech, her American attitudes, her *disdain*, was this the reason she irritated him so much?

He was chilled. He might have been immersed in cold water. His lungs flooded with frost. Momentarily he was unable to draw air into his body. Then the resemblance passed. He'd been mistaken. His myopic heart was always too quick to forge a counterfeit reality. Would it always be this way?

He turned to James Honculada and, thanking him for the food, said he wanted to return to his hotel, that he needed sleep.

"Lizzie will be happy to drive you."

Armando Teng said it wouldn't be necessary, he could take a taxi. The girl rattled her car keys, which were attached to a clear plastic cube in which a dead butterfly was entombed.

"We wouldn't hear of it," Honculada said. He walked with Teng to the front door, where they shook hands. "You need sleep, Raymond. Tomorrow's a busy day."

Teng looked at his host's eyes, the whites of which were slightly yellow from too many cigarettes. His skin, puckered beneath the eyes, had a drawn quality.

"What happens tomorrow?"

"Lizzie escorts you to Dallas."

"Dallas?"

Honculada smiled. "Dallas, Texas."

A certain tension touched Teng. He thought, *The clockwork moves. The cogs turn.* "Why do I need an escort?"

"Because we don't want you to get lost, Raymond."

"Yeah," said Lizzie. "We wouldn't want that to happen."

"I'd take you myself," Honculada remarked. "But I have some urgent business tomorrow in San Francisco, and I can't get out of it."

Teng stared at the girl. He wanted to say that he needed no guide, he could find his way to Dallas on his own, but he didn't speak.

"Take care," Honculada said as he opened the front door. The courtyard was white and stifling. Teng stepped out of the house as if he were passing from one dream to the next. The girl moved behind him, keys rattling. Teng turned to thank Honculada for his hospitality but the big front door was already closed and the faces of the saints were all that stared back at him, inscrutable and, from his angle of vision, stripped of any holy dimension.

"Where's your hotel?" the girl asked. She wore very black sunglasses now.

Teng had a bad moment in which he couldn't remember the name of the place. Then it came back to him, and he told her. She stepped ahead of him, pushed open the arched metal gate. In the light of early evening the yellow Volkswagen was bright in a primordial way, like a color newly discovered.

Inside the car Teng's fingertips collided with the smooth skin of the girl's outer thigh, but she didn't react. He drew his hand away, surprised by the softness of her flesh. *She doesn't look like*

Marissa, not even remotely. But her flesh felt the same to him, matching exactly the texture of Marissa's skin, his memory of which was infallible. He gazed at the butterfly inside the cube, which swayed to the movement of the car as if the creature had been stirred from death and was trying to free itself from the transparent little coffin.

"I'll pick you up tomorrow morning at ten," the girl said. "Be ready."

Teng gazed at a row of storefronts in which could be seen the yellow reflection of the car.

"I don't know what you're all about," Lizzie Honculada added, when she braked at a stop light. "My guess is that you're political in some way because my father, who has more money than sense, is always making donations to causes in the Philippines. He gives money to the nationalists. He gives to the churches. The poor. He gives to various political campaigns. Sometimes he helps people who turn up on our doorstep, like yourself. Except you didn't exactly turn up, did you? There was some cloak and dagger about you."

She looked sideways at him. "The bottom line is I really don't want to know why you're here. I do my father a favor, I take you to Dallas, and that's the end of it as far as I'm concerned. Clear?"

"Clear," said Teng.

Lizzie Honculada didn't speak again until she reached the parking lot of the Palms Hotel. She pushed her sunglasses up on to her head.

"Ten sharp."

Teng stepped out of the car. "Ten sharp," he said. He walked away.

"Hey, Cruz," she called after him.

He stopped, turned around.

"Learn to hang loose. You're in California now." She dropped her sunglasses back in place, laughing as she spun the little car in a tight circle.

After dark Charlie Galloway parked his Toyota behind a thirty-story apartment building overlooking a section of the San Diego Freeway near Torrance. A late 1950s building of obscene ugliness, its boxlike balconies had all been painted a different color, yellows, oranges, lime greens, sky blues. Seen from a distance, the block imposed a sense of apprehension because it suggested some form of psychiatric test, an evaluation in which you, the subject, were meant to respond to a random display of colored cards, on which basis your personality was evaluated by persons in white coats.

From a mile away, the place had made Charlie Galloway morose. He would have chosen sky blue. What did that make him? An incurable melancholic? A soft-hearted romantic? A fool to be dabbling in any of this? When he stepped from the Toyota he skipped around the swimming pool—a cracked affair of chlorinated water ringed by pale, globed lamps and deck chairs in which sat two or three red-skinned middle-aged women who eyeballed him with the lackadaisical interest of the bored—and headed for the main doorway, glass, also cracked, made safe by silvery duct tape in the shape of a St. Andrew's cross.

He walked to the elevators. He pressed a button and was conveyed sluggishly upward. He stepped out on the twenty-seventh floor, where many of the wall lights lacked bulbs and those that emitted illumination did so only sparingly, creating a Gothic effect, a corridor in a house of the damned or a lobby leading to the schizophrenic wing.

Apartment 2724 had an imitation-wood number plate fixed to the door. Charlie Galloway tried the handle. Locked as expected. Unless a deadbolt was in place, or a safety chain, he could easily fiddle the Yale and gain entrance to the flat. It was old stuff, cop stuff, and he'd done it a hundred times before in an incarnation more pleasing to him than his present one.

The trick was speed and silence and, that rarity for him, a steady hand. *Think of this, Charlie, as delicate neurological surgery. Think of this lock as Einstein's brain.* He slipped from his wallet a hatpin he'd bought at a junk shop an hour ago. A savage little instrument made of bright steel, it had a small plastic blueberry as a decoration at one end. Inserting the point into the lock, he held the blueberry between thumb and index finger and poked, then twisted, feeling the tip of the pin tangle with the locking mechanism. It was an ancient Yale, and perhaps had been forced before and never properly repaired, because it yielded with unexpected ease. Charlie nudged the door open about a half inch, seeing a darkened room beyond.

He entered the apartment, quietly closing the door at his back. The room in which he stood contained a sofa and a coffee table, on which lay an aluminum tray with the remains of a TV dinner, one dehydrated meatball that suggested a mule's ballock, and two small carrot wheels. He made his way around the sofa, drawn to a door on his left. Pale light emerged from the room beyond.

A woman's whispered voice said something Galloway couldn't quite catch. A man laughed in that intimate way suggestive of impending coitus. Galloway peered into the space between door and jamb. What he saw at first was a fringed lampshade on a bedside table and a plump white hand extinguishing a cigarette in an ashtray. Then yellow hair, a bare white back, well-fleshed shoulders, buttocks that were dimpled with cellulite.

"Slip it in." A man's voice. "Yeah. Oh. Like that."

The woman coughed.

The man said. "You make my balls ache when you cough."

"Poochie's sorry."

Poochie! Galloway, eavesdropper, voyeur, had the distinct sense of reaching the limits of his trespass. At any moment he was going to kick the door wide open. He hesitated. You gathered nerve, hoped for a rush of adrenaline. His forehead was damp from sweat. And yet. How could be intrude on this moment? How could he barge in, an agent of coitus interruptus?

Besides, the man had mounted the woman now. Having rolled over on her back with a grunt, her thick thighs spread to heaven and her fingers drumming her lover's spine, she gazed through half-shut eyes toward the door, where she appeared to see Galloway in the narrow space but didn't react, almost as if she were so far gone into screwing that the presence of a stranger might have been for her some form of sexual hallucination. She was straining through levels of increasing effort for orgasm and maybe she perceived nothing of the external world. Who knows?

It was a sight, Galloway thought, and it froze him. He couldn't take his eyes away. The little brown man aboard Brenda, a weird circus act, Human Fly Scales Impossible Cliffs of Flesh. Saddled, Freddie Joaquin thrust away without finesse but with appreciable abandon, even joy. His clothes, Charlie noticed, were hung neatly over the back of a nearby chair. Even his dark socks were folded, his necktie rolled up.

"Oooh, you fucker, you beauty fucker," the woman said. "You fuck me so good, babe babe babe, sweeeet baby, so good, oh fuck, oh Christ, ride me, Jesus, motherofgod motherof motherof."

Her coming was an event to witness. Charlie Galloway was transfixed. Fascinated, he saw the entire expanse of her white body shake, as if wracked by an internal quake of quantifiable seismic activity. Her veins became rigid in her neck and arms, a purple network of narrow elevated ducts through which her blood pounded and raced. Her jaw hung open and her face was tilted back and she cried out in the impenetrable glossolalia of profound orgasm, muttering words that were not words, but suggested instead the hissing of snakes or indecipherable Aramaic, the language of a religious experience such as one might undergo in the presence of death. Her hands contorted, became claws that raked Freddie's back, and her upraised knees, formerly locked around him, parted and wobbled and plopped flat on either side of the little man, and she sighed the longest sigh Charlie Galloway had ever heard in his life.

And then the woman plummeted back to reality and registered the stranger in the doorway. She shouted, "Hey! You! Asshole! What the hell," and raised her hand, pointing one thick white finger at Charlie Galloway, whose first reaction was the shame of the voyeur, the man caught with his face pressed against the greasy glass window of a private pube show, hands suspiciously tucked in the big pockets of an Aquascutum where he had scissored holes that gave him surreptitious access to his dick. He pushed the door wide, stepped toward the bed. Freddie Joaquin turned his face, simultaneously rolling off Brenda much as a man might dismount an awkward, dizzying fairground ride.

"I'm sorry," Galloway said. "I could have chosen a better time." Master of the understatement, he smiled wanly at the couple in the bed. He had the impression that the room was dominated by bare buttocks, random genitalia. *I came at the wrong time,* he thought. *The only one who did.*

"This is great, this is just fucking terrific," Freddie Joaquin said, and reached for a telephone on the bedside table. "This is what I call illegal. This is gonna interest Duffy."

"Who is this geezer?" Brenda wanted to know.

"He goes around saying he's a cop, but I learned different today. He's unemployed. Suspended. Right, Galloway?" Joaquin, drawing a bedsheet over himself, began to dial a number.

Charlie Galloway had absolutely no intention of letting Duffy learn of Evelyn Thompson's eyewitness account just yet, if indeed ever. Duffy was a twit, or, as they phrased it so cryptically in Glasgow, a *nyaff*. Galloway brought his hand down with no great force on the back of Freddie Joaquin's wrist and the little man dropped the telephone. Brenda lunged at Galloway with a foot. Tangled in the bedsheet, her foot was somewhat impeded, although a blow managed to land in Charlie's groin. It took the wind out of him briefly. He felt a weird implosion; in his testes some small tent had collapsed.

"Sick fuck," Brenda said. "Coming inside the privacy of somebody's bedroom. You do this a lot, mister? You *spy* on people? Go around pretending you're a cop just so's you can watch people make love?"

"What the hell do you want, Galloway?" Joaquin asked. Brenda was kissing his stricken hand like a woman comforting an ailing Chihuahua.

Charlie Galloway had his hands in his pockets, as if to prevent the pain he felt from spreading. The woman had clipped him nicely. Had her blow been uninterrupted he would have been leveled on the floor, eunuchoid. He whistled tunelessly, pretended nonchalance, walked to the window and looked out across the San Diego Freeway. Incessant traffic, almost two unbroken threads of light, flowed north and south. He sucked in some air and gazed down at the lit green water of the rectangular swimming pool. A swimmer kicked up froth and the underwater lights fragmented. Pain, such as Galloway felt then, dissipated all the quicker the less attention you paid it. *Granma Galloway's Household Book of Hints, page twenty-three, chapter heading, Sore Balls and What to Do with Them.*

He turned away from the view. The ache was fading. "Now we've got the violence out of the way, Freddie, let's get down to business. You said you saw Ella Nazarena for the last time the night before she was killed.''

''Sure. We had dinner. Pico Boulevard. Polynesian food. I told you all this.''

''Aye, I remember, and the food was unbearable,'' Galloway said impatiently. ''But here's the rub, Freddie. I've got an eyewitness that can place you at her house *last* night, at the time when she was shot.''

''An eyewitness? What eyewitness?''

Galloway sat on the edge of the bed. *An intimate threesome,* he thought. *Did you hear the one about the Scotsman, the big blond stripper, and the little Filipino?*

''You lied to me, my wee friend. And I'm bloody disappointed in you.'' He studied Freddie's face, trying to imagine him committing murder. But then Galloway couldn't imagine *anyone* killing Ella Nazarena. During his deskbound years, he must have lost touch with that whole world of serious brutality. He'd relegated to some cranny of his memory the darker urges of the creatures in the human zoo.

With emphatic scorn, Joaquin said, ''Listen to the man. He talks to *me* about lying. You're the liar, Galloway. You never said you were suspended. I don't have to answer questions. You don't have no eyewitness.'' Joaquin reached for the telephone with his uninjured hand.

Galloway said, ''Will you never learn,'' and twisted the receiver out of Joaquin's fist. He understood the Filipino's need to put on a manly show for the sake of big Brenda, but enough was enough. Galloway yanked the cord from the wall this time, a decisive gesture that gave him some quiet, transient pleasure. Basically, though, he didn't have the taste for violent displays. You needed to enjoy violence before you became good at it.

''Don't say a word, Freddie. Call your lawyer, you want my advice,'' said Brenda, who was still gently holding Freddie's bruised fingers.

This tenderness, obviously so genuine, reminded Charlie Galloway of how the varieties of love and compassion were infinite, a fact he sometimes forgot. In this rich world of love the most unlikely partners came together in the heart's strange mambo, some briefly, others for a lifetime. He'd always imagined he belonged in the latter category. Now he wasn't so sure. Certainty wasn't his forte these days.

"You don't want to call your lawyer, Freddie. And you don't want to call Duffy just yet. Let's talk, you and I. Man to man. Then we'll see where we are."

Joaquin rose from the bed, draped in a white sheet. "Who's your eyewitness?"

"You know I can't tell you that, Freddie."

"Somebody blind, I bet. Some *loko-loko* person," and here Freddie Joaquin tapped the side of his skull with a finger of derision.

"Call your lawyer, hon," said Brenda, staring fiercely at Galloway.

Freddie Joaquin stared at the woman. "Just keep your face out my business."

"Well, pardon me," she said, sulking.

"I don't need to answer anything this guy asks," Joaquin said. "He's bluffing. You can see that."

Charlie Galloway shrugged. "My eyewitness is prepared to swear in court you entered Ella Nazarena's house on the night of her murder. A court of law, Freddie. Think about that, my wee friend. Let that one sink in. And then if you still want to call Duffy, just plug the phone back in the wall and do it."

"Yeah yeah. You know what? I still think you're bluffing, Galloway."

"That's your prerogative, my man."

Joaquin opened the balcony door and the whine of the freeway entered the room. Pensively, he peered out into the darkness, flicking his cigarette away and watching it create deep red sparks as it fell toward the swimming pool. Then he turned to Galloway and smiled. "It would be your eyewitness's word against mine, Galloway."

"True. But juries take credibility into account, Freddie. My eyewitness has led a law-abiding life. Can you say the same? I don't think so. You've got a dirty wee secret here and there. Who's a jury going to believe? Twelve good folk and true, Freddie. Who are they going to listen to? You? Or my witness?"

The word *jury*, with all its implications of courtrooms and lawyers and immersion in a legal system Freddie had experienced before in his life, jolted the little man. A whole awesome world, defined by great leather law volumes that terrified him, opened out before him. Stern judges, skeptical juries, the confines of courtrooms, harsh interrogations. It was an unpleasant universe of booby traps and telltale witnesses. In a court of law people talked about you like you were absent. And nothing was simple in a court, nothing made any sense. Surrounded by gangs of dark-suited men talking about his fate in a language he didn't understand, he was lost.

And then the slammer—*Cristo!* How could he deal with that again? Barred, slung in a bare ten-by-ten room with some white racist—which was what had happened last time when he'd been locked away in the company of a big hairy man called Warren Schwerm, a member of the Aryan Brotherhood, who hated anything yellow, brown, or black, and had referred to Freddie as "his goddam gookness." *Is his gookness awake yet? Did his goddam gookness have a pleasant night?* A sadist of truly spooky proportions, Schwerm had once tried to carve a swastika in Freddie's chest with a carving knife. *It's a holy symbol,* Schwerm had insisted, *a fucking Christian sign, you pagan gook.* A few times he'd banged Freddie's head off the wall just because he was bored. And Schwerm wasn't the only one with a racial grudge to exercise. He had his Aryan brothers too, all of whom considered cruelty a way of life. These were men who thought Hitler was soft. Freddie was subjected to kickings, petty acts of viciousness, sexual harassment in the shower room, a whole slew of humiliations.

No way was he going back to that. No way. Uh-uh.

"If you want to talk, Freddie, I'm listening," said Galloway, wondering if any jury would *actually* believe his witness or simply consider Evelyn Thompson a senile English eccentric given to lapses of memory. "Remember. It's you against my eyewitness, and I wouldn't bet on you."

Joaquin's instincts told him that Galloway was no bluffer: He held the eyewitness card just like he claimed. But Freddie had a sudden notion that if he played his own hand properly he would face neither jury nor jail, which was why he'd slid the balcony door open in the first place, so that he might have quick access to a potted fern, in the mulch of which lay concealed a Beretta—

not, of course, the gun used on Ella Nazarena, a Colt purchased in the john of a bar in East Los Angeles from a black guy whose specialty was removing serial numbers from weapons. That particular Colt, wiped clean, had been wrapped in aluminum foil and tossed into a dumpster behind a Ralph's supermarket in West Hollywood, whence it would travel to the city dump or some faraway landfill.

The Beretta was handy. It made him feel secure. He had only to stretch a couple of feet. But he didn't reach because it occurred to him that shooting Charlie Galloway without further deliberation was a very wrong move, ill-considered, impulsive. The guy was the Law, suspended or otherwise, and you didn't go around killing cops except as a last resort. Such an act, Freddie was convinced, would bring down the wrath of God on him. He decided on a half-truth because he had a greater affinity with distortion than murder. Lies could be changed. Murder was final.

He turned, faced Galloway. "I never killed her, Galloway. I swear on my life." He crossed himself deftly.

Charlie Galloway sighed. "And you didn't go there last night, right? My eyewitness made a mistake. You can prove you were someplace else. As I recall, you said you were glued to *Wheel of Fortune.*"

Freddie Joaquin shook his head. "Lissen. I admit. I went to see her. I don't deny it. I got nothing to hide. I went to see her."

Brenda interrupted. "You don't have to talk to this foreign geek, hon."

Joaquin glanced at the woman without seeing her. "Only she was dead when I got there, Galloway. I swear. A guy like me, a prison record, we don't call cops. You understand that? I saw she was dead and I got out fast. Put yourself in my place, Galloway."

Galloway leaned against the wall, arms folded. "Bullshit. You killed her."

"Why, huh? Tell me that. Go on. I'm listening."

"Try this one. Let's say there was talk of marriage. Let's say she thought you were going to make her your wife." He paused a second, lingering over this last word, which echoed inside him like a harp string. "But you refused. Maybe you'd fallen out of love. Happens all the time. Nothing is forever. Romance over, violins back in their cases, dance hall empty. Let's say all the roses had withered for Ella. But she insisted. No, Freddie, she says, I still love you. Don't leave me. I'll do anything, she says. There was a bad scene. Violence. You slap her about a bit. Things get out of hand. You shoot her.''

''Sweeeet Jesus,'' Brenda said. ''What is this dickhead saying, Freddie? What romance? Who was this Ella anyway?''

Galloway said, ''There's motive, Freddie. It's plausible. Best of all, it has the squalid ring of truth.''

Joaquin said, ''Make it stick.''

Charlie Galloway smiled. Freddie's hard-assed line lost something when it was delivered by a man in a bedsheet. Outside, the freeway droned like some monotonous background gossip. Flying ants, a partnership of praying mantises, all drawn by light, flapped through the open door and went in search of the bedside lamp. Flustered, Brenda beat them vehemently away with a rolled-up copy of *People* magazine, the swish-swish of which was for a time the only sound inside the room.

Then Galloway said, ''Aw, face it, face it. You're up shit creek, Freddie. It's stacked against you. The time. The motive. They'll turn you into mutton pie in a courtroom. You confess, you might see freedom again in your very old age with the aid of strong bifocals. You stick to your denial, sonny boy, you're going away for the remainder, especially if the best you can afford is an overworked public defender in an off-the-peg suit. You're jail fodder, Freddie.''

Freddie Joaquin felt a weird pressure. Its source appeared to be inside his own head. A stroke? he wondered. A tumor? But it was plain fear, nothing else, an eruption of activity in that part of the brain where dread is manufactured by assembly lines working to a hellish production quota. He considered the Beretta again, but Galloway had moved closer to the balcony door and stood now only a few feet from him. The man's proximity paralyzed Freddie: How could he grab the gun *and* turn *and* fire without Galloway taking steps to protect himself? Was Galloway armed? Too many unknowns.

Freddie sweated. Moisture ran over his scalp, his forehead, collected in his eyelashes, slid down the side of his nose. The bedsheet stuck to him. Panicked, he decided to try another lie. He was buying time now. He was going to have to get the gun.

He couldn't let Charlie Galloway put him away. He wasn't going through all that crap again. A trial, a jail cell, never—especially for something as serious as first-degree murder. In his flustered state of mind he reached for the first plausible perjury that came to him, one with some minor element of truth to it. He had no real talent for embellishment, no gift at the best of times for spellbinding fabrication. And suddenly these were not the best of times. He tossed truths and half-truths together in a careless salad. All he could think of was the Beretta. *It's going to end real bad for somebody anyhow,* he thought, *but it's gonna be Galloway, not me.*

"I'll tell you who did it, Galloway."

Charlie Galloway said, "My antenna's up."

"The guy you saw in my car. Cruz. Cruz did it." Freddie had crossed a river and burned the bridge at his back and now he had to keep going toward an outcome that was inevitable. *Adyos, Galloway. Paálam.* Blame Cruz, take the heat off yourself for a moment. Fucking inspiration! If he'd stuck a completely unknown name in front of Galloway as a candidate, what good would it have done? Galloway would immediately have dismissed it as a wholesale fiction designed to save Freddie's ass. By placing a real person into consideration, Freddie, whose heart thumped in his chest like some trapped rabbit about to become *escalopes du lapin,* hoped to give the lie a tenuous connection to reality. Enough, at least, to distract Galloway for all the time it would take.

Galloway looked incredulous. "Now why the hell would Cruz kill Ella?"

Freddie shut his eyes. He imagined his hand on the Beretta. "Because she knew."

"Knew what?"

"Why he'd come to America."

"And why has he come to America, Freddie?"

Joaquin swallowed very hard. He had to get the gun. No two ways about it now. "The way I hear it, he's gonna kill somebody. Some high-up. I don't know who." He stared at the fern. It had begun to wilt in the heat.

"Fuck a duck," Charlie Galloway remarked. "First you deny you were in Ella's house. Then you say you were, but you didn't kill her. Now you tell me somebody called Cruz did it. Not only that, he's going to kill again. I'm reeling, my wee friend. I hear bagpipes and they're all playing different tunes."

"I'm only telling you what I know," Joaquin said in the manner of a man whose options are all about to expire. *Talk more, Freddie. Keep it rolling. Keep the cop interested. Enthrall him. Then go for the whole goddam thing in one swift move.* There was no way in the world Charlie Galloway could be allowed to walk out of here. *You killed before. You can do it again. Easy. Madali. Madalang.*

"I begged Cruz. Don't do it. Don't kill her. Nice lady, okay, she don't deserve to die. But he went there last night and shot her, because she was gonna talk to you about what she knew. Now he's gonna kill somebody else. I don't know who. I don't belong in any of this, Galloway. I wouldn't kill Ella. Word of God. I liked her. I told you before. I respected her."

And on and on. Freddie was speaking like somebody on a diet of white crosses. Amphetaminic little sentences, spurts, a babbling that made Charlie Galloway wary. His English was becoming careless. He'd fallen into the Filipino habit of confusing his *V*s and *B*s. *Give* became *gib, deserve deserb*. Men who sprayed you with words in unending gibble-gabble like wee Freddie were desperate about something.

Brenda said, "Whack!" and clocked a praying mantis with her rolled-up magazine. Half the bug was splattered to the wall. The other part adhered to the teeth of the person on *People*'s front cover, who happened to be Princess Anne. An odd conjunction, the choppers of English royalty and a battered insect, Galloway thought, then turned back to Freddie, who'd taken a step out onto the balcony during Brenda's massacre of the mantis.

"If I was you, I'd talk to Cruz," Freddie said, and he bent to tend to a bedraggled plant in the corner of the tiny balcony. "This goddam weather's killing everything, heh? Rain. We need rain, Galloway. Nothing grows, heh? Rain, rain. Come again."

Eberything. Joaquin, a lover of plants? Kneeling, looking faintly demented, Freddie turned his face up with a small smile. *It's the smile,* Galloway thought. *Transparent, devious, apprehensive. Whatever's going on, it's in that bloody smile.* Galloway flexed himself for something, anything.

"She's dying," Joaquin said of the fern, and he turned away from Galloway to probe the roots with his fingertips. He sang tunelessly under his breath as he dug. "Rain in Spain valls mainly on the plain . . ."

Galloway experienced one of those rare moments out of time, a kind of high in which you are aware of mortality and infinity at the same time, a second during which what rushes to your head isn't blood but the intense sensation that your demise is imminent. Call it primeval instinct, a leftover reaction from your reptilian origins, the sense, say, of a pterodactyl screaming toward you for a very quick lunch. Call it the warning whisper of that passing angel who is the *padrone* of drunks.

Charlie Galloway *knew.*

The gun came out of the roots and Freddie half rose with the thing in his hand, even as Galloway's leg was already moving through the air, foot aimed at Freddie's face. The contact was agonizing. Galloway felt a cartilaginous creak in the region of his ankle. Freddie Joaquin fired a single reflex shot which pierced the balcony immediately above and then, as the full power of Galloway's foot struck him in the larynx, the little man gasped and slanted backward with such force that the lime-green front of the balcony gave way, torn from its rusted anchorage of bolts and screws.

Freddie plunged out into the night, the white sheet resembling a great wing that might float him safely toward the ground; but then it came free rapidly from his body, flapping, rising upward like a misshapen parachute, while he plummeted down and down, faster, sucked by gravity, a roar of ineffable terror coming from him.

Horrified, Galloway saw him drop, strike the diving board head first, then rise again several feet before tumbling into the center of the pool, where his entrance shattered the surface of water and set the poolside women screaming. Brenda came rushing onto the balcony while Galloway watched the water begin to settle around the disturbance Freddie Joaquin had made.

"Oh Jesus, Jesus," she said over and over. She stared from the broken balcony at the sight of Freddie, diminished by distance, floating facedown. Galloway put out a hand to draw the woman away from the edge of the balcony, but she swiped him across the face and he backed into the room. She stalked him, lashing out again and again, slapping at his upraised hands. Eventually he caught her wrists and held them, while she swayed and shut her eyes and streaks of mascara slid down her plump cheeks to the corners of her lips.

"Jesus, Jesus," she kept saying.

Galloway led her to an armchair, gently made her sit, then covered her with a blanket. She stared at him. He felt more than merely awkward under her unblinking gaze. He might have been a disgusting mutant, something gone awfully wrong in a genetics lab, an amoeba to be incinerated.

"You fucking slimeball," she said.

It would do no good, he realized, to mention the fact that Freddie had pulled a gun on him. Truth was powerless against shock and grief. Silence was all he had.

He stared at the open door. Buckled lime-green metal hung from the balcony. The gun was nowhere to be seen. Perhaps it had gone with Freddie Joaquin and lay even now at the bottom of the pool. An expanse of white suddenly filled the dark beyond the balcony, a spectral thing drifting slowly downward. It took Charlie Galloway a moment before he realized it was Freddie's sheet, which had been caught on the railing, finally floating to earth, a shroud falling from deep space.

11

Under ordinary circumstances Charlie Galloway couldn't quite say what set him off drinking. He always claimed the reasons were so vague and various as to be indefinable, so why bother? Stress, glumness, a twitter of homesickness, even a good glow of well-being—how was he to pin down any single emotion or reaction as the one that launched him into that first drink, an orbit he took to with initial trepidation but whose trajectory, as it rose higher and his own afterburners dropped away, became one of light and glad recklessness? Watch Charlie glow! Observe the cinders! Up, up, and up into that place where the finite became uncharted and strange, and yet always familiar in some way, like seeing a very old photograph of your great-grandfather and recognizing in his ancient face the future architecture of your own.

Usually Charlie knew only that he was a prisoner of his needs, no matter what resolution he'd made. It was plain and simple. Nothing to analyze. Now, though, leaning upon the bar of a small tavern of minimalist pretensions he'd found on La Cienega, all he could think of was Freddie Joaquin falling through space and time to his doom, a memory that pitched him into a depression worth at least one small glass of amber fluid.

He ordered a malt whiskey, set in front of him by a bartender who might have been pumping gasoline, so little respect did he have for the nectar in Charlie Galloway's glass.

"On the rocks?" the barman asked. He was handsome and unworldly, yet another aspiring actor in the ongoing dream that was Los Angeles.

On the rocks, Charlie thought. A sacrilegious notion. He pulled the drink toward himself in a protective manner and the barman drifted elsewhere, muttering lines from Beckett's *Endgame* in preparation for an audition the next day. The play was only community theater in Sherman Oaks, the bartender had explained, but he had to grab whatever straws floated past on the river of fame. Otherwise, where was his identity? Like, he was only a stupid barman if he didn't act, right?

"But I feel too old, and too far, to form new habits."

I'll drink to that, thought Charlie, and raised the glass to his mouth, then set it down again without so much as a taste. The perfume, distilled perfection, bottled wonderment, magnetized him. The genie was roaring to be set free. *Uncork me, Charlie. I won't give you any trouble.*

The bartender, one hand flat on his chest in a thespian gesture, strolled back and forth. *"Then one day, suddenly, it ends, it changes. I don't understand, it dies, or it's me, I don't understand that either."* He paused. "What the hell does that mean?"

Galloway pretended not to have heard the question. He peered inside his glass. He'd never seen liquid so golden and pure as that distilled from the cold clear waters of Speyside by alchemists. Grapes made plump by sun only gave you wine, and what was that but a polite lubricant during a meal? A fine malt was something else, a triumph of nature; its drinkers were disciples, druids. Even the bloody names on the bottles were mystic incantations. Tamdhu. Tullibardine. Lagavulin. Strong Scots names that made Chateau This and Cabernet That decidedly unimpressive, sweet little drinks for dilettantes.

"This play's so negative," the barman said, glancing toward Galloway with an actor's tilt of the head. Everything was posture, every facial movement an eight-by-ten glossy.

Charlie was conscious of a faint ache in his ankle, a muscle wrenched during the encounter with Freddie. He had no heart to be drawn into a conversation with the bartender, so he carried his drink to a plastic cube that passed as a table. He set the glass down. He pulled up a matching plastic chair and sat hunched, staring at the malt as if he were a gargoyle perched for eternity on a roof.

Think before you drink. Good idea. He thought about Freddie in freefall. He thought about good-natured Ella and the bloodied sheet that covered her. He thought about Brenda's tears flowing through her mascara. A catalog of casualties. He lifted the glass toward his mouth, setting in motion a whole series of complex reactions. Should he drink? Could he take just one and then walk away a free man? How would his self-esteem be affected? Would his brain be insulted? *Charlie, Charlie. Could a man not drink without this kind of self-interrogation, for the love of God?*

Still holding the drink halfway to his face, he closed his eyes. He'd waited at Joaquin's apartment for the inevitable arrival of Duffy, who, after questioning him loudly about his *goddam raison d'être*—the French was an odd touch, Galloway thought at the time—had called Paffett to complain about Charlie's *extracurricular activities*, about the *dire consequences* of a suspended cop interfering in a *fucking* homicide case. Duffy had developed a fondness for speaking in italics, almost as if some invisible biographer were present whom he needed to impress. Loose talk was bruited about that Charlie, without provocation, had maybe tossed Joaquin off the balcony, but Kenneth Duffy saw no future in this line of inquiry, despite claims made by the hysterical Brenda, whom Duffy knew had a criminal record that included perjury. As a potential witness she had zero credibility. In any event, she had to be tranquilized. A physician came and shot her with liquid Valium and she flopped facedown on the bed. Charlie Galloway felt very sorry for her.

He opened his eyes. He held the glass against his lips, the rim upon flesh. It was a matter now of centimeters. He looked at the neon clock behind the bar. Midnight. The hour of downfall. He calculated he'd gone without alcohol for approximately twenty-nine hours. Wasn't that roughly an aphid's life-span?

Don't do this, Charlie. For God's sake.

But it's only one little drink.

Two long-legged, yellow-haired girls in fashionable summer rags sat on stools and prompted the barman when he faltered over his lines as he frequently did. Much laughter. An occasional squeal. The barman was in his element, having found an audience, better still, one without a brain and therefore no critical faculties. *What a gas,* Charlie Galloway thought—

—and the malt whiskey slipped over his lips and between his clenched teeth, propelled by a dynamic of its own, as if it were quicksilver now and not Macallan. He placed the suddenly empty glass on the table and stared at it in shock. Somewhere in his chest essence of Spey exploded.

What in God's name had he done?

He locked both hands together, imagining he'd cuffed himself and couldn't move, couldn't signal to the barman for a second. He was paralyzed. Disabled. A man in a wheelchair, victim of some wasting disease. But, lo, he contrived to raise one hand in a feeble gesture—a miracle, really! See how the formerly catatonic can be cured by an act of faith! The small glass was refilled and Highland waters, clearer than God's eye, streamed through Charlie's veins. He was home, though far from dry.

His mind entered its razor-sharp phase. Thoughts came to him without impediment. Such as: He loved his wife more than anything, and when he'd finished his second glass he'd go in search of her. But this was followed quickly by another thought, that he'd failed Karen and himself, and their marriage, by drinking again. A morose moment, filled with the awful pibroch of self-accusation. *Where do you go from here, Charlie Galloway?*

The barman was intoning, *"I say to myself that the earth is extinguished, though I never saw it lit."*

I've seen it lit, Galloway thought. *From very high places, I've watched it burn.* He had a third Macallan in front of him now, compliments of the bartender. Galloway closed his eyes again, seeing once more Freddie Joaquin in graceless, screaming flight. And where did Freddie's death leave him? Did it solve the killing of Ella Nazarena? What did it matter anyhow? That dear woman, his friend and fellow exile, was dead. And if Freddie was the killer, he too was dead.

If.

If, Mrs. O'Grady of the primary school arithmetic class had been fond of saying. *If is a very wee word with a very big meaning, boys and girls.* He hadn't remembered Mrs. O'Grady's narrow, skull-like face in years, her plain brown woolen cardigans and matching tam-o-shanters and her high-bred, West End, Presbyterian voice. Poor thing: Her husband had run away with the strumpet who ran the lady's shoe department in the cooperative near Govan Cross.

If.

How could he know now if Freddie had killed Ella? How could he take the mystery out of that? His quest, which had begun with the notion of repairing his dented spirit and finding Ella's assassin, had apparently ended in impending drunkenness and defeat, the same old withered garden, the same dead roots crushed underfoot, the same dreary dissatisfaction and failure. Redemption, it seemed, was for other people. Charlie Galloway, once a bright boy primed for a decent life, was an ill-fated fungus.

He picked up the glass, looked inside it. He'd guzzled the first two drams so quickly he was already beginning to feel their effects. He swallowed the third, asked for a fourth, cradled it quietly for a time, then shrugged and drank it. The boxcar effect, drink linked to drink, clank clank, the railway of doom.

He slid the empty glass across the satiny plastic surface of the table and watched as one of the adorable young girls slipped down from her stool and, adjusting a skirt that was too short by half a mile, did a heartbreaking strut toward the lady's room, smiling at Charlie with perfectly aligned white Californian teeth. She left in the air a musk that was sea salt and tangerine peel. How beautiful and bright she seemed in motion, as though she were tracked by a series of tiny yellow lights or fireflies.

He stood up. The floor had the feel of a trampoline. He no longer had the capacity of his youth. He walked to the bar, where he set down his empty glass. Did he want another? the barman asked.

Galloway answered aye, one for the road might be in order. And now, inevitably, his voice was funny. His words had the ring of empty beer cans rolling around in the back of a pickup truck.

The barman said, "You sure don't let moss grow under your drinks, sir," and poured a decent measure. Charlie Galloway, smiling politely though his heart was heavy with the weight of his own wretchedness, was aware of the girl coming back to join her friend at the other end of the bar. Both were astonishing beach creatures, sirens blown out of the white surf of the night. They put him in mind of lost youth, inverted hourglasses, a dead self.

Charlie Galloway, formerly romantic, now rusty. Solitude was dread. He was a candidate for a private box number in the Friendship pages of certain magazines. *Wanted: thirty-ish female bored by aqualunging and cross-country skiing. I am a white male, and an avid explorer of the farther horizons of exotic sex.*

Dear Karen, come home to me. I love you. But I am flawed.

He picked up his glass, turned it around in his hand. He concentrated very hard now. He couldn't stay here forever. He had no time to observe girls young enough to be his daughters, nor to involve himself in conversations during which he'd be treated kindly at first, then patronized, then ignored, then ultimately dismissed as a fortyish drunk who'd never heard of Oingo Boingo or The Cramps and thought Bob Dylan the last word in music. He had things to do. Places to go. Salvation yet to seek.

Consider Cruz.

In the book according to Freddie, Cruz was the alleged killer. Cruz, meaning cross. What if Freddie was being truthful? What if Cruz, brown-skinned and so stunningly blue-eyed, was Ella's killer? Charlie could make an inquiry of the man. He owed it to Ella and to himself. After all, how long would it take? The Palms wasn't a long way from here, if indeed Cruz was registered there, which was something he could check by phone. He sniffed the strong perfume of his drink, suddenly remembering Freddie Joaquin's panicky remark concerning Cruz's further murderous intentions. How much truth was there in that? Or had Freddie tossed that one out like a smoke bomb?

With some little difficulty Charlie Galloway walked to where a telephone was situated, got the number of the Palms, then dialed it before he had time to let it slip through the wreckage of his memory like a fish through a bum net. *He's gonna kill some high-up*—wasn't that what Freddie had said? Some high-up. In Freddie's world, what exactly constituted a high-up anyhow? A man with a four-chair barbershop? A bigger car than Freddie's? What?

When the hotel operator answered, she confirmed that Cruz was a registered guest. Galloway hung up, started back toward the bar. The two blond girls and the barman were huddled together, enjoying some quiet joke. Observing this comfortably pleasing moment, this lighthearted scene of Californian youth and beauty through the fine warmth induced by whiskey, Galloway realized something he frequently forgot.

He liked Americans.

He enjoyed them. For the most part they were friendly, open where Europeans were closed, and for that reason more accessible. If he ever suspected their facility, if he ever perceived their quick intimacy as shallow and glib and at times even childlike, then he overlooked the fact in the bloom of this particular moment. He leaned against the bar, bought two Mexican beers for the girls, left a fine tip for the barman and, suffused with sufficient electricity to light a small city, he smiled and stepped out into the darkness. Only when he reached his car and unlocked it and sat behind the wheel did he feel shame and guilt return; and although both reactions were at some remove from him, he knew they would sooner or later gather speed and come rolling toward him like great, barbed tumbleweeds in a storm of dust. So much for possibilities. So much for fresh directions and a new life.

In his small room on the top floor of the Palms, a chilly air-conditioned box, Armando Teng woke when he heard the knock at his door. He turned on the lamp, looked at his wristwatch. Twenty minutes before one A.M. He reached for his shirt and pants.

"Who is it?" he asked.

"Galloway."

Teng said, "Wait, please," and dressed quickly, even as he wondered why an agent of the Los Angeles Police Department should be calling at this time of night. He was very calm. He'd done nothing, he had nothing to hide. He opened the door after he'd buckled his belt, and Galloway stepped inside the room. It was immediately apparent the man had been drinking. His step was uncertain, his eyes unfocused, the smile friendly in a glassy way. He wasn't a dangerous drunk; he had no sense of menace about him, no vibration of violence. But he was having a problem aligning himself with his environment.

He lurched carelessly against the dressing table, spilling a waxen cup that contained the remains of Pepsi and ice. The liquid streamed over the wood surface, across the pages of the room-service menu, then dripped on the floor. Charlie Galloway caught the cup, set it upright a little too late, looking around the room without comment, as if the accident had never happened.

"What can I do for you?" Teng asked. He put only a slight note of irritation in his voice. It was that of a man disturbed out of sleep, though not too angry about the fact. To play the game with a certain detachment, a lack of concern, was the best way. He couldn't afford to show hostility to Galloway. He'd be vigilant but helpful.

Galloway sat on the bed rather heavily. His San Diego Zoo T-shirt hung outside his pants at one side and he stuffed it back in with a quick stab of his hand, like a man holstering a revolver.

"Freddie's dead," he said.

"Dead? How?"

"He had the misfortune to fall from a balcony."

"Was it an accident?"

"He took it into his head to point a gun at me, the silly wee bugger. In the ensuing contretemps, he went over the edge. It was a bloody long fall."

"Why did he point a gun at you?" Teng asked. He detected for the first time an inflection in the agent's speech that wasn't American.

"I suspect he wanted to win an argument," Galloway remarked. "Is there anything here to drink?"

Teng shook his head. "Room service stops at midnight."

Galloway sighed. "That's a bloody bore."

Teng moved to an uncomfortable chair in the corner of the room and waited for Galloway to continue. Had he come here at this hour simply to relay news of Freddie Joaquin's demise? No, there had to be more, and Teng sensed it. He'd wait. He'd say nothing unless it was in response to a question. Why volunteer anything? He observed Galloway closely, surprised by the man's disarray, the chaotic hair, the casual clothing that struck him as undignified. But then he wondered if the appearance might be designed to lull him, to infuse him with a sense of superiority over Galloway and so put him off guard. For that matter, maybe the inebriation was an act too. You had to be wary of traps. He lived constantly with the possibility of exposure and capture, something he felt in the Philippines more than he did here. Nobody was looking for him in Los Angeles. In Manila, though, in that city of rumor and fear, the constabulary by now would surely have a file on him, even if it was only a vague one. What did it matter if he was a long way from the Philippines? He couldn't afford complacency, regardless of his location. He always had to stand guard against the possibility of a slip.

"You don't seem unduly perturbed by the sad news of Freddie's demise," Galloway remarked.

Teng wondered how he was supposed to react. Freddie Joaquin meant nothing to him. How could he feign sorrow without a massive effort he didn't have the energy for? "It's terrible, of course," was the best he could do.

Charlie Galloway sat very still. He appeared to have become fused to the bed. His eyes scanned the room slowly. Teng followed the line of the man's vision, although there wasn't much to see. Some clothing, a *Los Angeles Times*, a passport issued by the Republic of the Philippines on the bedside table, a bottle of aspirin.

"You're the kind of man who keeps his feelings to himself, eh?"

"Not always," said Teng.

"Can we safely say you're not heartbroken, Ray?"

Teng smiled with what he thought was sympathy, but he didn't speak. He wasn't sure he understood Galloway's question, because of the man's accent and the way he ran words together or dropped letters.

Galloway noticed how light from the lamp created little oily slicks from the soda he'd managed to spill. He thought, *Not what you'd call an auspicious entrance, squire.* It might have been worse, it might have been the complete clown routine, waxy cup and soda *and* lamp to boot, the whole shebang upturned, then a trip on the rug and a great somersault across the narrow bed. He was no stranger to acrobatics. He shut his eyes a moment and sought a calm place in his mind, a clearing removed from all the moldering stumps and dried bracken.

"You mind if I use the bog?"

"Bog?" Teng's English was artificially correct, stilted at times, but it didn't run to Scottish slang.

"The wee boy's room." Galloway rose, went inside the bathroom, poured himself a glass of the most appalling water in the Western world. He rinsed, spat in the sink, looked at his face in the mirror. Spooked by his own image, which had the color of an apparition in spirit photography, he pulled the little chain that killed the bathroom light. Limping slightly, he went back to the room, where he sat on the bed and picked up the Filipino passport, whose pages he flicked. *Raymond Cruz.* In the pale red stamp of the U.S. Immigration Service, it was recorded that Raymond Cruz entered the country the day Ella Nazarena died.

"What time did your plane get in?"

"Seven. Seven-thirty. I'm not certain."

Ella had been murdered around ten, which gave Cruz more than enough time to get to her house from LAX. The problem was one of motive. Joaquin had made that off-the-wall claim about how Ella had died because she knew something concerning Cruz. How in God's name had Ella come into possession of the kind of knowledge that would jeopardize her life anyway? She was an unlikely candidate for embroilment in a wild world of hazard and deadly information. Had she become enmeshed in some peculiarly Filipino situation, perhaps a feud, a grudge, something rooted in a culture of which Charlie had no experience? What had Ella been so anxious to relay to him?

All speculation withered inside his head. *I am out of my depth,* he thought. As much a stranger to the circumstances behind Ella's murder as Raymond Cruz must be to the United States. A couple of strangers, Charlie and Ray, just passing in the night, accidental companions in a foreign land.

Galloway got up from the bed. "Were you and Freddie close?"

Teng shook his head. "No. We had mutual acquaintances in our province, that's all. But we didn't know each other well."

Galloway sensed an odd shift he couldn't altogether define, as if the world had slowed a microsecond and he was out of synch.

"As a matter of interest, Ray, where were you around ten o'clock last night?"

"In a motel room fast asleep."

"You remember the name of the place?"

"The Mandalay Motor Lodge. Near the airport."

"You were alone?"

"Yes. Why are you asking these questions?"

"Before he died, Freddie made an accusation against you. Claimed you murdered a certain Ella Nazarena."

"I did what? Murdered who? I've never heard of this person."

"He was adamant."

"But it's crazy."

"Crazy or not, that's what he said."

"I don't understand," Teng said, looking puzzled.

Galloway ran a hand across his dry lips, squeezing his face between thumb on the right, fingers on the left, as if his cheeks were lemons out of which he might wring that one last significant drop that will make a margarita perfect.

"Freddie also said you intended to kill somebody else, Ray."

Teng laughed in surprise. "Then it's obvious Freddie was an inveterate liar, Mr. Galloway."

"Probably." Galloway heard the drums in his head, his private Mau-Mau thirst ceremony. "I take it you *don't* have plans to murder anybody?"

Teng laughed again, a sound of restrained merriment, as if there were a curfew against fun, and he feared breaking it. "You may safely assume that."

"What line of work are you in, Ray?"

"I teach school."

"And you're here to do some sightseeing?"

"Of course. Los Angeles. Hollywood . . . so many things to see."

Galloway thought something was missing, some phantom core he kept circling, only he wasn't sure what. He wished he wasn't drunk, even as he longed to immerse himself in an ocean of booze, where tides and trade winds would carry him to shorelines of wonderful chaos.

"How long are you staying?"

"Until my money runs out."

"And you'll stay right here?"

"It's not expensive."

"I have to know where to find you . . . in case we need to talk again."

"Allow me a question, Mr. Galloway. Do you actually *believe* I had anything to do with killing this woman?"

Saying nothing, Galloway wandered across to the narrow window and looked down into the parking lot. The simplest conclusion was that Freddie Joaquin, in an act of cowardice, had tried to stick the blame for the murder on Cruz, to shove it up somebody else's arse and see if it fit. And it hadn't. The only peculiarity was that Freddie, for some reason, had gone on to make his second claim, evoking the death of what he'd called *some high-up.* Why had he felt compelled to embellish? Why the extravagance? The trouble with liars—they inhabited a world incredibly complicated.

"No," Galloway said eventually. "I think Freddie did it."

"I'm relieved to hear you say so."

Galloway looked at Cruz. Was there in that blue-eyed look something hidden? Something so guarded it was impossible to reach? He had the faint but distinct impression that Cruz was concealing a vital matter, although nothing so straightforward as the murder of Ella Nazarena. Another thing altogether. There were depths to the Filipino, clouded lagoons you couldn't see into, emotions masked by murky puffs of sand disturbed by formless creatures darting across the bottom of the water.

You're drunk, Charlie Galloway.

He moved back across the room. He opened the door, stepped out into the corridor. Cruz watched him expressionlessly. Whatever it was that had slipped Galloway's mind earlier remained mysterious. As he turned toward the elevator, conscious of Cruz closing the door of his room, the puzzle seemed to break loose from his brain and float away, something so trivial it did not deserve space in his head. The elevator plunged him down a shaft into the lobby, where a Japanese night clerk looked at him as if he were an escapee from the Camp on Blood Island.

"Where's the nearest watering hole?" Charlie asked. His T-shirt had come loose again and dangled at his thigh.

The young man, whose thick black hair was oddly cut in a modish style that suggested a hairdresser with a chamberpot, a carving knife, and three pounds of Dippity-Do, shook his head. "Watellinga-hall?"

"Never mind," and Charlie Galloway, who knew a few late spots, hurried out of the lobby, where icy air yielded to the dry gasoline-flavored warmth of the night.

Armando Teng watched Galloway, shirt flapping, cross the parking lot, weaving between motionless cars. Sometimes, like a man trapped in a pinball machine, Galloway appeared to ricochet in the narrow passageways of automobiles, here, there, forward, backward, lurching as he moved. Then Teng lost sight of him in the darker recesses of the lot.

He turned from the window, walked up and down the room, wondered at the desperation that had induced Freddie Joaquin to blame him for the murder of the Filipina. Had he been cornered, trapped, obliged to utter the first nonsense that had come to his mind? More an act of mindless despair than one of treachery? Had this same desperation led him to that other revelation—that Cruz had come to the United States to commit murder?

Teng roamed back and forth. He paused near the bed, laid his forehead against the wall, and stood motionless. Joaquin had known nothing, hadn't been in a position to tell Galloway anything specific; therefore, what point was there in worrying? Confronted by Galloway, Freddie—a man with little inner strength—had simply lost control. There was no more to it than that. Everyone had a point where they snapped. Freddie had reached his.

Teng lay down on the bed. He'd reasoned it out and perceived no personal danger to himself nor to his task: Galloway could establish no relationship between himself and the dead woman, because there hadn't been one. The letter that might have been incriminating lay locked in a safe-deposit box.

He should have been relaxed. Why wasn't he?

The strain of the task in front of him, the stress of shutting the past from his mind, an accumulation sometimes unbearable. He closed his eyes.

He knew it was coming.

It struck him as it sometimes did, out of nowhere. With no apparent connection to anything that had gone before, unless he counted the thin, even imaginary resemblance between Lizzie Honculada and Marissa. It came of its own fiery accord, the monster of memory. It locked his chest, seized his throat. He couldn't breathe, couldn't move. Turbulence beat against his brain.

The field. The stand of trees. The moon in fully ivory flight.

He imagined the noise made by shackles, like so many coins being dropped again and again in the darkness. He imagined Marissa, chained to the others, shackles bruising her flesh. He saw her being pushed forward through the grass. Perhaps the moon vanished then. Perhaps the sky blackened. The stars went out. Certainly the stars went out. He had no doubt of that. He had relived Marissa's death ten thousand times. And ten thousand times the stars had died.

In his reconstruction he did not immediately feel the revolver shot through the mouth that had ended her life. No, he entered the house of his personal demonology the way he always did, by the front door, at the very threshold where two uniformed men of the constabulary first seized Marissa from the streets of Baguio and dragged her to a jeep and, handcuffing her, drove her to an isolated shack where Captain Deduro "interrogated" her about her political alliances. Wasn't she a member of the New People's Army? Wasn't she involved in an assassination plot against their beloved President Marcos? Why didn't she admit it? What good was denial? He had proof, detailed evidence.

He tore off her blouse and applied lit cigarettes to her nipples. When she screamed, when this smart, funny, innocent girl screamed, she was punched in the face by the gallant captain. Half conscious, her teeth and jaw broken, her lips split and bleeding, that lovely face already purple and disfigured by swelling—this punishment was evident from the decomposing horror found weeks after her burial beneath the long grass—she was driven up into the fields beyond La Trinidad, where she was chained to a dozen others who had been rounded up the same night, under the same pretext of belonging to anti-Marcos groups.

Like herself, the rest had already been tortured, burned with cigarettes, or made to lie like human boards between two chairs spread five feet apart for hour after hour, a form of punishment

known as the San Juanico Bridge, and when they slumped or tried
to alter the positions of their aching bodies they were beaten with
rifle butts. One had been slashed repeatedly with knives and
sharpened bamboo sticks, another blinded, yet another had un-
dergone *falangas*, the constant beating on the soles of the feet
with wooden paddles. Another had been given the water treatment, bucket after bucket of water forced into mouth and nostrils
until suffocation was almost reached. And Joe Baltazar, the only
man to escape from the field that night, the only witness to
events, the only one to slip away unseen, uncounted, covered by
darkness, had had a lit candle held to his penis and staples fired
from a staple gun into his testicles.

Teng rebuilt this house of pain over and over. He visited all
its rooms, knew them intimately. He opened doors better left
shut. But how could he resist going back inside? It was his monument to horror, the place where he worshiped, his temple. He
couldn't turn his face away, or weaken.

He stared at the ceiling, unable to contain what he felt. He
covered his face with his hands and wept in a way that an onlooker would have found unusually disturbing, because it was the
deep, dry, silent weeping of a man unaccustomed to tears, a man
who refused to yield to a grief that was his constant companion,
his daily enemy.

He lay across the bed, facedown. When the torrent of an-
guish diminished, he was drained and cold.

Vengeance had an abstract sweetness about it and justice a
way of bringing small satisfaction, but what could ever replace
that part of him ruined by the violent act of irrational men?

What, he wondered, could replace that joy?

12

Clang! The sound of a swaying old Glasgow tramcar woke Charlie Galloway, who opened one dysfunctional eye. He could still see those trams, each with their destinations inscribed on the front. Rouken Glen. Riddrie. Paisley Road Toll. A memory came to him of placing a big old-fashioned penny in a tram's iron track and watching the great green and orange metal ship sail along in the rain, grind the trapped coin, bend it neatly in two and then, with dignity undisturbed, go floating on toward Springburn or Alexandra Parade or the Broomielaw. These were exotic outposts to young Charlie, foreign places as strange as Algiers or Tijuana.

But why did he hear tramcars now? He made a huge effort to focus his one open eye. He had the impression he lay on a sofa, because his cramped physical position suggested it, but he had no exact knowledge of his whereabouts.

Clang! Another tram shoogled past, rattling, faces pressed to steamed windows, the conductor moving up the aisle between the seats, issuing tickets from her little machine.

He tried again to focus. He got both eyes open. The pain that seared his scalp was one broad band from bridge of nose to nape of neck. But he saw enough to understand that he lay on the couch in his own living room, which was a good sign; he'd made it home somehow, although he had absolutely no recollection of anything except his departure from a late-night joint run by obese Greeks who played poker using Dexatrim capsules as chips.

Then darkness. No memory of coming home.

He understood he wasn't alone in the house, that the clanging he'd attributed to tramcars came from the kitchen, where somebody had been filling a kettle, rattling it in the sink, then banging it down angrily on the stove. Charlie sat upright, a grave mistake. His muscles ached, his head was not his own. He was totally dehydrated. His tongue had turned to Velcro. His throat was stuffed with cotton.

Blinking, he looked at the kitchen door. In the name of God, who had he brought home with him? He put a hand to his head and squinted at his wristwatch, the glass face of which had a mysterious new diagonal crack. Seven A.M. Through closed shutters some thin morning sunlight, already menacingly hot, made a sneaking pass.

There were voices from the kitchen. More than one person, or just some loony who mumbled alone? He slumped back against the pillow and sighed. Breakdown. Alcohol at toxic levels in the bloodstream. Amnesia. Muscular pain. A fever akin to malaria. Eyelids of lead. Atonal music playing in the brain. Tremors. Dryness. These things reduced Galloway to something less than human. He hated the small strident voice in his head that said, *You paid for this with your own money, Charlie.* It was the snide, sniping, snippy voice of the school prefect who appeared to have occasional squatter's rights in some pristine corner of Charlie's brain. *Your fault, your fault, yah yah yah.*

He groaned as he tried to get up. The sheet that covered him slipped to the floor. He wore only his boxer shorts, red and green tartan and faintly ridiculous, a silly present from Karen last Christmas. They weren't even a real tartan. Designer "plaid." Clan Bloomingdale. He rose, padded in his socks across the floor, paused in the open kitchen doorway, where he was obliged to lean against the jamb for fear of falling. *Consider it all from the viewpoint of eternity,* he thought. *You're one miserable wee speck in one miserable wee star system among billions, trillions, and your hangover's nothing in the great scheme of things.*

Sure. That helps a lot.

The kitchen was filled with small parachutes of sunlight floating through half-open drapes. The two figures in the room were shadowy and faceless with the windows behind them. Shading his eyes, Charlie Galloway realized the pair were familiar to him, although for a second he was so disoriented he recognized neither Clarence Wylie nor Karen.

He staggered to a chair, clasped his hands on the table, shivered despite the temperature of the room. It was going to be another day of blistering intensity in Los Angeles and across the entire nation, a day of searing meltdown and manic, bug-eyed meteorologists proclaiming record highs. It was a day of unreasonable tides and unpredictable currents, violent undertows in the affairs of men and women.

Charlie Galloway didn't open his eyes at the table. The kettle whistled, a strange uneven sound, like that of a small mouse freaking out on very bad speed. Then it stopped. A cup of hot coffee was placed in front of him and he sensed it as a blind man might. Shame and sunlight conspired against the notion of forcing his eyes open. How could he look at Karen or Clarence Wylie? How could he face them?

"Coffee," Karen said.

He sipped the coffee and tried to reassemble all the shards that would make up last night's ruined mosaic. A slab of buttered toast was thrust before him and he sneaked a look at it, seeing how hot yellow grease oozed down through the pores of the fleshy bread. *Bad close-up, Galloway. The stomach churns.*

"I know you won't remember, so I'll tell you what happened, Charlie," Karen said. "You called me at three A.M. You told me you loved me."

Galloway blinked at her. She seized some toast with her right hand and ate it as she talked. In her left hand she held a bunch of red grapes, a couple of which she popped into her mouth between bites of toast.

"You also told me, in that marvelously eloquent way you have when you're completely trashed, that you were going to drive home," she said. "When I suggested you take a taxi, since you were obviously in no condition to drive, you said you'd run out of money because you lost some kind of bet."

Galloway had a flickering memory, hand-shadows thrown on the dilapidated screen of his brain. He remembered an argument about American football with a man who'd made some spurious claim to Scottish ancestry. Charlie knew nothing about football. To him a tight end was a sphincter condition. Yet last night he'd made a bet, the kind that came from the assurance of alcohol. The wager concerned the name of the team that won the very first Super Bowl. Of course Charlie Galloway knew that one! He was infallible. Going full throttle. He'd put cash on it. Out came the wallet and down went his last twenty. The name of the first team to win the Super Bowl was . . . the Dallas Indians, right? No such team had ever existed. Charlie's twenty swiftly disappeared.

"I took a cab, Charlie, to some godawful place in Burbank, and I drove you back here in the Toyota. I tucked you up less gently than you might have liked. Then I slept upstairs." Karen stuck another grape in her mouth. "You manipulated me, Charlie. I knew what you were doing and I allowed myself to be manipulated anyway. And, as per usual, I rationalized it away like an idiot. I didn't want you to drive. I didn't want you to kill yourself or anybody else. I didn't want you to get arrested. Oh, boy, I know all the self-deceptions."

She put one hand on her hip and looked at him with animosity even as her eyes became moist. "I swore I wasn't going to be your goddam chauffeur ever again. And Christ, there I was, running to bail you out. I want a life of my own, Charlie."

Clarence Wylie, who had no desire to eavesdrop on marital discord, had slipped out of the kitchen during this conversation. From the corner of his eye, Charlie saw him go inside the living room and shut the door. How long had Clarence been in the house? he wondered. Why was he here? Enlisted by Karen?

The sight of Clarence jump-started a quiet turbine in Charlie's brain, and another memory of last night took on a shape of sorts. Something mortifying. Something not to think about. The blood of embarrassment rushed to his face. At some time after the ridiculous football bet he'd consulted his address book and . . . and called Eric Vanderwolf *at his private number!* Surely not! Disturbing the hotshot in his lair just wasn't done! Like many drunks, though, Charlie had a communicative urge mystical in intensity. He experienced overwhelming needs to make telephone calls for reasons too convoluted ever to be reconstructed in sobriety. Seemingly luminous notions occurred to him under the influence. Call this old friend in Yonkers. That forgotten cousin in New Jersey. His former French teacher in Glasgow. An old flame in London. The craving to make connections was a high, a drug, a speed.

And so after midnight, possessed, his mind congregated by demons who wouldn't be silenced, he'd called Vanderwolf. He couldn't remember why; perhaps something to do with a depression passing through him, an insight into his lack of future, of self-esteem, perhaps a highly unlikely wild-eyed notion of salvaging a pride much diminished by unemployment. What did it matter? He'd made the call and the conversation he remembered was a warbled affair, like voices on a distorted tape. *Didn't you once offer me a job, Mr. Vanderwolf? Something about me working for the FBI.*

Who the hell is this? Vanderwolf hadn't sounded like a prospective employer. Sleepy, not a happy man.

Charlie Galloway. Clarence Wylie's best friend. Remember?

Galloway? Oh, yeah. I have a vague recollection. You know what time it is?

What was time to a drunk? Dross, sand. *The thing is, I've been considering your offer during the past few years and I'm getting nowhere in my present position—*

What offer? What the hell are you talking about?

Remembering now, Charlie cringed. A mistake had been made. He'd misinterpreted a situation. Vanderwolf was angry, snappy. The job offer was a figment. But Charlie in his cups was a madman and couldn't stop rolling toward humiliation. *Clarence worked a long time for you, and I've got many of his qualities. You could find a place for me. I'm conscientious. Loyal. Punctual.*

And drunk, Vanderwolf said. *And unemployed.*

Not so, not so, hold on—

I hear things. Word gets around. You're a sot, Galloway. You're a waste of space. Dead air. I never liked you.

Clarence knows me, he can speak glowingly on my behalf—

I'm hanging up.

Well, fuck you.

A wit to boot, said Vanderwolf before the click.

Charlie listened to a wind of shame roar in the cavities of his skull. Why did he do these things? Why did he yield to such absurd promptings? If he wanted to self-destruct he could do it quicker with short-fused dynamite strapped to his chest and one burning match.

Karen was saying, "That was one hell of a good wagon you climbed on, Charlie. It didn't get you very far, did it?"

Galloway, dismissing the awful recollection of Vanderwolf, pushed his coffee cup away. He knew what he was going to say and couldn't help himself. The most abused word in all the English language, a word stunted by torture. *Sorry.*

"What's that you said, Charlie?"

In glum silence he stared at her, thinking how lovely she looked even with one cheek made plump by grapes.

"Did I hear *sorry,* Charlie?" she asked.

He knew it was coming, the sarcasm, the feigned astonishment, the rhetorical artillery wheeled into position for an assault on his nonexistent defenses. He watched her face. The explosion of hurt in her eyes was unbearable to him, all the more so because he caused it.

"Where's the Webster's, Charlie? I'd like to look up *sorry,* because it sounds familiar. I've heard it before but I've never actually understood it the way you use it, Charlie. Is there some special Scottish usage I'm not aware of? Is there some archaic connotation that eludes me? Or is it just something you tag on at the end of every drunk, like a belch?"

He looked down at the table, picked at the crust of his toast, wondered why in God's name he kept bringing this wonderful woman pain. Even after she'd walked out on him, he still managed to twist her heart. By using her, preying on her kindness and concern, he continued to victimize her. *Mea culpa. Piss off, Charlie.* It was worthless to confront the dragon of remorse with the sword of your good intentions because it always overwhelmed you with fire and black fumes. And it was worthless to say sorry because she'd heard it so many times the word had all the integrity of a used condom.

She wiped the cuff of her blouse across her eyes. The short

hair gave her a severe look, but didn't take anything away from her beauty. The jeans, he saw, were a little tighter than before. How many candy bars had she devoured since she'd left him? How many compulsive late-night sessions with Ben & Jerry's Heath Bar Crunch Ice Cream? He wanted to rise and comfort her—Christ, did he ever—but he didn't move. The total wreckage of self-esteem paralyzed him. Besides, he wore only the ridiculous boxer shorts and socks. Thus attired, how could he hope to be taken seriously?

He'd blown it. He'd fucked up. He'd chucked it all away—all his fine statements and grand designs were stillborn creatures. Having set out to prove himself, he'd reached only the most dismal conclusion. He was a sick fool destined to go through life like a man who, having no sense of delicacy or balance or moderation, nevertheless insists on frequenting china shops.

"I am so *tired*, Charlie," Karen said. "You know, when we talked the night before last, I left here feeling something . . . I can't explain it exactly. I don't want to overstate the case and say it was hope. No, that's too grand. What I felt was this tiny atom of optimism that maybe *maybe* you meant to quit this time. I drove away feeling surprisingly lighthearted because I thought I'd seen something on your face, a new determination, a resolve of sorts. I *thought*. I shouldn't think. Thinking screws me every time."

She paused and turned her face up to the ceiling. On each cheek there were tears. "I must be some kind of dimwit. Really. What is it about me that keeps me hanging on? Huh? What weakness? I don't know who's sicker, Charlie, you or me." She was silent a minute, looking at him as if she were seeing him through newly prescribed lenses. "I convinced myself the night before last that there was, well, okay, a chance, a glimmer. Now I see things for what they are. You've cleared my head, sweetheart, and for that I thank you." She smiled sadly. "I'm out of here, Charlie. For good."

"For good?"

"Somebody will come for the rest of my stuff. The lawyers can do the paperwork. I'm bored being your victim, Charlie. I wasn't born for that."

"Wait a minute, hold on," and he reached for her hand, but

she drew it away. He was trembling, afraid. He wished, as every hungover drunk wished, that clocks might be turned back and the immediate past rewritten by a tender, sober pen on soft vellum.

"This is it, Charlie. This is the point of no return. Face it, we don't have a hope in hell. I can't keep hanging in there, not after last night. It's always going to be the same. Even if you were sober for ten years, and we were back together, I'd still live in fear. I'd *still* wait for you to come through the front door drunk on your ass. You tell me, Charlie. Is that any way to live a life?"

"You make me feel like I'm some kind of monster," he said.

"Why not? There's a monster inside you, and you feed it, Charlie. The trick is simple: Starve it to death before it's too late for you."

He stood up, walked toward her. She allowed him to hold her only a moment before she stepped away. Her hair smelled of her favorite shampoo, a faint cinnamon perfume. Behind her left ear, half hidden by the fold of hair, was a tiny pink horseshoe of a birthmark. He had always adored this blemish.

She covered her eyes with her hands, lost her composure a second, leaned against the kitchen table. "This is sad," she said. "God, this is the saddest thing. I didn't expect to feel this bad."

Galloway tried to say something but his sentence fell off the edge of the world. "I've run out of . . ." He wasn't sure what he'd run out of. Time? Conviction? He was at some horrible new low here. He couldn't stop trembling.

Karen touched the side of his face with the palm of her hand. "I don't know what's worse. When hope dies or when love fades. Reality's a damn hard place to be at times. But you know that better than most people, don't you?" She took her hand away. "I don't have any hope and I don't believe I have any love left either. No hard feelings, but that's the reality. That's what I gotta face, sweetie. You too, any way you can."

Galloway tried again to speak but there was a catch in his throat. A small death was going on inside him.

"Your father has this terrific saying, Charlie. *It's a sair fecht.* Remember?"

Of course he remembered. Life's a hard fight. The old man was always saying it.

She said, "He's perfectly right."

Charlie Galloway made no response. This was new to him, this particular brand of unmerciful emptiness, this sadness. He'd been sad before. He'd lived for weeks in this empty house. But what was different this time was the absence of a future. The fine crystal that was hope had been shattered right in front of his eyes, and now the air crackled with all the small flying pieces. She'd said she was going for good and he had no reason to doubt her. There was a quality in her expression he'd never seen before, a hard, determined resolve in the eyes, as if she were already half-way to forgetting him. He knew she wouldn't change her mind. No glib rejoinder, no self-derision, no wisecrack was going to sway her.

"There's nothing left," she said, and her arms flopped at her sides in a gesture of resignation.

His voice was a very strange whisper. *"I can't stand to hear you say that."*

He listened to the kitchen door open. She went across the tiled floor of the living room, where she said something to Clarence Wylie. The front door closed quietly, a click of the latch, finality. He wanted to go after her, but there would have been a headlong quality of desperation in the move. She wasn't coming back. She wasn't coming back. *Think about that before you go chasing after her in your underwear and socks.*

He sat down at the table and held his head between his hands. How long he remained in this position he had no way of measuring, nor was he able to evaluate exactly how he felt. The best you could say of a hangover was that it blunted your responses, took some of the sting out of your emotions. Of course you felt physically sick, confused, depressed, remorseful, clarty. But the up side of all this bleakness was a certain numbness that rendered the complex equations of the heart as difficult to grasp as infinity.

His wife had just gone. She was never coming back. He loved her dearly. Therefore . . .

Galloway's Unfinished Theorem.

At the age of forty-three, that well-known mathematician of the emotions, Charles Galloway, formerly of Govan, succumbed to death by disappointment, his life's work incomplete.

Clarence Wylie entered the room, sat at the table. He wore a white shirt that looked as crisp as the inside of a Winesap apple, and his dark necktie was unobtrusive.

Say it, Clarence, Galloway thought. *Say some word of consolation, some kindly phrase. Something like, "She spoke in the heat of the moment, Charlie. Things will improve, you'll see. She doesn't mean it."* But Clarence Wylie, who preferred silent sympathy to an idiot platitude, said nothing.

Galloway got up from the table and poured hot water into his cup, then tossed in a spoonful of instant coffee granules, which he stirred in a manic way.

"You'll wear a hole right through that cup, Charlie," said Clarence Wylie.

Charlie went on stirring, stirring.

"Sit down, Charlie. Drink the coffee."

Galloway returned to his chair. He didn't want to talk. His hangover was giving out some weird visual vibrations and the air between himself and Clarence seemed to fill with oscillating lines. Each wave brought Galloway a flicker of pain directly behind the eyeballs.

His brain was broken. He saw in the distance the jagged rainbow of the old Migraine Express. He rubbed the sides of his head. He was going to pass out. The room tilted one way. The ceiling dropped a few inches. The window came zooming toward him. In the sensory chaos of hangover inner damage was inestimable. Millions of brain cells had been blitzed. Repair crews worked the main avenues but the side streets were still a disaster. Several zones had been sealed off entirely to prevent looting. Vandals stormed the various emporia that stocked memories, feelings, and reflexes. This was the ruined city inside Charlie's head, where what remained of the working gendarmerie was barely managing to hold back the attack of the great white slugs that burrowed through the suburbs of his cerebrum. Plump and sickening, tentacles upraised and quivering, they crawled behind Galloway's eyes, creating hideous pressure.

When his head cleared enough to see, he eyed Clarence Wylie curiously. "You're still here, then."

"I'll leave if you want," Clarence said in the manner of a man with no intention of going anywhere.

Galloway stared unblinkingly at the sunlit window. On the sill two peaches left to ripen had rotted, and flies pecked at them, busily regurgitating their food before they could swallow. Probably they were breeding too, producing their charming children in condos bored out of the decayed fruit.

"I heard about Ella Nazarena," Clarence said quietly. "I understand how upset you must be."

Charlie could still hear the echo of Karen's heels on tile. "I'm not over the moon about it, Clarence."

"I also heard about this . . . Joaquin incident."

"Christ. News travels."

"I got a call from Len Paffett."

"And what did Paffett want?"

"He's worried about you. Wants me to use my friendly influence to get you to cease and desist—his words, Charlie—from poking your nose into this murder. Otherwise . . ."

"Otherwise?"

"Dark hints were made. The legal process was mentioned. It didn't sound good. Stay away, Charlie. Leave it alone. Why did you go to Joaquin's apartment anyway?"

"I had a tip he killed Ella."

"And you wanted to play cop."

"I don't think that deserves a response, Clarence."

"Don't sulk at me, Charlie. Don't give me that protruding lower lip routine. You forget. I know you. I've held your head while you puked in more johns than I care to remember. I've listened to you babble for hours at a time. I'm an expert on Charles D. Galloway and his travails."

"What a burden for you."

"At times," Wylie said. "At times." He tapped the table with his fingertips. "Joaquin denied the accusation?"

"Sure."

"But you believe he killed Mrs. Nazarena?"

Charlie Galloway said, "An innocent man doesn't usually pull a gun on you."

Wylie appeared to consider this for a time, but in a detached fashion, as if he were trying to remember a life before retirement. He said, "Listen. Do yourself some good. Take a vacation, Charlie. Get out of LA for a while. Stay out of trouble."

Galloway thought of Greyhound buses and terminals and destinations, and all this depressed him profoundly. People rode through roaring dark wastes to places with names like Blythe and Twentynine Palms and San Luis Obispo, communities of mysterious decrepitude. He thought of airplanes and the peculiarity of suspension at thirty thousand feet and how the brown, arid landscapes below were always crisscrossed with inexplicable lines suggestive of Peruvian enigmas. He wasn't about to leap into the abyss of timetables and tickets and suitcases.

Wylie said, "Go to San Diego. Go to Vegas. Anywhere. Just get away."

"I'll think it over, Clarence."

A pain skipped through Charlie's brain, reminding him of the ritual he'd have to go through that would diminish, if not entirely alleviate, the hangover. The long shower. The shave. Pints of cold water. Alka-Seltzer. Vitamins B and C. Then, later, some starchy food, pasta, which filled the cracks in the stomach like cement. These palliatives made it possible for you to drag yourself through the day.

He sipped his lukewarm coffee. He wondered about Karen. Had she called for a taxi before leaving? Or had some friend, Justine, say, picked her up by prearrangement? He was afraid of life without her, the enduring emptiness of it all. He walked to the sink, filled a glass with water, swallowed quickly. He repeated the dose. Slicks ran down his bare chest. He drew the back of a hand that still shook across his lips. He filled a third glass from the faucet. His ankle ached and he rearranged his position for relief. A spectacular bruise was located just above his right hip, blue-yellow, as picturesque as a small tropical parrot; he remembered colliding with the dressing table in Raymond Cruz's hotel room.

This recollection spurred something else, but his memory, befogged now, was going nowhere. A mystery lurked in that pea-souper, as sinister as the shadow of Jack the Ripper, but he was damned if he could define it. Something to do with Cruz, with Joaquin, an account that didn't balance. But what?

What did it matter? He'd been banished, hounded by the forces of law and order. Wherever he went chaos stalked him.

Ah, wasn't that the siren song of his old companion in adversity, self-pity? Where the hell was his mettle? Where his back-bone? Where the strength of character to clamber up out of this stinking pit and get on with a life? *It's a sair fecht.* Right, but that wasn't an excuse to lie down and roll over like some dying dog. So you stumbled, you fell face-first into a pile of dung, but you didn't just lie there, did you?

Fuck, nooooo! You got up. You whistled. You tap-danced, even if your feet were killing you.

He felt cold water run to the waist of his embarrassing plaid shorts. It was a time, he decided, for a strategy of limited opti-mism, rather than the disappearance Clarence Wylie advocated. Physical relocation was the same as drunkenness: Both were forms of flight. Clarence meant well, but in this instance he was wrong.

Descended from a long line of gritty Lowland Scots, hardy shipyard men who'd lived through the deprivations of the Great Depression when the yards lay silent and rainy and people were hungry, Galloway wasn't going to be run out of his own damned home by anybody, nor was he about to accept Karen's last speech as the closing of the curtain on their marriage. He dried himself vigorously with paper towels. He was a Man of the Clyde. He had a life to work out. Yes. He had a life to lead and problems to solve.

"I'm a resilient bastard, Clarence," he said. "Knock me down, I bounce back. It's in my blood."

"And you just bounced back?"

"The alternative, old son, is bloody despair."

Galloway had a look on his face of forced cheer. How long could he keep this up? Did he really believe in this brave new front? Or was this more of that pox self-deception? He crumpled damp paper towels in his hands and tossed them in the wastebas-ket, remembering that these particular towels were the only ones Ella ever used when she cleaned. Everything else, she'd say, is inferior and falls to pieces immediately, and she'd demonstrate how water made pulp of cheaper towels, as if she were doing a TV commercial. She'd loved American TV, which she looked at every day with fresh eyes, as if it had been invented overnight.

Followed by Wylie, Galloway wandered into the living room, where his pants lay crumpled on the floor. He picked them up and asked, "Matter of curiosity, Clarence. If you were me, would you walk away from Ella's death?"

"I can't answer that—"

"Step in the bloody water, Clarence. Get your feet wet. Give it a try."

Clarence Wylie frowned. "What did the dead woman mean to you?"

"She was a friend. I felt sorry for her. I think a lot of her life was pure shit, but she smiled through most of it, and I liked her for that. She minded her own business and she wasn't judgmental. She didn't need to die the way it happened, Clarence. Somebody shot her, and he's out there in the streets right now. Does that answer your question?"

"Maybe."

"Don't maybe me. Just get back to me with a reply, for Christ's sake. Would *you* walk away from the whole thing? Would you let yourself be warned off by Paffett and that moron Duffy?"

"I'd want to know what 'the whole thing' means, Charlie, what's involved. I'd look deeply at my own motives—"

"Fucking *hell*. When did you turn into an old woman, Clarence? When you retired? I asked a straight question—"

"You're a pain in the ass, Galloway."

"Lemme tell you, Clarence. I know what you'd do. I know *exactly* what you'd do. You'd stick with it, wouldn't you? You'd see it through. You wouldn't let some eedjits put you off, not if you were determined enough, and curious enough. Not you, Clarence. You might walk in the shadows, but you'd hang in there. Correct? Correct, eh?"

"Maybe."

Charlie Galloway laughed.

"I emphasize *maybe*," Wylie said. "But not before I'd asked myself some damn tough questions first."

"Of course, Clarence. Damn tough. Self-examination and all that. Right?"

"Piss off."

They walked together to the front door, a curious pair, the tousled dripping Scotsman in his tartan boxer shorts, the retired

FBI agent in white shirt, dull tie, and navy blue, well-creased slacks.

Clarence said, "If you want my opinion, I don't like the idea of you trespassing, which is always a risky business. But do what you have to, Charlie. Because that's what you'll do anyhow."

Charlie watched his friend walk to his parked car. The brilliant morning sun transformed his shirt from white to some unnamed color beyond the spectrum, a phosphorescence that burned itself on Galloway's eyes.

Charlie shut the door quickly, climbed the stairs to the bathroom where he turned on the shower and, while steam was building, he took two aspirin, a handful of multivitamin capsules, and a glass of Alka-Seltzer. Then he climbed inside the shower, adjusted the nozzle, making the stream of water sharper. With closed eyes, he turned his face directly into the jet, which pummeled and jabbed him. It would be two, maybe three days before he was himself again. Over the age of forty, restoration from drunkenness was a chore, a terrible price you paid for a few dark hours of merriment you couldn't remember anyway when you woke up.

There was, he knew, little logic in that, but alcohol and reason made unnatural bedfellows, which was why you never went to bars to discover and revere sages, and the only philosophers you ever encountered in the kind of pit stops Charlie frequented dug ditches for a living, preferring to speak more of shovels and earth-moving equipment than of Socrates and Wittgenstein.

He leaned against the tiled wall, enjoyed the pinprick sensation of water on the surface of his skin. Then he stepped from the shower, wrapped himself in a towel, and walked back to the bedroom. He looked out at the small garden at the back of the house, where Karen had planted runner beans and begonias. Everything was in an advanced state of rot.

He remembered now what it was that had been troubling him about Cruz, an anomaly so small it required a microscope to see it, but it nagged him anyway, touching him with a sense of dissatisfaction that normally he might have ignored. But he was not these days a busy man, even if he wished to remain a determined one. And when minor incongruities flowed around him like shoals of tiny fish, he had all the time in the world to step into the water, no matter how shallow or unruffled, for a closer look. He took a fresh shirt from the closet, a pair of slacks, nonplaid boxer shorts, and his LAPD identification.

When you got right down to it, he had nothing much to lose and the leisure time in which to do it.

For a long time Joe Baltazar had been moving from one cheap rooming house to the next in various quarters of Manila. He left behind no obvious trail for anyone tracking him, even though he could never shake the sensation that somebody was close at hand. He'd spent some nights in Sampaloc, in a room occupied by three unemployed laborers from North Luzon, old Marcos loyalists who drank tuba and spoke bitterly of "the housewife" Corazon Aquino. Baltazar pretended to sympathize with them, but most of the time he feigned sleep.

After Sampaloc he'd crossed the Pasig River to the edge of Makati, where he found a crummy little room, six feet by five, alongside the noisy South Highway which rumbled with traffic *awra-awra,* an unceasing thunder. Then he'd drifted into Malate, to one small room after another, some shared with strangers from different provinces. Baltazar was polite to these people but encouraged no intimacies. He lived inside himself. His smile was a hermit's.

He was convinced he could live safely only in this wayward manner. When you couldn't predict your own moves, how could your enemies? He traveled dark alleys, rarely saw sunlight. He lay in stifling uncooled rooms and through open windows listened to the endless racket of life in the streets of Manila, jeepneys, roosters, street vendors. One moonless night he moved to a room over a restaurant in Chinatown, where the smell of garlic filled the narrow staircase at all times. He suffered insomnia. On certain days the pain in his groin was so bad he could do nothing but walk back and forth, moaning quietly, eyes watering. It was an old pain, but when it recurred it was as acute as it had been on the night of its affliction. He wondered if it had some magical capacity to renew itself, like a tumor. Perhaps it would never leave him in peace until the enemies were dead. He stroked the cat's eye amulet and often found a form of solace in this.

He left Chinatown and had moved north toward Tondo, believing the impossible maze of filthy alleys would afford him anonymity. Tondo was a blight, a plagued landscape of the worst poverty, shacks pressed against shacks, refuse piled in narrow alleyways, where it stank and seethed and came alive in the monolithic heat. Poverty in Tondo was more than just the lack of money and hope; here it became something else, a mutant social form, a deplorable new order.

He rented a room built out of corrugated tin from an old man who was also a moneylender. Prostitutes came to him to pawn their cheap jewelry for a few pesos. On the night after Teng's departure from the Philippines, Baltazar, numbed by loneliness, had taken one of the girls to his room and tried to make love to her, but even brief penetration caused him distress and he had to withdraw and roll away from the girl, whose name was Epifania.

After, the girl smoked a cigarette and dressed in silence. Then she sat down beside him and asked him who had hurt him this way, a question he didn't answer. She placed a hand softly between his legs. He felt the tips of her fingers on the welts that would always give disfigured contours to his testicles. The gesture was so unexpectedly tender it moved him. He gave the girl one hundred pesos before she left. Later, he lay for a long time thinking of Teng, wondering how Teng was faring in the United States. He closed his eyes and tried to picture the young man, but nothing would come to him.

The morning after the encounter with the girl, he left Tondo and went to Baclaran, to a pension house in a decaying side street. His few possessions he carried in an old canvas bag. His room was on the top floor. Open fires were lit among abandoned buildings nearby and raw smoke billowed inside the house through shattered windows. He locked his door, lay down on the narrow bed, but even behind locked doors in disintegrating houses he felt no safety. When he looked from the window along the smoky street he thought he saw people waiting for him in doorways. And those lovers who passed holding hands—who was to say they were really lovers and not agents of the constabulary keeping him under surveillance?

He read and reread old newspapers. He waited until darkness before leaving the house to walk to a nearby cafeteria for food, a quick, simple meal of pork and garlic rice. After he'd eaten he hurried back in the direction of his room. The streets filled him with fear, reminding him of a time when fear hadn't been a word in his vocabulary, when he'd been bold and headstrong. Look at him now. What had he become? Depending on Teng for his revenge—what did that make him? A form of parasite, somebody who feasted off the bravery of another? He'd planned it all, of course, but that was merely a matter of joining the dots. That was nothing.

A few yards from the cafeteria a cigarette vendor accosted him. Baltazar kept walking. He had to get back to his room. That was all he knew. The aimless crowds around him were illuminated only by sparse light falling from a few shop windows—a foreign exchange bureau, a *turo turo* restaurant, a fruit juice place. He smelled mango pulp and kalamansi. He kept going. Why was the cigarette vendor pursuing him? Baltazar turned to look. The vendor, who had a tray of Marlboro and Camel, grinned at him. Baltazar said he didn't want cigarettes, didn't need them. He turned a corner, found himself in a narrow unfamiliar alley. On either side of him were half-demolished houses in which squatters lived. Clouds of smoke thickened the darkness. Dense palm fronds, some strung with electricity cables, overhung the street. Beyond open doorways could be seen groups of people sitting at makeshift tables or squatting on old wood floors, smoking cigarettes, eating, drinking. Here and there black and white TVs showed a basketball game. Somebody plucked a chicken beneath a kerosene lamp. Feathers floated strangely in the blue-yellow light.

Baltazar hurried even though the vendor had disappeared. The alley seemed narrower now, enclosed by a darkness deeper than before. He stopped, realizing that he'd somehow lost his way. All this was unfamiliar to him. The alley. The buildings. The cigarette seller had upset him, that was what had happened. He'd allowed the man to spook him. *Coward,* he thought, turning back the way he'd come.

He passed the open doorway of a *sare-sare* shop, from which emerged two men in short-sleeved barongs. More shadow than substance, they converged on him as if they meant to rob him.

But they were not thieves. They were too well dressed, they lacked the stealth of bandits.

Baltazar understood. He knew what these men were. Alarmed, he moved sideways, thinking he might slip down a narrow lane that opened to his left. But it was busy with people crowded around a TV in somebody's doorway. The commentator spoke in the hybrid language of Taglish.

If he went into that lane, which was no more than four feet wide, Baltazar understood he'd be trapped in the throng. He turned this way, that way, indecisive, panicked; then he began to move back in the direction he'd first come to get away from cigarette seller, deeper into the unfamiliar alley, into the chaos of lives openly lived in houses with neither doors nor windows nor decent roofs. Lovers, widows, babies, grandmothers, children—they were framed in the ruin of their circumstances, forlorn still lives.

Baltazar hurried, but he knew he wasn't fit enough to outrun the two men following him. He stepped inside one of the shacks, knocking aside a doorway of corrugated tin, seeing it fall away from him and clatter against a table made of wooden crates around which sat two women—one old and toothless, the other a pretty teenage girl suckling a baby. The women cried out as Baltazar crashed into their flimsy little world. They moved aside for him, though not without protest, shouting at him as he strode across the room seeking an exit, a window, another door, any means of egress. But he should have known better. There was only one way into this hovel, only one way out. He had nowhere to run.

He stood with his back to the wall, gazed at the two large men in the doorway. He noticed how the very fine embroidery of their shirts diverted attention from the pistols they wore holstered at their hips.

13

Richard McCune, the President of the United States, was a trim man who kept in shape playing badminton and doing ungainly butterfly strokes in the White House pool. He was not popular except among his natural constituency of right-wing blue-collar workers, supporters of TV ministries, and the Cro-Magnon good old boys who ran the Pentagon as if it were a Saturday morning hobbyist's club. What the President had in common with the Joint Chiefs of Staff, apart from a deficiency of social vision, was a devotion to military hardware and a fascination with each killing novelty that came from the drawing boards of the architects of extreme destruction. New bombers, outer-space death systems, giant killer subs—one of which would have fed a million Appalachians or Mississippi Deltans for fifty years—enthralled him. His reading was dedicated to technological reports or high-tech thrillers, although little difference existed between these literary forms, since both were depopulated blueprints, rah-rah pamphlets for the ultimate mayhem. Reputedly the President was one of the few readers of these books who could go from cover to cover without moving his lips.

Jews considered him a closet anti-Semite, blacks a hooded racist. Liberals detested him because he represented the Worst-Case American, the arrogant *oinker* who shook the hands of visiting heads of state with the disdainful look of a potentate who expects no mere contact of fingers but full genuflection, and who, when he traveled abroad, took his own chef, bottled Saratoga water, and Nebraskan T-bones.

Moderate right-wingers found him old-fashioned and naive. Journalists were disenchanted with him because his press conferences often fell apart in tantrums and he behaved like the kind of spoiled American brat President who doesn't think freedom of the press has anything to do with him *personally.*

Fashion writers mocked both him and the First Lady, calling them the Sultan and Sultana of L. L. Bean. At gala occasions the President and Mrs. McCune were ridiculed; he for his bland, boxy tuxedos, Winona for what Mr. Blackwell, in his annual assassination list, tartly called the "sequined nightmares that make her resemble a spangled Vegas act from the 1950s."

The President at times perceived the world as a major metropolis and himself as policeman on a lonely beat. Gun holstered, badge gleaming, he walked dark streets, warily scanning shadowy doorways, looking at lights in shop windows, listening, wondering where trouble would come from first. This vision of the world, inadequate as it was, reduced things to manageable proportions for him. He could invade this or that neighborhood and kick ass, containing problems at their source.

As a corollary to this simple concept, he believed in a strong, well-behaved America with streets where people weren't mugged and little kids didn't buy and sell narcotics in suburban shopping malls. A sparkling clean, lemon-scented America, land of Ty-D-Bol and Doublemint Gum and the Colt Peacemaker. The republic, menaced as much from within as without, could not be allowed to go in a handbasket to hell because of crack dealers and oddball terrorists and people from such outfits as the Posse Comitatus who didn't believe in paying federal income taxes.

Richard McCune was the man Senator Byron Truskett had come to see. It was ten A.M. Eastern time when Truskett entered the Oval Office, remembering immediately his encounter there, more than thirty years ago, with Dwight Eisenhower. A kindly man of overpowering blandness, Eisenhower had the mannerisms of an absentminded uncle quick to hand out two bits to nephews and nieces whose names he always forgets. Ike had smiled, and patted young Truskett on the shoulder, and said something about the future of the nation being in good hands, yup yup yup. Cameras flashed, and young Truskett, anaesthetized by the fumes of power, was ushered out of the Oval Office, clutching his check.

Dick McCune was no Eisenhower, no Daddy to the nation, but an acerbic bully who owed his ascent to two things: the total ineptitude of his opponent, a droopy little man in ill-fitting suits who won only in the states of Massachusetts and New Hampshire, and the fact that, despite the prairie bleakness of his heart, McCune had projected throughout his campaign an image of common sense so acceptable to a slumbering America that he was voted into the White House by a margin only slightly smaller than the one received by Nixon over the doomed McGovern in 1972.

Besides, McCune was silver-haired and photogenic, and in the dank culverts of American politics how you photographed was a hundred times more important than whether you had a solitary policy you could call your own about *anything*. The electorate, bludgeoned by frantic TV images of party conventions, preferred Dalmane or Valium to the democratic process.

Now Truskett shook the President's hand, which was always cold, no matter the weather. Truskett understood there was some circulatory problem. On McCune's desk were three red-tagged manila folders, each stamped STATE, a framed picture of the President and Mrs. McCune taken in the Rose Garden, and a rectangular blotter across which lay a badminton racket and shuttlecock.

Truskett sat down at the President's bidding. Behind the President stood Farley Kusik, chief of White House staff and known around town as The Shadow, because he never left McCune's side. Kusik was a very tall, silent figure whose characteristic stance was that of stooped listener. His eyes were two small pools of black oil. He had a way of fiercely clutching his chin with his undertaker's white fingers as he concentrated.

"Byron," said the President. "And how are we this very hot morning?"

"Well enough, sir," Truskett answered. He thought it a sorry state of affairs that such a mediocrity as McCune had risen to the Oval Office. One consequence of awfulness at the top was the way in which everything else deteriorated from there on down, stratum after stratum of increasingly witless attachés, counsels, lawyers, assistants, deputies, secretaries, until you finally reached the mail room, where things were misdirected by hapless messengers.

"Sorry to hear about Bach," said the President.

"He'll be missed," Truskett replied.

"Indeed," McCune said in that hollow, windy voice of his.

Although Truskett and McCune belonged to the same political party and subscribed to a shared patriotism, they stood far apart on certain basic issues, some highly emotional, like abortion, some both fiscal *and* emotional, like increased military expenditure; McCune opposed the former and ejaculated over the latter. On the other hand, Truskett thought vast quantities of money had to be directed away from the Pentagon to mend the chancres that festered in American society, although he didn't favor the kind of laissez-faire programs that had unglued the Democrats in the late sixties and early seventies.

The rich, middle, and working classes had to be protected from increased taxation; the destitute had to be raised up from despondency. Truskett still considered America the land of opportunity—God's own apple, as it were—but more money had to be channeled into social programs run by efficient specialists instead of well-intentioned amateurs. And there was only one place to get the kind of cash his ambitions demanded: the Pentagon, where military spending had reached surrealistic levels, as if all requisition forms were made out by the Three Stooges.

Besides, the enemies of the United States at this stage of the twentieth century were mainly crazed dictators or Banana Republic Communists unable to directly menace the U.S.A. with the kind of warfare that justified the outrageous financial demands of the petulant coots running the Pentagon. The real threat to U.S. security, Truskett thought, was terrorism, which could be countered more by strong intelligence than advanced weaponry.

It was a time, he'd said in many speeches, for new "alignments" among the various strata of society, a time for education, pride, an end to the humiliation of homelessness. He avoided such phrases as the "redistribution of wealth" because in American politics you might as well slit your wrists in a public place as use such "radical" talk. He implicated nobody in these speeches. He took huge pains to avoid criticism of McCune, for which the President, a beleaguered figure, was grateful. The speeches were little gems of moderation, and at times even the light of kindness shone through. Some people in Truskett's own party were wary of him; they thought he was peddling his own brand of snake oil, Byron's Presidential Panacea Elixir.

"The file on Laforge," said the President to Farley Kusik, who produced a charcoal-gray cardboard box that contained the history of William Laforge. He glanced at Truskett. "We're prepared, you see. We did our homework."

"I can see that," Truskett remarked.

The President tapped the box with one finger. "And this is your boy, Byron?"

"I consider him the best man for the job, sir. Far and away."

Farley Kusik, who always spoke in a clipped way, said, "Two strikes against him. One, Iran. Two, Marcos. Not squeaky clean. Not squeaky clean at all."

Truskett was prepared. "I don't have to remind you, Farley, that both the Shah and Marcos were allies of the United States at the time when Billy Laforge was deployed in their countries."

"We're well aware of this," said the President.

"Allow me to point out the fact that after the fall of Marcos, Laforge worked efficiently for Corazon Aquino's administration."

"Point acknowledged," Kusik said.

"At every turn, Laforge has done everything his country asked, without complaint."

"Loyal," said Farley Kusik. "No denying it. No denying it at all. Loyal as the day is long. Sun never sets on his patriotism."

"We might get some flak about the Shah connection," McCune said, and tapped the box once again.

"We can handle that, Mr. President," Truskett said. "There's absolutely no evidence Laforge had anything to do with the Shah's secret police. Knowing the man as I do, I believe his high professional and moral standards would prohibit him from acting in a way contrary to any reasonable man's sense of decency."

"Ummm." McCune picked up his badminton racket and

swiped the birdie across the room, where it struck the door and fluttered to the carpet. There was silence after this eccentric little outburst of energy, which seemed to deplete the President momentarily.

In this silence, at some sublevel of awareness, a faint electronic hum was audible. Truskett understood the entire conversation was being taped, one of McCune's presidential whims.

"Home life above reproach?" Kusik asked.

"Indisputably," said Truskett.

"That counts," said McCune, a great believer in conjugal virtues ever since Winona McCune had caught him, some twenty years ago, in a Ramada Inn bedroom with a seventeen-year-old political groupie's face buried in his groin, and had threatened to have his balls for doorstops if such a thing ever happened again.

The President went on. "Sandy Bach was sick for three long months. During that time, his office has been run by his deputy—whatsisname?"

Kusik supplied it. "Jerry Slotten."

"Right. That's the fella," said McCune. "Now the way I see it, Slotten's been doing a competent job, Senator. What's wrong with giving it to him permanently?"

Truskett had expected at least token resistance. The trick to winning lay in the right phrasing. "I'm not going to badmouth Jerry Slotten, Mr. President. After Laforge, I'd say Slotten's the next best choice. But Laforge has it over him in field experience. And I believe Laforge can get the numbers required for nomination."

"Possibly," McCune said. "But Slotten's been in the hot seat for three months, Senator. That counts for something."

"I'm not denying it," Truskett said. He hesitated before his next utterance. His head was filled momentarily with an image of Carolyn Laforge—golden, wonderful. *Do it for me, Byron. You can do anything you want. For me and to me. Eat me. Go down on me hard. Yes,* he thought. Carolyn Laforge was a whole world of possibilities. "What worries me frankly is the risk of division, Mr. President. I've counted some heads and I know Laforge can muster what he needs for his nomination."

"You mean *you* can muster, don't you, Senator?" McCune asked. He knew Truskett coveted the Big Cheesecake, this office and all its trappings. He also knew that one day Truskett would probably get it, Rose Garden, swimming pool, paper shredders, and all. McCune, halfway through his final term, had to be circumspect: A probable future President was someone you disregarded at your own peril. Although he didn't much like Truskett, whom he thought a trumped-up young jackanapes he would have enjoyed seeing fall flat on his tush, he understood that in politics you were often obliged to choose between evils. You never knew when you might need, say, a favor in your old age. Retirement could be a chilly place. What did Ford do except play golf and give speeches? And Carter created a flimsy illusion of keeping busy with some Nice Guy projects. Ronnie Reagan was dragged out, blown up, dusted off, had his head dipped in black dye and was sold to the Japanese for propaganda reasons. And Nixon was completely pathetic, a sad old liar seeking respectability. Screw all that: McCune wanted to keep busy even as he desired to be perceived as a man who had the President's ear and offered smart counsel. He wanted to be the wise old owl of his party.

Truskett smiled his modest smile. "My own contribution isn't really significant, sir. I've recommended Laforge here and there and the response has been favorable. Now, with all due respect, if you place Slotten into consideration, I think you'll find those supporters of Laforge unwilling to back Jerry—no matter how good a man he is. Either they'll vote against him or they'll abstain. Same difference in the end. A few will vote for him, of course. But you see the problem. The risk of division in the ranks is very real. It doesn't reflect well on the presidency if you send Slotten's name up only to have it rejected."

"In other words, why not send the right man up in the first place?" said McCune.

"Yes."

The President was quiet for a time before he asked, "You'll walk the line for him, Byron?"

Truskett nodded. "Of course."

"You'll go to the wall?"

"If necessary."

"I admire your conviction, Byron."

"In this case it's not difficult."

McCune glanced at Farley Kusik. Something passed between

them, some current that put Truskett in mind of the eye contact made between a ventriloquist and his dummy. Who was ventriloquist and who dummy in this situation was unclear. McCune looked as pensive as he had on campaign lapel buttons.

Finally he said, "Okay. I'll nominate him, Byron. I'll get behind him. I'll make my announcement this very afternoon."

"Thank you, Mr. President." *Before Sandy Bach is even cold,* Truskett thought. McCune did business with a swashbuckler's sensitivity.

"Lemme warn you of something, Byron. I'll pull the rug out from under him at the first sign of an indiscretion. Keep that in mind. My support goes only so far. If he's a bad apple, he don't go in my pie."

Truskett rose. He was no lover of the folksy imagery and grammar McCune occasionally endorsed.

"Keep this in mind also, Senator," said the President. "You're standing on the same rug as your boy Billy."

Byron Truskett smiled, but neither McCune nor The Shadow returned the expression. In shade, they seemed to fuse together, as if some sinister trick of light had welded them into one entity—a moment of pure science fiction, and it left a vaguely disturbing impression on Byron Truskett that lingered long after he'd stepped from the Oval Office.

Thomas Railsback took a telephone call from William Laforge at ten-fifteen A.M. in his Dallas home, which lay north of University Park and south of the Lyndon B. Johnson Freeway, a good neighborhood severed from the Northwood Country Club by the artery of the highway. Although there were some shade trees on the street, the sun had made an arid mockery of them. A few leaves, dead long before their time, had fallen from branches and lay listless on bone-dry lawns.

Railsback's study, a glass extension at the rear of his home, overlooked a half acre of yellow Bermuda grass. Four elm trees and a cedar fence marked the boundary of the property; in the center of the lawn stood a small statue of a woman holding a cornucopia in her arms. Even the pears and grapes that flowed from this plaster horn seemed, to Railsback's bleak eye, withered.

He sat at a large laminated desk which held a computer

terminal, a fax machine, and a printer. He was conscious of his teenage daughter Holly padding barefoot along the hallway on her way to the kitchen. School was out for the summer, a state of affairs that always struck Railsback as slightly unnatural. He was so accustomed to having the house to himself at this time of day that his daughter seemed like an intruder, albeit one he adored—even if her lovely oval face always served as a painful reminder of his former wife, Eve, who had run away with some muscle-headed Popeye who worked a charter boat out of Savannah. Railsback looked at Holly and sometimes, no matter how he struggled, the resemblance caused old resentments to strut in front of him. It was a circus that had never quite left town.

"I wanted you to be one of the first to know, Tom," Laforge was saying. "I just heard I'm going to be nominated for Bach's job."

Was Railsback supposed to act surprised? "Didn't I tell you?"

"And you were right."

"You'll do a hell of a job," Railsback said.

"If I get it."

"You'll get it."

"I appreciate your confidence, Tom."

There was a lull. Railsback had the distinct feeling that this news wasn't the entire reason for the call. Something else lay in Laforge's tone of voice, a touch of concern, whatever.

"How are things deep in the heart of Texas, Tom?"

"Everything's just fine," Railsback answered.

"Nothing unusual? Nothing out of the ordinary?"

Of course. What else? Clearly Laforge was still chewing on the notion of an avenger from Benguet, an idea that in the hot, severe, frazzled light of a Dallas morning seemed even less realistic than it had in the gloomy, humid woods of Bucks County.

"Like I said, everything's fine," Railsback remarked. "Nothing out of the ordinary. Same old, same old."

"Do me a favor. Keep me posted, Tom. If anything strange happens, even if it seems only minor . . ."

"Sure." Strange, Railsback thought. Like how? How strange was strange? What was minor, what major? How did you quantify Laforge's anxieties?

"You think I worry too much, don't you?"

Yes, Railsback thought. "I didn't say that."

Laforge was quiet for a few seconds, perhaps reflecting on the insincerity in Railsback's answer. Then he laughed, a flat tinny sound reminiscent of a coin dropped inside a Salvation Army can. "You think I'm a fussbudget."

"I didn't say that either."

"You didn't have to, Tom. I see danger where none exists, isn't that how you feel?"

Jesus Christ. Exasperated, Railsback gazed out of the window. "Look. You're this close to a job you always wanted, and quite naturally you're stressed in case something goes wrong. That's it. The rest is pure imagination."

"It's just that something in the air is different, Tom. I can't define it. It's like a charge of electricity. You know that way the air changes when there's about to be lightning. Still. Heavy. It's like that."

"Try to relax," Railsback said quietly. What else could he say? Take a trank, lie down for an hour? Forget all about this charge of fucking electricity nonsense?

"Relax? Yes, you're right. Of course you are."

"I'll call if anything comes up. I'll keep in touch."

"Do that, Tom. Please."

Railsback said good-bye and hung up the telephone. *The way the air changes. . . .* The anxiety in Laforge's voice had been unmistakable. Billy normally displayed no emotion at all, unless you counted a kind of smile that wasn't really worth counting because it was ambivalent. Railsback had seen stress in him only once, and that was during the meeting in Bucks County the other day. Maybe it came down to this: Tie game, bottom of the ninth, bases loaded, and Billy, walking to bat, victory within reach, didn't have the nerve for the big moment anymore. Some men just couldn't cut it after a certain age.

Or perhaps Billy was having bad dreams, dark visitations in the night. Railsback knew a thing or two about those, about the chills, the way old images resurfaced in spooky new forms. These dreams didn't come often to him anymore, but when they did they were always zingers, bloodcurdlers that woke him in fever, sheets glued to flesh, hair damp, strength depleted.

Holly put her face around the door and blew a large pink

sphere of bubble gum. She wore an old lightweight coat of Rails-back's, which swept the floor, and a strange thrift-shop hat, a 1930ish trilby pulled down over her forehead. Half woman, half child, nymph.

She was fourteen and no longer a virgin, a fact she'd announced in a forthright manner only the day before. A part of Railsback thought rage and shotguns; another part conjured up detailed drawings of his daughter's defloration, which had happened at the hands, so to speak, of a seventeen-year-old high school dropout who—O Christ, what else?—wrote poetry and loved the stars at night. No redneck parent, Railsback did his best to absorb this business in a way he considered enlightened. He'd sighed and hoped she'd had the good sense to take precautions against pregnancy and, these days, fatality.

Her bubble gum popped and the deflated structure clung like an exploded web to her cheeks and nose. She made no attempt to scrape it off. She asked, "Is it okay with you if I go to the Galleria and hang out later?"

It was odd, Railsback thought, how his daughter—having shed her virginity, smoked pot and dropped acid, having in a sense grown up—could still ask permission to visit a shopping mall. She had one foot in her childhood, the other God knows where.

"You look ridiculous with that gum all over your face."

"It comes off."

Railsback stood up and walked across the polished pinewood floor to her. How long had it been since she'd had plump cheeks and chubby knees? She had her mother's blue eyes and that same way of looking at you with her face turned just slightly to one side, as if some mischief was taking place that could either be innocent or harmful, and it was up to you to guess which. In Eve's case, Railsback had figured wrongly.

He placed a hand upon Holly's arm. "You'll need money." He took a couple of fives out of his wallet and gave them to her.

She stuffed them in the pocket of the oversized coat. "I'll be back around six for supper, okay? Listen, I'd kiss you, but you'd only get sticky and hate me forever. Later, pater, potater."

And she was gone, coat flapping, leaving behind the gibberish of adolescence. He watched her disappear along the corridor, then went back to his desk. He sat still for a time, looking out at the statue, the trees, the cedar fence of the property that adjoined his. At various points along this fence he'd installed an electronic sensor system. Anyone climbing the fence would trigger an alarm inside his bedroom, where he kept a shotgun and a pistol. The front entrance of the house was protected by an invisible beam of light that, if broken, caused another set of alarms to ring. The windows were wired into the system. If anybody tried to force one open, not only would bells sound but floodlights immediately blaze around the house. It was a strong system, certainly enough to foil your average burglar.

He heard Holly singing in the kitchen, although he couldn't catch the words. A purity about her voice aroused that blind, unanalyzable love of a father for his daughter, a fathomless, immutable feeling that isn't menaced by passing years or enforced absences or the loss of a child's innocence. It was so unexpected that when she stopped singing and the emotion withered away, he was left with a mild sense of displacement, almost a despair. In a few years she'd be gone from this house—perhaps, as he quietly hoped, to college, perhaps to do Europe in a van, if that's what kids still did these days.

He rose. It was almost time to drive to his office on the third floor of an old building overlooking the dreariness of the Trailways bus station downtown, a scene that always depressed him with its decrepit, aimless air. In his office he usually shut the venetian blinds and read the overnight dispatches from the intelligence operatives he ran inside Central America. That was his assignment these days, gathering and interpreting material from the men and women, some of them bogus priests and nuns affiliated with supposed "church missions," under his command in Nicaragua and El Salvador. This information he analyzed and sent by scrambled modem to the Office of Central American Analysis in Virginia. The material usually concerned reports of ordnance deliveries and guerrilla maneuvers in rebel-held regions. Anything deemed inimical to American interests—anything, that is, of a left-wing nature, or hostile to the CIA—was relayed in detail. On occasion, Railsback was obliged to fly to Mexico City or Belize for personal meetings with staff members, but increasingly nowadays he managed to stay right where he was, at home with his daughter in Dallas. Which delighted him.

He stepped into the corridor, where he looked in the direction of the kitchen. The door lay open, revealing the girl standing at the sink, peeling gum from her face as if it were a layer of skin ruined by overexposure to sunlight. He watched for a moment, enjoying the role of unseen observer, then he turned away.

Unhinged by the clarity of daylight, bewildered by the energy of his own motorized slipstream, Charlie Galloway drove down from the hills and through twisting canyon roads with an expression on his face of one demented. He had no way of ignoring the hangover, which periodically issued its own strident list of demands, as if it were a terrorist who had hijacked his body:

1. *Douse me with cold water.*
2. *Feed me more aspirin.*
3. *Put me back to bed.*
4. *Free me with a couple of fast beers, sonofabitch, or I'll squeeze your brain out through your earholes.*

On Sunset Boulevard morning traffic was tangled in smoky sunlight. Already the day was one of disconnections. Men drilling a great, meaningless hole in the concrete beneath traffic lights had caused a detour. A woman in an orange hardhat directed traffic unsmilingly with purple tattooed hands, but everything was stalled. A dwarflike vendor of puckered little apples weaved between motionless cars, and somebody in very black glasses tapped on Charlie's window to panhandle a buck, which Galloway, always charitable, gave him. No sign of gratitude was shown. This was a world wherein the beggars were surly, always looking for bigger handouts. The man sniffled, then spat, and the disintegrating arc of his saliva sent tiny drops of moisture across Charlie's windshield. Hollywood! Sunset Boulevard! Nine-thirty A.M., outside temperature ninety-two degrees, and already you've been touched for a buck, offered a doubtful secondhand apple, and spat upon! Was this some odd third-world dream? Had he somewhere crossed a borderline without seeing it? Or was America, a cumbersome giant with a sciatic creak and severe schizophrenia, disintegrating in front of his very eyes?

Dying, he rolled down his window, but the syncopated roar of two pneumatic drills churning through cement made him shut it again. The hot air was thick with dust. He turned up the air-conditioning. His head absorbed without discrimination all the stimuli rocketing toward it. No editorial process was going on. The internal filter was fucked up. When they were handing out afflictions, he wondered, why had he been given alcohol? Why wasn't he a workaholic? A religious zealot? An obsessive wanker? Why had this particular weakness been implanted in him?

Traffic moved. Stopped. Moved again. Galloway made a right turn, found himself in a sequence of side streets, assailed by white and yellow and pink apartment buildings that resembled fussy confections of the fake kind you sometimes saw in the windows of old pastry shops, bleached by sun and covered with dust. Two junkies in tattered fatigues emerged from the bomb shelter of their nightmare and wandered in the general direction of Gallo-way's slow-moving car, as if they were intent on stopping him to squeeze a little dope money out of him, but something appeared to snap simultaneously in their synapses, perhaps a form of shared hallucination, and they veered off unexpectedly in another direction.

The Palms Hotel came in view. Galloway parked the Toyota, then hurried out of the heat into the building. He was spared an elevator ride because Cruz was sitting in the lobby, a newspaper open in his lap and a small overnight bag on the floor between his feet. He had the restless look of a man waiting for somebody, absently tapping one foot on the carpet as he read. When he became aware of Charlie Galloway crossing the lobby toward him, he folded the newspaper and frowned, but this expression was brief and yielded to a smile that brought the strange blue eyes alive. Galloway had the feeling they weren't Cruz's eyes at all, but brightly colored contact lenses—another disconnected moment, nothing more.

"I'm surprised to see you again so soon," said Cruz, and looked at his wristwatch. "I was preparing to leave."

"Running out on me?" Charlie asked.

Cruz laughed in his shallow way. "No. Nothing like that."

"I was under the impression you planned to stay here."

"I was obliged to change my mind," Cruz remarked. "A simple budgetary matter. But I would have telephoned you, of course, as soon as I found new accommodation," and he looked sincere, as if to deter any impression of subterfuge on his part.

Galloway wondered why the notion of Cruz disappearing into the maze of Los Angeles troubled him. The Filipino had done some arithmetic and hadn't been able to balance his books, so he was shuffling off elsewhere, which was surely all there was to this. But hadn't Cruz called the Palms "cheap" only last night? Okay, he was no grandmaster of the checkbook, which wasn't a crime. You're searching too hard, Charlie, turning over tiny stones, digging away, bare fingernails in the black earth, acting more from desperation than doggedness—and you don't have a clue what you expect to find. Everything you do is grounded in desperation, both your own as well as that left you, like some unwanted legacy, by the babbling last words of Freddie Joaquin, by the mysterious, undelivered message of Ella Nazarena.

"Do you know where you're going?" he asked.

"I haven't decided," Cruz answered. He discarded his newspaper on a coffee table, picked up his bag and clutched it under his arm. He was getting ready to go.

"Do you know your way around this town? Have you been here before?"

Cruz shook his head. "I have a good sense of direction, Mr. Galloway."

"This is a very weird city, Ray, and you might end up in some undesirable neighborhood." Charlie made a small gesture of concern with his hand.

"I appreciate your concern, Mr. Galloway. I'll be fine. Believe me." Cruz smiled, shifting his bag from one hand to the other. "What can I do for you anyway?"

Galloway sat down. "It's nothing. Just a loose end I want to clarify, Ray."

Cruz glanced in the direction of the front doors, where the sun on glass suggested a photograph of an exploding nova. It was clear he expected somebody. Galloway wondered who.

"It's a small discrepancy, Ray. Something Freddie said."

"Freddie again," Cruz remarked, more to himself than to Charlie Galloway. A note of slight annoyance entered his voice and a tiny agitated muscle pulsed in his jaw. For the first time Galloway had the feeling he caused this man some minor discomfort, which didn't necessarily mean Cruz had any great secret to conceal; people were usually perturbed by the appearance of cops. But it was interesting to discover that Cruz's external control had a slight structural weaknesses, uncertainty at the heart of self-assurance.

"According to Joaquin, you were one of his dearest old friends."

"Is that what he said?"

"Effusively. He gave me the impression you and he were like that," and Galloway pressed his index and middle fingers together in a gesture of close bonding. "But last night, if I remember correctly, you told me you barely knew the man. You had 'mutual acquaintances' in your province. Wasn't that what you said?"

"Yes. That's true. Why? Do you believe what Freddie told you?" Cruz asked, as if the possibility were preposterous.

"I didn't say I *believed* him," Galloway remarked. "I was merely . . . intrigued by the difference between his version and yours." He gazed for a time at Cruz, whose face registered the expression of someone offended. Freddie said one thing, Cruz another. How could you believe Freddie, who'd pulled a gun with the intention of killing you? Cruz hadn't tried to shove a pistol in your face. Cruz was reasonable, articulate, personable if not quite successfully affable, a man who gave Galloway the impression of a constant undercurrent of loneliness that would always spoil his efforts at social ease. He was the one more deserving of belief. Freddie, on the other hand, seemed to have found truth a strange country, a hinterland with which he had merely a passing familiarity.

And yet. And yet. Galloway was restless, dissatisfied.

Cruz mystified him more than a little. The Filipino had none of that unfocused curiosity of the foreign tourist in Los Angeles, the fatuous awe of Hollywood that brightens the eye, the charged look of expectancy agitated by celluloid legends and dreams. No little maps to the Homes of the Stars protruded from his pockets, no camera hung around his neck. Cruz struck him as more purposeful than a common sightseer, as if he had some singular thing in mind. But what?

"Where did Freddie take you yesterday afternoon?"

"To the ocean."

"Then he brought you back here?"

Cruz hesitated over this simple question. There were only two possible answers, neither of which involved any complexity as far as Galloway could see. But Cruz missed a beat for some unguessable reason. "No. Freddie said he had other business. I came back in a taxi. May I speak frankly?"

"Be my guest."

"I fail to see the importance of your questions, Mr. Galloway." Cruz raised a hand as he spoke, touched the lid of his left eye. "If you suspect me of the murder of this woman—I am sorry, I forget the name—you should say so. Last night you said Freddie was responsible, but if for some reason you've changed your mind I think I have a right to be told. Otherwise, you know, I'd like to leave."

Galloway stood up. *The importance of your questions:* How could he explain to Cruz or even to himself? Tiny disparities acted upon his mind as poison ivy to the skin. Perhaps the hungover brain was a big empty auditorium in which whispers were magnified into great rumbling echoes. *Did you suspect Cruz of something? If Cruz and Freddie weren't the old pals wee Freddie had said, then what were they doing together? What did they have in common? Chauffeur and passenger? Guide and tourist?* Cruz neither looked nor sounded like a man who'd have a great deal in common with Freddie. You couldn't see Cruz, quiet-mannered, rather proper in manner, being very comfortable in a strip bar, surrounded by knockers and ass and spangle. Ray and Freddie had made an unlikely pair.

But so had Freddie and Ella. The whole business was fraught with incongruities.

Cruz looked at his watch again. "It seems to me everything comes down to the fact Freddie lied habitually, Mr. Galloway. Such people are not unknown."

Was that it, then, Charlie? Was that the end of it? Freddie a psychopathic liar, Cruz an angelic teller of truths. Is that your little discrepancy explained away, boxed and buried? He felt suddenly depressed, empty of purpose, like a man who reels in his line and finds not a fish but a discarded tire iron or a hubcap circa 1946 or a fragment of a downed satellite.

"Are we finished?" Cruz asked.

Before Charlie could respond, the elevator disgorged four Korean men rattling golf bags and carrying bright, rolled umbrellas. They were followed by four Caucasian hookers in tight shorts and black shades, astonishingly lovely, lipsticked, well-built girls who clutched the men in the possessive way of expensive prostitutes who haven't yet been paid for their comprehensive services. This crew created a noisy, energetic diversion and even as Galloway was distracted by them, Cruz shrugged and began to walk away. Although there was no sense of urgency or slyness in Cruz's movement—perhaps he thought he'd been dismissed—Charlie started after him, brushing past the golfers and their perfumed girls. He collided with one of the men, whose bag fell over, releasing a half dozen orange golf balls that bounced across the floor. The Koreans and their girls found this hilarious. All eight laughed with the uncontrollable merriment of people sharing a funny acid trip.

Cruz was still heading along the lobby without looking back. Before he reached the door a lovely Filipina girl stepped into the hotel and greeted him with a cool, indifferent, LA flip of her hand. *Like, hey.* She was short and black-haired, her skin an enviable tint neither chocolate nor tan but a color white American women basted long hours in the sun to achieve without ever getting it right. She wore a black silk shirt and baggy white pants in a carelessly rich manner, but her clothes didn't conceal the firmness of her slender body. *A looker,* Charlie thought.

Cruz clasped a hand around her elbow and ushered her out through the glass doors. She seemed a little surprised by his decisiveness, as if she were unaccustomed to being manhandled.

Galloway considered it altogether an odd moment, like a bad rehearsal, a flaw in a director's blocking. Girl walks in, Cruz grabs her, walks her out again immediately. Why the hurry? Some uncharacteristic moment of consternation on Cruz's part? Maybe Raymond simply hadn't wanted to go through the rigmarole of introducing the girl. Inscrutable Raymond, darkly purposeful, a loner.

Just who the hell are you, Ray?

Galloway went outside. He saw Cruz and the girl go across the parking lot to a yellow VW convertible with the top down. The girl climbed behind the wheel, Cruz sat in the passenger seat. The car backed up. Charlie Galloway looked at the California license plate, then walked to his Toyota, which sat shimmering in the rich mixture of sunlight and pollution like a combustible extension of his hangover.

Before he reached his car his stomach had contrived to rise up into his mouth and, as if he'd been struck by lightning, he slumped to his knees beside the Toyota, where he retched dryly, miserably, bringing up nothing save some sickly, thick saliva. A volcanic pain erupted in his head. He thought of a wandering thrombus clamped under his skullbone like a crab, creating the kind of pressure that made death seem a prospect to be welcomed by carnivals and calypsos.

Even when he managed to stand, he was unable to stop trembling. Under the white sky he stood shaking, deceived by the notion that the roar of passing traffic was a bizarre tide rattling down on a beach, and the squeak of brakes the squeal of outraged gannets, an illusion that had to be the harbinger of delirium tremens, but then the moment passed, and his head cleared somewhat, and he opened the car door with the relief of a man returned to reality after a trip down the fissures of his own dementia.

14

Larry Deets caught a shuttle from Washington and arrived at La Guardia Airport shortly after noon. It took almost two hours to reach Manhattan by cab because traffic had been diverted around the scene of a highway murder. Apparently an altercation had taken place between the drivers of two cars, which had resulted in a black family of three, each covered with a bloodstained sheet, lying dead on the shoulder of the road, and a Caucasian man dying from a wound in his neck. Paramedics streaked with blood labored to save his life while a hysterical black girl, a relative of the three dead, was furiously trying to attack the wounded man, but she was restrained by uniformed cops.

Two dented cars, one a station wagon with a bumper sticker saying VIRGINIA IS FOR LOVERS, the other a rusted old Camaro, straddled the highway. Ambulances, police cars, sirens in the sunlight, a fire truck, broken glass, and blood—all the elements of a tragedy Deets thought pointless, even as he realized how his life and ambition had anesthetized him to any sense of horror at such slayings.

Washington had insulated him. The rest of America was as

distant to him as another country, a land of suburb and prairie, dams and power plants, rivers with unpronounceable Indian names, men in baseball caps and women in hair curlers, small ghostly mill towns and great electric-orange cities you saw in the dark from airplanes. This second, shadowy America was good only for one thing. It would supply the numbers required to put Byron Truskett in the White House.

Deets got out of the cab in lower Manhattan. He went inside a small neighborhood bar, a place called McGloan's selling Guinness and Irish stew. The tavern was air-conditioned and dim. A few men and women sat on stools and concentrated with Celtic intensity on their pints of stout and shots of Bushmills. They paid no attention to Deets, who, in a gray seersucker suit, was incongruous among T-shirts and jeans and coveralls. The Irish had a talent for absorbing the unlikely without comment; it came with their general delight in idiosyncrasy.

Deets wandered into the narrow dining area beyond the bar, where large booths looked murky under smoke-stained lampshades, and menus, soiled with brown sauce, curled in their plastic holders. He sat down, placed his briefcase on the table, waited. He had the back room to himself. He checked his watch. He was about forty minutes late and wondered if his contact had already gone. For a while he studied the Aer Lingus wall posters.

He ordered a Beck's from the waitress, who was Welsh and spoke in the singsong way of Harlech people. Irish bar, German beer, Welsh waitress, and Deets himself, who was three-quarters Prussian, one-fifth Serbo-Croatian and a fraction Finn: The melting pot frotheth. Deets sometimes thought that the phenomenon of the deep genealogical curiosity that affected millions of Americans indicated trouble in the national psyche, a sense of something missed, similar to the ache people feel when they learn they've been adopted.

Five minutes passed, ten; somebody punched money into the jukebox and the room filled with the sound of an Irish tenor singing "She Moved Through the Fair." Deets appreciated music about as much as he had dancing lessons at Arthur Murray's. When the gods were handing out an appreciation of music they gave Deets something else instead, the gift of knowing whose coattails to ride to high places, the eye for the main chance—and he was damned if he was going to have it wrecked by anybody or anything.

He sipped the cold beer and thought resentfully about Byron, who'd gone ahead with his plan to put Laforge's name in nomination, *despite* the information Deets had supplied about the errant behavior of one Eugene Costain, a man under Billy's command in the Philippines. A rumor, admittedly, but in Deets's world you never got smoke unless there was fire somewhere. He'd gone to great lengths to unearth the material. But Truskett hadn't acted prudently. At the very *least* he should have waited a few days before seeing the President; he should have weighed the implications of the rumor and perceived a possible danger in it and instructed Deets either to substantiate the story or demolish it—but Byron, like some panting, overheated schoolkid, was thinking with his weenie. He was in an indecent hurry to satisfy Madam Laforge, which meant pleasing Monsieur Billy too.

Deets finished his beer. He hated the sense of his world hanging in delicate balance. He didn't like to think the eight years he'd spent working with Truskett, encouraging and supporting the man's ambition twenty-four goddam hours per goddam day, lying to Miriam, covering up the affair with La Laforge, juggling appointments, composing speeches, analyzing strategy, sitting up late into the night and listening over bourbon to what Truskett would do if he ever reached the Oval Office, years of counseling and comforting and flattering, years of chasing his own dreams of glory and influence—he was terrified to think all this might be headed for the disposal chute if it turned out that Laforge had indeed been bad in the Philippines and the Senate found out.

He should have acted differently himself. He should have *insisted* that Truskett wait. He should have been adamant. *Should, should, should.* You could *should* yourself into an early grave.

Later today the announcement of Laforge's nomination was going out into the world. The President considered the post of director of the CIA too important to leave vacant, as it had been for all practical purposes during Sandy Bach's protracted illness. So, with a decisiveness and speed unusual for him, he was calling a press conference at which he'd express his regrets over Bach's death with lengthy platitudes and then introduce the nominee, as if to reassure a fretful nation that somebody was now at the helm of the great ship Intelligence.

The music on the jukebox stopped. The narrow gloomy bar was silent. How much longer could he sit here? A telephone rang in an ill-lit recess, somebody answered it quickly, a terse conversation took place. Deets eavesdropped some guff about a bet on a horse that was, *ah, to be sure, jaysus, a dead cert,* then he picked up his briefcase to leave. A very fat man, blocking the sunlight, shuffled through the front door and made his way slowly into the back room.

"You Deets?"

Deets nodded.

"I came before, waited, then I figured a delay." Sweating heavily, the fat man squeezed himself into a booth. His enormous stomach overhung the waist of his burgundy polyester pants. He wore white shoes and a pink and red striped shirt with sleeves rolled up to reveal huge arms at the end of which were small chubby white hands that didn't quite belong. They resembled boiled squabs. The man's black hair was wet from perspiration and he wheezed as he breathed through his mouth. Deets thought he had to be about three hundred pounds plus with a fifty-six waist.

Deets was offered a slack wet handshake that felt like a swampy armpit.

"Call me Gregory," the man said. He had a rasping voice. It reminded Deets of the sound a kid made when his straw got to the bottom of a milkshake.

"I'd like some verification," Deets said. "Some kind of ID."

"You outta your mind? In a situation like this you don't ask for stuff like that."

"I don't need mysteries," Deets said. He opened the briefcase and took out an envelope to remind this blubber that a commercial transaction was going on, and that he, Deets, was calling the shots. He placed the envelope on the table and covered it with his hand.

The fat man smiled. He had little pointy teeth, as if they'd been filed down for maximum biting potential. "That the money?"

Deets said, "That's the money. Ten grand." He opened the envelope to display hundred-dollar bills. The money was his own. He lived frugally and invested with prudence. He'd briefly considered skimming the cash from the senator's campaign fund, but larceny unsettled him.

"Nice," said Gregory, and his eyebrows made an appreciative arch. With considerable grunting and twisting of the body, he produced a brown wallet from a hip pocket. A New York driver's license was flashed in front of Deets, who looked at it briefly; there were also Discover and Visa cards in the name of Gregory Redlinger.

"Fair enough?"

"I just like to make absolutely sure I'm talking to the right man," Deets said.

"They could be forgeries, of course," Redlinger said.

"Yeah. I'll take your word they're not." Deets had no great regard for those nefarious individuals, such as Redlinger, who gathered around the edges of the intelligence community like dullards drawn to the lights of a passing carnival. He had an aversion to the way they loved to create an aura of mystery about themselves. They needed the reinforcement of believing in an exclusive club named Espionage, of which they were happy to be members on first-name terms with the doorman and the maître d'. It was pathetic, and it worked better when there had been a Cold War and America imagined itself imperiled by the penny-dreadful threat of an international Communist conspiracy. Now, much of the intrigue people like Redlinger enjoyed was either nostalgic or imagined, or at best played out in shabby third-world arenas. Spying, like vaudeville, had declined with the times.

The fat man flapped his shirt collar to circulate air about his neck, and the movement sent a smell of sweat and yesterday's cologne wafting toward Deets, who turned his face slightly away.

The fat man said, "What I hear is you need more information about a certain situation that occurred a few years ago in a far-away land to the east."

The coy language! Deets said sharply, "I want facts. No hearsay. No faraway lands to the east crap. I can't eat pie in the sky, friend. I like stuff that can be corroborated, if need be."

"I dunno about that," said Redlinger, sounding sulky and

tugging at what turned out to be a small gold earring in his fleshy right lobe.

Deets sighed. "I don't want to sit here and listen to some story you might just have made up, Gregory, because you have a burning need for the loot. I want truth and I want detail. I wouldn't like to think I'm wasting time and money. You catch *my* drift?" Deets settled back in the booth.

Redlinger had ordered an appetizer of fried chicken pieces, which now arrived. They were shrouded in misshapen batter. He stuffed them into his mouth between words. "See, I don't want my name dragged into a situation that could turn out inconvenient for me if there was, you know, publicity. In my business, you need integrity. You don't go shooting your mouth off. You got an image to maintain. I'm an indy con, my word's gotta be money in the bank."

"An indy what?"

"Independent contractor. I'm known and respected throughout the trade because I can keep a secret." Wheezing, sucking air, the fat man finished his chicken, licked his fingers carefully one by one. "Which is why I got to be careful, know what I'm saying?"

Men like Redlinger always felt obliged to tell you how their word was their bond before they actually embarked on giving you information they'd probably sworn never to tell a living soul. Deets shut his eyes, thinking that Redlinger represented a step along a line of inquiry into Laforge which he'd begun weeks ago on his own initiative—an act, admittedly, of self-preservation—among fringe figures with tenuous connections to the CIA. Some of these were known to him through the activities of the Joint Select Committee on Intelligence, while others such as Redlinger were acquaintances of acquaintances of acquaintances, free-lancers who sold their services in distant countries, usually as couriers of one kind or another.

He'd reached Redlinger through learning about Gene Costain from a former State Department functionary, a man retired and mostly fishing his days away in Venezuela, an old Far East hand called Kelvin Wax, who'd known Costain the way expatriate Americans get to know each other in lonely tropical outposts, over scotch and soda and sharing outdated newspapers from

home and musing about the autumn they were missing, the last
gorgeous days of the baseball season, the crack of ball on bat and
the glorious whiff of a hot dog, Indian summer, the first crisp
snow that came soon after the melancholic flight of migratory
geese.

According to Wax, Costain had once talked in a vague way
about an incident that had happened in the Philippines during
the last few months of the Marcos regime, an event Gene appeared to take in his stride but one Wax thought might have
depressing implications if the whole story were told. Some Filipinos, suspected of anti-Marcos activity, had been mistakenly arrested and deprived of their basic human rights. A few, it seemed,
had been beaten. Of course, Wax remarked, you had to read
between the lines when Gene spoke because he liked to play his
cards close to the chest and when he told you a story he never
told you everything because he'd been trained that way. He'd
been a stickler about observing discretion in professional matters,
although he'd screwed up his personal life, said the angler, by
having his nuts well oiled by some beautiful number in Manila.
For heaven's sake, even Gene's wife up in Poughkeepsie had
known about the little chickadee in Manila!

Over cocktails the night before last at the Colonnade Room
in downtown DC, Wax had brought up the name of Gregory
Redlinger as the man most likely to know the whole truth about
Costain's tale. Redlinger and Costain had been close for years.
Gregory knew more about Gene than Gene had known about
himself. He also understood the Philippines as well as any American, but he'd need a little *grease* to talk. Was Deets prepared to
pay? You bet your ass he was. A phone number was scribbled on
the back of a coaster and slipped across the table to Deets. And
Wax, winking, had gone out into the draggy heat of a Washington
night and back to the draggy heat of Venezuela to catch fish.

"I want to know exactly what happened in Benguet," Deets
said.

"Well now," said Redlinger. "Let's start with what you already know and go from there."

Deets said, "According to my information, Costain was instrumental in rounding up Communist suspects in the province."

The fat man's eyes closed. "Are you fucking kidding me?"

"I don't follow," Deets said.

"You did say rounding up, right?"

"Right."

"We're not talking rounding up, Deets. Ha! We're not talking some picnic situation where somebody swipes an extra drumstick and gets his wrist smacked. *Rounding up!* I like that. I like that one. Jesus Kay-ryst." Redlinger opened his eyes, which reminded Deets of the fakes a taxidermist might use when he readied a dead rodent for posterity.

"Deets, Deets." The fat man leaned across the table as far as he could. "Gene was one of my oldest buddies. He confided in me. He told me shit I didn't want to hear. You know what I'm saying? So when you sit down here and talk to me about 'rounding up' I have to laugh. What we've got here is fucking cold-blooded murder, Deets."

Deets was quiet for a moment during which he heard his heart as surely as a grandfather clock. The fat man laughed, a coarse hiccup. *Eh-heh eh-heh eh-heh.* He couldn't get over the phrase *rounding up* and he said it quietly to himself a couple of times as he laughed.

"Listen. They took maybe a dozen of our little brown brothers and sisters up into the hills after the local constabulary had had their fun and they blew them away. See what I'm saying? After the sport, da-drum de-dum, the coop de grass."

"You're not making this clear, Redlinger. Spell it out for me."

"Oh, you're slow, Deets. Torture. With a capital *T.* Electricity where it causes the most pain. Some of the old water stuff. The bridge treatment, very unpleasant. They used some of the Flips as ashtrays. Sticks. Bats. Needles. Broken glass. Whatever causes pain. Now, this ain't pleasant to the ear, especially to a guy behind a desk all day. But what do you know about the real world, Deets? Games is what you know. Whose buttons to push. Whose ass to kiss. You don't know shit about what really goes on."

Deets said, "The idea of torture doesn't faze me, Gregory."

"Christ, you're a tough guy. I'm impressed." The fat man smiled, or so it seemed. His lips moved and cavernous dimples appeared in his cheeks. "You don't know torture from toothache,

Deets. Ever seen a torture victim? It's like a light goes out. They don't sleep. They have nightmares. Long after the bones mend and the bruises go and the wounds fade, they're basket cases. They never make it back all the way. Fucking twilight zone."

Deets chose to ignore the fat man's taunt; he wasn't interested in diversions. "Who instigated the torture?"

"Instigated?" Redlinger shook his head as if he couldn't believe this Deets and the words the guy came up with. "You don't *instigate,* Deets. Something just kinda happens, and sometimes it gets out of hand, and it grows, and before you know it you're overboard. You've gone too far and you can't go back to where you were before. You get me?"

Deets nodded his head slowly. "Was Costain involved in the torture?"

Redlinger was quiet for a while. Somebody put a coin in the jukebox and then it was Bing Crosby singing "When Irish Eyes Are Smiling."

"Let's say he didn't stop it. Let's say, *maybe,* he could've told the constabulary to ease off. On the other hand, maybe he got into the spirit of the thing and did some things himself that weren't righteous. But you gotta get a perspective, Deets. The times were fucking evil. Marcos wanted examples made of the Commies. And sometimes mistakes happened and the wrong saps got it. Gene had to bury some evidence, if you see what I'm saying."

Deets was quiet a moment. "What part did Laforge play?"

"Bashful Billy?" the fat man asked. "So far as I know, he sent the orders down. He was Marcos's pipeline. That's why he went to the Philippines in the first place. To shape up the constabulary where it needed it. Which was practically everywhere."

"Did he know there was torture?"

"What do you think? He'd have to be blind and deaf."

"Did he know about Costain's role in the killings?"

"Listen. The night you're talking about, there were two of our guys in Benguet. Gene Costain one. And a guy called Tom Railsback. He's still with the agency. Works out of Dallas. Both these guys took orders directly from Billy. What does that mean exactly? Did Billy order the deaths? Did he say *Turn your face to the side and act unconcerned if you happen to see some torture, guys?* Who the fuck knows? Billy was in charge. Billy's responsible even if he didn't pull the trigger himself. Sure he knew people had been tortured and he knew people were shot and buried. He could have reported it. He could have reprimanded his men. He didn't. So what does that tell you?"

"Everything," Deets said quietly.

Redlinger looked at the envelope. Drops of sweat rolled from his hair. "Take a thing like My Lai, Deets. Guys get out of hand. Carried away. Basically decent guys who happen to be on a roller coaster ride. Blood rushes to their heads because that's what blood does. It's over in thirty seconds. Then they laugh like they're really nervous. Then they don't say anything for days. Then they stuff it. And that's where it stays. Stuffed. In a deep-down place."

"Did Costain tell you all this?"

"It's the kind of thing a guy likes to get off his chest, I'd say. Sure he told me. You think I made it up?" Redlinger reached out and snatched the envelope from Deets in a move of surprising agility. "I think I just earned this."

"Is there anything else I should know?"

Redlinger redistributed his weight. The Naugahyde beneath him farted quietly. "I go to the Philippines three, four times a year. I'm in touch with what's going on. It's still possible to be an American over there if you keep a low profile. I rent an apartment in Parañaque, which is livable. So people know me. I'm the fat American who's kind to the barefoot kids. That's who I am, Deets. Santa. I sit down with the locals and we eat boiled rice together. They're nice people and they accept me."

"So?" Deets asked.

"I sometimes hear fascinating stuff."

"What stuff?"

"Look. Is this Laforge important to you?"

"In what way?"

"They say he's going to get the nod for Bach's job."

Deets said, "Maybe."

"And that means a lot to you?"

Deets made an ambiguous gesture with his hand.

The fat man looked sly. "See, I might have some other information for you, Deets. I mean, if you're interested in Laforge. . . ."

"I'm listening."

"It ain't that simple," said Redlinger. "You gotta understand my business, man. You want what I got, you pay some more." The fat man shrugged, the gesture of a trader who regrets market forces—but, jeez, what can he do about them? There was a whiff of the bazaar about Redlinger.

"Uh-huh," Deets said. "There's no more money, Gregory."

"Well, that's too bad." Gregory began to slide out of the booth.

"I don't see it quite that way," Deets said. "In your shoes I wouldn't be in any great hurry to flee, my chubby amigo."

"Meaning?"

"Meaning you tell me anything else you know, and you tell it for free this time. I've been generous. But the coffers are empty, Gregory. The well is dry. You're out of luck."

"And you're outta your skull, Deets. You must live on another planet. Nothing gets you nothing."

Deets smiled at the fat man and grabbed his wrist. "Not this time. Just sit down."

"What the fuck." Gregory pulled his arm free and, looking sullen, sat reluctantly.

"That's better. Now satisfy my curiosity on a couple of things. Tell me how it's possible for a man to avoid filing federal income tax returns for the last eight years. I'd like to know your secret, Greg. What moron wants to pay taxes anyhow?"

Gregory blinked slowly. "I got a hotshot accountant."

"Sure you do. Okay, let's try this one. Clue me in on how a man on parole for peddling pornographic videotapes of Filipino children performing unnatural acts manages to flit so freely between hemispheres. Your parole officer know about your globe-trotting?"

Gregory sighed. "You done your homework, Deets."

"Force of habit. I was an A student."

"Hey-ho. It was worth a try. Nothing to lose, huh? You might have laid some more bread on me."

"Count yourself lucky you got what you got, Gregory. Now talk. I'm all ears."

Redlinger looked thoughtful, as if he were still trying to concoct a scheme to force further payments out of Deets, a con, some fiscal acupuncture. Eventually he forced a small flabby smile of resignation. "Jeez. You got your act down sweet, Deets. You look like a DC bozo and come on like a fucking gangster. Okay. There's a guy just arrived in this country. Name of Teng, which sure as shit wouldn't be what it said on his passport. He came in through Los Angeles. He's here to hit Laforge. Soon."

"Hit as in . . . ?"

"Hit as in," said the fat man.

"How do you know this?"

"A stoopid question, Deets. You don't believe me, watch the papers. Especially the Dallas ones. Look for the murder of Tom Railsback. Then if you still don't believe me, sit back and wait for Laforge to get his too."

Deets watched the man struggle out of the booth, a battle between flesh and Formica. For a second Redlinger appeared to have lost and he swayed a little, as if he were about to be sucked back down into his seat, but he prevailed and shuffled toward the door, wheezing miserably with every small step he took.

Deets didn't move for a while.

On the flight to Dallas, Lizzie Honculada said nothing for a long time, affected as she was by the dour manner of her traveling companion, who sat in the aisle seat, flipping the pages of the airlines magazine faster than he could possibly read. When he got to the end he started at the beginning again. Snap, snap, snap. Somewhere over New Mexico she politely asked him to stop, and he turned his blue eyes on her as if in a pinch he'd crack her head open without further consideration. She thought they should have been lovely eyes, but they were too . . . *elsewhere.* Coldly attractive, okay, if you went in for that sort of faraway look, which she always associated with zealots, raving men wandering in deserts, seeing things and talking to snakes and coming back to tell people about bliss. Besides, a small light of contempt lay beneath the blue, like a lamp beyond opaque glass.

He'd been more than usually distant since the hotel in Los Angeles, when he'd hurried her across the parking lot and told her to drive. She'd looked back to see a disheveled character walking after them, but then the man vanished. All the way to the airport her passenger kept turning around, afraid of being followed.

"Who was he?" she asked.

Snap, snap with the magazine.

"God," she said. "Quit it. Quit."

Teng rolled the magazine into a tube and tapped it on his knee.

"Who was the guy back at the hotel?" she asked.

"Nobody."

"For nobody he sure had an effect on you."

Armando Teng looked out into the blue magnificence of the late morning, the cloudless stretch of sky that suggested a great limpid lagoon in which you might simply float. Sunlight came back off the silver wing of the plane, blinding. The vibration of the engines coursed through him, churning his stomach, and the girl annoyed him. But these were superficial—what really bothered him was Galloway. He tried to remember what Freddie had said about the omniscience of the LAPD—surely a superstitious exaggeration—and he wondered what Charlie Galloway knew, if indeed he knew anything. The chances were good that he didn't, otherwise Teng wouldn't be flying to Dallas without hindrance. But he couldn't shake the feeling Galloway was on to *something*, and it nagged at him. Three or four times on the way to the airport he thought he saw Galloway's car behind; even now he imagined the cop was sitting some rows back and watching. *Turn and look,* he thought. But he wouldn't give in to the impulse.

"I don't want to know," Lizzie Honculada said. "Forget I even asked, okay?"

Teng stared along the aisle at the stewardess, a slender blonde plumping up pillows for an old lady. He'd never flown first class before and the indulgence troubled him. You were pampered here, and fawned over by the servile blonde, and the drinks came in real glass, not Styrofoam. He felt trapped in what seemed to him a flying cylinder of privilege. Lizzie Honculada looked perfectly at ease. She probably never traveled any other way. She was spoiled, buffered against the real world, and even now lost in the glossy fashion magazine that lay across her lap, brightly colored pages of gaunt, unsmiling women in clothes that cost an extraordinary amount of money. How simple her life had to be, how lacking in substance. What to wear. What color of lipstick. Such strenuous philosophical inquiries.

Teng felt rage flare up in his head. But what was the point of directing it at the girl? He was angry because he'd lost control in Los Angeles and allowed Galloway under his skin. He should never have turned and walked away—that was the behavior of a person with something to hide. How could it fail to alert Galloway to the notion that Raymond Cruz wasn't the simple tourist he claimed to be? But what could Galloway conceivably know? Okay, so Freddie had run off at the mouth. He'd become a talkative gossip, a *daldalero*. But it wasn't possible Galloway could have believed him. *No, no. You worry too much. You're in a strange country and you're nervous. You see things that don't exist. The secret is to relax.* Wasn't that what Lizzie Honculada had told him yesterday? *Hang loose.*

How did you learn to do that? How did you set aside your purpose, even for a moment, and pretend you were carefree and easygoing? He was tight, coiled, muscles stiff. It was what hatred did. It locked you in. Your flesh was a coffin. You thought of nothing but revenge and it consumed you.

"I wish you'd stop tapping," Lizzie said.

He opened his eyes. The magazine was going up and down, down and up, on his thigh. He hadn't been aware of it. He stuffed the thing into the seat pouch and tried to smile.

"Did anybody ever tell you your face really changes when you smile?" Lizzie asked.

Marissa—the very name seemed to chime delicately in his head—had said once he had the kind of smile that could charm flowers out of the earth, if he learned how to use it. Why in the name of God had she died? Why hadn't *he* been the one tortured and shot that terrible night? He had a deep black reservoir of guilt. On the day of her death he'd been in Manila to look for a rare book, something that didn't matter a damn in the long run. He could have postponed the trip and stayed with her and maybe they wouldn't have taken her away. But no, he'd gone to Manila, browsed in the Solidaridad Book Shop on Padre Faure Street and then he'd walked along Mabini Street to a restaurant, whittling time away until the departure of his bus back to Baguio in the late afternoon. He'd reached Baguio shortly after midnight.

By then she was already dead.

The sound of the engines changed now, the modulation from major key to minor that accompanies descent. Lizzie closed her magazine. Her fingernails were painted a shade of red and she wore two rings, one of which had rubies matching her nails.

"We're coming down," she said.

Teng was quiet for a moment. "Then where?"

"I have instructions to take you to a certain place. And that's the end of the road for me, thank God. I'm not what you'd call thrilled to be here. It's not like I don't have things to do."

"Painting your nails," Teng said. "Choosing your rings."

"Up yours too."

Teng crumpled a napkin in his fist and said nothing.

"I never met anybody as tense as you, Cruz. You give uptight new dimensions. The sooner you're off my hands, terrific, fabulous, I'm out of here."

Teng felt the fuselage shiver and heard objects slither in overhead compartments as the aircraft dropped into a pocket of turbulence. A sense of alarm went through him and he touched the back of the girl's hand very lightly, as if the shudder of the plane and Lizzie's outburst had combined to unsettle him and he needed the touch of another person—perhaps to calm him, perhaps to offset the isolation that accompanied him with the constancy of a big sad dog. Then the plane trembled again and the FASTEN SEAT BELTS sign flashed on and off and the big aircraft took on the pall of a skyborn death trap. The tremors reminded Teng of the fragility of human life, how easily the skin of this flying whale might peel away and send people out into the finality of the great blue spaces.

"You're right, I'm tense," he said. "I'm sorry. I'm very sorry." A dry apology, uttered quietly; but he meant it. It was useless to let his resentments control him. The girl couldn't help what she was, how she'd been formed. She could no more deny those forces than he could forget the background that had shaped him. He took his hand away from her and fumbled for his seat belt buckle, embarrassed by his own gesture of companionship— or was the touch meant to be a truce? He wasn't sure.

Lizzie looked out of the window. Dallas lay spread some thousands of feet below, like a balsa-wood scale model of a city.

Cruz's touch had taken her off guard but it didn't alter anything. In the right circumstances, maybe, *just maybe,* by moon or surf or candlelight, she could warm to him, but this was all speculation since he was about to split. And that would be an end to him. Which was well and good. You could practically smell danger and destruction on the guy. The gesture, though, had been a surprise, and not unpleasant. And now he'd actually apologized!

Teng said, "If you knew more about me, perhaps . . ." He left the sentence dangling. Candor wasn't wise. To talk about himself openly would make him vulnerable.

Lizzie said, "I really don't want to know, Ray. You. Your business. I like being kept in the dark, okay?"

"Yes. I understand."

The plane landed smoothly in clear light. Beyond the air-conditioned terminal heat shimmered everywhere, rising from the gloss of cars and buses, from molten concrete and glass, as if Dallas and Fort Worth were enormous smithies where thousands of furious hammers rose and fell on overheated anvils. A black car, driven by a uniformed man from a limousine service, picked Teng and Lizzie up and headed in the direction of downtown Dallas, where the temperature was one hundred and six degrees. The highway went through a landscape of monotonous flatness wherein suburbs and shopping malls, bombarded by intolerable rays, suggested the shells of hermit gastropods. Flags, Texan and American, were motionless on high white poles. Rich suburbs and poorer ones lay close together in uncertain arrangements. Teng surveyed it all from the cool tinted darkness of the big car, surprised by the enormity and space of what he saw. Cities had always meant Manila to him, where the sky was crowded out either by high-rise buildings or massive pollution, and streets were traffic-choked boulevards or cramped pedestrian corridors. Here, though, was Texan bravura, a sky bigger than any he'd ever seen before, unblemished to infinity, and great flat highways running to God knows where. And then in the distance appeared the skyline of downtown, towers and turrets, black stone and pale, castles of crystal, a city struck out of dirt and raised upward to dominate the flatlands like a series of oversized oil derricks. To Teng it had the substance of a vague dream, an unnatural city in a landscape dry and ravaged and far too bright.

The car entered downtown, where the streets between the high-rise buildings were in shadow, suggesting gullies. The driver parked in front of an old red-brick building, got out, held the back door open for his passengers. On the sidewalk Teng clutched his small canvas bag and sweated miserably. Lizzie told the driver to wait, then led Teng inside the building toward an elevator, which conveyed them rapidly and silently to the sixth floor.

"What is this place?" Teng asked.

"An American history lesson," Lizzie replied.

The elevator opened. A ticket desk and a turnstile lay ahead. Lizzie bought two tickets from a clerk. Teng followed uncertainly, his eyes as yet unaccustomed to the change from sunlight to shade. He stood in a large room filled with posters and television screens and for a second he was puzzled until he saw an enormous picture of John F. Kennedy and, to his left, a glass cube inside which were boxes of books and a window. Between the boxes was a space where a man might hide. From the window, sealed in its own prism to keep the public away, Lee Harvey Oswald had allegedly fired the rifle that killed John F. Kennedy in Dealey Plaza below.

Teng knew this piece of American history well because he'd learned about it at school, where the textbooks were written to persuade you that Kennedy was some kind of saint. Teng tried to imagine the gunman crouched by the sill, rifle in hand, while the caravan of official cars and police motorcycles went past outside. He tried to feel Oswald's urgency, his apprehension, his state of mind. Was there uncertainty? Some last-minute indecision? Perhaps there was a high, a rush of conviction that took him beyond all doubt. Teng was familiar with that, the acceleration of the pulses, the pounding.

He stepped back from the display and walked past the various exhibits—photographs of Kennedy and his wife, TV consoles that played film of the assassination—to the other side of the room, where Lizzie stood. She was looking down at Dealey Plaza, where the road ran past the grassy knoll, an insignificant rise in the land made notorious, even spooky, by history.

"Why are we in this place?" he asked.

"Because it's where my father said to bring you, Ray. I'm doing my duty. Make sure you take him up to the sixth floor of the depository, he said. Well, here we are. Sixth floor. Okay?''

Teng watched a couple of Scandinavian tourists stroll past a large photograph that consisted of stills from film of the assassination. One blurred picture depicted Kennedy at the moment of a bullet's impact, another Jacqueline Kennedy scrambling over the trunk of the big convertible. *Why this place, of all possible places?* he wondered. Why this huge chamber of death and dismal recollection, this assassin's room? If it was intentional irony on somebody's part, he didn't appreciate it. Meet Lee Harvey Oswald. Remember what becomes of assassins. To his left was a blow-up of the famous photograph in which Jack Ruby shoots Oswald, the victim's contorted features filled with horror.

This place, this shrine to violence, was unnerving. Teng looked at Lizzie Honculada, who was still watching traffic go past in the plaza. Any moment now she'd return to the car downstairs and he'd be alone again until the new contact turned up, the next in Baltazar's chain of messengers. Why hadn't there been a single contact only? Because it was safer when no one person knew everything. That was how Joe's ruined mind worked. The generosity and amiability of his character before his torture had changed, yielding to a meanness of spirit; and his natural trust had deteriorated into a paranoia that made a labyrinth of his thinking.

Tired, overheated, Teng placed his face upon the warm pane of glass and closed his eyes.

''I should be going,'' Lizzie said. ''I have a plane to catch.''

He drew back from the window. He wanted to say something, he wasn't sure what. He realized he didn't want to be left alone. He blamed his mood on the room, which was riddled with currents of violence and conspiracy and murder. It was almost as though the place were a tiny heart, an American heart, and it beat with depressing arrhythmia in the core of this large Texan city, like a tempo still haunting after almost thirty years; and America danced yet to this erratic, violent measure, guns in glove boxes, missiles in silos, bases in reluctant colonies. There was never enough violence. How could there be? When you were addicted to a thing, how could there ever be enough of it? The gunfire that echoed through this room was the same as that which had rolled through the trees in the fields beyond La Trinidad. The very same. Violence, Teng thought, was useless except as the currency with which to pay old debts. When they were paid, you owed nobody and you had no more need of it.

"I don't know what you're here for, but I hope it works out for you," Lizzie said, and she stepped away from him.

"I hope so," Teng said quietly.

She turned, moved in the direction of the exit. She had a graceful way of walking. Her black hair was momentarily tossed by a current from an air-conditioning grill and it rose in gleaming disarray before falling back in place. Teng had the urge to go after her, not because she bore some fanciful resemblance to his dead love but because he dreaded the demons of isolation. He could stop her, talk to her: simple human intercourse. He'd smile and kindness might prevail.

He did nothing. He watched her go. His life was empty because it had to be. He walked slowly around the room, moving to a corner where a TV screen was tucked away in shadow. It showed a black and white news report broadcast on the day of the assassination. The man reading it was Walter Cronkite.

Teng studied the worried features, the thinning hair, the small mustache. The voice was sonorous, heavy with dismay. *The President is dead.* He thought of his mother in a frayed hotel room in Olongapo, knees raised, legs spread for her American lover, her beloved Walter. He thought of Walter's hands on his mother's little breasts. How frail she was. She must have been crushed under the tall American's body. He imagined he heard the American cry out, then roll away satisfied, reaching perhaps for a cigarette, a Lucky Strike, a Camel, on the bedside table. There might be a lamp making his mother's eyes reflect light. Light and love. Dear Walter. She would wait for him *pagputî ng uwàk.* Until the raven turns white.

15

By six o'clock in the evening Charlie Galloway was in Santa Monica, driving through the quiet streets of a rich neighborhood where large houses, rendered stark by sunlight, suggested abandonment, empty rooms, furniture covered by dust sheets, grand pianos nobody played. Earlier, he had telephoned the Motor Vehicles Division of the state of California because it was the easiest game in town to get a name and address on the basis of a license plate number if you knew which buttons to push. A certain Elizabeth Honculada of Santa Monica popped out of the computer as the VW owner that had ferried Ray Cruz out of the Palms Hotel.

The address turned out to be an impressive house in the back streets of Santa Monica. He parked, walked through the welcoming shade of a leafy courtyard, rattled the brass parrot-head door knocker a couple of times, but nobody answered. Fine. He'd wait. He had the time. He found a stone bench under a palm tree and sat down.

What did Elizabeth have in common with Ray Cruz? Where were they headed? Where in the great blistering scheme of things had they vanished? After they'd left the Palms, Galloway had gone looking for them too late. He'd prowled here and there, tooling fruitlessly up and down streets for such a long time he felt irrevocably trapped in the mysterious grids of Los Angeles and quite unable to find his way back to the place where he'd first begun.

It seemed to him now that the manner of Ray's disappearance was just as important as the fact of it, the quiet way he'd decided to walk out of the hotel, then picking up speed when the girl had materialized, hustling her out across the parking lot with less than his customary insouciance. It was hard to avoid the impression that the Filipino, packed and prepared, hoped to skip cleanly away and Galloway's unexpected appearance had knocked the props out from under him. Why skip, though? Why the haste? What had Ray done?

Charlie shut his eyes. His thirst was unslakable and maddening, the kind that conjured oases out of still air. Now, with its usual intensity, came the crucifixion inside his head. The jeering Romans. The knock-knock of the hammer, the nail through the brain, the taste of vinegar at the back of the throat. Nearby, a sprinkler system hissed restfully.

He opened his eyes abruptly. Had he dozed? Must have. An hour had dissolved. It was five past seven suddenly and the shadows in the courtyard had stretched, although the day was still wretched.

His bladder was under extreme pressure. A quick scan of the yard revealed one likely spot in which to relieve himself. He stepped behind a clump of assorted bushy plants, dwarf lemons, pomegranates, succulents of one kind or another, and unzipped his fly with the universally stealthy gesture of a man about to have a jimmy riddle on somebody else's property. What was he supposed to do? Suffer? Explode? He aimed directly into the fleshy succulents, contented, ah, hearing the splatter of his own water drum upon thick, unflappable leaves.

He neither saw nor heard the girl who came across the courtyard. He was halfway through the process of emptying himself when she said, "Let me get you a towel and soap, why don't you," and he jumped in astonishment, his urine leaping in a dying arc, striking leaves and branches and backsplashing against his pants.

He stuffed himself hurriedly inside his zipper, painfully snagging a stray pubic hair in the vicious little metal teeth.

"Look—" he began to say.

"Why look? I saw all I wanted to see. To be frank, I wasn't impressed."

Charlie Galloway felt lame. "I didn't just wander in off the streets to use your courtyard, you know."

"No? Somebody invited you?" she asked. "Can we expect more people to show up? Is this going to be a party?"

"This isn't what it seems," Galloway said.

"You mean there's a subtext?"

"Look, I'm sorry. I was desperate. What the hell can I tell you?"

"Who are you anyway?" the girl asked, brushing a length of black hair from her face.

"Charles Galloway. Here," and he dragged out his ID, which he passed under the girl's eyes. Unhappy with the speed of his movement, she caught his wrist and studied the badge carefully before she released him.

"So. The LAPD is using my garden as a toilet. I'm honored. You don't look like my idea of a cop."

Charlie knew what she meant. "Are you Elizabeth Honculada?"

The girl said she was. She plucked a leaf from one of the orange trees, crushed it between her fingers, and smelled the odor released by the fragments. "What can I do for you?"

Charlie Galloway felt the moment of his embarrassment pass. Now the idea of exerting some control over the situation occurred to him, but Ms. Honculada was a toughie whose dark eyes were hard with resolve. Her Malay attractiveness could either be tender or determined, but it was only the latter Galloway saw. He ran a fingertip through the layer of sweat on his forehead and hoped the girl would suggest they go indoors, but she saw his discomfort and clearly enjoyed it so much she'd keep him outside and suffer.

"The man you were with today—" he began to say.

She interrupted fiercely. "What the hell has happened to civil liberties in this country? What makes you think you can come in here and pee all over my plants and ask me personal questions,

Galloway? Is this the way our country works these days? Some new law got passed and I didn't notice it? The Freedom to Piss Act? Listen, I'm bone-tired on account of this weather, so unless you got a real purpose being here, excuse me, I'm going indoors."

Weariness overwhelmed Galloway. "You left the Palms Hotel with a man called Raymond Cruz this morning."

"Raymond Cruz? Oh, yeah, right. You were in the parking lot. I remember you. I thought you looked familiar."

Galloway returned to the bench and sat down. He tried to recall everything he'd ever learned about the techniques of interviewing, but all that had slipped his mind—the logical arrangement of questions, one question supporting another, one step leading to the next in the sequential dance of interrogation. Gone. Flushed out of his head. What he had left wasn't technique but scattered instinct, blunderbuss intuition. Sometimes he had the feeling he was shadowboxing, an old pugilist now punch-drunk, clenching his fists every time a telephone rang. *Ding!* and off he went.

"Where did you take Cruz?"

"LAX."

"And you left him there?"

"Right."

"And he caught a plane?"

"I believe that's the reason most people go to airports," she said. She yawned at Charlie.

Galloway stared across the courtyard. The lengthening shadows turned purple, but they were hardly less warm than the areas the sun still penetrated. Dehydrated again, he had a moment when he saw himself in long shot, and what he resembled most was one of those disgusting shrunken heads morbid people bring back from jungle towns.

"Do you know Cruz's destination?"

"No."

"You drove him to the airport and he didn't tell you where he was going? What did you talk about during the ride?"

"The weather, Galloway. The climate," and Elizabeth Honculada gestured toward the blue sky that created a rectangle above the courtyard.

"And he didn't say where he was going?"

"Nope."

"Hard to believe."

"Believe what the hell you like. I'm going inside." She stuck her hands deep in her pockets defiantly.

"Wait." Galloway stood up. He infused his voice with a decisiveness he didn't feel. "Sometimes people don't tell their stories straight the first time and that puts me to a whole lot of bloody trouble. Now I'll have to contact the airport, get the ticket people to check their passenger lists and then spend ages looking for Cruz's name. I get pissed off, frankly. If people just told the truth straight off the bat I'd have some kind of personal life."

The girl put one hand upon her chest. "My heart goes out to you."

"Where did you leave him? What airline?"

"Delta. Or was it American? No, wait, it was Eastern. It might have been America West or Continental. I don't remember."

"Right at the crucial moment, most of the people I ever speak to get bloody amnesia. Why is that?"

"Something in the air affects them," said the girl.

"The only thing in the air right now is the smell of manure."

"No kidding? I was under the impression all along it was wee-wee. Silly me."

Charlie Galloway thought that if Elizabeth Honculada were a wall, she'd be Aberdeen granite with sharp glass attachments and rolls of barbed wire. "What's your relationship with Cruz?"

"I don't think that's your business."

"Just once I'd like an answer, Elizabeth."

"Just once I'd like to think you deserve one, Charles."

Galloway experienced a familiar desperation. He had a brief unlikely notion that he might reach out and snatch the girl's purse and rummage through its contents, possibly finding receipts for an airline ticket, or some form of evidence he could consider hard, something definite. Right now he was getting nowhere. He looked at the sky, blue yielding to a darker blue; then he gazed at Elizabeth Honculada, wondering what would get past her defenses. A wrecking ball, wire cutters, blowtorch, demolition instruments he didn't have.

"Who is Cruz?" he asked. "Old family friend from the provinces? Is that it? You were showing him around, eh? Is that the story? Or is it something else altogether? You and Cruz have a thing going. Is that a fair assumption?"

The girl looked at him with an expression of disdain. "Your time's up. I don't have to answer your questions. I'm calling my lawyer, Galloway."

Lawyers, always lawyers, incubi ascending from hell with new ordinances tucked beneath their sulfuric wings. Galloway was frustrated by the girl, by everything. "Call your damn lawyer," he said, and his voice rose. "Tell him you harbored a man I suspect of being involved in a murder. Tell him you were instrumental in transporting a possible felon."

"You're bullshitting me, Galloway."

Galloway smiled secretively and leaned upon the trunk of a tree. He folded his arms. A cat slunk across the courtyard, black and shiny, regarding the little human drama before him with feline indifference. A broken-winged robin shivered under a bush, awaiting extinction.

Elizabeth Honculada said, "Okay. I'll buy a ticket. Who did he allegedly murder?"

"A woman here in LA."

"And you've got proof?"

"I'm *that* close," Galloway said. It was bluff, and he enjoyed it, all the more so since it briefly deflated Miss Honculada. It was a contest now of Charlie's rusted will against the girl's, his ruse pitted against her stubbornness. She was staring at him, assessing him, testing his depths. He could almost feel her litmus paper dipped in his bloodstream.

She smiled and shook her head in amusement. "Galloway, you're so full of shit it's a wonder your eyes aren't brown." She moved past him toward the front door, where she turned back. "Let me say it one more time for the record. I took Ray Cruz to the airport. I dropped him off. The end."

Galloway sighed. "Have it your way. I'll start checking the airlines. I might get lucky right away. You never know. Unless Cruz used an assumed name, of course. On the other hand, maybe *you* paid for his ticket. And just maybe"—here he raised a finger in the air, a joker approaching the punch line—"you even bought it for him with your own credit card. After all, he told me he was short of money."

"And just maybe," the girl said, "I didn't even go to the airport at all." She gave Galloway the kind of look that might poison wells, then unlocked the large, impressive door and stepped inside the house. Galloway walked across the courtyard and through the metal gate to the street, which was empty and secretive, a Californian pop-art painting of arched doorways and palms and orange trees, hypnogenetic in the razzle-dazzle light. An outrageous squeal caused him to look back and he saw the black cat emerge from the shrubbery with a dying bird shuddering in its jaws.

He had all kinds of sympathy for that bird.

Carolyn Laforge, shortsighted, too vain to wear spectacles, had to narrow her eyes to watch the television picture in her hotel room. She lay on her stomach, face propped in her hands. On the floor was a tray that had recently been sent up by room service. A half-eaten smoked-salmon sandwich, a bottle of Chablis, and a slice of melon, barely nibbled, lay in disarray. She gazed at the TV picture, which depicted a commercial for a disposable feminine douche called Summer's Eve, available in different fragrances.

"I hope you never use that stuff," Byron Truskett said. He lay alongside her, one bare leg set across her spine.

"Why?" Carolyn asked.

"It might spoil the taste of you."

Carolyn said, "I understand douches destroy natural bacteria."

The senator, far removed from bacterial notions, had on his face the satisfied smile of a man whose leaves have just been raked in no uncertain terms. He was the cheerful proprietor, one languid leg bonding him to the woman, imprisoning her on the large bed of this hotel in Alexandria, Virginia.

Earlier today, in the Oval Office, all the old desires had come back to him with renewed intensity, magnifying that unequivocal sense of destiny he'd first felt many years before. He would run this country, goddammit. He'd make this nation work again, by God! No more stupid police actions, no more global interference, no more bully-boy in the schoolyard of Latin America and else-where. He'd set about his task with that mixture of practicality and compassion he considered so essential to the job. He'd run things with both a data base and a heart, because heart alone was the road to ruin. You needed the kind of precision in the political process that raw emotion was unequipped to provide. You needed computer technicians as well as poets, economists as well as vi-sionaries. Soft-headed liberalism was a dinosaur, and the notion of a welfare state, which had never played in Peoria, a sure avenue to bankruptcy. There was a middle road, and that was the one President Truskett would walk. And in those places where that road forked, hell, he'd just stray off the beaten path if that's what it took.

He laid his face now against Carolyn's spine, placing a hand around her buttocks, which were well toned, soft without flab, luscious, gloriously feminine. He was very afraid of loving this woman. Like other men who have abdicated power for the sake of love, he had a sense of going over Niagara Falls, not in a barrel but in bikini briefs, unprotected, flailing air, choked by spuming water. He lowered his face, kissed that sensitive spot where spine meets the first soft rise of ass, the gentle pillow of flesh covered with almost invisible down. He raised little goose bumps in Caro-lyn's skin.

"It's almost time for the news," Carolyn said.

Truskett adjusted his position only slightly, because he was reluctant to move. He gazed at the TV in the manner of a man who has swallowed one too many downers. Everything beyond the immediate vicinity of Carolyn wasn't very interesting. Was he hypnotized? Bewitched again? Lust assailed him suddenly. He was on the rise.

"Not now, wait," Carolyn said, even as she wrapped her cool palm around his agitated penis, a touch both of exquisite sexual-ity and deferral, joy delayed. Truskett liked to look down at the head of his cock protruding from the clasp of her white, ladylike fingers because the juxtaposition thrilled him—his anxious mem-ber, inherently so unmannered and hasty, palmed by a pale, smooth aristocratic hand. He could come like this, eyes shut, a moan in his throat.

"Byron, I want to see the news. Then you can fuck me until kingdom come. Or you do. Whichever is first."

On screen was a film of boat people attempting to reach Hong Kong from Vietnam. Blown off course, they had drifted for twenty-two days, hungry and dying, in the South China Sea. This tale of human tragedy dissolved into the next item, which was what really interested Carolyn, and she gazed intently at the box to see a not very good photograph of William taken last year in Bucks County. The photograph gave way to tape of President McCune announcing his nomination for the post "made vacant by the tragedy of Sandy Bach's death yesterday," blah blah, fee fi fo fum, "urgent need for continuity and purpose," rhubarb, rhubarb. Cut back to studio where the anchorperson, an aggressive toothy woman with yellow hair, uttered a few words about William's background, accompanied by another photograph. And that was it.

Carolyn zapped off the TV with the remote control, then turned on her back and looked up at the ceiling. Even as she lay here naked with Truskett, William was at the White House with the President, discussing policy, shaping the Central Intelligence Agency. She was immensely proud of him. For a moment she imagined the penis she held was his, not Byron Truskett's.

Truskett had his face buried in the hollow of her throat, the tip of his tongue moving lightly upon this sensitive area of flesh. He had one exploratory hand tracking the contours of her inner thigh. She raised her hips a little, readying herself to receive him, but he delayed the moment of entry, lost as he was in the study of her flesh. This vein, that vein, this hair, that—Truskett might have been an algebraist of surfaces, so avidly did he probe and touch, kiss and admire, a man utterly adrift in the intricacy of love's complicated formulae.

His mouth closed around a nipple. He really was a most tender lover. Carolyn shut her eyes, drifted. Directing Truskett gently, she slid her body beneath his, and he entered her with a suddenness she found breathtaking. She clasped her hands around the back of his head as they rocked together, fused for so short a time Truskett was always disturbed by his lack of self-control—but what could he do? This woman thrilled him as no other ever had. Being inside her was as close to perfection as he was ever likely to get. Abstract notions he'd normally dismiss as pretentious—oneness, transcendentalism—took on concrete qualities. The top of his scalp began to come off his skull. Hairs on the back of his neck tingled. Blood went through his veins with ferocity—then that first astonishing sense of coming disintegrated him.

Feeling him grow, Carolyn locked herself harder to him. An amazing thing happened. For the first time she was being carried along by Truskett's intensity, she was taking the same mountainous route with him, up and up, a singing in her ears, a pressure in her head, lava flowing through her. Swept along in his excitement, stripped down, disassembled, hearing herself cry aloud, she realized, in a moment of extraordinary intimacy, that she'd come with him, revealing a hidden aspect of herself to him. She gazed at him with unexpected fondness, more than she'd ever wanted to feel, and her eyes filled with tears. By her own standards of fidelity, she'd never truly betrayed William before.

"What's wrong? What's the matter?" Truskett asked.

"You wouldn't understand."

"I might." He rubbed her neck softly. He thought she had a luminous quality, an aura in which he basked. How could he ever tire of this woman? How could he ever let her drift from his life?

She had turned her face to the side.

"Did I do something wrong? Tell me." Truskett was worried.

"I'm fine. Really I am." How touching his concern was, she thought. How pleasing. "I love my husband, Byron."

"Yes."

"What you and I have is good. Wonderful."

"But."

"An enormous but."

"Insuperable, right?" Truskett asked.

Carolyn thought of the house in Bucks County, the beech trees, the creek, she imagined herself looking from her bedroom window and seeing William walk across the meadowland, butterflies disturbed into erratic flight by his movement, the whinny of horses. How could she *possibly* jeopardize her own little world? She could never hurt William. *"Insuperable* is a good word, Byron."

He was about to respond when the telephone rang. Since nobody knew he was here, he was reluctant to pick it up.

"It has to be for you," he said.

Carolyn reached for the receiver. A man's voice asked to speak to the senator. When she denied Truskett's presence, the caller identified himself as Larry Deets. She passed the phone to Truskett, who took it with a mild expression of puzzlement.

"Senator, we have to talk," Deets said.

"Why?" Truskett asked. "Is there a problem?"

"That would be an acceptable description," Deets replied, "if your forte was understatement."

The darkness falling upon Los Angeles seemed to Charlie Galloway an illusion, a magician's silk drawn across the sky, soon to be whipped away to reveal—abracadabra—the same old golden egg of the sun. The night had a tenuous hold. The emerging stars looked timidly distant and the moon, waning from fullness, was half turned away in what might have been caution, like that of a man averting his eyes from an open furnace.

People moved in the darkening streets in shirtsleeves, bare feet in sneakers and sandals. Divine girls in skimpy tank tops or thin cotton blouses caused Charlie to ache for Karen. The severity of separation was killing him.

On Melrose Avenue he wondered if the world was always going to be this stifling. Perhaps if you were a stern-faced fundamentalist sitting on the porch of your chicken farm in darkest Alabama and resisting, with great difficulty, some lunar urge to bite the head off a rooster, you might think the apocalypse had begun. This very day, hadn't the newspaper reported that a group of religious zealots, allegedly hearing the hoofbeats of the Four Horsemen in Coldwater Canyon, had taken to the Santa Ana Mountains, there to be safe and multiply?

Upscale boutiques jostled funky run-down stores on Melrose, where a furtive kid pressed a leaflet into Charlie's hand, a Xeroxed sheet with the information that a certain punk-rock band known as Hepatitis B (formerly Chancre) would be playing for one night only in a bar nearby. Pity to miss it. Charlie kept moving, passing open stores filled with granny-style clothing, 1940ish wristwatches and fountain pens and old Bakelite radios.

Near the corner of Crescent Heights Boulevard, Clarence Wylie waited outside a record shop. He looked luminously incongruous, a solitary white-shirted figure milled around by assorted punks and greasers with spiked hair, spangled eyelashes, and surly expressions. Clarence noticed Charlie and raised a hand in weary greeting.

"You're late, Charlie. You said eight-thirty when you phoned."

"Sorry." Galloway looked at his watch, which had finally quit. He wondered if it had been a good idea to call Clarence—but where else could he turn? He couldn't go to Len Paffett or Duffy, who'd clap him in irons at once. Elizabeth Honculada had stalled him, and he didn't like the sensation of defeat.

Music roared out of the record shop, the lyrics unintelligible. "Let's stroll," Wylie suggested. "This music unnerves me. I never got beyond Sinatra. Even Elvis baffled me."

Both men walked until they came to a coffee shop, a place of chrome and exposed ductwork. Wylie suggested coffee. A waitress brought cappuccino.

Wylie sipped his carefully, then set the cup down. "You said you needed help, Charlie. I hope it's something extremely simple, like money. But why do I feel it isn't anything that straightforward?"

Charlie Galloway looked around the coffee shop. A multitude of mirrors reflected his image to glassy infinity. How bedraggled he seemed, a crumpled wreck zooming back from those callous, silver surfaces. "I need information."

Clarence Wylie sipped his drink. He dabbed milky froth from his lips with a paper napkin. "Information? Money's easier." Clarence took out his wallet. "Look. I can give you two hundred. If we go to the automatic teller, I can get you another two. Enough for a ticket to Vegas, Charlie, a couple of nights in a good hotel."

"Clarence, I told you. I'm not going anywhere."

Wylie, shrugging, put his wallet away. The enormous espresso machine issued a vast cloud of steam and for a moment all the mirrors clouded. "All right, Charlie. What kind of information are you chasing?"

"There's a guy who calls himself Raymond Cruz. He came here from the Philippines the day Ella was killed. He was with Freddie Joaquin for a few hours the following day. I don't know what they had in common. They had slightly different versions of reality." Charlie ran a hand through his unruly hair. "Today Cruz slips out on me and takes off with a girl called Elizabeth . . . Christ, the last name escapes me, Clarence."

Broken brain syndrome. More leakage from the banks of memory. Data vanished into the ether. Galloway was embarrassed.

"Take your time, Charlie," Clarence said patiently. He noticed a slight tremor in Galloway's fingers, not a great sign.

"Okay. My feeling is Cruz left town, but the girl won't say where or why."

"And?"

"I'd like to know if you have anything on Cruz inside the machine."

"I'm retired, Charlie. You don't seem to grasp that. And even if I wasn't, how could I justify a computer search? On what grounds?"

"I don't have particular *grounds.* I only have this sense that Cruz isn't who he seems to be. Clarence, I need to know. It's that simple. He tried to walk out on me after I told him to stick around. If I hadn't turned up when I did, he would have hiked clean away. People don't do that if they're beyond reproach, now, do they?"

Clarence Wylie said, "I can't do anything, Charlie."

"That's codswallop. I'm not buying that. You could make a search. You know what buttons to press, Clarence."

Clarence leaned across the table. "Charlie, listen to me. You're in a bad state. Your marriage is unglued. You're out of work. I know it's a goddam awful time for you—"

"Thanks and amen, brother."

"Hear me out. You're walking a thin margin with all this stuff. You're not yourself."

"Okay, I'm having an identity crisis, I'm coming apart at the seams, I need a fucking drink I know I can't have, and I'm not included in Jesus's sunbeam quota, okay, okay, let's accept all that as given—will you help me?"

Clarence Wylie slumped back in his chair, puffed his cheeks, expelled a stream of air in exasperation. "This Cruz. Do you suspect him of the woman's murder?"

Charlie Galloway wasn't sure how to answer. Vague notions crossed his mind, but he couldn't track them with anything like certainty. They were erratic, wild comets in his private firmament. He fidgeted with sugar cubes, unwrapping them, building them into a precarious column. The whole clamjamfry was about to topple.

Wylie asked, "If you don't suspect murder, what *do* you suspect? Complicity?"

"Complicity. I don't know. I think he's involved in something, Clarence. But if I knew what it was, I wouldn't be asking you for information, would I? Joaquin made some off-the-wall accusation about him, and that's what keeps sticking in my mind. Now, it might well be the kind of thing somebody says in sheer desperation, so it has to be taken with a few grains of salt, but it's like a rotten taste in my mouth."

"Involved in 'something' isn't overwhelmingly helpful, Charlie."

"It's the best I can do."

"What was Joaquin's allegation specifically?"

"That Cruz had come here to kill somebody."

"Who?"

Too many questions, too few answers. Galloway sensed an imbalance in the world; questions came faster than answers could be supplied. "I don't fucking know who. I was hoping you could help me with that one."

Clarence Wylie said, "I wish your marriage was in better shape. Karen's a wonderful woman. If you could get her back—"

"Aw, Jesus, Clarence. Is that what you think this is all about? I pull something off, and maybe Karen's going to come back to home and hearth? She's gone, for God's sake. You were there. You heard the last post. I'm doing this for me! For C. Galloway. I mean, look," and Charlie held out his shaking hand. "I'm a mess. I admit it. And this hand's only the outside, Clarence. You should see it from inside. Even my mind's bloodshot. The only thing I've got going is this Raymond Cruz business, and I don't even know what it is, or if it's anything at all. Give me a wee bit of direction. That's all I'm asking. I'm damned if I'll beg, Clarence. You won't see me rattling the old tin can at you. I'm down, squire, but I'm not out."

Wylie was quiet for a while. He picked up his cup and finished his coffee while Charlie added one last lump to the pillar of cubes. Clarence's face was tense. He wondered why he allowed Charlie to get to him this way. Christ, what was the basis for this friendship? It wasn't as if Charlie had saved his life, hauled him out of a burning building, dragged him from quicksands. He didn't owe Charlie. So why hadn't he let Galloway just drift out of his private orbit years ago? One answer presented itself, but Clarence didn't want to accept it—the idea that Charlie Galloway introduced an element of uncertainty into a life that was nice, a life pleasantly humdrum, that to befriend Charlie was to accept a certain unpredictability into one's world, an edge, a glimpse of the abyss. Was that part of it? Vicarious thrills? Clarence didn't care for this particular boulevard of self-dissection. For one thing, it led to the conclusion that his own life was dull—which was far from the truth. Happily married to a woman he loved to distraction, he considered the moments of his life, even in retirement, well filled. So why did he need a flake like Charlie? Why would anybody in his right mind need Charlie? Christian kindness? Brotherly love? *Blessed are the drunkards, for they need a whole lot of goddam help.* It was probably very simple when you got right down to it. He liked the man. He liked him very much. Why analyze that? Why lose yourself in wandering around in the maze of your own feelings, looking for meaning? You didn't always get to choose your friends. Sometimes you just stumbled into them, or, in certain cases, over them. What the hell?

Clarence put his cup down. "Raymond Cruz, you say."

"According to his passport."

"A Philippines passport?" Clarence asked.

"Right."

"You know anything else about him?"

"I can describe him."

"Fine."

Charlie did so.

Clarence had taken out a small black notebook. He wrote with a Parker fountain pen on which his initials were inscribed.

Galloway suddenly remembered the girl's name and said it aloud.

"Where does this Elizabeth Honculada live, Charlie?"

Galloway had that information scrawled on the back of a crumpled slip of paper. He removed it from his pocket and slid it across the table to Wylie.

"Good neighborhood," said Clarence as he wrote. He shut the notebook. He stared at Galloway a moment, feeling a familiar bond with the Scotsman, as if this particular situation reminded him of the occasion when they'd first worked together years ago, the young LAPD cop and the older Fed, a team, a damn good team. Despite remarks to the contrary, Clarence missed the action at times. "I'll see what there is. You go home. Don't drink. Just wait. You'll hear from me."

"When?"

"Give me a few hours. But don't hold your breath, Charlie." Clarence Wylie dropped a five-dollar bill on the table and turned away. "I don't know what a retired agent can still do. I don't know if I can find my way around Vanderwolf's security. I don't know if he's changed the system, altered the passwords."

"I want to thank you," Charlie said.

"I haven't done anything yet."

"I was being grateful in a general kind of way, Clarence."

Clarence Wylie smiled and walked out, leaving Galloway alone with the mirrors and the infinite reflections of his face. Somewhere in that plethora of images, he felt, was the real Charles Galloway; all the rest were counterfeits, rogues, rapscallions and piss artists.

16

It was almost dark when Holly Railsback punched the five-digit code into the electronic pad that unlocked the front door. She stepped inside the house, closed the door firmly behind her and pushed the button that activated the alarm system. Her father's need for security, she thought, bordered on the wacko. He was preoccupied with switches and floodlights. She knew he worked for the federal government in a capacity that was highly—what was his word?—*sensitive,* but she thought he took things a little too far at times. This house had to be almost as bad as Fort Knox. She sometimes wondered what it would be like to see the world through her father's eyes and just maybe understand his obsessive need for a citadel—but it eluded her. She was an easygoing girl and her dad's siege mentality bugged her.

He was a nice man, and all her friends considered him cool, but there was a side to him they never saw, a spacy aspect, those times when he'd get a faraway look in his eye and drift off God knows where. When he was in flux he had this real strange habit of chewing the inside of his mouth, as if an invisible plug of tobacco were hidden in his cheek.

She loved him, but he sure had a distracted side to him.

She kicked her shoes up in the air and caught them on the way down. Then she flopped on the sofa. A hard day at the Galleria tired a girl out. She'd bought a new CD of a band called Violent Femmes, but she didn't feel like playing it right then. She just wanted to zone out before her father came home. He was due in about twenty minutes. She stretched her arms, yawned. After a few minutes she became restless, wandered the room, paused by the big bay windows that faced the darkening street. She reached for the cord that would draw the drapes.

Halfway down the block, beneath the overhang of a tree, a white pickup truck was parked a little way from the nearest streetlamp. She looked at it absently. In this neighborhood trucks weren't commonplace unless they belonged to landscapers or pest-control outfits or plumbers. Almost everybody around here drove European or Japanese cars, although you sometimes saw the occasional Cadillac. Through failing light she thought there were two men in the cab of the truck but she wasn't sure.

She was about to close the drapes when the telephone rang and she walked across the room to answer it. It was Graham Bisby, the seventeen-year-old light of her life, her deflowerer. He'd just written a new poem proclaiming her radical beauty. He had a velvet way with words. Would she like to hear him recite it? You bet, oh God, she'd die to hear it.

"If you were treacherous to me," he recited, *"my heart would be a slaughterhouse. I held your hand at Six Flags over Texas. And I knew then I loved you."*

Seduced by his voice, she shut her eyes and quite forgot about the curtains.

The man who wore the Stetson hat and cowboy shirt with fluted pockets was called Johhny Ko, a Manileño who had lived in Dallas for fifteen years and now considered himself a native, a lover of rodeos and country music and Tony Lama snakeskin boots, a pair of which he wore when he'd met Armando Teng on the sixth floor of the old book depository building. They'd walked to Ko's pickup truck and, to pass time, driven through downtown Dallas, where Teng noticed a crowd of rather bedraggled people outside the blood plasma center on Elm Street. Past the west end historical area where a part of old Dallas was preserved, past the upmarket restaurants, Ko drove out by Turtle Creek, where enormous houses overlooked a stream muddied by nightfall and depleted by drought.

The cassette deck in the truck played Merle Haggard and Tammy Wynette and Tanya Tucker. Ko, who drummed his fingers on the steering wheel in time to the music, pointed out this building or that with the pride of a true Texan. He mouthed facts and figures attesting to the state's size and its preponderance of colossi—this freeway took x years to build and used y number of men, that building is the largest convention center in the USA, there's the tallest flagpole in the state.

They drove the endless flat freeways out past Love Field and Texas Stadium, then north through darkness to Farmers Branch, where Ko headed west on the LBJ Freeway, talking all the while about how great a country this was, and how readily he'd been accepted and his hand-crafted leather goods business had prospered. Of course, he missed the old country, and his family, he wouldn't want to give the wrong impression, no way, he was a Filipino first and foremost. He missed the *lechon,* the suckling pig, in Baclaran, the action on Ayala Avenue, the crowded streets of Chinatown. He missed the *atmosphere,* hard though it was to define.

Teng, who felt the tension of a man traveling with no visa toward a border crossing, watched the lights of passing suburbs and barely listened to Ko's anthem of praise. He thought Ko, with his Chinese blood, looked all wrong in a Stetson and cowboy shirt and the garish yellow- and wine-colored boots. He'd sold himself to America, like James Honculada. And how many others? The ironic thing was how people like Ko and Honculada imagined they were free members of a free society. They counted their money and watched their bank balances grow and paid their taxes to feed the U.S. machine, but never once did they stop to ponder the illusory nature of their liberty. A country that enslaved others could never itself be free—but, blinded by cash, befuddled by possessions, big houses, and automobiles, Honculada and Ko failed to understand this, or chose not to care.

Teng shut his eyes. Now Johnny Ko talked about how he used to be a movie extra in Manila and how close he'd been to

Joe Baltazar, his best friend from way back, they'd been like brothers, no, more like twins, in the days when Joe had hung around the movie studios looking for carpentry work. When Joe had been in the United States in the late 1970s, Ko had found him a small apartment in Arlington and a job digging ditches, even though Baltazar had no green card, not even temporary legal status.

"He never did take to the States," Ko remarked. "It's a whole other way of life. Either you want what it has to offer or you don't. And Joe didn't. He didn't get along with Texans. Had trouble with English. But I think what really bugged him was the immigration bit. Undocumented workers got to keep one step ahead of the *migra.* Naturally he was jumpy. When they finally caught up with him, he'd been here three years, most of them miserable for him. Deportation was like a relief, you know? Considering what happened to him when he went back home, I guess he wished he'd stayed here."

Ko was mercifully silent for a couple of miles after he came off the freeway system into a network of lamplit suburban streets, where darkness imposed itself on pleasant houses and a sense of comfort, even complacency, prevailed. Teng gazed at the frowning Madonna hanging from the rearview mirror.

"This guy you want," Ko said. "Now he's not always predictable, you unnerstand. I been watching him for a few weeks. He works in an office downtown but he drives home always a different route. He gets home usually, say, between seven-thirty and eight. My understanding is his house is wired like the fucking utility company. You can't get in. So you have to act like real fast, and take him just before he gets his car in the garage. If he gets inside the garage, forget it."

Teng considered this a moment. "Is he armed?"

"My bet is he's carrying."

Ko slowed his truck at a four-way stop sign. He took the opportunity to change the tape from Merle Haggard to the Flying Burrito Brothers. More quiet streets, more soft lamps barely penetrating the dark. "Check under the seat," said Ko.

Teng reached down. He found a sawed-off shotgun on the floor. He raised it up, set it in his lap.

"Walk in fast. Get as close as you can. *Pow,*" Ko said. "What am I telling you this for anyway, eh? You know how to use a gun."

"Yes," Teng said.

"With that gun," Ko said, "you can blow a man clear into the next country. Or the next world, hah-heh."

Teng studied the houses that went past. Fragile archipelagos of light. Illuminated windows. TV screens. Plants flourished in pots or hung from ceilings in macramé slings. The gun he held in his lap threatened the orderly nature of all this. These quiet streets would echo to the roar of the blunted weapon. A woman might look up from a letter she was writing, or a man raise his face from a newspaper. A kid splayed on a rug might turn from the TV and ask, *What was that?* and somebody would say, *Backfire, I guess,* and then in the newspapers next morning they'd know differently. Teng saw a man on a stepladder hang a picture on a white wall. A snapshot, an icon that passed out of existence as Ko's truck kept rolling, perhaps something unreal, imagined, dreamed up by Teng, who felt his brain kick into some higher level of perception, that hard place where anticipation and dread were both companions and jailers.

I am afraid, he thought.

Johnny Ko whistled annoyingly.

"Don't," Teng said.

"Yeah. Sorry. I wasn't thinking, *kaibigan.*"

Teng tapped the stock of the shotgun. He remembered what Joe Baltazar had said: *There were at least two Americans that night, Armando. And one of them shot Marissa. One of them shot her in the mouth.* Teng froze these words out of his mind. He was propelled now by an abstract sense of hatred, something pure, but in the process of distillation detached from its original source, from the particulars of a dead girl in a black field, a girl he loved. But what did he know of love now? He understood only the shotgun in his lap. He was defined by it. It circumscribed him.

He placed his palms under the weapon, raising it up from his lap and feeling the deadlines of its weight. Then he put it back down against his legs. Why was there no comfort to be had from the feel of the weapon? Why no security? His fear was like a tide in his blood, rushing, roaring in his ears, the violent whisper you heard in seashells sometimes. He tilted his head back and closed his eyes. *Remember. Remember,* he told himself. *Why you are here. Why you have come all this way.*

He was conscious of Ko steering the truck from one street to another, a route the Filipino cowboy had clearly traveled many times before because the street signs were mainly unreadable in the dark. And then Ko stopped the truck and cut the engine. Teng stared up into a streetlamp, the globe of which glowed with uncertainty, as if the dark were too much for it. The light cast a peculiar shadow, reminiscent of an abnormal hand, through the branches of a tree and onto the sidewalk.

"That's the house," Ko said. "You see the bushes there. By the driveway."

Teng saw not only the shrubbery but also the bright light that burned in the front window of the house.

"You might think different," Ko said. "But when I checked this place out, it looked to me you could hide yourself pretty damn good in the bushes. It's the only weak spot in the whole setup. See, the guy has to drive his car past the shrubs to his garage. You step out. You got the gun . . ."

Teng was hypnotized by the white window, the rectangle of light that carved a slice out of the dark. Somebody moved in the room beyond.

"Who else lives there?" he asked.

"The guy's daughter," Ko said.

Teng, who had somehow imagined an empty house, said nothing. He put the sawed-off gun inside his pants, against the outer thigh. He closed one hand around the grip. Ko looked at the luminous digital clock on his dash.

"Go now," he said.

Teng opened the passenger door and stepped down. The night had a perfume to it, the scent of an unfamiliar blossom that surprised him. He walked across the street, drawn to the phosphorescent window. The shotgun pressed against his flesh and he altered the rhythm of his movement. He paused once, turned to look back at the truck, and wondered why he half expected it to take off. *Good people,* was what Baltazar had said. *Not professionals, but they're on your side.* He saw Ko's face in shadow through the windshield. *He's on my side,* Teng thought. *Don't forget that. He's with me.*

He kept moving. When he reached the driveway of the house he crouched in the shrubbery, removing the shotgun from his pants and holding it ready. He had a bad moment, similar to the feeling in Los Angeles when he'd hurried away from Galloway; he wanted to get up and walk out on this before it was too late. What good was another death? It didn't bring equality. And revenge was merely a passing satisfaction, a momentary sweetness that dissolved in your mouth as quickly as chocolate.

No. You've come all this way to bury your dead. You don't walk out on a funeral. You do it. He gazed at the light from the window, seeing a shadow pass back and forth and then crystallize in the shape of a pretty young girl who held a telephone to her ear, and she was smiling in a dazzling, impossibly youthful way, the kind of radiant look that belonged in only one time of your life, and that was when you first discovered love, because you never smiled like that again no matter how often or how well you loved afterward. You restrained your face, practiced control. You pretended and dissembled and took less risks with your heart. But for this one splendid fraction of time you loved unconditionally, like the girl in the window, who was clearly listening to a boyfriend's adoration of her. Teng was touched more than he wanted to be. Had Marissa looked that way when she'd listened to his own declarations of love? Dear God, he couldn't remember, it faded, it dissolved.

He tightened his hold on the gun. The girl's face was turned slightly away from him now. The window was a mere ten feet from the shrubbery. An unexpected breeze of some delicacy flitted across the night, enriching the dark with the perfume he'd smelled before. And then stillness returned, and silence.

But the silence was brief, interrupted by the sound of a car coming along the street. Teng saw the headlights, heard the change of gears, and knew that this particular car was coming into the driveway. He saw it turn and move slowly toward the garage door, which, remote controlled from inside the vehicle, was already opening soundlessly to reveal a large space lit by a fluorescent tube, a room of hammers and screwdrivers and wrenches hanging from pegboards, a workbench with a lathe, paint cans in a tidy arrangement on a shelf. Teng leveled the gun.

The car rolled toward the garage door. Teng stepped out of

the greenery and he fired the shotgun twice through the driver's window. Beyond surprise, beyond fear, beyond even the fragment of time it took in which to register any reaction, the man received both shots in the face, then slumped sideways. Was he the one? Teng wondered. Was he the man who had put a pistol between Marissa's lips and pulled the trigger? Teng realized he felt nothing now, neither nervousness nor fear. What did it matter if this man was the killer or if the other, Costain, had actually fired the gun? They had been accomplices in destruction and so vengeance was allotted with scrupulous equality.

The car kept going toward the open garage, where it scraped the right wall, bringing down shelves, tools, old coffee cans containing nails, bolts, screws. It moved sluggishly to the far wall, stopped there by oil drums and a pile of cinder blocks. A green plastic bag burst open against the car's bumper, disgorging a bunch of old soft toys: bears, monkeys, battered dolls, the rejects of a child grown into her teenage years. They had an air of pathetic abandonment.

Teng gazed at the house. The girl in the window had dropped the telephone and was screaming at him and pounding the pane with her fists. He raised the shotgun in her direction. Why should he kill this child? Why should her life be brutally ended? He stared at her stricken face, feeling an unexpected bond with her, a kinship; they were both fellow travelers in a world of violence. He wished he could in some way console her. But what was there to say? *This is the way it has to be? There are no other choices?* Sympathy was useless. Words were sounds signifying nothing.

He turned and ran toward Ko's truck. But he carried the girl's expression with him, a memory of her open-mouthed horror scorched into him. That she could quite possibly identify him was something he didn't stop to consider, didn't care about. All he wanted was distance between himself and the girl.

He climbed hurriedly into the cab. "Drive. Just drive."

In the basement office of Byron Truskett's Georgetown house Larry Deets gazed at the senator, who sat morosely in a dark green leather armchair by the fireplace. On the mantelpiece were framed photographs of Byron and Miriam, two happy people in the sunshine, a big Winnebago in the background, mountains and fir trees—the traveling honeymoon couple, fishing rods and floppy hats and the sheer simplicity of early marriage.

The photographs were deceptive; even then, Truskett hadn't been the innocent novice he appeared, because he was already well versed in, and somewhat sullied by, the politics of the Iowa state legislature, where he'd served his political apprenticeship. Now, of course, these old pictures suggested a time of great purity, but that was only because Washington is to Iowa as snuff films are to soft-core porn; as death is to life.

Truskett looked into the empty grate with the expression of a man who wishes it were cold enough outside to warrant burning a couple of logs, toasting a few marshmallows. Deets got up, paced, paused by the fireplace, and leaned there in an unrelaxed way.

"How do we know this character Redliner—"

"Redlinger—"

"How do we know he's telling the truth?"

"I ran a check of his background," said Deets. "He has connections. He's authentic."

"Authentic," Truskett said, as if the very word annoyed him. The senator had moments in which he yielded to the kind of petulance bred in the blood of the rich. He could sulk furiously.

Deets remembered, for no good reason, the sleek black-haired senorita who had tried to teach him the mambo, and he slid one foot slickly across the tiled floor of the study in the manner of somebody involuntarily practicing a dance step. It was called muscle memory. That's what the senorita had tried to instill in him. *Muskell memory, Meester Deetz!* Thoughts of the dance teacher segued into an image of La Belle Laforge, the great Carolyn, who had brought Truskett to this sorry pass with some intimate shimmies of her own. Had Byron remained faithful to his devoted little wife, had he eschewed the prime beef that was Billy's missus and kept his pickle in his pocket, then Truskett would *never* have thrown his weight behind Billy and none of this would have come about.

Deets said, "Let's look at the options, Senator. One. Billy comes through the nominations unblemished because nobody has found out about his . . . let's say unacceptable behavior. Two.

Somebody *does* find out, and Billy is crucified, and you along with him as his prime booster. Don't underestimate the gravity of that. We are not discussing some random ass-kicking in the boondocks of the Philippines, Senator. We're looking at behavior universally condemned by our allies everywhere. Torture isn't an A-list word. The United States doesn't approve of it. No more White House breakfasts. No invites to foreign embassies. No gala receptions. Say good night to your dreams." *And mine*, Deets thought. He placed a pinky in his ear and shook it vigorously a second, as if already he heard the clamor on the Senate floor.

Truskett said, "Even if the first option worked and Billy came through the nominations unscathed, it's still a minefield. Six months, a year down the road, your man Redlinger decides to drop a dime and sell his Filipino yarn to one of those hotshot investigative snipers on some goddam city desk—what then? The wall collapses. The crap hits the fan. And we're covered in bricks and shit, Larry."

"True," Deets said. If Laforge won the nomination and sat behind the big desk at Langley, there would always be Redlinger's unpredictable shadow in the background somewhere. That kind of tension was unacceptable. "Okay," he said. "Option three. Billy withdraws of his own free will."

"That's about as likely to happen as Jimmy Carter getting his mug on Mount Rushmore, for Christ's sake. Laforge *wants* this goddam job so badly he gets a hard-on when he thinks about it. What's he going to do? Turn it down? Say thank you but no thank you? No way, Larry."

"You overlook the power of coercion, Senator. Go to Laforge. Tell him what you've learned. Explain his candidacy is down the tubes on account of his past indiscretions. Toss in the word *heinous*. That's always a kicker. You turn up the heat and Billy, being smart, steps out of the kitchen. Too much pressure. He can't take it. So he tells the President reasons of health, whatever. Sudden murmur in the heart. Angina politicalis."

Truskett shook his head. "You know how he'll react to that, Larry? Denial. Plain. Simple. But very shrill denial. He'll act like he's just had a testicle severed. It's his word against Redlinger's. And who's going to believe some grubby free-lance spook? Billy, on the other hand, is a class act from top to bottom. He's the closest thing to landed gentry there is in this republic. Coercion isn't going to work with him. Maybe with somebody else it would be a piece of cake, but not with him. He's unreal, I swear to God."

"Try it," Deets said.

"No."

"It's worth a shot. Talk to him. Persuade him."

Truskett, hearing an unusual persistence in his assistant's voice, waved a hand dismissively. "It would be a total waste of time. Drop it."

Deets experienced a rush of frustration. His usually pale features flushed. A redness occurred along his hairline. "You know why you won't try it?"

"You're going to tell me, I suppose?"

"Because your gonads have made a unilateral declaration of independence, that's why."

"You are *way* out of fucking line, Deets."

Deets knew he'd overstepped the mark. He'd known it before the words were halfway out. The outburst, fired by all this menace to his ambition, left a vile taste in his mouth. He attempted a quick repair. "You're right. Absolutely right. I take it back. I apologize from the bottom of my heart."

"From the bottom of what, Larry?" Truskett, sulking more darkly than ever, stared into the middle distance. He wasn't going to absolve Deets immediately. Let him simmer awhile, do him some good. Even special assistants were not indispensable despite the fact they sometimes considered themselves, as Deets did, kingmakers. They had no mandate to trespass on personal matters.

"It's this whole business, Senator. I'm jumpy. I'm not myself. I'm sorry."

Truskett watched Deets prowl the room back and forth, window to door, hands clasped behind his back. For a while there was the kind of silence that follows the demise of somebody believed to be in splendid health who drops dead in the middle of the street after playing three sets of squash, would you believe it? Poor bastard had everything to live for.

In a quiet voice Deets said, "Consider this. Option Four. The Humble Pie Agenda. You go to McCune and tell him that in the light of new, shall we say, evidence, you no longer think Laforge a worthy candidate. You say you consider it 'prudent' that the President withdraw Billy's name from nomination. And when McCune asks why—tell him there's something fishy about Billy's sex life. Make it up. Invent a lover. Preferably a boy. McCune hates faggots.''

"How would that make *me* look, Larry?"

"Flexible. A man who admits mistakes. A big man. All too human. . . . Alas." Deets smiled sadly. "Excellent qualities if you happen to be a priest on his way to a bishopric, but when you're after the Oval Office, less than admirable. To be successful in politics you have to be intractable. The least desirable quality for a politician is overt flexibility because it makes him look indecisive. Wimpy. When did you ever hear a President or a presidential hopeful admit to a mistake, for Christ's sake? You're above mistakes of judgment. You can't afford to be wrong.''

"By the same token, McCune wouldn't be ecstatic about having to change *his* mind.''

"With a mind like his, there isn't much changing room anyhow,'' said Deets. "But you won't get anything from him in the future, we may be sure of that. No merry backslapping at the next convention. No words of praise. No commendation that you carry the party's banner into the presidential fray.'' *Kiss it off,* Deets thought. *Everything, everything we worked for, lusted after.*

Truskett sighed, raised his hands in the air in a gesture of despondency, then let them flop back in his lap. A timid knock sounded at the door. It opened a little way and Miriam looked into the room, a tentative smile on her lips. Was she intruding? She wondered if she might make sandwiches, since the midnight oil was obviously burning—deferential smile, a movement of the head akin to a curtsy—there was some nice cold beef they might enjoy. Truskett, who perceived his wife only dimly, declined the offer of food with a dimissive gesture. Deets, always pleasant to Miriam, turned her down more effusively. Miriam withdrew, closing the door quietly. A sad little mouse had come and gone, Deets thought.

Truskett rose, stopped by the bookshelf where a framed photograph of Truskett Senior, who resembled a walrus, looked at him with prim midwestern disapproval. It was the expression of a banker who sees no evidence of collateral for a loan. Truskett Senior had been fond of aphorisms, little verbal tonics. *Even bruised grapes yield a little wine, son.*

Yeah, sure, sure. But what kind of wine, Pops? What kind of wine can I get out of these babies? How could he go to McCune and admit that a bad error of judgment had been made, that he was to blame? There had to be some other way.

He considered Billy Laforge a moment and felt rage. The gentleman, squire of goddam Bucks County, horseman, every inch the country aristocrat—how was it feasible that this man could have become involved in something as squalid, as deplorable, as downright goddam sleazy, as the events in the Philippines Deets had described? Okay, so Laforge hadn't been *physically* involved, but that was a damn fine hair too thin to split. It boiled down to the fact Laforge had been lax, blind, indifferent to human suffering, unmindful of the behavior of his subordinates. There was a sense in which his contribution was even more terrible than if he'd pulled a trigger himself. He'd failed in an unsurpassingly dismal manner to keep brutality in check. And when he knew, he'd turned his face away and looked elsewhere. He'd committed that most ordinary, that most appalling crime: neglect.

An exemplary life. Yes, Carolyn. Oh, yes. The man is a saint. Truskett slumped in his green leather chair and stretched out his long legs before the cheerless fireplace. *I need another course of action, Pops. I need inspiration. Show me.* He closed his eyes, remembered the showroom of Truskett Senior's original funeral parlor in Cedar Rapids, the smell of fine wood, the dull glow of brass and the brightness of silver, the way a reel-to-reel played organ pieces, the Muzak of grief. At the age of seven Byron had climbed inside one of the coffins just to get the feel of the thing, and he'd imagined the great heavy lid closing over him, slam, just like that, consigned to oblivion. You had to respect the sheer *heft* of death after that.

He recalled the downstairs room where the morticians worked at prettifying corpses, injecting tints into dry veins so flesh would appear lifelike, applying makeup to faces in a clownish attempt to salvage expression from the expressionless, pomading hair, clipping fingernails. He remembered sharp chemical smells mixed with the stale aroma of dead flesh. On one occasion a putrefying body had been brought in from a forest where it had lain for many days and Truskett recollected that odor even now with a clarity that astounded him, rotten old pork, humus, moss, something gaseous, a terrible fart trapped in an airtight box for centuries. Larvae worked busily in the flesh, colonizing the veins, gnawing and burrowing. When a layer of papery blue-black flesh was peeled away by a mortician's knife an astonishingly busy cross-section of decay was revealed, dung beetles, worms, ants, slugs, spiders, a massive crawling and feasting, a hungry celebration at the decomposing heart of things.

He opened his eyes and looked directly at Deets, who sat on the edge of the desk and swung one leg back and forth in an absentminded way. Deets, you could see, was concentrating ferociously, his thoughts as busy as the larvae inside that putrefying corpse. A bright idea was needed. A means of salvation.

Deets tilted his head to one side in the attitude of a man listening to something he alone hears. At precisely the same moment Byron Truskett had a lucid insight that caused his heart to rise up from gloom. In one of those rare alignments of rumination, the senator and his aide had the same notion simultaneously, a mutual murderous dawning, as if what really fueled their ambition were a cynicism so black and deep it was the grandfather of outright anarchy.

Truskett gazed into the grate for a moment. "Tell me. Is anyone out there actually *looking* for this . . . alleged Filipino killer?"

"Funny. I was just asking myself that very question." Both men were again silent for a short time.

Then Truskett said, "I am wondering . . ." He paused, gazing at Larry Deets in the fashion of men so familiar with one another that sometimes finished sentences were needless.

"It could be very neat and tidy," said Deets.

"It could indeed," Truskett remarked. "I would need to approach Hugo Fletcher, of course. . . ."

Deets assumed a little grin like a man trying on a radical new style of necktie. "How would you explain the details to him?"

"Details? What details?" Truskett asked. "I don't know what you're talking about, Larry."

And he winked, turning his face to the side the way William Laforge, in other circumstances, might have turned his.

17

Galloway, waiting with nervous impatience for Clarence Wylie to get in touch, spread the meager pickings from his mailbox on the kitchen table. A picture postcard had come from his father. It depicted a slightly fogged view of the Finnieston Quay Crane in Glasgow at dusk. The sky in the background was lemon and fanciful, unlike anything ever seen above the city save by persons who spiked their milk with methylated spirits or hair lacquer: electric soup.

Charlie studied the picture for a minute, noticing high-rise slabs beyond the enormous crane, the Cathcart Hills in the fuzzy distance—altogether a dour portrait, reminiscent of Gdansk ship-yards. He flipped the card, examined the message, which was written in red ink.

I never told you your sister Martha Had Quite A Serious drinking PROBlem that caused her delusions. She had a Brief Affair with a Pakistani chemist in the Gorbals, a TOTAL disaster. Keep in mind that what's in the blood is in the BLOOD. Your Loving FATher

Charlie had never had a sister. In senility Dan had taken to constructing a family tree rooted in imagination more than reality. It was a strange thing, the old man's tapsalteerie re-creation of the past. *What's in the blood is in the blood.* Was he trying to convey a cryptic message? Galloway set the card aside. He already had more perplexity than he could deal with; if he started to analyze the old man's utterances for even more . . . It didn't bear thinking about.

He examined the empty refrigerator. O bleakness. He filled a glass with cold water and ice, then stood at the window, drinking quickly. Karen was out there somewhere in the neon city, perhaps slinking with friend Justine through the sexy night places, the singles bars, a look of availability in her eye and a white mark where her wedding ring used to be. Galloway's mind was all at once filled with ruined conjugal pictures, flaxen crumbs of a three-tier cake trodden into red carpeting, little bridal figures made of smashed frosting, a bouquet of roses stuffed in a trash can. Memories of a wedding came down to that chaotic place where what might have been and what actually was formed a fork in the roadway, signs pointing the wrong way, travelers tearfully lost. He had to speak to her. Had to. Couldn't let years of marriage blow themselves up. Couldn't let her drift, just drift away.

He dialed Justine's number, expecting the inevitable answering machine, but Justine herself picked up on the first ring. Justine emitted politeness, oozed concern over the fate of the Galloway union, then said that Karen was unavailable. *Unavailable?* This word was a Popsicle pressed upon Charlie's heart. What did *unavailable* mean? It was the most sinister word he'd ever heard.

"Don't upset yourself, Charlie," Justine said. "She'll be back later."

"Later? How much later?"

"Don't force me into being a go-between, sweetie," said Justine. "I resent having roles thrust upon me. In any case, I understood you and Karen were in disarray permanently."

"Did she say where she was going?" he asked.

"I don't police her movements. She's a big girl."

Galloway fought for control over the images that assailed him. "Is she . . . I mean, is she out on . . . a, what's the word, date?"

"Sweetie, she'll get in touch. I'm sure."

"You didn't answer my question, Justine."

"Good night, dahlin."

"I need to talk to her, Justine."

Galloway heard the line die. He dropped the receiver back in place. *Okay. Okay. Put Karen out of your mind. Set her aside. Pretend she doesn't exist, never has, she's a product of your brain on overtime. Some illusory being decorated this wigwam of a room in which presently you stand on the panicky margin of hyperventilation. Gasp.* He kicked the door open, breathed the heat into his chest. This was no way to live. Without Karen. Not knowing where she was. Or what she was doing. Or with whom.

A mature man would not be bothered by these dire possibilities, Charlie. A mature man would not be lingering over pictures of his estranged wife seated at a candelit table in some uptown restaurant with a Mister Smoothcock, footsie under the hanging linen. A truly mature man would be planning his life, assessing this factor, weighing that, making absolutely certain he had some control over his future—unlike you, Galloway, you who are destiny's air-filled pigskin, kicked up and down the rutted playing fields of your own sorry ways. He drew more stale oxygen into his lungs. God. Bring her home. Bring her back.

The telephone rang. Such were the irrational leaps of faith a sad-hearted romantic drunk made that he assumed at once it was Karen getting back to him. His second thought was that it could be one of the airlines responding to his inquiries. Earlier, he'd begun calling airline desks at LAX in alphabetical order to see if there were records of tickets purchased by Raymond Cruz and/or Elizabeth Honculada. But the computers were down, as computers tended to be. He was informed that maybe in an hour or so they'd be up again, but it was, *gee,* hard to predict; could be tomorrow, he was told, real sorry.

He snatched up the receiver and was assaulted by loud music, over which a woman's voice was barely audible. It wasn't Karen. It took him a few moments to recognize the woman and when he did he was tempted to hang up.

"You bastard, you miserable fuck. How the fuck you sleep last night? Huh? Huh? Huh?"

"Brenda, listen," he said.

"Don't Brenda me, I saw you, slimesucker, I saw you push Freddie off, I was there."

"I didn't push anybody—"

"Eat it, Galloway. Eat it and choke. Choke, scumbag. You think you can push my Freddie off some goddam balcony and walk away, huh, huh, that what you huh think—"

Shaken by the woman's inebriated rage, Galloway put the receiver down. Lord, yes. What he really needed was abuse. He went into the living room and watched the sluggish moon climb over Los Angeles, passing through skimpy cloud cover—the first clouds in how many days?—and then reappearing, surrounded by rust-colored haze.

He stepped outside. He stuck his trembling hands in his pockets and wandered toward the avocado tree. A toad croaked, leaped toward him, stopped. It had barely any spring in its jump. Charlie found the garden hose, turned on the tap, sprayed a good-sized puddle of water around the creature, and watched it immerse itself. He felt merciful, brimming with infinite compassion, St. Charlie of the Hollywood Hills, savior of toads.

A slight sound made him turn, a dull thump caused by a premature avocado falling to earth. Why couldn't they just hang in the branches long enough to ripen? What the hell was going on in the world? He went back indoors, telephoned the airport, asked about the condition of the computers, but no change— Eastern was down, and so was Continental and Delta and American, even All Nippon Air. The female voice that informed Galloway of this unhappy state of affairs might have been relaying the temperatures of a patient in an intensive care unit. *Down, sir, and still plummeting. We can only pray.*

As Charlie hung up, the lights of a car illuminated the front yard. He looked out to see Clarence Wylie approaching the house. As soon as he entered the living room Clarence sat on the sofa, undoing the knot of his tie. He removed his notebook from his hip pocket and laid it on the coffee table. He looked, Galloway thought, very uneasy.

Clarence stared at his notebook. "It took some effort, but I managed to get you something," he said. "I warn you, now. I think it's unhealthy. What you've walked into is a pile of shit."

"Not an unusual phenomenon." Galloway, balanced on the arm of the sofa, glanced at the hieroglyphics that covered the pages of Wylie's notebook. They were unreadable.

Clarence removed his tie completely. "This is what I have. From the description you gave me, I think the man you know as Raymond Cruz is also known as Arturo Paz and Joseph Salongo and quite a few other names as well. His real name appears to be Armando Teng. The Philippine Constabulary have a warrant out for his arrest on charges of killing three of their cops a few days ago. We have this information because Teng is *also* suspected of murdering an American national called Eugene Costain in Manila recently. Our embassy there was advised. Routine in such matters."

"Who was Costain? Why was he killed?" Charlie asked. He was eager, anxious for Clarence to finish. A vitality possessed him, a sense of being close to the heart of a mystery. It was as if a formerly bare room had become furnished all at once. There were particulars now. Things to touch. Windows and skylights to look through.

"I'll get to Costain," Clarence Wylie said. "Teng first. Sometime yesterday, and this is hot off the press, Philippine Military Intelligence arrested a man called—" here Clarence checked his notebook, "Jovitoe Baltazar, who was wanted for questioning in connection with your Mr. Teng. This same Baltazar was deported from the United States in the late 1970s as an illegal alien. I put that in parentheses because I don't know if it has any bearing on this."

Clarence played with his tie, the label of which said MADE IN THE USA. "Jovitoe Baltazar, it would seem, was happy to 'cooperate' with Philippine authorities. I use *cooperate* loosely. Bones might have been broken, a bruise or three inflicted. Who knows? According to Baltazar, Teng was dispatched to the United States to do some killing. Which is what Joaquin told you."

To do some killing. Yes. *Yes.* What came back now to Galloway was the first impression he'd had of the man he knew only as Raymond Cruz. *This one's a killer*—wasn't that what he'd thought when he'd shaken hands with him through the open window of Freddie Joaquin's car? Charlie moved around the room like a loose particle, readjusting things for no real reason, just an overflow of energy, a discharge of electricity. A matchbook here, a vase there, a copy of *Good Housekeeping.*

"Dispatched by whom, Clarence?" he asked.

"By Baltazar himself, presumably. But I also figure there's a group of some kind helping out here in the States. If Baltazar spent time in this country, he could have a number of acquaintances in place assisting Teng. Your Elizabeth Honculada, for instance, turns out to be the daughter of a certain James, who, according to the Treasury Department, has been known to transfer large sums of money to bank accounts in Manila. He could be Teng's financier. That's a guess."

Wylie was quiet, inward-looking, as if he'd left some part of himself elsewhere and couldn't remember the precise location. "Now let's go back to Costain. According to our vague information on him—supplied, I may say, by a so-called information officer at our embassy in Manila—Eugene Costain sold securities to Filipino businessmen. Trouble is, Costain had no affiliation with any corporation doing business in the Philippines, nor is there any evidence he operated in a self-employed way. No tax ID, nothing of that kind in the IRS computers, which I was able to access."

Charlie Galloway had an uneasy moment during which he considered the nature of privacy in the United States. He thought of computer linked to computer, one police department to another, one federal agency to the next, privileged information freely sent back and forth across the electronic linkages of the land, wires abuzz with names and addresses and income tax returns and who was sleeping with whom and whether somebody's sexual preference was for sheep or stirrups. A massive federal ear eavesdropped on everything—tax accountants, psychiatrists, physicians, debt-collection agencies, the offices of archbishops, probably even confessionals. Was it any wonder there was such anxiety loose throughout the land? That paranoids roamed the streets and people sought safe harbor in booze and drugs? America was a listening post, a Big Ear.

Clarence said, "Costain had a wife in Poughkeepsie who might have been in a position to tell us more about her husband's activities in Manila—except she OD'd on Tuinal a couple of days ago. Not the kind of slumber you come back from. Odd business.

She also snuffed about a dozen spaniel pups by poisoning their chow, a demented act. If you want my informed guess, Charlie, Costain was CIA, or at least one of its nebulous branches, but that hasn't shown up on our computers. Some stuff the bureau just doesn't have access to, because our stepbrothers at Langley, typically, aren't into sharing. They like secrecy. They can cloud a glass of water just by looking at it."

"Is that a way of saying nobody knows who Teng intends to kill?" Charlie asked.

"No," Wylie said. "According to Philippine MI, Baltazar named two men, one of whom was shot dead four hours ago in Dallas. The description of the assailant—provided by the victim's daughter, poor kid—matches Teng. The victim was a certain Thomas Railsback, whom we know to have been a CIA contract employee, or at least somebody with Langley connections. That much is in the data banks."

Dallas. Cruz had flown deep into the dark red heart of Texas. "What's the CIA doing about the murder?"

"To the best of my knowledge, nothing. They'd probably deny a connection with Railsback anyhow."

"So Ray, or Armando, or whoever, has a vendetta against our beloved Central Intelligence Agency."

"It would appear."

"What about the second proposed victim?"

"Agents have been assigned to protect him."

"Who is he?"

"This is where it gets heavy, Charlie. I think this is where you have to draw the line and walk away." Clarence hesitated. "Have you been watching TV?"

Galloway shook his head.

"Then you missed seeing William Laforge. The President just nominated him for the directorship of the CIA."

Some high-up. Sweet Jesus, Freddie. The wee man hadn't been yanking Galloway's string after all. Charlie looked through the window at the moon, whose aura suggested some kind of illness. Perhaps it had been surveying Mother Earth, the sick old hag, too long. Charlie tried to imagine Cruz under this same diseased moon, stalking dark places with a gun, bearing violent grudges against the Central Intelligence Agency.

But who in the third world didn't? Who in the decaying cities of Central and Latin America, in the Middle and Far East, on the Pacific rim, didn't think the initials CIA stood for one of the many secret names of Satan? Who, bathing in some shit-infested river or scrubbing clothes where macheted bodies floated blithely past, or slaving in the blistering heat of a sugar cane field or sweltering in a hellish basement sewing silk dresses they could never themselves wear, didn't believe that the CIA was a labora-tory where atrocious schemes were hatched to overthrow unac-ceptable governments and assassinate the alleged opponents of American democracy? Who didn't believe crackpots walked the corridors of the Langley complex, soft-skinned, pink men who emerged from think tanks with a deranged, pumped-up vision of a planet dominated by U.S. policy and backed by U.S. guns?

Never mind the goddam *third world!* Who in these *United States,* in this loose federation of dismaying contrasts, didn't consider the CIA a law unto itself, a secret nation within a nation, beyond the reach of the Supreme Court and the Constitution and the Bill of bloody Rights? Who didn't believe they kept the dark-est of dark secrets? Who didn't deem them masters of conspiracy who had hoisted into power some of the most appalling villains to have darkened this miserable century? And who didn't believe that the CIA controlled the United States and with it the presi-dency?

Charlie wondered what in particular had set Teng's clock running, what infraction, what personal injustice Langley had enacted upon him. "I assume there's a full-scale search on for Teng?"

"Any moment. Vanderwolf is probably busy assessing the data himself, then he'll consult with Washington before any decision is made. Since he's only director of the western region, he won't wipe his nose without talking to Hugo Fletcher. I wouldn't rule out a massive operation within the next few hours, Charlie."

Although a diazepamed aging preppie called John J. Coleman was the titular head of the FBI, it was Hugo Fletcher who made all the decisions that actually mattered, because Coleman was frequently hospitalized in serene locations where he was treated for his addiction. Fletcher, whom Charlie had met only once in those distant days when his star inside the LAPD had not begun to fizzle, had a shark's easy grace, a hardness of eye, a predator's razor-edged benevolence. He'd smile as he throttled you, no doubt.

"What are the Dallas police doing?" Charlie asked.

"They're treading water because they've been told to."

That figured. A call comes down from the Feds and the Dallas cops back off whistling happily. One less homicide was one less burden. If the Feds wanted to hog the Railsback murder, happy trails to them. The Feds could do what they liked.

"What you're saying, Clarence, is that Teng is out there somewhere and nobody is looking for him yet."

"It's only a matter of time."

"How much time?"

Clarence shook his head. "I don't know. It depends on a number of things. How Vanderwolf reacts. How quickly Washington responds. When Washington says go, then Vanderwolf phones Dallas and floods the place with agents."

"Where does Laforge live?"

"Pennsylvania."

"Then Teng could be headed there already."

"If he is he'll walk into a small army because Laforge will have protection. Teng will be cut to ribbons before he gets anywhere near Laforge. And if he hasn't left Dallas yet, he'll be picked up as soon as Vanderwolf gets his hordes into the field."

A limp breeze shivered among the brittle leaves of the avocado, then died, and the night was still again. Charlie thought of Cruz, and the people who had helped him, from Freddie Joaquin to Elizabeth Honculada to whoever supplied him with a gun in Dallas. Now, if he read Cruz with any accuracy, he imagined the man had already been assisted on his way out of Dallas and was headed east—by road, rail, air, perhaps some intricate combination of the three. But he couldn't be sure of anything. Cruz was elusive, guarded, and moved quickly even when he seemed languid and detached. That was his cover, his protection, that camouflage of aloofness—and it was a good one too. Charlie shut his eyes, picturing Cruz as he'd last seen him in the parking lot of the Palms hotel. *He's mine. Nobody else has a right to him.*

He gazed at Clarence Wylie. "I deserve a chance."

Clarence shook his head. "Don't tell me. You want to go out there and look for this guy and bring him in like some goddam hero?"

A hero. No. That wasn't it. Charlie didn't want to be a hero. It was quieter than that, far less grand. It was a question of finishing something, a matter of ending what he'd already begun, an orchestration of all the half-heard notes that had been playing inside his head ever since Ella had died, symphonizing them into one well-structured tune, a beginning, a middle, an end—that was what it came down to. Heroism was for heroes, not drunks, whose aims were less lofty. To stay sober. Finish a job. Wake without a hangover. Live a life free of chaos. These were surely modest ambitions. For Charlie they were matters, quite simply, of life and death. Sobriety required a form of courage he wasn't sure he possessed. Even now, taunted by the ruin of a hangover, he wanted a drink, something to steady his hand. One small nip. No more.

"I'm not hero material, Clarence. But I need Teng. I need to get to him."

Clarence walked up and down the room. His expression was one of frustrated sympathy. "Look, I understand how you feel. I know you think Teng is your personal business. You discovered him, Charlie. I know that. You need something to run the right way for you—"

"Is that pity I hear in your voice, Clarence?"

"Screw you, Charlie. You know I don't pity you. I think you're an ass at times, but I also think you'll do just fine if you ever get your shit together—but this isn't anything for you to get involved in because it's too big and you don't understand how the game is played at this level."

"Give me the address, Clarence. That's all I ask. Give me Laforge's bloody address."

Clarence Wylie sighed. "Listen. Teng's probably in Dallas. He probably hasn't left Texas. If he's smart, he'll lie low there until he imagines the heat's off—then and only then he'll go on to Pennsylvania."

"I think he's more desperate than smart. And I think lying low isn't on his agenda."

"Since we're talking desperate, Charlie, go look at yourself in a mirror."

"So what? One desperate man looks for another. Don't you appreciate the symmetry?"

"What would you do with him, Charlie? Bring him in with cuffs on? Take him prisoner? Is that the notion?"

"Something like that."

"Teng's armed. He's a killer. Do you even *remember* how to fire a pistol?"

"I hate guns."

"Whether you love 'em or loathe 'em isn't quite the point here, is it? You can't go unarmed against a man with a gun. Be reasonable."

"Okay. Watch me. I'll get my gun. If that's what you call being reasonable, in your funny Yankee way, reasonable I'll be." The gun to which Galloway referred was a Colt Government Model that lay on top of the piece of bedroom furniture Charlie knew as a wardrobe but which Karen called an *armoire.* He had absolutely no enthusiasm for guns. Although he'd cheerfully returned his police pistol to the department, he owned the Colt because Karen had insisted, during a spate of muggings and rapes, that home and person had to be protected from the menace that lurked in Los Angeles. So Charlie reluctantly purchased the weapon even though the fatal American infatuation with the pistol bewildered him. People were encouraged by an outmoded Constitution to use guns in defense of their liberty, which was clearly jeopardized on a seasonal basis by ducks, moose, and deer. Sometimes people just got in the way—say during liquor store holdups and burglaries and muggings. But the right to bear arms was inviolate. So be it. Charlie moved to the foot of the stairs, put his hand on the rail and prepared to climb.

"Charlie," Clarence said. "You're making me miserable."

"I'm going for my bloody gun. You told me to be reasonable. So I'm showing maturity, Clarence. As if by magic, the Scotsman turns before your very orbs into a man of admirable responsibility. The Colt awaits me on yonder *armoire,* Clarence, old chap, old pal. See me climb. Up and up. *I have a sense of purpose.*"

"Wait, Charlie. Let's talk."

Galloway paused on the stairs, turning to look down at Clarence Wylie, who asked, "Even if you knew where Laforge lives in Pennsylvania, how do you propose to find Teng? Where do you start looking?"

Galloway felt an odd little dizziness dance through him. Hunger, imbalanced chemistry, too much alcohol in the bloodstream aggravated now by a blast of adrenaline. He had the sensation he was crazy, that the tiny germ of insanity he'd carried around for years was suddenly full-blown, and yet when he heard himself speak he thought how rational, how *sensible,* he managed to sound. "If Teng has a specific location in mind, then it's not so hard. You try to think the way he'd think himself. You put yourself in his situation. If you know where he's going, you imagine how he'd try to get there."

"Oh, that's rich, that's a great speech," Clarence remarked. "The reality isn't going to be anything like that."

"I'll take the chance, Clarence. I don't have a lot on my plate at the moment. You might have noticed. So what about that address?"

Clarence shook his head, chewed his lip in the manner of a man warring with himself. Jesus, how was he going to resist that imploring note in Charlie Galloway's voice, that lost look in the eyes, the suggestion of despair about the mouth? How was he supposed to withstand all that? "No, Charlie—"

"Clarence, please."

"Don't put me in this position—"

"A favor, Clarence. That's all. One last favor. For auld lang syne. Don't leave me hanging."

"God help me," Clarence said. "God help me if this is a mistake, because I'll never forgive myself if anything happens to you." He scribbled in his notebook and tore out the page, holding it aloft before setting it down with great reluctance on the coffee table. Raggedly perforated, it had an innocuous, improvised look to it, the casually insignificant presence of a grocery list.

Charlie walked to the table. He looked at the paper, then folded it twice before pocketing it. "Nothing's going to happen, Clarence."

Clarence said, "No more favors, Charlie. Okay? I had a problem getting what I already got. I think I used up any leftover clout I might have had in the office. Too many new faces there. They see me as some kind of dinosaur. A lot of the old crew have taken their pensions. I'm going back inside my nifty little shell of retirement, away from it all. I like it there. I don't like it where you live, Charlie. I've had it with danger."

Danger. The word did a little hopscotch step in Galloway's head. He placed a hand on Wylie's shoulder, a gesture of gratitude. Clarence walked to the door, where he paused to look back. "Keep me informed. I want to know everything that happens. Where you go. What you do. You owe me that."

"I'll be in touch," Charlie said.

"And *please* don't let me live to regret this," Clarence added. A voice nagged him in his mind: *You've made a big mistake, Wylie. Your biggest.*

The dawn that broke over Bucks County was the color of a ripened peach. The day, barely begun, was going to be as torrid as the one before, and the one before that. From the window of his bedroom William Laforge watched the specters created by the trees, the flattened shadows that spread across the grass and under the picnic table.

Already dressed, Laforge stood with hands in the pockets of his cotton slacks, his pale blue shirt open at the neck. He'd been unable to sleep, tossing, turning, his mind a hare chased by the hounds of the upcoming Senate hearings. Then he'd risen and showered and was halfway through shaving when the telephone had rung. The call was from his assistant at Langley, a pleasant apple-faced young man named Frank Christian.

Only bad news came at dawn, Laforge thought. Nobody called at that time of day to say you had won the lottery.

There had been an incident in Dallas, Christian said. *An incident.* Christian had a way with euphemisms and doublespeak and would inevitably go far in the Company. An incident in Dallas. Laforge had listened in silence and then put the telephone down. His face was still covered with shaving cream, a fluff of which he left attached to the receiver.

Tom Railsback was dead, shot in his own driveway. It was an awful blow to absorb even if Laforge had known it was coming. Railsback had scoffed, that was the worst of it. He hadn't listened. It's only Billy behaving like some goddam housewife, that's probably what he thought. Fussy Billy. If only Tom had paid attention. But he'd blustered. *Nobody's going to get me in my own backyard.* Poor Tom.

Laforge changed his angle of perception. Beyond the beech trees, where the gravel driveway led to the stables, a dark car and a van had been parked. Inside the larger vehicle were two men, an array of communications equipment, TV consoles depicting images relayed from cameras strategically located around the estate. In the car sat a couple of armed guards, men in white shirts who didn't conceal their weaponry. On the backseat lay several rifles. The trunk doubtless contained tear gas, grenades, more firearms. Out of Laforge's view, at the place where the old bridge straddled the creek, three men armed with rifles and carrying walkie-talkies patrolled the area. This was the protection afforded the man nominated to be head of the CIA. What had happened to Tom couldn't happen here. A killer could not get close to the house. There was simply no way.

It was difficult not to be impressed by all the security, the attention, Laforge thought, hard not to yield to the notion that you were a man of some consequence. He was excited by the idea of running the show at Langley, impatient to forge a different, sharper intelligence agency out of the blunted intrument Sandy Bach had left behind. Hadn't McCune said as much?

I want an agency with teeth, William. I want intelligence with some bite to it.

I'll give you that, Mr. President. And he knew he could because he knew how the agency worked, where it was weak, where strong, he knew the men who deserved promotion and those who were time servers and clock watchers; above all else, he knew secrecy, a favorite old mistress whose hot embrace never failed to enthrall him.

Now, as he studied this brand-new dawn and tried not to think of poor Railsback, he recalled President McCune also saying that the Central Intelligence Agency, if it was to have goddam fangs, needed a strong man at the helm. *I believe you are that man, William.* There, in the Oval Office, McCune had smiled, offering a brief handshake of extraordinary firmness, like a steel gauntlet to which Laforge was obliged to yield; a crack of finger joints, the pressure on bone. Laforge had smiled dutifully, knowing in his heart that he didn't like McCune, that the President was crude in ways Laforge found offensive. It was more than the handshake, the insincerity of the smile, the strange way he sometimes had with syntax. There were reprehensible jokes of an ethnic nature, told with an air of WASP confidence. There were, surprisingly, Havana cigars. *Blockade isn't worth a damn,* McCune had said, winking, nodding. Laforge, a dedicated nonsmoker, had had a hard time breathing. Tension, smoke, the sense of place and occasion—and the upsetting feeling he kept having that this was all an elaborate joke and he was going to be found out and dragged from the White House by Secret Servicemen. *On your way, asshole. Take your act down the road.* The evening had been surreal.

Laforge's mind went back inevitably to Tom Railsback. Despite the rising sun, he felt cold. He toweled soap from his chin, then continued down the hallway to Carolyn's bedroom. As he walked he thought, *Any invader on this property would be shot.*

Asleep, one arm curled characteristically around a pillow, Carolyn looked like an angel who had fallen only a short way from grace. He loved her: a simple perception. If it could not be love of any common kind, it was the only form he was capable of feeling. He knew she'd been with Truskett last night. And why not? They had something to celebrate, after all. He reached for her hand, held it in his own, squeezed.

Carolyn slowly opened her eyes. "Is something wrong?" she asked.

Laforge shook his head. "Absolutely nothing. Why do you ask?"

Coming out of sleep, she always appeared very young and fragile. "You look . . . troubled," she said. She raised her arm, laying the warm palm of her hand against his cheek. He shut his eyes. She made him feel secure in a way no battalion of guards could ever do.

"I'm not troubled," he replied. *Railsback is dead and I'm not troubled.* "It's just very strange to look out of one's window and see a detachment of security personnel."

Carolyn smiled. "Did you really think your life would go on as before after last night?"

"I don't know what I thought."

"You're an important man, my love. You need protection."
She tossed her bedsheets back. She always slept naked. He gazed
at the flatness of her stomach, the delicate shallow of shadow
created by her navel, the deeper shadow between her legs. Her
skin was impressively smooth, unmarked as yet by age.

She said, "You have nothing to worry about now."

Laforge didn't speak.

"You'll make an enormous contribution to this country,"
Carolyn said. "Do you doubt that?"

"No."

"Do the hearings trouble you?"

"Of course not."

"Then stop looking so grouchy." She rose from the bed and
stood before him, running the flat of one hand through her yellow hair. Not for the first time in his life did he wish he felt the
sexual desires most men feel; the urge to reach for her and draw
her to him was very strong. But he was disabled, crippled, a fact
he reflected on with a sense of ironic detachment: While he was
perfectly capable of running the Central Intelligence Agency, of
operating the great machinery of secrecy, he couldn't muster
what it took to satisfy his wife. It was an irony whose deeper
levels he had no urge to probe.

"McCune wants the hearings to begin next week," he said.

"The sooner the better. Then you won't be mooning around
the house waiting. You'll be running Langley."

Laforge wandered to the window. He saw the van move and
for one heart-turning moment he imagined it was about to leave,
that all the security on the property was being stripped away from
him because he'd been found out, his secret had unraveled—but
then the vehicle stopped and the engine died. It had simply been
changing position, perhaps to better monitor the estate. That was
all. A brief panic passed out of Laforge, but his hand, which had
become a claw upraised to the windowpane, remained inflexible,
as if it had atrophied in fear.

Carolyn said, "You must relax, William."

"I am relaxed," he insisted. *Railsback, Costain, and Deduro.
All dead.* He stared over the meadow at the stand of trees, which
looked different to him just then, unfamiliar, altered overnight.

"And I'm from Missouri," Carolyn remarked, thinking how

very proud she was of William, and of how little he might have achieved had it not been for her unselfish dedication to his career. Now she need never see Truskett again, a realization that caused her relief and, to her surprise, regret in equal measure. She gazed at William as she drew her robe on, and she remembered her extraordinary flight with Byron, the thrill, the deprivation of air, the frightening, powerful sense of unity with him. All that was over. All that was done.

And she would miss it.

18

It was seven A.M. when Byron Truskett parked his car under a stand of fir trees at the edge of an isolated lake in Prince Georges County, some thirty miles southeast of Washington. He scanned the water, which was still and very blue in the morning light. He got out of his car, put on dark glasses. Underfoot, dry pine needles crackled. He walked to the water's edge in the wary manner of a man concerned about putting a fine Italian shoe into an unspeakable pile of shit.

About fifty yards along the shoreline a decrepit jetty jutted into the water. A small sailboat was tethered to this uncertain anchorage. A big man in a bright yellow T-shirt and dark blue shorts was visible on board. As Truskett got closer to the pier he saw discolored light streak from the man's green plastic visor.

Truskett reached the jetty. Planks of gray wood were here and there rotted through. Silvery minnows darted in the shallows, where a collection of old Coors cans lay in silt. Truskett, his shirt already soaked with sweat, noticed that the boat was called the *J. Edgar.*

Only now did the man in the yellow T-shirt look up. He had

been undoing a knot in a length of rope, and he tossed the rope aside, indicating with a gesture of a large hairy hand that Truskett should come on board. The man, Hugo Fletcher, vanished inside the tiny cabin, leaving Truskett to board without assistance. The boat swayed slightly as the senator clambered into it. He stooped, stepping into the cabin, conscious of how close to his skull a kerosene lantern hung. Brass fittings, hemp coasters on a table of ancient oak, Bavarian beer tankards, a pistol holstered and slung over a cross beam—a mariner's world of weathered surfaces and hard objects.

"Brewsky?" Fletcher asked.

"It's a little early for me," said Truskett.

Fletcher opened a Styrofoam ice chest and took out a Budweiser, which he tossed into the air and caught on the way down. Its contents fizzed out when he popped the tab. "Never too early for American beer, Senator," he said. "Horse's piss. Drunk stronger water in my time. Anyway, this is supposed to be my one day off per month. A man's got to get away. If possible. If he isn't hounded."

Fletcher gave Truskett a funny little look, knowing and supercilious, unsmiling. Hugo wasn't renowned for his mirth. He had reputedly been heard to laugh in nineteen hundred and seventy one when Richard Nixon had uttered the phrase "peace with honor," but this was apocryphal. He had in common with Nixon one thing—a problem with facial hair, which grew at such a rate he was obliged to shave two or three times a day. The visor cast a pale green pall over his complexion, giving the impression of a malignant illness.

Fletcher thunked the can on the table and stared at Truskett, who noticed a curious irregularity in the pigmentation of Fletcher's eyes. The right eye was blue, the left gray.

"So," said Fletcher, languidly scratching a hairy black leg. "This the day of reckoning, is it? Calling in your marker?"

"That's one way of putting it, Hugo," Truskett replied.

Fletcher made Truskett feel like a debt collector of the worst sort. But Truskett had nothing about which to be ashamed. Fletcher owed him, it was that simple. A few years ago Byron Truskett had convinced John J. Coleman to promote Fletcher to the number two spot inside the bureau at a time when Coleman was undergoing one of his regular "retreats" at a cosy clinic in the Berkshires. Like many people, Coleman had a hunch that Truskett would be the next President, and therefore a man to oblige; even if he considered Fletcher a threat to his empire, he'd honored Truskett's request. Tranquilized, indifferent to his surroundings, how could Coleman have made a sound judgment in any case? He'd never been known to make solid decisions, straight *or* zoned out. He'd risen to the directorship of the FBI through the rapid transit system of the old boy network, correct prep school, grammar school, Ivy League university, the proper clubs. His competence was of less importance than his connections, his weakness for soporific drugs less significant than his reputation for bonhomie and clubmanship.

Hugo Fletcher was an altogether different kind of animal from his nominal superior. Unlike Coleman, a gregarious raconteur, he was perhaps the most secretive man Truskett had ever met. He was never photographed, frequented neither fancy restaurants nor nightclubs. He had never married. It was rumored he kept a woman on a country estate somewhere near Wheeling, West Virginia, but nobody had ever verified this. A mystery, self-perpetuating.

Truskett said, "There are certain aspects of the national interest at stake."

"And some of your own, no doubt," Fletcher said, and crushed his beer can cheerfully.

"My concerns often coincide with those of the nation." Truskett said this with due gravity, giving it the timbre of a campaign pledge.

"And so do mine, Senator." Fletcher ran fingertips over his bristled jaw. "From the tone of your phone call, I'd say you're anxious to get me to cover your ass in the matter of a certain individual, am I correct?"

Truskett said, "So to speak, Hugo. A security detachment—"

The word *security* appeared to act on Fletcher like a convulsant. With a sudden chopping motion of his hand through the burnished air, he forced Truskett to leave his sentence unfinished. Fletcher gazed from the porthole in a manic way. Sun, glittering on water, made him blink rapidly. "This place give you an impression of isolation, Senator?"

"I'd say that."

"You casually parked your car. Strolled right up on the dock. Stepped on board. Just you and me and the lake and some trees, right?" Fletcher turned from the porthole. *"Right?"*

"Right," Truskett said.

"Wrong, wrong, wrong. Oh, very wrong." Fletcher broke open a new beer. "There are four men concealed out there. You wouldn't notice one of them, Truskett. They're hidden in trees. They're on the other shore. They're lying in reeds. They have one function."

"To protect you."

"You're a quick study."

"I didn't see them," Truskett said.

"Damn right you didn't," Fletcher said. "You noticed one of them, I'd have his ass."

Truskett looked suitably impressed, although he was anxious to be gone from this place. He wasn't happy in nautical situations.

Fletcher said, "Security! I know security, Senator! I can give it or I can take it away. I can order it in place or I can disperse it."

"Dispersal is what I have in mind," Truskett said.

"Doubtless." Fletcher waved the hand that held the beer. "You don't have to spell it out any further, Senator. No names. That's not how I play marbles. You think *careful* is just a word, don't you? You say things like *Oh, be careful* or *Let's do this in a careful way,* don't you? Horseshit. To some of us, Senator, careful's a way of life. Careful's a goddamn religion. You don't bandy it around. You handle it like goose feathers."

Truskett was quiet for a time, pondering Fletcher's relationship with reality.

"I know the identity of the candidate," Fletcher said. "I know he has a cadre in place. It can be rendered ineffective, at least for a short time."

"Can this be achieved without, let's say, difficult questions rearing their ugly little heads later?"

Fletcher said, "Anything can be achieved, Senator. Nothing is impossible in my line of business. I have networks you wouldn't begin to understand. You wouldn't want to."

The senator felt the boat shiver just a little, knocked against the pier by some mild chop. "About this foreigner who has entered the country . . ." he said.

"You want him to have a clear run at his target, correct?" Fletcher asked, although it wasn't exactly a question. "You don't want him impeded. You don't want a manhunt. He should be allowed to complete his task here. Right?"

"I see that as the general goal."

"Easy," Fletcher said in a casual way.

"I'm glad you think so, Hugo."

"In fact, Senator, I already set a few things in motion just after you called." Fletcher was quiet a moment, looking dourly satisfied with himself. "We're quits. Account settled. Okay?"

"As you say." Truskett stood up. He had one more request to make. "The woman . . ." He was briefly uneasy. He thought he saw a tiny smirk on Fletcher's green-tinted face, and he didn't like it. "I don't want her hurt in any way. Not in any way."

"She'll be safe," Fletcher said. "I assure you."

"Thank you, Hugo." Carolyn's image drifted before Truskett. He wondered if obsession had a cure.

"One final thing, Senator. The assassin. Disposal after completion?"

Truskett made a brief affirmative gesture of the head: the execution order. How simple. What scant involvement he felt.

Fletcher said, "I wouldn't want any misunderstandings. Loose ends. I like things tightly wrapped."

"Yes," said Truskett. "I can see that."

The senator made his way out of the cabin and stood, a little unsteady, on the deck. He looked across the lake. He saw no sign of life, no evidence of the men Fletcher said were hidden in the landscape. The world seemed quite empty, save for himself and Hugo.

"Jerry Slotten's a dear friend of mine, Senator. I've always thought he was the best candidate for the job," Fletcher remarked.

Byron Truskett clambered up to the jetty. A sliver of wood punctured his thumb. Pressing the throbbing thumb against his lower teeth, he looked back down into the boat and said, "He's the only candidate now, Hugo."

* * *

Because it was dark in the back of the van, Teng had no notion of time or distance. He'd lain down among some packing material and tried to sleep, but what he kept coming back to was the sight of the girl's face in the window of the house in Dallas. He had brought sorrow to her; he'd scarred her because of sins her father had committed. What justice was there in that? You didn't seek revenge against the innocent, the relatives of the guilty, those who survived. The argument for vengeance was inevitably flawed. The terrorist who blew the plane out of the sky killed hundreds to get one man, and those hundreds swelled to thousands when you considered the way grief spread like water disturbed by a seabird's claw: a small ring, a larger one, then others larger still. A great pool of suffering—and for what principle? What point?

He closed his eyes. He forced the joints of his fingers into the sides of his head until there was pain. He pushed so hard it seemed the skin would surely be pierced. He felt the rage of his blood, his pulses driven. How could he deliver himself from grief? from guilt? A child's face in a window. Was anything worth that expression of terror and loss?

He felt like a blinded animal inside a sweltering trap. Somewhere on the outskirts of Dallas—Teng recalled a sign that said Balch Springs—Johnny Ko had driven his pickup into a garage and both men had transferred to this large furniture van. Ko, who was driving, had instructed Teng to get in the back, where it smelled of cardboard. Empty crates and boxes slithered here and there. Plastic packing pods spilled from sacks and attached themselves by static to Teng's clothing and the hairs on the backs of his hands. It was as if lifeless white leeches clung to him. He turned on his side, drew a flattened cardboard box beneath his head, but comfort was out of the question. The van rocked, swayed, sending reverberations through his bones.

He sat upright, jammed himself in a corner, fought against the depression that assaulted him. To detach yourself was the only way. To remain disinterested. He thought of the dark swarming with police cars. He envisaged Galloway, strangely dogged even in his inebriation, as if some corner of him were always sharp and sober, some inviolate place in his brain forever absorbing information. Where was Galloway now? *Looking for me,* Teng thought. But what did Galloway know? Had he learned of the connection between Costain in faraway Manila, Railsback in Dallas, and Laforge? Suddenly it didn't matter what Galloway knew or didn't know. Teng would finish what he'd begun, without opening the awful door that allowed emotions to gate-crash; he'd go through events the way Baltazar had planned them. He didn't exist except as an agent of vengeance. What did the expression on a young girl's face matter? What concern was it of his to realize that for the rest of her life the girl would carry in her memory the echoes of two shotgun blasts?

The van shuddered over what felt like a series of metal rails, and Teng was thrown to the side, rattling his head upon bare metal. Pain flashed briefly; small meteorites sparked in the blackness. He moaned, rubbed his skull gently, changed his position. He tried to imagine himself elsewhere, but it was hard at first to force his mind beyond some vague images of Baguio, a mist rolling on dark green hills, and a few poorly developed pictures of Manila. Then they became clearer, like Polaroid photographs flooding slowly with color.

Years ago, in the company of Joe Baltazar, he'd walked through the somber, overwhelming streets of Intramuros, the Spanish walled city within Manila, a place smelling of aged stone and death, holy relics locked in glass cases, crannies out of which enormous wooden saints regarded you with the benevolence the pious keep for the profane. He remembered gazing from an open window into a courtyard below and seeing barefoot kids beg coins from a middle-aged American couple, the man in a plaid jacket, the woman in Bermuda shorts and orange chiffon scarf. The more the Americans refused, the harder the kids persisted. A conflict of wills, Teng had thought at the time. Now he saw it as a collision of economic cultures, the needy interacting with the fortunate, the hungry with the providers, the tugging of small brown hands on seersucker sleeves and a silk blouse, the shrugs of the American couple as they tried to liberate themselves from an uncomfortable situation. As the new overlords, they'd come to see the relics left behind by the previous colonists of the Philippines, not to be waylaid by two tiny brown goddam nuisances. The kids pursued the Americans all the way across the courtyard until finally the woman relented and opened her purse, drawing out a handful of coins and bestowing them on the boys even as she kept moving away. Her husband harangued her. *Don't encourage them, honey. That's the last thing you want to do.* Neither American understood a simple fact: Begging was no longer a stigma in Manila; it had become a tourist industry, like weaving, leather shoes, handbags.

Remembering Manila disturbed him. He had the unwelcome instinct that it would be a long time before he saw the city again. The return trip was something that hadn't been discussed with Joe Baltazar. Teng assumed Joe had made arrangements to get him home, if not to Manila—where his situation might by now be thoroughly compromised—then to some other part of the archipelago, Northern Luzon, perhaps, or Palawan, even Mindoro. Uncertainty possessed him. Momentarily he experienced a panic growing out of the notion that Joe Baltazar *hadn't* made plans for his return, that he'd be abandoned here in America. And then what?

No. Baltazar wouldn't desert him.

He wondered what Joe was doing now. Waiting, living anonymously, with worried impatience, in some narrow room at a pension house in Manila, newspapers scattered on the floor beside a small electric hot plate on which he brewed coffee, a fan that turned slowly in a window. Waiting for the end. For the completion. For the guilty to be dead and buried.

The van stopped. Teng heard the door of the cab slam shut. Then Johnny Ko unlocked the rear of the vehicle and told Teng to come out. The place where Ko had parked was brown and still, a wilderness in the slatted early daylight, a flat stretch of dry earth, here and there a feeble shrub casting insubstantial shadows. How far had they come from the expansive conurbation that was Dallas? Teng wondered.

"What now?" he asked.

"We wait," Ko said.

"For what?"

"The airplane."

"I knew nothing about a plane," Teng said. But why should he be surprised by any of Baltazar's arrangements now?

Ko gazed up at the sky. In silhouette, there was nothing

oriental about his features. He might have been a drugstore cowboy with his wide-brimmed Stetson. Teng wondered about the
depths of Ko's assimilation into a culture he'd been obliged to
learn. Had it come to him easily? Perhaps America was something
you absorbed, a medication, a bromide; the faster you absorbed
it, the faster it worked. You toiled hard, and you dreamed, and
if your goals were prosperity and comfort you had a good chance
to achieve them.

Prosperity and comfort. Teng thought these words rang like
two unfamiliar bells in the distance. But people like Ko and James
Honculada and Freddie Joaquin obviously understood the sweet
little melody they played. They knew the bells. They knew the
tune. They'd heard the music of America—at the cost of forgetting the simpler native songs of their upbringing.

"Why are you helping me?" Teng asked. "You like America.
You said so. You make money here. You're happy. So why are you
running this risk?"

Ko tugged on the brim of his hat, a gesture he might have
learned from a western movie. "It's not so hard to figure. I don't
owe nothing to the guy you killed. What difference did he make
to my life? He didn't come in my shop and buy stuff, did he? Joe
Baltazar, now, he's a friend. He asks me for some of my time, I
give it. Joe's enemies are mine too. I look at the situation, I don't
see any real scary risk in it for me, if you want the truth, so I help
out. There's no mystery, *kaibigan.*"

Teng silently watched the sun rise on the flat landscape.
Already the day's warmth was evident. He stretched his arms. He
was hungry, but he knew the sensation would go away if he
didn't think about it. He had been hungry before in his life when
Teresita hadn't been able to afford basic foodstuffs like rice or
fish. Hunger clawed for a while, then receded.

He gazed into the sky, saw nothing. *He didn't come in my
shop and buy stuff.* This line echoed in Teng's head, a distillation
of a philosophy he found hard to understand. Railsback wasn't
a good customer, therefore his death was of no importance to Ko.
Capitalism. America. The Dollar.

"Look," Ko said.

Teng stared into the cloudless span of sky. The plane was
barely a fleck, like a flaw in your retina. The sound of the twin

engines was low and rasping, growing louder the more the small craft dropped in the sky and came down, mosquitolike and frail, toward the place where Ko had parked the van. Teng thought of a kite as he observed the aircraft shudder through a layer of clear turbulence—paper stretched between wood struts, played out on a length of string and the wind's whim. Gray-skinned, a faded number on the fuselage, the plane kept descending, and when it hit the ground some quarter of a mile away it raised devils of dust that were instantly scissored by the propellers and dispelled in fantastic patterns.

"Your plane," Ko said.

The craft skidded slightly to one side, then rolled to a halt a hundred yards from the van. Small shrubs blew sideways in the breeze, disturbed in their tenacious somnolence.

Teng, whose life had become filled with entrances and departures, took Ko's extended hand in his own and shook it a moment.

"So," Ko said. "I don't know where you're going next, but good luck."

Teng walked toward the small plane. The propellers were still now. Sun glistened against the fuselage which Teng saw had been patched here and there with fiberglass. At one time or another this slight craft had been in some kind of collision. It wasn't an idea Teng intended to entertain for long. He thought of heights and far horizons, propellers beating air, the upward rocketing of turbulence. Flying wasn't his favorite means of transport. He stopped, turned to look back. Johnny Ko was already inside the van and wheeling it around in a storm of brown dust. Brown dust and farewell.

Weary, feeling depression force itself back into his head, Teng climbed up into the cockpit on the passenger side. He glanced at the pilot even as he reached for his seat belt buckle in the manner of the obedient passenger who knows his very life depends on the flying skills of a complete stranger. The pilot, a straw-haired man, an Anglo, said nothing. Teng looked out of the window, imagining that the expression on his face might, to an imaginative onlooker, bear some slight resemblance to that of Railsback's daughter, frozen behind the pane of glass in the house in Dallas.

* * *

At seven-twenty A.M. Pacific time, Clarence Wylie stood in Eric
Vanderwolf's living room, where he'd been summoned by a
phone call just before dawn. Retired, Clarence was under no
obligation to comply, but some old nerve in him seemingly still
responded to Vanderwolf's edicts, a conditioned response he
hadn't yet expurgated. Vanderwolf wore striped pajamas and a
robe the color of burgundy. His slate-veined feet were bare inside
his leather slippers. He walked up and down the enormous den
of his large house whose windows had what avaricious realtors
called "spectacular" views of Los Angeles. Little of spectacle
could presently be seen. Already a tide of malodorous smog was
rolling complacently across the city.

Clarence Wylie listened to the slap-slap made by Vander-
wolf's leather slippers and gazed at the illustrations that adorned
this paneled, masculine room. Western oils, cowboys on frozen
horses perched on the snowy banks of an icy creek, badmen with
Pancho Villa mustaches. These paintings had titles like "Man and
Beast Defeated by Winter" or "Wranglers Working at Sunset."
They were photographic and sentimental, and not to Clarence
Wylie's taste.

A child cried in some recess of the huge house. Vanderwolf
said, "My youngest. Twelve. She has nightmares."

"That's too bad."

"She dreams she's being attacked by seahorses, of all things.
What I did was to put an aquarium in the kid's room," Vanderwolf said. "I filled it with seahorses. You don't face your fears,
you don't overcome them. I keep the aquarium next to her bed.
It's lit all night long so she can see it. She can hear the pump
running constantly. Those seahorses are always right there."

"I see," said Clarence Wylie, though he really didn't. "Why
did you call me down here at this time of day, Eric?"

Vanderwolf turned from the window, his hands clasped behind his back. "Don't trifle with me, Clarence. You know better
than that."

"I still don't follow," Clarence said.

Vanderwolf's great white brows came together in a fierce lock
and the shallow scar that creased his right cheek deepened to a
small trough as he scrutinized Wylie. "I was under the impres-

sion you'd retired, Clarence. I was under the impression you'd given up the right to use office facilities."

Wylie suddenly knew where this was leading, and he didn't like it. Obviously he'd been reported by one of the anonymous courtiers in the Vanderwolf palace. How could he have deceived himself into dreaming he'd walk away clean? He tried to remind himself that he'd left the bureau, he was no longer Vanderwolf's minion. He'd taken his pension and quit. Vanderwolf had no hold over him, not now. But some ghost of a grip remained, and it made him apprehensive.

"So what makes a retired agent ransack the data bank, Clarence? Did you think I wouldn't find out? Didn't you stop to consider the fact sooner or later I know everything that goes on in my own territory? What the hell does a retired agent want with privileged information, for Christ's sake?"

"I was just curious about something, Eric."

"In a pig's ass," Vanderwolf said. "I know you got it for somebody else, mister. You got it for that cop you're so thick with, didn't you? What do you feel you owe that asshole? He blackmailing you or something, Clarence?"

Of course. All this led back—where else?—to Charlie. Charlie had the unsettling knack, sometimes found in drunks, of getting you to do things you wouldn't usually do. Friendship with Charlie was sometimes as demanding as a tax audit. "He asked for some information," Wylie said quietly.

"And out of the kindness of your heart, you got it for him."

"Right. I got it for him."

Vanderwolf shook his head in disbelief. "Soon as you left the building you were followed to Galloway's house, Clarence. I think you must have a deficiency in the brain department these days. Did you think you could just walk in and play with the computers and drift away without somebody asking questions? Retired federal agent plunders computer to get information for a suspended LAPD cop! What next, Clarence? You planning to give out private data on the corner of Hollywood and Vine, huh?"

"I was trying to help Galloway, that's all." Wylie cursed himself for underestimating the cyclopean Eye that was Vanderwolf, the horrible orb that observed everything occurring within its dominion. You scanned a computer and the Wolf found out because internal control devices recorded computer activities. You were logged and charted, mapped and checked, tracked and pinned and, like a forlorn shrimp, butterflied.

"Galloway's an asshole. Did he tell you he called me night before last?"

"Called you? What for?"

"Who knows? He was incoherent, it was past midnight, I wasn't listening. He rambled on. Something about a job. I never understood his accent at the best of times. Drunk he's incoherent. I hung up on the idiot."

Clarence knew the black level of inebriation that led Charlie to make unreasonable phone calls. He'd been the recipient of more than a few himself. "He was helpful to the bureau once, Eric."

"Back then maybe. Back then, oh he was a local hero. Hot stuff. That was before the sauce. He went downhill faster than shit through a greased goose. Personally I was never fooled by the guy. He always smelled of anarchy to me. Always had that deep whiff of trouble about him. He doesn't belong in law enforcement. Frankly I think the LAPD ought to revise its policy. Only native-born citizens should be eligible. None of this imported, naturalized scuzz. They don't have that gut feeling about America a good cop needs. They don't know what it means. They think it's all barbecues and swimming pools and such. They don't feel that tug of the old heartstrings on the Fourth. Hell, we can't expect it of them. It isn't built into them."

And Vanderwolf, Clarence Wylie supposed, was a good American name, probably Navajo. Clarence loved America and American values as much as any reasonable patriot, but he disliked Vanderwolf's form of chauvinism, a grunt, redneck, myopic love of country that suggested some misshapen child incestuously bred and hidden in a shack. If you happened to criticize this disagreeable infant in front of the Dutchman, he would snarl at you and you would sense the hair trigger drawn in his dangerous heart.

"I understand the information you dug out concerned the activities of a Filipino national," Vanderwolf remarked in a rather dry way. "One Armando Teng."

"Yes." Clarence saw no point in denying anything, if Vanderwolf already knew.

"Why the hell would Galloway want to know about some Filipino?" Vanderwolf asked. "I was stationed at Subic in 1960 and I never met a Filipino good for anything except knowing how to launder shirts and clean shoes and cook. As a race, Sucksville. Not too bright," and Vanderwolf tapped the side of his large head.

Clarence Wylie, allowing a vague irritation at this ethnic slur to pass out of his system, stared at the western paintings for a moment. He knew that Charlie Galloway was urgently trawling his character for some depth of purpose to put his life back together. He wanted his job, wanted his wife, reasons to go on. He wanted love. What could Vanderwolf, master of insensitivity, know about any of this?

The child continued to whimper in her distant room. Vanderwolf had clearly tuned her out. Background noise, the Muzak of a kid's nightmare.

"So what else did you give Mr. Galloway, Clarence?"

"Nothing much."

"Okay. Let me put the question another way. If I were to remind you that the theft of data from our computers is a federal offense carrying one hell of a heavy sentence, how would you feel about that?" Vanderwolf sat on a sofa, crossing his legs, tapping his fingers on his thighs. "With that pleasant prospect firmly in mind, Clarence, I'll ask again: What else did you give your dear old pal Galloway?"

Clarence pondered the question, remembering that one of Vanderwolf's ploys was to ask questions to which he already knew the answers. Sometimes, of course, he fished—but you could never tell by looking whether he was rummaging or whether he was trying to catch you out in a lie. After all the years Clarence had spent in Vanderwolf's employ, he still couldn't read the man's face, the shrouded eyes, the secretive mouth, the mysterious scar on his cheek.

Vanderwolf leaned toward him. "Don't fuck with me. You might be retired, but I don't give a shit. I have a long reach, mister. Speak to me. What else did you tell Charlie Galloway?"

Clarence remained silent. Vanderwolf's physical presence always stifled and overwhelmed him. He knew that if he spoke now he would say nothing convincing. Was there any point in further lying on Charlie's behalf?

Vanderwolf's black pinky ring glinted. "Okay, I understand loyalty, Clarence. Loyalty to a friend is admirable even if it's misguided. So I'll say a name. I'll make it easy for you. Laforge. William Laforge. Familiar?"

Clarence raised his face and looked at Vanderwolf, whose white eyebrows, fused as they were, suggested the result of somebody's deranged knitting.

"If you told him Laforge, Clarence, the consequences for your man Charlie could be . . ." Vanderwolf appeared to choose his next word with great care, skimming through his private thesaurus of menace. "Terrible."

"Okay," Clarence said. "I told him Laforge was Teng's target. Godammit. I knew as soon as I said it, I knew it was all wrong for him—"

"And did you hand out some personal data? Address and phone number and such goodies?"

Clarence whispered yes. His head had begun to ache.

"So now Charlie Galloway is out there chasing the Filipino, who is in all likelihood headed for the Laforge residence in Pennsylvania."

"Yes."

"What does Galloway intend to do, Clarence? Catch the guy? Make himself a hero? That the game plan?"

"Something like that." *You wouldn't really understand, Eric,* he thought.

"I want Charlie Galloway out of the way, Clarence."

"Out of the way? In what sense? I mean, I don't, wait—"

"Christ, not like that, Clarence. Not permanently. I want him out of action for his own sake, that's all. I'm talking about protection, not termination. I just don't want him around fouling up this whole operation." Vanderwolf smiled. It was the somewhat placid expression of a man who considers his realm inviolate, his position secure beyond sabotage, political upheaval, palace coups, earthquakes, or other assorted acts of God.

"Then you better bring him in," Wylie said.

"That's precisely what I have in mind, Clarence," Vanderwolf said. "Bring him in, save him from a bad situation. So you believe he'll go to Pennsylvania?"

"I'd guess he left already." Even as he spoke this sentence Clarence wondered if it could be construed as a betrayal of Charlie. If so, it was for his own good.

"An early bird," Vanderwolf remarked, looking thoughtful and sly. He closed his eyes, clasped his hands, rocked his head slightly. The impression he gave was of unfathomable cunning.

"You'll intercept him," Clarence said.

"Somewhere along the way, certainly."

"Before he gets himself into an even worse situation. . . ."

"Trust me, Clarence. He won't be allowed to interfere."

Trust me. The pain drummed more devilishly in Clarence's head. Why had he ever let himself get talked into giving Galloway the information in the first place? Why had he fallen for that lost look, that hopelessness in Charlie's eyes? An excess of mercy and compassion, the urge to rescue the stray that was Charlie Galloway—these were flaws, not virtues. He'd made a grave mistake with Charlie, setting him loose instead of dragging him back to the clinic. Killing him with kindness. Charlie needed one thing: to be saved from himself. To be pulled from the half-demolished building of his life before every worm-eaten timber collapsed about his head.

"What would happen if Charlie gets to Teng first anyway?" he asked.

"I don't think that would be very good," Vanderwolf answered.

"If Charlie finds the guy, what's he going to do with him, Eric? He'll just hand him over to you or the cops. So what difference does it make who catches Teng? You, Galloway, the cops, whoever. So long as he's caught. Isn't that what matters?"

Again Vanderwolf appeared to choose his words with care. "Let's just say we don't want Galloway to apprehend the Filipino."

Clarence massaged the sides of his head. He heard the tiny rolling coin of revelation. "I get it. *You* want the credit. *You* don't want Galloway to get there before the mighty FBI. Is that it?"

"Ah, Clarence. Always perceptive. Always on the ball."

"Then it's a PR matter. It's image, Eric. The FBI can't be upstaged by some poor alcoholic schmuck of a cop."

"In a nutshell." Vanderwolf smiled patiently. "I think that about wraps everything up, Clarence. You've told me where Galloway's headed. I needed to be sure, and you've confirmed it. He'll be quite safe. We'll find him. Thank you, Clarence. You can go now."

Wylie was dismissed with a slight gesture of Vanderwolf's silver-haired hand. But he didn't move immediately. A small sense of dissatisfaction bothered him, although he couldn't say why exactly. Was it the unexpected compliment from Vanderwolf? *Always perceptive, Clarence.* In all the years of their relationship Eric Vanderwolf had never said a kind word to him. Why begin now? Clarence, suspicious, took a step toward the door, then turned to look back. Vanderwolf, a lofty creation of the federal government, a supernatural being who surveyed his terrain as if it were his personal property and not something merely entrusted to him by the citizens of the land, those minnows in whom he had absolutely no interest, had always perceived himself as both permanent and immortal, and the games he played were usually complex. Gods or devils, after all, couldn't be content with simplicity.

And this was all just too simple for Clarence to buy now. He was certain more was involved here than the bureau's PR image. Vanderwolf's bland compliment concealed something else—but what? It eluded Clarence, who had spent too much time lost and bewildered in the Dutchman's world, a place where Vanderwolf was both magician and master of physics. He gave the impression that he sat in his office and said *Let there be rain* and, wow, rain there was. Or he commanded gravity to be suspended and suddenly objects floated through the air like weighty items moved by unseen hands during séances. There was a diabolical quality in his expression. The eyebrows helped. They were those of a man who purchased souls from lost people in flophouses and blood donation centers.

"Incidentally, I hope you're enjoying your retirement," Vanderwolf said. "You earned your pension. But in future don't go where you don't belong. Oh—if Charlie Galloway calls you, tell him this: Drop everything and come home, Charlie. Be a good boy and come home."

Clarence opened the door. "You're not telling me the whole story, Eric. You're holding back. I sense it."

Vanderwolf stuck his hands in the pockets of his robe. "Go home, Clarence. Go home. You don't work for me anymore. You're not paid to sense things."

Obstructed by his own suspicious thoughts, perplexed, Clarence heard the sad sound of the child sobbing and imagined seahorses fluttering dreadfully in an aquarium; and he thought of Charlie adrift in America—beyond reach, out of touch, endangered.

19

Tanned men and women in sombreros and bright shirts drank from little bottles of premixed margaritas on the plane. A fine-boned bleached blonde of about forty shook maracas in the aisle, swaying her hips as she worked the gourds back and forth. *La cucaracha, la cucaracha,* people sang over and over, as if this were the only word they'd learned during their vacation in Mexico. There had to be at least thirty sombreroed persons in various stages of early morning post-holiday inebriation and they controlled the plane, ignoring the pleas of the cabin staff to sit down and buckle up. *La cucaracha, la cucaracha,* they kept singing, while the dyed blonde with great hooped earrings went sashaying back and forth, shaking the maracas now in Charlie Galloway's face, tempting him to join in, join the party, be a sport, hon!

How easy it would be, Galloway thought. How simple, how escapist, to put on a funny hat and swill the margaritas and samba down the aisle with the blonde, singing about cockroaches, and perhaps even find himself drunkenly locked in carefree intimacy with the woman inside a john at thirty-five thousand feet above Kansas or somewhere.

He blinked at the sun that struck the wing. Glinting, it blinded him like a camera flash. He had no notion of time; zones confused him. He'd taken the first available flight out of Los Angeles, changing at Dallas, where the cockroach crew from Acapulco had come rowdily on board, bound for Philadelphia. His watch was broken. The woman with the maracas wore no watch and wouldn't have known the time if you took her up in a helium balloon to the face of Big Ben. And the cabin crew, confronted by their inability to control the party, had taken refuge, along with their wristwatches, in a curtained galley. Charlie, in this timeless condition, knew only that it was morning, too bright, too blue.

He hadn't slept. After Clarence Wylie had gone, he'd quickly studied a Rand McNally road atlas, looking at Pennsylvania with the kind of curiosity Dr. Livingstone might have brought to an early map of Africa. Then he'd driven by a circuitous route through the predawn streets of LA and boarded this flight. Going through these motions had imposed a sense of reality on him, as if he were victoriously stepping out into the world after long solitary confinement in a dark room. The dreamlike quality of everything slipped away for a while; the world became hard-edged, and Charlie Galloway a man with a definite mission, definite goals. Businesslike in dark blue suit, a tad of brilliantine applied to his wayward hair, a scrap of loose toilet tissue over a razor cut on his freshly shaved chin, he'd strolled confidently through the airport, paused to purchase a newspaper, scanned the headlines, *did things other people did every day of their lives without a second thought.*

The sheer magic of the ordinary. He was touched by it, and moved. *Welcome to the species, Charlie. Welcome back.*

But that was three hours ago—before the Mexican gang came on board, before the margaritas started flying, before the blonde went up and down the aisle and the threat of a conga line became increasingly feasible. Three hours ago: eternity.

Now he had the thought that what he was doing could only be some form of madness, a delusion of grandeur brought on by booze. He'd finally succumbed to the inability to differentiate the perceptions of sobriety from those of alcohol. They were flawlessly seamed. You couldn't say where one began and the other ended. It had been years in the coming, and had involved much abuse of the brain, but now it had happened: *He couldn't tell the difference.* In sobriety he'd come up with the idea of capturing Teng, a notion that surely belonged in a drunkard's dream of self-aggrandizement, the lush as winner.

Catch Teng?

O dear Christ, what was I thinking?

Closing his eyes, tilting his head back, listening to the *whooom* of the great aircraft, he realized now that his bravery and ambition had been a device to offset the shitty feel of dread and contrition, those evil wizards in the pageantry of his hang-overs. He was now at that junction where the hangover had diminished from nausea to discomfort to disconsolation.

Where was the joy in sobriety? Where that glad glow people reported? That sense of pink well-being? He felt none of it.

Catch Teng? Bring him in, shackled and chained, to rounds of applause? Had that been the childish momentum of his imagi-nation? *Dream on, Charlie Galloway.* He was bereft, adrift in the heavens, flying toward a destination in which he wouldn't find Teng but would come only face-to-face with his own disinte-grated self, a burned-out character, captain of a sad misadventure.

Even the name of your destination is a bloody joke, Charlie.

New Hope, Bucks County, Pennsylvania. New Bloody Hope!

Aye. It had all seemed so right a few hours ago, so apt! A man might refresh his life there, or rearrange his old one into more pleasing patterns. He might discover himself in a place called New Hope. He might *achieve* something. He wasn't likely to redeem himself in places with names like Sulphur, Oklahoma, or Broken Bow, Nebraska. New Hope was replete with possibilities. So it had seemed to Charlie before depression had set upon him.

Fighting the dismay that mobbed him, he turned his thoughts to Teng, wondering where in this vast continent the Filipino might be. If he was headed directly for the heart of the matter, he would be traveling east just as Charlie Galloway was. Though not by commercial airline. Charlie thought. He'd be afraid of exposure by now, especially after hitting Railsback in Dallas. He'd fly in a private aircraft or by car. But which? Who could tell? Teng was still an enigma to him, a closed book, and all that blether about trying to imagine himself into Teng's mind, those brave words he'd spoken to Clarence Wylie—that was just so much hot air. He couldn't read his own damn mind. By what miracle of telepathic engineering could he transport himself into Teng's?

Teng. The unfamiliarity of the name, the strange brittle quality to it, underlined Charlie Galloway's general puzzlement. What did he know of Filipinos? What did he know about the Philippines except that the Americans kept bases there and Corazon Aquino was the stressed-out President and that the women were said to be as beautiful as the country was impoverished? He ransacked his slender depository of knowledge, lamenting his own ignorance. He'd heard of the loveliness of the landscape from Ella Nazarena, and she'd once or twice shown him photographs of smiling people standing outside a bamboo and cinder-block house—her family in Baguio—but that was it. You could draw a black heavy line right there. End of entry.

The merrymakers from Acapulco had broken open party favors and were blowing reedy sounds from tubes of silver paper. The blonde, weary at last, was sprawled in her seat, long legs dangling into the aisle, high-heeled shoes hanging off her feet. Charlie shut his eyes, dozed for a while. He woke abruptly, dry, baffled by his whereabouts and why his ears were filled with the drone of engines. Then it came back to him and he wondered if it might be possible to parachute out somewhere over the heartland and forget he'd ever undertaken this idiot journey. Down and down, held in place by harness and a mushroom of strong cloth, drifting slowly to the warm earth, hitting Main Street, Buckhannon, West Virginia, or God knows where. There he'd assume another name, find a room, a quiet job as a clerk in a grocery store, and live a life of rewarding anonymity—there would be peace, and a picket fence, and sobriety, and Karen would come back and maybe they'd have a kid, it wasn't too late, and Charlie could learn to raise it, changing diapers, singing lullabies, staring lovingly at the child while it slept. It would be a plump kid, healthy, a delight. They'd take it to Scotland and show it to Dan and it wouldn't matter a damn if the old fella was deranged. Charlie would say *Here's your grandson, Dad,* and maybe the old man's eyes would fill with tears.

"This is your captain speaking, ladies and gentlemen."

Charlie listened.

"We'll be on the ground at Philadelphia International Airport in about thirty minutes. The temperature in Philly is ninety-four degrees, folks. Another hot one."

Charlie walked to the lavatory. He slid the lock in place, the light came on. He urinated in a nervous, trickling way, his bladder coy. Then he washed his hands and ran wet fingers through his hair to smooth back an unruly tuft. After that, he dropped the lid of the toilet in place and sat down, thinking, thinking.

Okay. He'd come this far. Incontrovertible fact. What could he do now? Fly back to the West Coast immediately and write this trip off as a boozer's delusion? That was the easy way. Besides, the bureau probably had Teng in custody already. Then why worry? Where was the problem in getting off the plane in Philly and just turning right around? No sweat. Nothing to reproach himself for. He wasn't a hero after all.

So, Charlie. Disembark in Philly. Have a cup of coffee, a sandwich, then take the next flight back to Los Angeles. Screw the coffee. Have a beer. And then what?

What do you do in Los Angeles? In the city of death, in those hard sunlit streets where shadows of palm were thrown on pastel stucco, what do you do? Drive past the place where Ella was killed, maybe? Wonder what it was she wanted to tell you but never got the chance? Remember her corpse, the bloody sheet? Perhaps ride the freeway alongside the tall building from which Freddie Joaquin took his last plunge? Keep trying to hunt down Karen? It was endless, around and around; in Los Angeles he would become a man trapped on a circular sightseeing tour of his own recent history, a prospect of hell and sunshine. That's how LA would be, and he knew it.

He stood up, unlocked the door, walked back down the aisle to his seat. The plane tilted a few degrees and an empty miniature margarita bottle rolled along the floor, stopping at Charlie Galloway's foot. He reached down, picked it up, closed the palm of his hand around it.

A few rows in front of him the blonde's legs still dangled in the aisle. One of her high-heeled shoes slid from a foot and clattered to the floor, but she made no move to retrieve it. In a very weary manner she sang two words—yes—*La cucaracha.* The tone of her voice had changed now, all effervescence having escaped. She mouthed the words in the manner of one coming down from a high.

Somewhere inside the plane a party favor farted once miserably, more squeak than thunder.

Galloway changed the position of the overhead nozzle so that cold air hit him directly in the face. Poised in a difficult, slippery place between retreat and advance, an old life or a new route, he felt as if the familiar huskies that hauled his sled were warring with one another, going off in a dozen different directions at the same time—and he was dumb to command them otherwise.

He knew what he ought to do. He knew which way the huskies should be made to run. But the reins, which had made the palms of his hands raw and bloody, kept slipping, slipping away from him.

I am out of control, he thought.

Under the noonday sun Laforge walked as far as the old bridge. He wore a floppy fisherman's hat to keep the light from his eyes. The scent of cigarette smoke, so alien here, drifted toward him. He heard the crackle and hiss of a walkie-talkie. From the ferns that grew densely along the banks of the creek a man in a green shirt emerged and gazed at Laforge without expression. He wore a pistol in a shoulder holster; under one arm he carried a rifle. His walkie-talkie was strapped to his hip.

Laforge smiled in his patrician fashion. He introduced himself. The guard, a muscular figure who wore an abbreviated mustache, said that he recognized Mr. Laforge from the photographs the security team had been given. A short silence followed these introductory remarks while Laforge ransacked his mind for something to say—a witticism, a throwaway joke, anything to suggest he lived on the same planet as everyone else. How did people handle cocktail parties, for God's sake? He could talk of the weather, he supposed, or say how poor the fishing had been this year, small talk. He said nothing. Why was it so damned hard to make trivial conversation?

The guard's walkie-talkie croaked and he slid it from his hip and raised it to his mouth. "Vespa here," he said. "Over."

Vespa, Laforge thought. *Was that a code name?*

Out of the hideous static he heard Vespa's communicant say, "How is it down there?"

Vespa said it was fine, turning away from Laforge slightly as he spoke, as if trade secrets were at stake here. Laforge understood that men like Vespa and his colleagues were accustomed to concealment and stealth. They spoke a different language from everyone else. They looked at a clump of shrubbery and saw, not leaves, stalks, roots, but the potential for menace. Vespa attached the instrument to his belt again and looked at Laforge.

"Everything okay?" Laforge asked.

The man smiled. He had small yellow teeth. "Just the way we like it, sir."

Laforge made a gesture of approval. He stared down into the stream, where thin froth floated through reeds and a spent match, presumably tossed into the weak current by one of the security men, drifted. Water beetles buzzed the surface, skimming back and forth.

The bridge creaked. Laforge raised his face toward it. A second man stood there, armed as Vespa was. Unlike Vespa, he was dressed in a brown shirt and slacks. Green, brown, Laforge thought. Earth tones. Camouflage. Laforge lifted a hand in greeting and the man on the bridge, tall, powerful, with the kind of face that disappeared into broad shoulders with no apparent neck, returned the gesture without much enthusiasm.

The man stepped off the bridge and drew Vespa aside and they conversed some yards away in whispers, while Laforge felt curiously uncomfortable, as though he did not belong on his own property. The muscular man in brown clothes glanced at Laforge once during the inaudible conversation with Vespa, but the dark eyes pierced Billy as if he weren't there at all.

Laforge moved away quietly. He knew that these men had come from the Office of Security at Langley, but what he couldn't understand was why they whispered so. When they addressed him they were polite, of course, but he was just a job to them. A body. An object to protect.

He took off his hat, which he thought made him look pretty silly anyway. It was a countryman's hat, rustic, shapeless, the kind to which you expect to see attached fishing flies and hooks, perhaps small enamel badges attesting to membership in this fishing club or that. There was nothing *distinguished* about the headgear. Sunlight screamed down through the branches of trees and burned his scalp and sweat ran into his eyes. He was apprehensive, as if the sun had singled him out for personal abuse. And the guards—why had they unsettled him?

He was still upset by Railsback, that was what it all came down to. He was trying not to think of Tom dead. It should have been easy. He was accustomed to the suppression of unpleasantries. He had a talent for introducing light into dark landscapes, a swift brush stroke of amnesia—and lo! the storm clouds rolled away.

No. It was more than Tom Railsback, and he knew it. He didn't want to think about it. Why did he need to remember Benguet now? The memory lay in a remote drawer of his brain where, undisturbed, it had gathered dust. Every so often the drawer, as though shaken by a tremor of sorts, seemed to slide open and a mildewed scent rose from within, an offensive, sickly smell that came and went, leaving in its silent passage a vague feeling of doom.

He moved across the meadow as quickly as he could. Distorted by light, the two security vehicles parked close to the house appeared to have fused together, melted by the sun then forged in an unnatural way, a weird sculpture in the landscape. Everything shimmered. The ground reflected heat in rays that gave the grass an oceanic effect, as though a soft tide ran through the stalks. For a second Laforge felt he was walking under water, a sensation emphasized by how much he perspired. His shirt stuck to his flesh, his pants to his thighs.

He reached the house finally but didn't go inside at once. He saw the door of the van open. A man stepped out. A cheerful figure, unlike the pair by the stream, he came toward Laforge with a confident stride, a hand extended for the future director of the CIA to shake. He had a bright reliable face, tanned like Laforge's, a large, good-natured mouth; you could imagine this man, who introduced himself as Ted Arganbright, telling jokes at parties, being the life and soul of things, guardian of the barbecue pit.

"I hope all this isn't too disruptive, sir," he said.

"No, not at all," Laforge remarked.

"We don't like to take chances, so we tend to poke around

all over the place," Arganbright said. "If we get in your hair, you just shout."

"No, really, everything's fine. Your men are unobtrusive."

Arganbright looked up at the sky briefly. "Some of them are a bit on the grouchy side. It's the job. It makes them testy at times. It's a great quality as far as your safety's concerned, of course. It means they're vigilant." And he said this last word proudly.

"Of course."

Arganbright had threadlike red veins in his big cheeks. "You're in good hands, sir."

"I know that," said Laforge, and he stepped toward the house, disturbed still. The memory of Benguet wasn't fading. Persistent, it wasn't going to be defied admission.

In the kitchen, he poured a little mineral water into a glass, gazed from the window in time to see Arganbright pause by the car, lower his face to speak to the two overheated men inside, then return to the van. What had they talked about? Laforge watched the van door open, then close with a certain finality that made him feel, not the security Arganbright had emphasized, but a sense of aloneness, as if he'd been abandoned all at once in a precarious position. Which was a stupid notion, considering the amount of security on the estate. And yet. He drank the water, set down the glass on the table. Click. The sound irritated him. *The memory was a migraine,* he thought. *You could always feel it coming but there was nothing you could do.*

The telephone rang. Thankful for the interruption, Laforge picked up the receiver quickly. Byron Truskett was on the other end of the line.

"I intended to call you earlier, Billy," said Truskett. "But I've been busy with this and that. You know how it goes."

Laforge said he understood.

"Congratulations!" Truskett sounded enthusiastic. "I'm sure the hearings will be a breeze."

"I appreciate your optimism," said Laforge. "And your support."

Truskett emitted a brief little laugh, a way of saying, *Think nothing of it.* "I've been talking with my colleagues, Billy. Sort of taking an informal head count. The numbers are looking very good. Very good indeed."

"I'm happy to hear that."

"So how does it feel to be surrounded by security forces?"

"It's rather strange."

"They'll take great care of you."

"I'm sure they will."

"You better believe it. You're an important man. I'll be in touch."

"Thanks for calling."

Laforge set the receiver down. He stood in the window and he had the thought, *I am vulnerable. Here, standing in this window, I am vulnerable, a target of whoever killed Railsback and Costain and Deduro.* When darkness fell across the estate, what did the security men do then? How well could they protect him on a moonless night? Did they have arc lights? Did they flood the property with great white lamps? Did they see what lingered behind every dark tree or bush? Did they have radar inside the van? Could they truly stop a determined assassin, somebody driven by a hatred beyond understanding, somebody made cunning by the demands of vengeance?

He stepped back from the window. He found it difficult to breathe for a moment. It was in his head again, that field in Benguet. He remembered how he'd assigned Gene Costain and Tom Railsback to assist Captain Deduro in training his men in the task of capturing "Communist insurgents" in the hills beyond La Trinidad. He remembered the reports he had received from Costain and Railsback after the event, the typed sheets of which no copies were ever made, the terse description of events.

> *Subject, male, age middle 50s, resisted arrest, tortured by members of the constabulary, executed.*
> *Subject, female, age approximately 23, resisted arrest, tortured, executed.*
> *Subject, male, resisted arrest, tortured, executed.*
> *Subject, et cetera, et cetera. . . .*

These flat statements of fact were all the more graphic for their lack of detail, as if the absence of particulars rendered them concrete and terrible. That girl, for instance, aged "approximately" twenty-three—what did she long for, what did she dream? She was a featureless entity in a dark field, and yet this being with no face tormented Laforge more than if he had known her name and age and desires.

He opened the freezer compartment of the refrigerator, swinging the door back and forth as though it were a fan. Chilled air blew softly upon his face. But he sweated anyway. He put a finger between collar and neck, closing his eyes and swaying a little, a man made dizzy by a memory so wretched he hardly dared claim it as his own. The buzz in his head was louder.

He couldn't get away from it. It returned when he least needed it, the only entrapment in his life from which he hadn't found some means of escape or compromise. He could displace it to a certain degree, sure. He could addle it, scramble it, upset its chronology, alter a detail or two. Sometimes he succeeded in attributing the experience to an imaginary other, somebody else who'd gone that night to the field above La Trinidad. Not himself but a stranger who moved in the sweltering dark Philippine night, unseen, hidden from the view of Costain and Railsback, invisible to the constabulary, a mere passerby who had stopped to look.

And what had he seen, this other man? Silhouetted, shackled prisoners, some screaming, others begging to be spared, were led across the grass to the place where they were shot, a dozen or more people gunned directly in their skulls—this is what he'd seen. And what had drawn him there from the safety of Baguio City and his suite at the Hyatt, what lurid interest had compelled him to drive in a dark car to La Trinidad long after he'd dispatched Costain and Railsback? What malady had seized him and locked him into the overwhelming need to witness death and destruction?

He'd stood in the dark, detached, hypnotized by monstrosity, the unseen spectator at a bloodletting, a man imprisoned by his own absorption with savagery. He'd stood motionless, feeling absolutely nothing, wanting to feel, wishing he could experience outrage and emerge from the night and put a stop to the massacre, but he was restricted by a sense of inevitability, by the fact he hadn't the urge to act.

He wanted to see people die. He wanted to watch. He was

fascinated by slaughter. He had no idea what the price of admission might ultimately be, but he stayed, and he watched, and he felt nothing when the pistols went off—not with the sharpness he expected but rather quiet explosions. When the silence came afterward, the enormity of it was appalling, and it jolted him back to self-consciousness, to incredulity, as if what he'd seen had been a shadow play upon a screen, a kind of bloody masquerade, a brutal puppetry.

He closed the freezer door, pressing his face against it. His eyes were damp. He raised his fingertips to them, remembering now his confrontation with Railsback and Costain the next day in Manila, how calmly reasonable he had been, failing to mention his own silent presence. He justified the behavior of his subordinates by placing it inside a framework that made torture and murder to some degree acceptable, comprehensible. After all, the Communists were armed and bloodthirsty. They killed without asking questions. After all, U.S. assistance had been pledged to Marcos to fight the insurgents. A foreign country, a strange environment, an American commitment, men lost their nerve and behaved atypically—the excuses went on and on, you could conjure them out of the thinnest air. *And you, Laforge, you shredded the reports. You destroyed the documentation. You obliterated the records. And then you closed that drawer in your brain, locked it, tossed the key away, and for most of the time contrived to forget.*

Torture and murder to some degree acceptable. . . .

A great despair touched him. What if they found out, the senators who would pass judgment on him, who would cast their votes for or against him; what if they learned of his presence in La Trinidad that night? They would see it as an impassive disregard of human life, an act of brutality by omission, coldhearted negligence. They would call him psychotic, a monster. They would not be persuaded that what took him to La Trinidad that night was a sense of duty, a devotion to seeing wrongs righted, and America's enemies . . . exorcised. *I did what I had to do in the national interest, gentlemen.* He wasn't even able to convince himself that this was the reason anyway, as if what lay enclosed inside him were a black impenetrable emotion, beyond understanding, a complex configuration. There was a part of himself that he did not know and might never know. He shut his eyes and thought, *I am not a monster. I want to feel. I do not know how.*

Carolyn entered the kitchen, singing some tuneless ditty. She stopped when she saw him standing against the refrigerator. She came close, placing her hands on his hips, pressing her thighs against his, as if even now, after all the dry years between them, she thought a fusion possible. Laforge remembered Costain saying, *I shot the girl because she could identify me,* and these words echoed inside him and he was ferried back to his office in Manila, the room that overlooked Roxas Boulevard on one side and the bay on the other, and Costain and Railsback were seated around the conference table and out on the ruined, lovely, rust-colored bay the air was implausibly dense with smoke from the stack of a steamer. He heard himself tell Costain, *It doesn't matter, don't worry about it, we can handle it, unfortunate things happen in a war, and that's what this is, Eugene, a small war we're helping to contain. . . .*

He'd carried it off very well, he thought. He'd managed to look shocked by the turn of events. He'd managed to look quietly horrified while remaining eminently practical. *Leave it to me, I'll deal with it. . . .*

Carolyn poured some coffee into a mug on which was inscribed, in delicate floral fashion, her name. "Who was on the phone?" she asked.

"Truskett."

"What did he want?"

"To congratulate me."

"How thoughtful of him." She sat down at the table. Steam rose over the lip of the mug. "I don't think I'll be seeing him again."

"I imagined as much."

"He has a reckless streak," she said. "It's hard to explain. But I sometimes have the distinct feeling he would throw everything over if I asked him. Wife, career—the whole thing. I don't need to encourage this kamikaze side to his character, William. He needs stability more than anything else. Miriam is probably the one to give it to him."

She looked into her coffee, then raised her face and turned

it toward her husband, who thought her beauty had a wistful quality he rarely saw. He walked to the table and, standing behind her, laid his hands on her bare shoulders. The bond between them was at that second strong and uplifting, as if they had just transacted an especially lucrative business deal on behalf of Laforge & Laforge, Inc., which was true enough—but there was more, an intimacy beyond the corporate superstructure of their marriage, that special closeness which defies definition.

Then he saw at the juncture of her neck and shoulder a red-blue contusion, a love bite, Truskett's mark—and he made a connection he didn't intend, wondering how many marks had blemished the body of the girl Gene Costain had shot dead, what discolorations had been left by passion of a different order.

He dropped his arms to his side, turned to the window. Both car and van glowed in the noonday furnace as if they were about to explode.

The pilot of the twin-engine plane gave Teng no name, barely addressed him except with an occasional grunt, and even when he landed to refuel at a field near Frankfort, Kentucky, said only that he wanted a cup of coffee, without inviting Teng to share one. Teng wandered around the edge of the field. A leaden quality affected his limbs and his eyes ached from the brightness of the sun, which had seemed to trap the plane in a lozenge of intense light and hold it aloft. Toylike, it had floated, puttered, droned, as Teng slipped in and out of shallow sleep, dreaming sometimes of rain and typhoons.

At the Kentucky airfield he went inside the men's room, washed his face and hands, and wondered about the pilot, who was presumably a mercenary Baltazar had arranged, perhaps a man accustomed to transporting illegal cargo without asking questions. The mute arrangement suited Teng admirably. He had no urge to speak. He wanted no company. When the plane took off from Frankfort he looked at the clock and realized he'd been flying a little over three and a half hours.

Below him lay arid fields, desolate hills, great forest tracts where here and there smoke from picnics or barbecues drifted in an indolent manner skyward, farmlands, meadows, cattle and horses, hamlets, villages, towns—all America, it seemed, had unfolded beneath him, and he had a sense not only of its vastness but its variety. He saw the blue swimming pools of suburban houses, the flat discs of reservoirs, here and there the meandering line of a river forging its way through greenery, isolated farms located amid mazelike dirt roads.

Cramped, harnessed into his seat, he pondered this diversity—rich and poor, rural and urban, black and white, desperate and complacent. What did these people so far below him, so busy with their lives, care about American misadventures on the Pacific rim? What did it matter to the farmer in that Kentucky field that Americans were despised in the foreign lands they conquered with their New World amalgam of naïveté and cunning, generosity and self-interest?

Teng studied the pilot's firm hands on the controls. He looked at the meaningless little dials and gauges, the pilot's dirty fingernails. He felt an inner drift. Vaporous clouds streaked past, but then the sky was monotonously blue again all the way to Pennsylvania, where the great conglomeration that was Philadelphia darkened the sky, sullying it with acids and smoke, an artificial mist engulfing the small plane. But then the air cleared and the craft started a gradual descent about forty miles beyond Philadelphia, down toward green countryside and white houses and clustered villages. In the distance Teng saw the broad, greenish Delaware River crossed here and there by bridges. And still the craft dropped, landing finally at Central Bucks Airport on the edge of Doylestown, a harsh landing, a skip and a bump, a second skip, a second bump.

When the pilot had brought the plane to a halt he turned to Teng. He took from his pocket a car key. He said, "It's a 1984 Chevy. Black. New Jersey plates. 7DCD 655. You'll find it parked in the lot. Look in the glove compartment. That's it. That's all I got to tell you."

Teng closed his hand around the key, unbuckled his seat belt, opened the door, jumped down. Light-headed, giddy from many hours of flying, he went to look for the car. The plane had already begun to move again, rolling away from him, taxiing back to the position for takeoff.

Teng walked through the heat to the parking lot. He found the Chevy, unlocked it, tossed his overnight bag on the backseat.

Then he opened the glove compartment. Inside, wrapped in a leather pouch, was an automatic pistol. There was also an envelope, which Teng unsealed. It contained a detailed map of the vicinity, with arrows drawn carefully in red ink. His route. An arrow larger than the others indicated his destination; an exclamation point had been inscribed beside it. On the margin of the map was written the address in capital letters, and stapled to the very edge was a color photograph of the man called Laforge. He had smooth features, a face reminiscent, Teng thought, of a priest, a man to whom you might unburden yourself, if absolution was what you sought. Teng gazed at the white hair neatly combed, the perfect set of the mouth, the firm jawline. Here was a man who took some pride in his appearance.

What you couldn't see in the picture was cruelty. But how could you photograph evil?

Teng felt revulsion. He removed the photograph from the map and put it down on the passenger seat. He spread the map open over the picture and studied it, the thin veins of country roads, the yellow geometric shapes that designated towns, the red triangles that were libraries, the blue stars where courthouses stood—a map of considerable detail, almost intimate in the way it revealed the contours of Bucks County. He looked at the red-inked directional arrows and saw how they ended in the bold exclamation point on the edge of a town called New Hope. New Hope was also the name of a district of Manila. Bagong Pag-Asa. New Hope.

His route, his weapon, his victim. What else did he need for revenge but the courage to go through with it?

He inserted the key in the ignition and turned it. The car at once came to life. Teng's hands were locked a little too tightly on the wheel. He hadn't driven in a long time, maybe a year, fifteen months, when he'd been employed as a taxi driver by the Blue Cab company that serviced the Philippine Plaza Hotel in Manila. He listened a moment to the engine, studied the dash. The Chevy was automatic, unlike the troublesome cab he'd driven.

Nervously he put the vehicle in reverse and backed out of the lot, concentrating so hard on the act of driving that he failed entirely to notice the gray car about a mile behind him as he headed out of Doylestown.

All airports in the vicinity had been placed under surveillance by order of Hugo Fletcher. All bus depots, railroad stations, car rental offices—wherever Teng appeared, Fletcher needed to be sure he was spotted, followed, and logged. The man in the unremarkable car, a dogged time-server named McTell, used his car phone to call the Philadelphia office of the FBI with the news that Teng had shown up and was heading east on Mechanicsville Road. Twenty minutes later McTell called again to relay the information that Teng had checked into a room at a motel, looking—as McTell phrased it—"a very tired guy."

It was Teng's intention to spend a few hours in the motel, shower, refresh himself, and then when it was twilight and some of the heat had gone out of the day, to leave for New Hope, where he'd observe Laforge's property before deciding the best plan of action. What kind of security did Laforge have? How many men? Were there dogs? He needed to know what lay ahead of him.

He slid the chain on the door, drew the curtains, and lay on the bed, eyes open, following the scar of a crack in the ceiling. In one hand he held the gun loosely, getting the feel of it, aiming it idly at the crack as though it were a vein in Laforge's head. He imagined pulling the trigger once, twice, three times, emptying the chamber into Laforge's face, leaving him disfigured in death as Marissa had been left.

20

Under an extravagant sun Charlie Galloway drove a rented Nissan along Interstate 95, which skipped the edge of Philadelphia and followed the western bank of the Delaware River, passing a massive cluster of ships in the naval yard, power stations pumping grimly away, abandoned warehouses reminiscent of toothless crones lamenting a tragedy so old nobody can quite remember it exactly. He had the feeling the air was dead and if he rolled down his window he'd smell camphor or embalming fluid or something equally noxious.

A vast poster loomed over him, throwing a great velvet shadow. GOLDEN CRADLE. UNPLANNED PREGNANCY? LET US HELP. His head was filled with visions of unhappy girls knocked up by boys who had promised, in the spur of passion, marriage and dignity and two cars in the garage. By a stroke of the irony that lightens all our lives, a nunnery lurked beyond the poster, an ancient ivy-covered building in whose sunny grounds a couple of black-garbed nuns strolled arm in arm. Brides of Christ here, unclaimed brides over there. The juxtaposition pleased him.

Close to the Benjamin Franklin Bridge, Galloway put his foot down hard on the gas pedal. In a few minutes Philly was gone and countryside zoomed in, and Charlie Galloway came off the Interstate at the exit for New Hope.

The English had left an indelible mark on this part of the world. There was yearning here, a longing for a society different from America's own, a sense of Ye Olde This and That, expensive enclaves of large houses, developments called Hunter's Crossing or Fox Hollow. If you listened hard enough you might imagine the yap of unleashed hounds, horses crashing through thickets in pursuit of a sorry fox. Englishness permeated this landscape. Did they partake of afternoon tea in these large houses? Scones? Sherry at twilight? *I say.*

Galloway came to the town of New Hope. If he'd entertained the notion that this place might raise his spirits he was mistaken. It wasn't a town in which he felt inclined to get out of the car. A settlement of exaggerated quaintness, history in formaldehyde, its sidewalks were mobbed with tourists, ice-cream suckers, purchasers of maps and prints, used books, browsers peering through windows in which whole zoos of soft animals existed in gingham, glass-eyed, hand-stitched horror, bears and cows and pigs, funny-faced dolls, mutant offspring of long-forgotten Cabbage Patch kids, that made you want to throw up because your system couldn't ingest this much cuteness in one go.

He drove on. New Hope wasn't his kind of town after all.

Away from the center, the cozy yielded to the banal, the quaint to the hyper-ordinary—supermarket, gasoline station, dime store, pharmacy, the kind of utilitarian hard-edged buildings you saw anywhere in America. He could handle this. Pickup trucks, baseball hats, plaid shirts, blue jeans, this was unpretentious, simpler than the main drag of the town, with its claim on history and the tourist dollar.

He saw a Holiday Inn and was delighted by its familiarity, by the simplicity that, when you got down through the crap, was perhaps the true heart of America. What pleased him most was the stark purity of place, a functional motel at the edge of a functional highway, nothing hidden, no shadows, no undercurrents. He parked his car, went inside the lobby, helped himself to a free map of the area, and studied it for a while over a cup of coffee which shook in his maddeningly unsteady hand. Would a day come when he'd be still? When pulses and quivers wouldn't rack him as they did?

After considerable scrutiny he found the poorly marked road that led to the Laforge property, folded the map, finished his coffee. He walked around the lobby, gazed from the window at the highway shimmering in heat, then went to the pay telephone and dialed Clarence Wylie's number.

"This is your wandering Scot keeping in touch, as promised," Charlie said.

Clarence Wylie was muted in a fashion Galloway found disquieting. Clarence usually answered his telephone in a hearty manner, a bark. "Charlie, listen. Vanderwolf called me in."

"And?"

"He knew I'd been digging, he knew I was feeding the stuff to you. I'm rusty, Charlie. I underestimated the bastard's omniscience. A few years ago I would've known better."

"Does he know where I am?"

"Generally speaking. And he doesn't want you getting near Teng. He wants you out of the picture. Tell Charlie to come home. That's his message to you. You could be in trouble. I get the impression he used a capital *T*. It doesn't sound like a picnic in the park. He wants Teng before you. That's what it's all about. You might manage to get in the way of the great machine. He doesn't like that idea."

"He believes I could steal the bureau's thunder?" Galloway observed a black truck screaming along the highway, squandering in its passage a pall of noxious smoke.

"That's what he says anyway."

"And you're not convinced."

"I don't know what to make of it. I really don't. I get the feeling he's keeping something back. But what? On the one hand, it's hard to buy the idea that Vanderwolf would worry about one lone cop. No disrespect, Charlie. But I can't see him losing sleep over you. On the other, what else could be worrying him? I can't read his mind. I've been through the alternatives, and they're pretty damn slim. He doesn't want you up there in Bucks County. Why? Because there's something you're not meant to know? Like what? Has Washington warned him about something? Is Teng important to somebody? You figure it. I'm tired."

Charlie said nothing. He thought of beveled mirrors wherein reflections were distorted. He thought of the FBI, a gallery of such mirrors, where distortions passed as reality and perversions of language masqueraded as truths. Masked prestidigitators in gray suits and button-down shirts claimed to keep America safe. *Safe from what?* Charlie Galloway wondered. *Errant Scottish boozers?*

"I assume agents are looking for me," he said.

"You can be sure they'll have their eyes open," Clarence said. "In your shoes, I'd take Vanderwolf's advice. I'd pack it in, Charlie. I'd come home."

"Fuck Vanderwolf."

"I hear bravado, Charlie."

"You hear determination."

"Listen to me. Get the next flight back. Leave it alone. Why don't you work out your life some other way, Charlie? Walk away from Teng. It's a bad situation."

Galloway didn't respond to Clarence. He couldn't.

He'd come all the way across the continent on a drunkard's prayer, ill-considered, unplanned, a compulsion. But when you were a drunk only the compulsion mattered. Only the grand picture, not the details. He couldn't walk away from Teng, who had become his redeemer, the other half of his survival equation. Without Teng, how could Charlie Galloway be complete?

He hung up with no good-bye. He gazed out at the highway. If agents were indeed looking for him, then his only plan was to find an obscure place and wait for dark, because he understood that Armando, like all assassins a night creature, would make no move against William Laforge until the sun had gone down.

When Armando Teng woke in his motel room he checked the time at once. It was almost seven o'clock. He'd meant merely to rest but sleep had overwhelmed him. He'd dreamed of the young girl in Railsback's house in Dallas, the face in the window, the beautiful soft open mouth. In this strange slowed-down dream he'd stepped inside the house, whose rooms were galleries rising up and up into clouds, and he'd clutched the weeping girl, holding her, comforting her, speaking very quietly to her in a language of dreams she couldn't understand. She changed, became Marissa, but the dream disintegrated in vapor.

He rose, rinsed a towel in cold water and pressed it to his face. With some sad element of the dream still dogging him, he gathered his few belongings. He walked to his parked car, scanning the parking lot as he moved. A score of cars lay under a film of sunlight, all of them—as far as Teng could tell—empty. He got inside his Chevy, rolled down the windows. How stale the air was inside the car. Unbreathable. He spread the map on the passenger seat and drove out of the lot.

He thought it strange how little apprehension he felt. There was no nervousness in him. It was as if he'd done the killing already and was remembering it the way it had been. So powerful was this sense that even the road seemed very familiar. The houses he passed, the small tourist shops here and there, the fruit and vegetable stands, a tavern that stood crooked against the skyline, a motorcycle repair garage—he'd absorbed all this before. And in a sense he had. He'd slain Laforge time after time in his mind.

He looked in his rearview mirror. The traffic behind him was sparse on the blacktop highway. A cement mixer. A pickup truck. Behind that a couple of private cars. Teng glanced at the map, seeing the red-inked arrows pointing south, noticing how close he was coming to the exclamation point that marked his destination, six miles, perhaps seven.

His calm abandoned him briefly. The inside of his mouth was dry, his heart palpitated, a pressure built in his chest. At a stop light he braked, breathed deeply, tried to relax. Five miles now. Maybe less. He looked down at the picture of William Laforge that lay on top of the map; man and map became indivisible a moment. The light turned green and Teng drove forward, looking for the next turn the inked arrows indicated—a narrow road cutting through high trees on either side, shaded, sunlight locked out.

Stone walls imprisoned woods and fields. Here and there fine old houses were visible through trees at the end of long driveways. Teng looked in his rearview mirror. He saw nothing. The road was narrow, the canopy of trees more dense, creating a premature twilight at ground level. According to his instructions, a left turn was coming up very soon. He slowed, careful not to miss it. The road was called Valley Mill and badly signposted, perhaps deliberately so, to discourage riffraff from coming this way.

Teng made the turn. He drove a half mile, then parked the Chevy off the road, in a narrow lane dense with ancient mossy trees. He spread the map on his knees and traced the route with a fingertip. Laforge's property, consuming perhaps a hundred acres *(for one man!)*, was three-quarters of a mile from his present location. He'd walk the rest of the way. If it looked safe, if he saw no impediment and sensed no peril, he'd do what he'd come to do. If not, he'd withdraw and consider his options, formulate a plan of approach. He was calm again, lucid.

He put Laforge's picture in his back pocket. The map he folded and stuffed under his shirt. In his right hand he carried the leather pouch that had the gun. He walked two hundred yards or so, impressed by the silence that began with true twilight. A darkening blue filled the spaces between the trees. Quiet, serenity. Even the heat gently slackened its grip on the day.

Armando Teng listened. From beyond the stone wall to his right came the quiet sound of slow-running water, a stream rolling over pebbles.

The man known as Jack McTell, who from a suitably discreet distance had followed Teng from the motel, used his car telephone to contact Ted Arganbright. He announced the presence of Teng in the vicinity, and Arganbright thanked him for the information. McTell continued to drive in the direction of New Hope. He'd dine in the area somewhere before returning to Philadelphia. He had absolutely no idea who Teng was, nor would it ever have occurred to him to ask, to say to Arganbright, *Hey, what's going down,* because McTell had long ago learned the elementary principle that you never asked anyone anything in the Office of Security unless you had permission to do so. A vicious little circle: To get permission to ask, you had to ask permission. This paradox wasn't Jack McTell's concern. His empty stomach was a more immediate problem. He'd done his job and now he was clocking out and thinking that a delightful meal at the Lambertville Station, across the Delaware River from New Hope, might be just the ticket.

The rock music had become very loud and repetitive, banging against the dwindling light of day like a broken shutter in a wind. William Laforge, who had been taking congratulatory phone calls most of the afternoon from friends and enemies pretending to be friends, heard it vibrate through the old house. When he could stand it no longer he left his small office and, passing the closed door of Carolyn's room, went downstairs to the living room, where Nick lay on the rug by the fireplace, his eyes shut, his arms limp at his sides, his fingers tapping in time to the music. How could he look so relaxed in this din? Music shook lampshades. Porcelain figurines shuddered on shelves.

Laforge turned the volume down. "I can hardly hear myself think," he said.

Nick Laforge looked at his father with an expression he'd begun to use increasingly of late, a kind of exaggerated sympathy that was pure sarcasm. "I wouldn't want to interfere with your state of mind, Pops," he said, and he smiled innocently.

Laforge wondered why he could never fashion a truce between himself and his son. The barricades were so firmly in place they seemed impregnable. What did one do with a son? What was a child *for?* That odd half-yearning, that desire to understand the boy, touched him unexpectedly—and as he turned to look at Nicholas, he was seized by an urge to hold the boy, prompted in part by the sudden recollection that Tom Railsback had a teenage daughter—a child he'd never seen. (What was her name? Ivy? Holly? Cherry?) He wondered about her now, and her grief, and who was looking after her. Was she alone? Had her mother returned to take her away? Tom's marriage had been a dreadful mess.

"What's it feel like?" Nick asked.

"What does what feel like?"

"The hype. The attention. The chance of the big job." Nick made quote marks with his fingertips around the word *big*. "You'll be America's chief spook, Pops."

"I see it as an opportunity to serve my country at the highest level," Laforge remarked. There was gratitude in his voice, and pride.

"Fuck me," Nicholas said.

"Save that kind of language for your friends, Nicholas."

"You sound pompous, that's all."

Pompous! Laforge restrained the tiny fury he felt. "I wasn't aware of it," he said in a controlled manner.

"*To serve my country at the highest level,*" Nicholas said. "You really don't hear yourself?"

"Is there something wrong with the idea of serving the United States?"

"It depends on how you go about it, I guess. Your way, you really wanna know, I find shitty."

Laforge had no wish to prolong a conversation that would ultimately only underline the differences between father and son. If you pressed him beyond his customary sullenness, Nicholas would tell you the United States was run by an illicit affiliation of government, organized crime, and law enforcement agencies, a back-scratching system in which all these parts were interlocked to their mutual benefit. All were beyond the reach of the courts. Ergo, those who served in government tacitly or otherwise approved of a stinking, self-perpetuating system. When Ronald Reagan had once referred to the Soviet Union as an "evil empire," Nick had thrown a sneaker at the television and shouted, *"You got the wrong country, dickhead dinosaur!"*

Nick believed there were vast conspiracies, which he apparently found all over the place. The Rand Corporation, the Trilateral Commission, the CIA, the FBI, the Internal Revenue Service—all these organizations were in one another's pockets, shaping America as they saw fit.

How does it all work? Laforge had asked, trying to sound concerned but coming across as patronizing. *What are the mechanics of this enormous conspiracy, Nick? Do hundreds of people get together in some secret place and plan everything?*

They go underground, they have these deep caves in Colorado and Wyoming, the boy had answered with such obvious sincerity Laforge was appalled and just a little scared by what the young man so unquestioningly believed.

Do they also have a flying saucer and the bodies of dead

aliens they're keeping from the U.S. public, Nick?

The boy said yes, they did. He'd read it in a newsletter, one of those Xeroxed pamphlets that came to him in the mail from Boulder or Butte, issued by fellow travelers in the realms of conspiracy fantasy. The UFO conspiracy was one of the big ones. Laforge tried to see America through his son's eyes and what he perceived was a cavernous place in whose empty spaces could be heard the echoes of madmen whispering. His own faith in America was so strong, so demanding, he couldn't begin to understand an opposing point of view—especially one like his son's, which was out of control, twisted, a portrait in black.

Laforge had tried at the time to defuse Nicholas's infatuation with conspiracy theories, saying that while minor intrigues undeniably went on, and connivances took place at all levels of society, vast conspiracies of the kind to which he subscribed were practically impossible. How many men could keep a secret for years and years? It was against human nature.

Whatever, Nick had said. It was his favorite word with which to end a conversation. Whatever. A full stop. Sometimes a retreat. At other times an expression of pity. *Whatever, Pops. Whatever, whatever.*

Now Nick rose from the rug and stretched his arms. Laforge looked at him, wondering how long it would take for the boy to attain that age of reason wherein one saw things with the clarity of disinterest and put aside such easy notions as conspiracies. America worked. That's what the boy had to learn. It worked like no other country in the world because inherent in its structure was a system of balances. No despot could rise to supreme power. No dictator could take control. By the same token, no organizations could conspire together in massive plots and unbounded schemes to shape the nation, an idea that belonged in the hinterlands of lunacy, that interior region where the John Birch Society collided with Charlie Manson.

Laforge said, "I don't feel like arguing today, Nick."

"Why should you? This is a big day for you. Let all be calm. Let serenity prevail. I'm all for that."

The boy even managed to weave sarcasm into his cordiality. The telephone rang in Carolyn's room, and Laforge raised his face, staring up at her closed door. He wondered who was calling.

"Okay with you if I play my music again?" Nicholas asked.

"Quietly," said Laforge. "Very quietly."

He watched his son go to the CD player and insert a disc. At the same moment Laforge turned on a small fringed lamp on the coffee table. It glowed rather forlornly in the twilight that had filled the room with the consistency of a bluish gas.

Then it went out, dead.

"CD's not working," Nick said, fidgeting with the machine.

With an unexpected sense of alarm, Laforge gazed at the unlit lamp. "Perhaps there's a power cut."

"Hey, maybe you forgot to pay the utility bill, Pops."

Nick had no sooner spoken than the lamp came back on and the little red digital lights on the stereo console glowed.

"Just a minor power failure," Laforge said, thinking of darkness thickening over the property—but what did he have to be afraid of? A simple light bulb goes out. Why should some minor power alteration trouble him? Perhaps it reminded him again of the fragility of things, the thin skein separating security from uncertainty. He realized now he'd been anxious about nightfall all day long. He thought of the gun upstairs in his drawer. The idea consoled him.

"When you're director of the CIA, I bet they put in some kind of emergency backup generator for you," Nick remarked. "One of the perks."

"I seriously doubt it."

The phone call was from Truskett. Carolyn's head ached and she was tense. William's uneasy mood had affected her. Why was he so out of sorts? Possibly there had been too much excitement, the visit to the White House, the long confidential chat with the President, the phone calls that kept coming on his private line from various Washington power brokers and well-wishers—William was accustomed to a quieter kind of life. This attention jarred his system. Besides, there had to be an anticlimax factor too. You wait years for a job you think you deserve and finally it comes your way—there had to be a letdown. The morning after syndrome. Flat champagne. Even so, she had seen a look in William's eyes unknown to her. A haunted quality, a depression, she didn't know what.

She tried to concentrate on what Truskett was saying. He sounded breathless, hurried.

"Meet me," he said. "I want you to come and meet me."

"When?"

"Now."

"But why? Why the urgency?"

"You need to get out of the house."

"You're horny, aren't you? It's in your voice."

"Where you're concerned it's a permanent condition. Come as you are. Don't even get dressed up. Just meet me."

"You expect me to come to Washington at this time of day?"

"I'm in Philly."

"Whatever for?"

"A crazed urge to see you. Sheer lust. I'm blinded by it. Goddammit. Just come."

Carolyn turned on her back. She raised her knees. She imagined Truskett between her thighs and she was moist. Dear Byron. "Why are you in Philly? Tell me the truth."

"I told you. To see you. Come to me. Get out of that boring old house. I'll meet you anywhere you like. I'm in the Penn Towers on the University of Penn campus. If you don't want to meet there, pick a place. I'll be there."

"You sound like an adolescent boy, Byron."

"Just say you'll come."

"I don't know. . . ." She thought of Byron's mouth lost in the tangle of her pubic hair. She closed her eyes. "I would have to think of a wonderful excuse."

"You're creative."

"It would still take me at least two hours to get there," she said.

"I happen to know it's forty-five minutes by car from your house to here. An hour tops."

"I'd want to shower, get dressed—"

"No. Now. You must come now."

"Oh, you exasperate me." *I shouldn't go,* she thought. *I want him. But I should not go.*

"Listen. Hang up the telephone, Carolyn. Leave the house. Do it now."

"I just don't understand your urgency."

"Carolyn—"

The line went dead in the middle of whatever Byron Truskett intended to say. Irritated, Carolyn put the receiver down. She waited for it to ring again. If she knew Truskett, he would dial her back immediately. She waited. And waited. Perhaps he imagined *she* would call him. After ten minutes or so she gave in. She picked up the receiver, intending to call information for the number of the Penn Towers, but the line was dead in her hand. She tapped the reset button several times. Nothing changed.

A dead telephone had a menacing quality. Were you to cry aloud for any reason, the only person to hear you would be yourself. She sat up, smoothed her dress down over her knees and thought she'd check the other receivers in the house. Perhaps hers was the only phone not working.

After he quickly climbed the wall, Teng waded the stream because he considered the old bridge a few yards away a risk. Timbers had decayed and the structure was certain to creak beneath his weight, announcing his presence to anyone nearby. When he came up on the other bank, he slid, half crouching, through rushes that snapped back whiplike and damp-smelling at his face. The bank rose, the rushes thinned, the incline led to a stand of trees. Teng, surrounded by quiet twilight, enveloped by a stillness he could feel press in upon him, moved swiftly to the cover of the trees. Before him lay a large meadow, here and there a small summer flower, a daisy, a dandelion. On the other side of the meadow was a house, one window lit.

Teng lay flat. He didn't like the meadow. He would be exposed if he should cross it. What other way might there be to the house? Darkness was beginning to gather in folds, like a drape drawn slowly between the trees. A butterfly came up out of the grass and winged against his cheek so lightly he hardly felt it. He watched it go, red-winged, yellowy, almost luminous at the close of twilight. A joyful flutter of color and life. Why did this gladden him? He wasn't concentrating, he'd begun to drift, and drift could be lethal.

He looked to his left. The meadow ended in a white fence around a paddock. No cover. To his right the grassland gave way to a small area that had been cultivated for some agricultural purpose. A crop grew against wooden stakes. He wasn't sure what. Flowers had been planted along the edge of this cultivated plot, but they were wilting for want of moisture. Bleached of color, they suggested the resignation to death of patients in a terminal ward. Petals were folded like dried white hands.

Nothing moved in this landscape. No sentries patrolled, no guards waited. Straight ahead, Teng thought. Straight across the meadow to the house. Waiting, listening, cautious even though the property seemed defenseless, he stared at the light in the window for such a long time that it began to dance and disappear. And then the house itself moved, as if its foundations, like the bridge straddling the creek, had begun to decay. Another trick of the eye. But he thought, *There's decay all over here. The dying flowers, the dry earth, the rancid smell released by the reeds Teng had disturbed*—in what other kind of place could Laforge live? Wherever, he would bring death with him, death and rot, all windows drawn down, all air sucked out of the house, blinds nailed to wood, glass painted black, shutters drilled to brick—it would always be dark and awful where Laforge lived and breathed.

Teng moved slightly. Then he was still.

Phlott.

The sound came up from the creek, something over and above the regular rhythmic utterance made by water flowing slowly across pebbles. Perhaps a bird had landed, a night forager, an owl seizing a mouse from the water's edge. Teng listened. The sound came again. A man untuned to the murmurings of the landscape might have let the noise pass without question. But not Teng. He pressed himself flat to the ground and turned his face toward the creek and waited to see what might emerge at the top of the slope. Now, as twilight thickened, he had to strain to see. He aimed his gun toward the rise. If anyone had forded the creek and was climbing the bank, he would emerge a mere twenty or thirty feet from the place where Teng lay—gun in hand, tense, prepared, ready to kill, ready even to die.

21

Down Charlie Galloway went, the soles of his shoes failing to grip slick moss on the bed of the stream. The water was a mere three feet deep, but it soaked him to his chest when he lost his balance, and he came out on the bank bedraggled and unhappy, remembering times when he'd gone swimming in the sea off the Ayrshire coast and returned to the sands where, wrapped inside a towel, lay a bottle of scotch. Nothing, *nothing* on God's earth warmed a man like scotch.

He lay among the reeds a few moments, feeling mud soak through the material of his trousers. He'd whiled away hours that afternoon hiding, skulking in a country inn five miles from New Hope, watching the door and drinking cranberry juice and soda and studying the array of liquor bottles on the bar shelf. A gantry-ful of dreams and wishes. He wished for some of that long-dead, seaside scotch now. Despite the heavy warmth of the oncoming night, his legs were chilled.

When he'd left the inn he'd driven unmarked back roads, avoiding main highways where he could, finally parking his car four miles from the boundary of the Laforge estate and taking to woodlands through which he passed cautiously, drawing on reserves of stealth and cunning long inactive. Once, he'd seen a Range Rover parked in a clearing and he'd circled the vehicle at a safe distance, half expecting, with a tension that made him ash dry, to be apprehended. Half a mile on he'd heard voices through a thicket of trees, the words incomprehensible but the tone hardedged, like the language of fishermen who have seen a large silvery catch elude their lines. He moved with fearful caution, bent, scrambling, pausing when he imagined a threat, holding his breath when a bird shuttled overhead or a branch rattled, hurrying when trees yielded to the exposure of meadowland.

When he came to the edge of the Laforge property he'd waited a long time concealed in undergrowth—sickened by the smell of some freshly dead rodent rotting nearby—before carefully scaling the stone wall at a place where the overhang of trees created a fine dark-green shroud.

Onward, Charlie. Now he sat upright. The stench of mud was reminiscent of bad meat. He gazed toward the bridge, which he'd failed to notice before. He ran wet fingertips over his face. Three mallard ducks, insubstantial in the fading light, floated in peaceful formation under the bridge. They ignored him with the aplomb of duchesses.

He stood up, dripping. Clutching reeds for assistance, he slithered to the top of the slope, where he paused, drained. The smart thing now would be to turn and go back the way he'd come, all the way back, beyond Los Angeles, beyond this maddening continent, beyond beyond, back to Govan Cross and forget your whole American interlude, and years later, if you brought it to mind at all, it would be like poking around inside another man's memories.

But he was here in bloody Bucks County and he had business to finish. No matter what. *Keep bloody going, Charlie.*

He made it to the top of the slope and moved toward a clump of trees, which afforded him concealment. Beneath the trees lay a meadow. Beyond, a house was located. A couple of windows were lit.

Now he was puzzled by the apparent absence of security. He'd neither heard nor seen anything, no shadow, no flutter of a walkie-talkie device. The night that fell on the Laforge estate might have been entirely empty, and yet he had a sense of presences nearby, an awareness that the landscape concealed people. The men guarding Laforge—where were they? Where was the small army Clarence Wylie had said would be in place to protect Laforge from Teng? Hidden, of course, secreted in the innocuous shadows around the house, or in the barn beyond, or perhaps they sat, rifles in their laps, in the two parked vehicles some yards from the house. If they were good at what they did, they could be camouflaged anywhere—and yet that in itself was a source of puzzlement: If they were nearby, and watching, why had Charlie Galloway been allowed to pass unhindered?

Luck, maybe. He hadn't been seen. Hard to believe.

No. Something was off center here. The night had an imbalance to it. He stepped lightly between the trees, trying to slow his rapid breathing. He experienced a sensation of imminent menace, something perceived in the corner of an eye but unregistered by the brain—a tightening of nerve, the heart seeming to recoil.

The sudden chokehold made him gasp. He struggled, kicked back with his heels, then tried to bend and haul his assailant over his shoulder, but he didn't have the strength for it. He was being snapped like some huge wishbone. Breathless, blacking out, he raised his face to the sky, imagining he saw in a deformed way streaks of blood race through the heavens. His larynx felt like a pebble on which he was doomed to choke. And then abruptly he was released and thrown forward on his knees, a doglike position he maintained for a long time because he didn't have the energy to rise. Coughing and spluttering, fingering his neck, he had the odd sensation that his internal organs had risen to his mouth in raw conglomeration—kidney, liver, lungs.

His gun had been taken from his waistband. He turned his face slowly to look at Teng.

"I expected guards. Why do I find only you so far?" Teng asked in a whisper.

Charlie couldn't get his voice to work. It came from his mouth half strangled, like the effort of a novice ventriloquist. "I suppose they're hidden."

"Where?"

Galloway rolled over on his back. His head ached and spots cavorted in front of his eyes. "I don't know where . . . down there," and he gestured feebly toward the house.

Teng turned away briefly, gazing across the meadow.

"They'll wait until you get in close, Armando. Then they'll blast the fuck out of you. You'll be a bug on a windshield, my friend." Galloway managed to sit upright. He was still probing his neck, dogged by the notion that it had been bent out of shape and lay at an unlikely angle to his shoulders. Night had finally fallen and the darkness that consumed the Laforge property seemed to have penetrated Charlie's head to an equal extent.

"I have no choice, Galloway," Teng said.

"Why is it so bloody important for you to get Laforge?"

Teng looked sad, a man carrying an old sorrow like a pouch of stale tobacco whose dead scent hangs in all the folds of his clothes. He told his story in four, five sentences, impatiently and without emotion. Listening, absorbing a dark tale, a girl's torture and death, experiencing her pain in Teng's detached monotone, Charlie Galloway felt like a family historian entrusted with a burden. He was being made the keeper of bones, the curator of a place where petroglyphs that defied understanding were stored. He listened to Teng's terse narrative and he was moved. In a stand of trees in a Pennsylvania night transfigured here and there by the glow of fireflies, he perceived the tragic way disparate lives became juxtaposed. Laforge and his prosperous estate in the rich heart of Bucks County, Teng's girl in the impoverished Philippines. The director-designate of the CIA, and a young Filipina tortured and killed. A misguided arm of the self-righteous United States government reaches out and creates crazed, bloody chaos, and as a result a young man travels many thousands of miles with only an arctic hatred to sustain him.

The world, Charlie Galloway thought, was out of whack. People were dreadfully flawed. They inflicted pain on one another without thought. *Take yourself, for instance. When love held out a hand, you slapped it drunkenly away. And when you did love it was with a drunkard's kiss, a soak's paw, and you woke fevered in a twisted bedsheet upon a bed from which your wife, your Karen, had vanished.*

"If you go across that meadow you'll die," he said.

"Dying will be acceptable," Teng answered, "if I get Laforge."

"You won't get within spitting distance."

"I have no choice."

"And I don't have any choice either, Armando. I have to stop you."

"With what?"

With what indeed? A stick? A fallen branch? Galloway clenched his hands uselessly. Was this how it ended now, standing here, watching Teng walk the meadow to the house, to his death?

Teng said, "Laforge doesn't deserve your heroics. He doesn't deserve martyrs."

Galloway turned his face to the sky. "Laforge's life means sweet fuck-all to me, Armando. I have no bloody intention of becoming a martyr for the CIA. I don't want you to get killed. I want you alive."

"In your custody."

"Yes."

"In the long run, it doesn't matter what you want."

No, Galloway thought. *It really doesn't matter.* He couldn't stop Teng. But he had to try. You might understand, Karen. Later, if they ship you my remains and you learn only half the truth, you might understand. *Here Lies Galloway, Better Dead than Dead Drunk. In Loving Memory of Charles D. Galloway, Who Took the Long Road to Sobriety. Kind but Misguided. He Never Meant to Hurt a Soul.*

Teng stepped away. "Stay where you are. Don't follow me."

"Why? Will you shoot me? Can you afford to make all that noise, old son? Draw attention to yourself?"

"Don't do anything unwise."

Don't do anything unwise. When had Charlie ever avoided that gauntlet? It was now or never or nothing. Victory or death. With the heightened recklessness that is the prerogative of the brave and the mad, he sucked in as much air as his enfeebled lungs could hold, tensed his muscles and lunged, throwing himself hopefully through space in the fashion of a rugby player. He thought he heard the crowd roar in approval, imagined he'd made contact with Teng, arms around the Filipino's waist, bringing him to the ground, pinning him victoriously.

But all this went seriously wrong as a fantasy. Teng, deft,

lithe, sidestepped, hammering the back of Galloway's skull with the butt of a gun. A severe pain traveled like a fast subway directly to Charlie's brain. He fell down, rolled a few feet, came to a stop against the trunk of a tree, experienced a druglike moment of sheer silliness, stoned and cheerful, and then the subway gathered speed, rocketing through tunnels where lights intermittently glowed, passing platforms from which disappointed commuters gazed flatly at the fleeting express whose only passenger was Charles D. Galloway. Somehow a postcard from Dan fluttered into Charlie's hand and he read the sentence *I always thought you'd Go far ONE day if only you took the right train* before he surrendered to the complete disarray of consciousness.

How long did the blackness last?

He wasn't sure. When he opened his eyes Armando Teng was gone and the sky brilliant, streaked with nebulae. He struggled to rise, so jarred by pain he imagined his skullbone must have splintered from Teng's blow. He remembered once, when he was perhaps seven or eight, falling from a stepladder and landing directly on his noggin and his father saying, *I hope that knocks some sense into ye, Charlie.* But blows on his head seemingly never achieved that effect, neither thirty-something years ago nor now.

He moved between the trees, down into the meadow, zigzagging, moaning quietly as he went.

"The phones don't work," Carolyn said. "I wonder why the service has been interrupted."

She made this announcement from the foot of the stairs, having tried the various extensions in the upper part of the house. Laforge went immediately to the receiver located by the living room window and picked it up. He rattled the bar on the handset a few times. Nothing, no dial tone.

"The phones *always* work," Carolyn said. "They never just die like that."

"Perhaps somebody is repairing the line somewhere," Laforge answered. He was thinking of how the electricity had flickered out before. He went across the room to where Carolyn stood. She was distracted. Her vagueness made her appear very delicate.

"Do you think the security people have anything to do with this?" she asked.

"I don't see why, dear."

"You know, perhaps they have to put a tap on the line or something, and service is temporarily disconnected—oh, I don't know."

"I can go out and ask."

"Would you? Please?"

Laforge, curious about his wife's apparent distress, wondering what had upset her customary calm—surely something more grievous than a failed telephone—moved to the front door and opened it. He stepped out into the night, turning his face this way and that like a nocturnal creature measuring the air. He moved toward the place where the van and car were parked, passing the picnic table, hearing a raccoon scurry away.

He reached the car. It was empty. Perhaps the occupants had gone inside the van. Yes. That had to be it. They had gone in there to confer, some procedural matter, something like that.

The cab of the van was empty. Laforge moved to the side door of the windowless vehicle and knocked. Ted Arganbright opened the door. Behind him were four monitors, darkened TV pictures of the estate relayed by cameras. Laforge saw his own face on one of the screens, his white skull flaring in the lit doorway of the van. He blinked, conscious of a table at Arganbright's back, a jar of instant coffee, a container of nondairy creamer, an open package of chocolate chip cookies, Styrofoam cups—incongruous domestic items.

"Our telephone has gone dead," he said.

Ted Arganbright smiled in his ingratiating way. "Nothing to be concerned about, sir. We've been patching our own lines into yours. That must have caused a glitch."

"That's exactly what my wife thought," Laforge said.

"I apologize. I'll have it seen to."

Laforge had the impression that Arganbright was alone in the van. But then he heard a slight cough, and the motion of a foot upon the floor, and he understood that at least one other person was in the van with Ted. He couldn't see. The angle of door, Arganbright's bulk—these obscured his view. Were all his guards in the van? Could that be possible? Perhaps a discussion of security tactics was going on.

"You don't have to worry about anything, sir," Arganbright said.

Laforge was somehow reluctant to terminate this conversation. He wanted Ted Arganbright in full view, tangible evidence of the security arrangements. He wanted to go inside the van and reassure himself that there were no more than two men in there, that the others were on patrol. Ted Arganbright didn't move.

"Everything is under control, sir," he remarked.

"Yes. Yes, of course."

"We're the best in the business. Keep that in mind."

"Where are the other guards at present?" Laforge asked.

"We change shift, sir," Arganbright replied, which didn't really answer Laforge's question. "We rotate."

"Change shift?" Laforge wasn't sure he understood this, and yet it seemed so terribly simple. People worked x number of hours, then they went home. That's all there was to it. Somehow he'd imagined that his security people would be a permanent presence. Nothing so commonplace as counting hours could possibly affect them. Apparently it did. He felt diminished by this knowledge, a prop kicked from under him.

"Don't look so apprehensive, sir," Arganbright said, turning his face away and looking at the other man inside the van. "Vespa and myself have everything under control. Believe me." He checked his watch. "The new detail is probably in position by now," and he waved a hand around the estate. "You're secure."

Laforge turned toward the house. The door of the van closed softly behind him. Despite Ted Arganbright's reassurance, he felt abandoned to uncertainty. He moved a few paces back, paused. Night crowded him. He became immobile, standing between the two parked vehicles like a blind man whose dog has fled. Caneless, unsighted, his senses redundant. What noise was that? What did he hear? No wind, certainly. No breeze. The crackle of dry grass stalks. Perhaps it was a sound made by the security people in the darkness of the meadow. But why couldn't he see them even though he narrowed his eyes and strained to look?

He walked to the house quickly. What he'd do would be to go inside and lock the door. A simple precaution. But he was

overreacting. He knew it. He'd been badly affected by those needless memories of Benguet. The uncertainty he felt, this intolerable sense of exposure—it all came down to those bleak recollections. He opened the door, closed it, turned the key.

"You're right," he told Carolyn. "They've done something
to the phones. They say normal service will be resumed soon. It's
nothing to worry about, dear. Just relax."

"Good. I'll go up to my room and read."

Carolyn went toward the stairs. She was still thinking of
Philadelphia. She was tempted. Would Byron be waiting for her
at Penn Towers? Or might he have gone? Perhaps he'd been trying
to ring through and hadn't been able to. It was such a damned
nuisance, this interference. But necessary, of course. Necessary to
William. She climbed to the landing. She would wait until the
phones were in working order again, then she'd call Philadelphia,
and if Byron was still there she'd go.

She opened the door of her bedroom. The window was wide.
She couldn't remember having left it like that. Huge furry moths
that made her skin crawl flapped all around her head in panic.
Some were the size of small birds. She couldn't stay in the room
with these monsters. She stepped back, drew the door closed. She
backed across the landing.

The man was in shadow. When he stepped toward her she
received a variety of impressions simultaneously, the frosty blue
of his eyes, the high cheekbones, the gun in his pale brown hand.
His intensity was such that he seemed to glow. Faint, she leaned
against the wall for support. It crossed her mind, with more hope
than confidence, that he was one of the security team who'd come
indoors for some reason, but he didn't look the part, he had
desperation on him, and a determination she'd rarely seen before
in any person, and besides the gun was leveled straight at her face,
which no security person would ever do. What did this man
want? How had he managed to get past the guards?

"Call your husband," the man whispered.

She shook her head. He pushed the gun directly to her forehead. It hurt her, metal pressed on bone.

"Call him."

"William," she said very quietly. "William. . . ."

Laforge heard her. He moved across the living room, reached

the bottom of the stairs, looked up. The smile he'd prepared for her disappeared from his face. He faltered. He caught the ornamental orb of the handrail, the ornate wooden globe in which some eighteenth century craftsman had carved petals. He was very conscious of the texture of this work against his skin. For a moment he had a curiously complete awareness of the whole house, and its details flooded him all at once, ceiling beams, plaster cornices, the random-width pine floorboards, dark crannies, the little surprises that even now pleased him—the exquisite woodwork of a mantel, a design etched in a pane of glass. The house filled him. The sensation was dreamlike. Even the gun in the young man's hand was more illusion than thing. *I am not here,* he thought. *None of us are.*

Then what rushed through him was the notion that this man's entrance was some form of security test, nothing more, that he'd found a weakness in the system and exploited it, and pretty soon Arganbright would come through the door and everything, everything would be hunky-dory. Shipshape. *We found a flaw, Mr. Laforge,* Arganbright would say. *We like to check our own strengths, sir, we like to probe and probe—*

But this was all so much wishful thinking, and Laforge knew it. So much fancy. He watched Carolyn come down the stairs, the young man moving just behind her. He was real. *Yes, he's real.*

"William, I do not understand this," Carolyn said.

She said it two or three times. Thinking he might halt her growing hysteria, Laforge made a comforting gesture with his hands.

"William, who is this man?"

"He knows who I am," the young man said.

Laforge had a weird feeling, a sense of implosion, air escaping from his body, as if he might shrivel like a balloon, casting off all responsibilities, all the flaws of his history as he dwindled into nonexistence.

"William, what is he going to do?"

Nick had come to the foot of the stairs, drawn by the sound of the intruder's voice. The appearance of the gun paralyzed him.

Teng smelled the woman's perfume. She stood one step beneath him, so close he could see the faint hairs on the back of her neck. Her yellow hair was long but she had it pinned up. A mole was visible on the right side of the otherwise unblemished neck. He couldn't remember Marissa having any blemishes. But some panicky slippage was going on inside him now and he realized he couldn't remember Marissa at all, neither face nor hair nor smell, the way she felt, nothing, everything had disintegrated so completely he experienced a solitude unlike anything in a life that had mainly been one of absences. It cut the way a surgeon's knife did, straight into his heart. He thought how little was left to live for.

"I gave no orders," Laforge said. "You understand that? I did not order Costain or Railsback—"

It was useless. Laforge knew it. Useless to protest.

"You can't get away from here," Laforge said.

Teng came down a step and shot William Laforge directly in the face. Laforge was thrown back against the wall, where he slid to the floor. Teng stood over him. He fired again into Laforge's face, which was deformed, unrecognizable, something from a child's dream of a thing that lurked in a cellar. It was done now.

The woman screamed. Teng, thinking of what had been done to Marissa, bringing it to mind with overpowering clarity, shot Laforge's wife in the side of the head. And when the young man shouted aloud at him—Teng understood nothing, he was beyond language, he heard only clamor—he raised the gun and fired into the boy's chest.

He stepped over the fallen woman, who lay at a strange angle on the stairs, thighs apart, knees uplifted, eyes shut. The young man had been knocked on his back, fetal in death, almost touching.

Teng remembered for some reason the young girl in Railsback's house, the beautiful young face in the window, the innocence he'd ruined in a fraction of time. Then he walked out into the night, which seemed cold to him, as if vengeance had lowered the temperature and justice were a chill affair.

Charlie Galloway was running toward the house when he heard the first shot. His coordination was poorly wired and he weaved from side to side through the long grass, panting as he ran. The second shot appeared to explode inside his own brain. The pain in his skull clawed. His internal compass was dented, his gyroscope out of alignment. The house at times seemed to be straight ahead, at other times left or right. He kept running. Sweating, he heard another shot, then another.

The house became abruptly silent, although not tranquil; the light that burned in a downstairs window looked like a raw eye newly blinded in an act of violence. Twenty yards from the front door Galloway crouched among an unruly outgrowth of brittle shrubbery, his chest aching from the effort of movement. He saw Armando Teng, pistol in one hand, step through the front door.

Where were they? Charlie wondered. Where the guards? Where the cavalry? In that shocked space beyond time, beyond reckoning, he wasn't sure how many moments had passed since the first shot—perhaps thirty seconds, perhaps less, he couldn't say. Violence had a clock all its own. Where was the small army? Did it exist? Was it composed entirely of deaf men?

Teng took a couple of steps from the house. He appeared unhurried, slightly dazed, as if having accomplished what he set out to do he'd shed all sense of purpose. He stared toward the shrubbery where Charlie Galloway was half hidden, but gave no sign of recognition. He turned his face to the left in the direction of the parked vehicles.

The van door opened. A rectangle of brilliant light flooded the dark.

Charlie took a step back, drawing himself down into the shrubbery. When six or seven rapid gunshots came from the direction of the van and Teng fell—first to his knees, then face-down with the slack finality of death—Galloway immediately hunched, sliding into the long grass and moving back across the meadow to the trees. He climbed the slope quickly, looking back only once before scrambling with heartbreaking speed down the incline to the creek.

Breathless, he stepped onto the bridge, hearing a fish feebly disturb the surface upstream. Somebody else stood on the bridge.

''Been a long time, Charlie.''

Charlie Galloway looked at the outcropping of white eyebrows, all that was visible of Vanderwolf's face.

''We had men out looking for you. I'll say this: You're slippery and persistent.''

"Is that meant to be a compliment?" Charlie asked. His voice had a tremor.

Vanderwolf came closer. The smell of his cologne was strong and citric. He peered disdainfully into the darkness and shuddered. "I hate the countryside. How can people live here?"

Depressed, Charlie Galloway said nothing. He thought, *They live here, and they die.* The night had gone all wrong, tilting on an axis he couldn't understand.

Teng was dead. Charlie Galloway had failed. He thought of Karen. He would go in search of her and explain his failure. She'd understand. He'd make her see how hard he'd tried. She might be convinced by his effort. She might see fresh beginnings, new possibilities.

"What a tragedy," Vanderwolf said. "Laforge had everything to live for. Along comes some fanatic and shoots him." And he shook his head, as if saddened. "Kamikaze type. You can't take protective measures against that kind of killer."

"I didn't notice protective measures," Galloway said. "Teng apparently strolled straight inside the guy's house and shot him and . . ."

He let the sentence hang. The obvious dawned on him: Nothing had been done to protect Laforge from Armando Teng. Absolutely nothing. The game was fixed, the outcome bought and sold. And now Charlie realized why he himself hadn't been apprehended on the estate, because such an event might have been noisy, might have forewarned Teng, whose destiny, alas, had not been his own. Sad Teng. Poor sad Teng.

CRAZED KILLER STRIKES IN BUCKS COUNTY. Tomorrow the world would read the story and then forget it immediately in the great amnesiac flux of things. Because life rolled on.

A very soft breeze came up through the reeds, dying before it had begun, stillborn. He had an image, plundered from God knows what source, of Karen standing on some breezy California cliff, a paisley scarf caught by bluster and tossed back from her slender neck. He loved that neck, the angle of her shoulders.

"Security can't be everywhere, Charlie. You understand that. What we have here is a tragedy," said Vanderwolf. "Psychotic killer on the loose. All too common, unfortunately.

I guess an examination of the killer's background will yield some useful clues about his motive. Who's to say?"

Charlie heard the fish again. In the beeches an owl cried.

"Well. What plans do you have?" Vanderwolf asked. "What next in your illustrious career? You ought to lay off the booze for openers. Give yourself a break."

"I think I'm going home," Charlie replied quietly.

"*All* the way home?"

Charlie stepped toward the end of the bridge without answering.

Vanderwolf said, "What's America got to offer a man like you anyway? You never struck me as a New World kind of guy."

Charlie still made no response. He had the feeling he was going to be shot in the back. His neck turned cold. Then the sensation passed, because he understood there was really no need for Vanderwolf to have him killed. What danger did Charlie Galloway represent? He had a story of sorts to tell, but who'd listen? Who'd publicize it? As soon as he tried to open his mouth he'd be discredited by the bureau, by the LAPD, by the testimony of paid experts. *History of alcohol abuse, drunken incidents, car accidents, hospitalization. You see how it is. Troubled.*

And what would his story consist of even if anybody listened? All he could say was that a person or persons unknown, clearly in positions of some influence, wanted Laforge dead. Otherwise, why was the man's official protection so ineffective? Charlie perceived complexities, questions to which he would never find answers because none were to be had. They would be buried in the heart of the capital, in quiet wood-lined offices, expensive houses, prestigious private clubs where powerful men made murderous decisions. Truth lost its gloss and faded into rumor. Rumor, in time, became apocrypha, beyond substantiation. Theories would arise, as they always did, and interested persons, some of them loonies, would pick at the fabric of these hypotheses, obscuring with paranoid conjecture what little remained of truth until finally veracity had vanished without leaving even a whisper behind. Speculation was a hall where meaningless echoes rolled back and back. Who was behind the murder of William Laforge? Was the standard-issue lone assassin theory going to suffice?

There was never any truth, never a core one could touch and say, *Yes, this is it.* America was obfuscation and shredding machines and people in political office who had raised denial to the status of a masonic ritual.

The country filled him with despair. He wondered if he'd carry his gloom with him if he went back to his origins. Would despondency always turn out to be his luggage, permanently attached to him? He imagined himself strolling through Govan on a white Friday night in summer, feeling that other-dimensional nature of a Glasgow weekend, that gateway into labyrinths of possibility amid the magic gray and ginger tenements—all this came into focus, drawing him back to his place of birth like a stranded sea thing reclaimed by a tide. But would he feel a weight and look down and see the sinister black suitcase chained to his wrist anyway?

"Charlie," Vanderwolf said. "One last thing."

Charlie looked around. He had time to think, *I know too much, although I really know nothing.* The gun in Vanderwolf's hand went off, a report in a minor key. Charlie felt the pain in his chest, but it was a bizarre sensation, his and not his, close and far away. He lost balance, slithered down the bank into the stream, disturbing the mallard ducks. Distressed, they squabbled around him, wings violently thrumming water. They clacked and pecked and harassed him. With one eye open, he watched them settle again. Recomposed, they sailed, over water already turning blood red, downstream.

Vanderwolf had gone. The bridge was empty.

Half submerged, Charlie rolled on his back and looked up at the stars, which appeared to be rushing away from him, sucked out of the galaxy.

This is a hell of a way to go.

He raised one hand up out of the water, imagining he was reaching for his wife, for a shadow of love, but then his strength faded and the hand dropped back to his side and he thought, *Karen. Karen, let me explain myself. Let me tell you how it is. How it will be in the future.* But she wasn't listening. He closed the one functioning eye. The lid fluttered gently, a tiny spasm.

After that, Charlie Galloway no longer moved.